蛇警探

PRECIOUS DRAGON

Other books by Liz Williams include:

Detective Inspector Chen:
    Snake Agent
    The Demon and the City
    Precious Dragon
    The Shadow Pavilion (Forthcoming)

Banner of Souls
Bloodmind
Darkland
Empire of Bones
The Ghost Sister
Nine Layers of Sky
The Poison Master

The Banquet of the Lords of Night and Other Stories

蛇警探

PRECIOUS DRAGON

A DETECTIVE INSPECTOR CHEN NOVEL

Liz Williams

NIGHT SHADE BOOKS
SAN FRANCISCO

First Edition

ISBN: 978-1-59780-082-2 (Trade Hardcover)
ISBN: 978-1-59780-083-9 (Limited Hardcover)

Night Shade Books
Please visit us on the web at
http://www.nightshadebooks.com

To Trevor

With special thanks to:
Shawna McCarthy, my agent
Jason Williams and Jeremy Lassen and the great team at Night Shade
Marty Halpern, my editor
Everyone in the Montpelier Writing Group and everyone at Milford
...and the oncology team at Musgrove Park and Bristol Royal Infirmary.

ONE

The spirit was singing her heart out, her ethereal voice soaring up into the air. Uneasily, the demon peered sideways, trying to see, but his view was impeded by a crimson edge of rock. He stamped from one foot to another, trying to concentrate, but the spirit's voice seemed to drown out the whole world. Beside him, his demonic kin swayed in a ferocious display of hatred, surging forward to follow the dragon as it charged toward the singing spirit. Soon, it would be upon her...

The demon, hopeful, looked up and to his intense relief saw that the hero's feet were now visible, descending rather jerkily from a cloud. With a sweep of his wand, the hero (mighty Xu Xiao, whose eyes flash pinwheel lightning and whose voice makes a whisper of storms) summoned the Storm Lord King onto the stage. The demons danced back as the Storm Lord advanced. The great creature, twisting and turning to conceal the sweating stagehands beneath its many-legged sides, batted at the dragon, causing the latter to dance with anger and return the compliment with a wave of its clawed foot.

The two beasts circled one another warily for a moment, then as the orchestra soared to a crescendo they leaped, screaming, to collide in the middle of the stage. Storm Lord King and Celestial Dragon tore at each other's throats, the centipedal king at last gaining an advantage. It seized the dragon's head between its jaws and pulled. The head came off, like someone decapitating a large shrimp. The Storm Lord rolled acrobatically backward and tossed the head into the air. Snapping in outrage, the dragon's head trailed sparks into the upper reaches of the dome, narrowly avoiding the chandeliers. There was a thunderous firecracker bang, which made the audience squeal, and all the lights went out.

The audience rose in applause as the opera thundered to a close and the curtain fell; not a moment too soon, the demon thought. He frowned be-

1

hind his heavy mask, longing to take it off and transform himself back into fifteen-year-old Pin, the chorus boy. His face felt as though it had melted. What were the stagehands thinking, to leave the hero's descent so late? Pin peered into the shadows at the back of the stage, but the curtain was already rising. His hands were seized by demons on either side as the cast rushed forward to take the first bow. A moment later, the lights came back on to reveal the whole cast, manifested in the aftermath of the divine battle and singing their hearts out.

The lights had gone up now, revealing the auditorium in all its vulgar glory. Pin blinked up at the audience, automatically noting who was there and who was absent. The box belonging to Paugeng Pharmaceuticals was not empty. The demon—the real one—was there again.

Along with a bunch of elderly Malay executives, the dark, golden-eyed figure was standing next to Paugeng's heiress, and the opera's sponsor, Jhai Bhatya Tserai herself. Rumors traveled fast in Singapore Three and Pin had heard a lot about Jhai's demon. It was said that she had traveled to Hell, fallen in love with him, and brought him home as her consort. Hell had half-destroyed the city as a consequence: it had only recently been restored after all the earthquake damage. Other rumors contested that Jhai had summoned the demon herself, down in the rebuilt labs of Paugeng, where no one who was not indentured to the company was ever allowed to go. And there was another, even weirder, rumor that said that the demon had something to do with the police department, and had met Jhai in the course of his enquiries. Pin did not know the truth of the matter, but as he was still something of a romantic at heart despite everything, he preferred the first theory.

He was so busy gazing at the demon that he almost failed to notice the snapping string of firecrackers as they detonated above his head. The cast bowed once more, then retreated backstage to enjoy their success.

As they began changing out of their costumes, the choreographer, Miss Jhin, came into the dressing room and clapped her hands for attention. There was to be a party at Paugeng, to honor the visiting Malay dignitaries, and certain cast members had been invited. They were waiting for the invitations now. Miss Jhin was excited by this brush with the cream of society, and fluttered about adjusting people's costumes.

"So pretty, and they noticed you especially!" she gasped. This last was directed at Maiden Ming, the sweet-voiced, sweet-faced, and evil-tempered singer who led Second Chorus. Delicate in her gauzy costume, Ming smiled daintily and bowed her head.

"Old perverts," she muttered when Miss Jhin's back was turned. Her face was flushed beneath the layer of powder. "I'll bet they noticed me. And I suppose the flute player intends to live up to his name?" She gave Pin a nasty look. He mumbled something, and turned to the mirror to adjust his make-up, seeing a young man with a soft mouth and almond eyes underneath a sideways fall of hair. He practiced a soulful expression, wondering doubtfully whether it would convince anyone that he was really a thoughtful, intelligent person and not merely some frivolous actor. Those looks won't last much longer, he thought gloomily, seized by a familiar sense of anxious desperation. He must find a patron soon, before his face failed him.

Pin dreamed of finding a patron, just as a wealthier young man might have yearned to find a lover, and the two were not exactly unrelated, as Pin's embarrassing nickname suggested. He could cheerfully have murdered Maiden Ming for bestowing it upon him. Until that throwaway and unnecessary remark, tossed over one exquisite shoulder and accompanied by Maiden Ming's ethereal laugh, his name had been Ryu Tang. It might have been a rather prosaic name, perhaps, but at least it was his own. Pin had, however, been searching for a stage name, something alluring and mysterious, and he had been unwise enough to mention this in company. It had sparked off Maiden Ming's famous comment, which had contained sufficient truth to stick.

"How about 'Pin H'siao'?" Ming had asked. "A charming name, 'The Flute Player.' " The name did have that literal meaning in Cantonese, but it also meant something rather more lewd, and since Pin's youth and good looks had made him popular at some of the city's more decadent parties, not entirely inappropriate. Miss Jhin, being a woman of almost supernatural refinement, had overheard Ming, however, and had taken the new nickname at face value.

"Why, how charming and cultured! I had no idea you were a flautist."

Fourth Chorus, to a person, had fallen about in laughter.

"He keeps his talent well-zipped up, Miss Jhin," someone said.

"Yes, he's supposed to be really accomplished at blowing," added someone else, to the accompaniment of hysterical mirth. Pin H'siao, formerly known as Ryu Tang, had listened sourly to all this, but dared not protest. He knew what would happen if he did: they'd flog the joke to death; but if he kept quiet, maybe it would wear thin. Unfortunately, it had been too good a joke, surviving no less than two cast changes, and Pin doubted now whether he'd ever shake it off. He tried to be graceful about it, with minimal success. At least he'd managed to abbreviate it to "Pin." The humiliation, however, added to his most cherished desire: find a patron and escape from these vulgar surroundings.

Pin had nursed a hidden hope that Paugeng's Jhai Tserai might be that patron, an expectation that he now realized to be completely unrealistic. Halfway through the first aria he had glanced up and seen that Jhai's face was as closed as if a shutter had fallen in front of it. In fact, sitting in tedious splendor as the complicated plot of the opera unfolded around her, she had looked downright bored. So, no chance of patronage there, Pin admitted to himself, but there never had been, really. It was all in his dreaming, hoping mind. In his saner moments, indeed, the thought seized him with a *frisson* of horror. And Jhai already *had* a consort, if the rumors about the demon were true. With a sudden terrified bound of his heart, Pin realized that the demon might very well be at the party. Miss Jhin was coming down the stairs with a handful of invitations; Pin went to see if his name was on the list, and found that it was.

Half an hour later, waiting on the curb outside the Opera House, Pin was joined by a smaller, cloaked figure. Resentful eyes glared from beneath a brocaded hood. Pin crowed.

"You got an invitation, too!"

"I don't think it's funny," Maiden Ming said. "At least you deserve your nickname."

"Well, *Maiden,* you certainly don't," Pin countered, delighted to have scored a point.

A car stopped, and the back door opened.

"Ladies first," he said, with a flourish. Maiden Ming climbed stiffly inside without a backward glance.

It was a long drive to Paugeng. When they reached the complex, all the lights were blazing, but not a sound could be heard above the heavy thud of construction work, somewhere toward the back of the building. The complex was being rebuilt, the work almost complete. The driver led Pin and Ming across the forecourt to the atrium, and sent them up in the elevator. The party was being held on the fiftieth floor, in Tserai's own ballroom, and appeared to be in full swing. As the door of the elevator opened, a man in his forties, with a wide, glazed smile, approached and then kissed Maiden Ming on the cheek. She gave a small trill of laughter and threw off her cloak, holding her arms wide. Pin had to admit that she was an excellent actress, particularly once she was off the stage. Her new friend drew her into the crowd. She did not look back. Pin sighed and stepped through the door.

To Pin's relief, the demon was nowhere to be seen. Instead, the huge room was filled with Singapore Three's elite: executives from the corporations that ran the city, stars from screen and opera, visiting dignitaries from other nations. Servants moved among them with engineered grace, exciting little flurries of interest as they passed; they were joined by the human whores, who had their own admirers. Pin realized without enthusiasm that there were many people whom he knew, but it was unlikely that anyone would remember him. No one would recall a mere rent-boy. As unobtrusively as possible, he collected a drink from a nearby servant and walked across to the window, where he stood looking out across the immense span of the city.

Immediately below, lay the dark pool of the harbor and the curving emptiness of the ocean beyond. From this height, the harbor looked no bigger than a puddle. Pin traced the streets that ran in all directions in a series of diagonals. He could see the main artery of Shaopeng, which, so the Feng Shui dowsers said, mirrored the line of energy called the Great Meridian. Pin was never quite sure whether he believed in *feng shui*, but the corporations took it very seriously and the temple of the dowsers, the Senditreya Endo, had wielded a great deal of power in the city until its recent disgrace. Sometimes, too, it seemed to Pin that he could feel something when he walked in certain places, like a current of electricity stirring under the earth. There were places that caused a curious sense of comfort and security, but others where he did not like to go, because they made him uneasy. Pin shivered, thinking of a little square at the back of Ghenret, which he was afraid to walk through because it produced such a feeling of chilly horror. The dowsers said that such places were closer to Hell than the rest of the world, but Pin put this thought swiftly aside. It did not do to think too much about such things; it was unlucky.

He had wondered, at times, whether he might be sensitive enough to be a dowser. It paid good money, and used to be pretty much a job for life, but Pin thought you had to come from one of the old families to be an initiate into the temple, and besides, it was dangerous. Dowsers walked with one eye on Heaven and the other on Hell, or so it was said, and Pin had a healthy respect for the sanctity of his own soul. And lately there had been some very disturbing stories about the Feng Shui Practitioners' Guild and the earthquakes that had devastated much of Singapore Three. Yet he couldn't be too much of a coward, he thought to himself…and then he looked up and saw two bright pinpoints of light, reflected in the smoky glass of the window. The demon was standing behind him. Pin turned, his mouth suddenly dry.

The demon's pointed face was pale, and his eyes were a fiery gold, rimmed with a dark contour as though he had lined each eyelid with kohl. Perhaps he had, Pin thought in a daze of admiration. It was impossible to tell his age; the demon's hair was dark and slick, his face unlined. He did not look much above thirty. He gave Pin a smile that managed to be simultaneously engaging and predatory, revealing sharp teeth.

"Good evening," the demon said, in accented Cantonese.

Pin swallowed hard and managed to find his voice. "I—I hope you enjoyed the performance, sir."

"I enjoyed it immensely," the demon said, "but I'm not sure I entirely understood the plot." His smile widened. "Perhaps you could explain it to me?"

"Oh," Pin said, beginning to babble. "It's really very simple. You see, it's a story about the Tao. There's positive energy, of course—*ch'i*—and negative energy, *sha*. They have to be balanced in order to generate good fortune. In the opera, Celestial Dragon represents the positive energy, and Storm Lord King represents the negative, but that's only one way of looking at it. In some of the operas it's the other way round. And the hero of the opera is a priest who believes in balance. When the Storm Lord conquers the dragon, it symbolizes the balancing of energy. Negative and positive, you see. And balance." With an effort, Pin forced himself to stop wittering repetitively on.

"I see," the demon said, very seriously. One sharp canine caught his lower lip. "Thank you for your explanation. What's your name?"

"Pin," he said, before he could stop himself.

"Pin," the demon repeated. "And my name is Zhu Irzh."

There was a short silence. Pin opened his mouth to say something but at that point a voice purred from behind him

"Why, *darling*…" Pin felt his elbow taken in a steely hand, and suddenly he was staring into the dark eyes of Jhai Tserai. He had thought that the heiress of Paugeng Pharmaceuticals would be taller, yet she was close to his own height; a doll in a silken sari. Her intricately braided hair lay close to her head like a nest of snakes.

"I see you're making friends, dear," Jhai said, with an arch of her eyebrows in the direction of the demon. With a pinch, she released Pin and stepped to take Zhu Irzh's arm in her own. Zhu Irzh looked down at her with an expression that Pin was unable to interpret: a kind of amused tolerance, perhaps. Attuned to malice, Pin schooled his own face into a bland semblance of politeness and gave his hostess a low bow. When he straightened up again, Jhai had already turned away, whispering something to the demon. Zhu Irzh was drawn forward with her, but as he did so he looked back over his shoulder and smiled at Pin.

Pin turned back to the window, feeling oddly shaken. Over the short course of his life, he had met many people and done many things, some of them he would have preferred to have left in the realms of imagination rather than those of experience, yet the demon was different. It was not simply a question of attraction; Pin felt that Zhu Irzh would be able to explain things to him somehow, to make sense of the world.

Pin gazed around the room and realized that his life, which he had previously accepted as a matter of fate and therefore something which one could do nothing about, was no longer the one he wanted. He supposed the impression had been growing for some time—his thoughts about dowsing had indicated that—but the demon seemed to have catalyzed it. Restlessly, he put down his empty glass and wandered across the room to the huge double doors, avoiding those who tried to catch his eye. He needed to be alone for a while.

"Where's the bathroom?" he said to a little servant at the door. The thing turned smoothly and raised its childlike face. Pin caught the antiseptic smell of engineered flesh and automatically took a step back.

"Down the corridor and on the right," the servant said in a sweet, whispering voice. Pin could see its vocal mechanisms stirring in its throat, but the rosebud mouth did not move. He made his way in the direction indicated by its pointing hand.

Even the bathroom was magnificent. Pin spent a moment exploring, then went over to the wall unit and splashed his face with water. He stared at his own reflection in the mirror, wishing that the glass was a gate to another world, and he could step through and walk away. There had to be more than this, but if it were a choice between either corporate indenture, or Fourth Chorus and occasional bouts of prostitution, he'd take the latter options. At least he got to go to parties, he thought dismally.

From one of the cubicles there came a sudden rustle of skirts and a stifled laugh. The door of the cubicle began to open. Pin recognized the laugh; he'd heard it often enough. So that was where Maiden Ming had got to. Having no desire, in his current mood, to encounter his rival, he stepped swiftly into the nearest cubicle and closed the door. There was the murmur of conversation, which Pin could not hear, and then a brief flurry of movement. Pin raised his eyes to the ceiling and waited. He heard the door swing open, and a grunt of exertion as someone emerged. Then the bathroom door whirred open and closed. Cautiously, Pin pushed the cubicle door aside and peered out. The bathroom was empty. He stepped out and paused: on the floor, just in front of the cubicle, was a single drop of blood. In the pallor of the surrounding room, it seemed almost to glow.

Pin knew that there was always the danger, in this particular kind of environment, that one would meet people whose tastes ran to extremes: his own memory winced from certain recollections. He despised Ming, but she was a member of the opera, and therefore one of his own. He ran to the bathroom door, listened for a moment, then stepped carefully through. The corridor was empty. Pin took a deep, steadying breath. Something had happened to Ming, presumably at the hands of one of the guests. Pin thought fast.

Appealing to his hostess was out of the question. The role of chorus people, during their off-hours, was to attend social functions, to be amiable and amusing, and to provide discreet services for the guests, for which they would be handsomely paid. They were also supposed to keep their mouths firmly shut. If Pin started making a fuss, he'd be branded a troublemaker, and why would Jhai Tserai care, anyway? Why would *anyone* care what happened to some little chorus girl? People like Ming and Pin went missing every day. Sometimes they turned up alive, but usually they did not turn up at all, and one was obliged to shrug one's shoulders and carry on as usual. Pin was suddenly sickened by his environment. He considered going alone in search of Ming, but surely the place was a hive of security cameras, and he had no wish to be found somewhere that he shouldn't be. Indecisively, he bit his lip; the impulse toward heroics warred with self-preservation, and the latter won. Guiltily, he made his way back to the party.

Back in the ballroom, the party was getting into its stride.

Pin found Zhu Irzh sitting on a couch, talking to a middle-aged man whom he evidently knew. Pin appraised the stranger with a practiced eye, and noticed two things: firstly, the man was entirely unremarkable, and secondly, he did not appear to be enjoying himself. As the demon talked, the stranger's gaze roamed around the room with ill-concealed distaste, which did not alter substantially when it focused on Pin.

"Ah," Zhu Irzh said, with apparent pleasure. "The young man from the opera. Chen, this is Pin, from the Pellucid Island Opera Company. Pin, this is my colleague, Detective Inspector Chen, who works for the police force."

"Delighted," Pin said, faintly. So, those odd rumors about the demon's involvement with the police were true. That wasn't reassuring. Chen nodded, amiably enough, then turned back to Zhu Irzh. Pin sat down on a nearby chair and pretended not to be listening to their conversation, which was about the weather, all the time thinking: *What has happened to Ming?* At last, shame overcame his natural caution of the police and he blurted out, "I think something terrible's happened."

Zhu Irzh and Chen looked at him, startled.

"What? Why?" Chen asked, blinking. Having begun, Pin could hardly retract what he had said. He explained.

"And you're sure it was your friend in the cubicle?" Chen said.

"She's not exactly—yes. And there was blood on the floor."

Chen sat forward in his chair and massaged his forehead. "All right. What are we going to do?"

The demon said, consideringly, "I have a certain amount of license to roam the premises. I'll go and look for the girl. You stay here; pretend to have a conversation."

Pin and Chen looked at one another with a mutual lack of appreciation, and reluctantly agreed. Zhu Irzh vanished in the direction of the door, and Pin and Chen embarked upon a desultory discourse about the opera for the next fifteen minutes, whereupon Zhu Irzh slid back onto the couch like a ghost.

"She's not in the apartments," the demon said. "I can't sense her anywhere, either. I don't think there's more you can do for your friend, Pin. Maybe you should go home. I'll try and find out what's happened to her."

"I can't go," Pin said. "I'm contracted for the evening."

"You're for hire?" Chen asked. Not looking either of them in the eye, Pin nodded.

"All right," Chen said grimly. "Consider yourself hired. I'll take you home myself. Don't worry," he added, "I meant *your* home, not mine."

Zhu Irzh nodded. "I'll make sure Jhai doesn't ask too many questions."

Pin saw Chen give the demon a long look.

"Not as long as you're still here. I should think she'd be delighted to have the competition removed… Come on, Pin. Let's get out of here."

They took the elevator to the atrium in silence, and flagged down a taxi. On the way down Shaopeng, Pin turned to Chen and said, "Detective Inspector. Thank you."

Chen said quietly, "I just wish, Pin, that I could do more. That people like you didn't have to do what you do. I understand the reasons for it, but that doesn't mean I approve of the circumstances which generate it."

Pin glanced at him. The policeman's face was downcast, banded in light as they passed beneath the neon towers of the city. He was quite an attractive man, Pin decided, more because of his kindness than his round-faced, stocky appearance. One learned to notice these things. Shyly, Pin said, "If you'd like to—I mean, I wouldn't mind if I really was for hire. I mean, for free."

Chen gave him a startled glance. At last he said, "Oh, no. No, that's quite all right."

"I'm not a child," Pin said, feeling oddly rejected. "And I'm not cheap, either." He might be a prostitute, he thought, but he still had his pride.

Gently, Chen said, "I know. But it's not my thing. I'm married, you see. And I meant what I said; I'm taking you to your home. Where do you live, anyway?"

"At the Opera."

"You actually live in the Opera?"

"We all do," Pin said, and glancing out the window he saw the familiar rotund shape of the Pellucid Island Opera House rising behind the go-downs and teahouses of Shaopeng. He discovered with surprise that he was almost pleased to be back.

"We're here," he said.

"All right. I'll make sure Zhu Irzh knows where to find you, if he discovers anything." Chen turned to him. "I'm sorry about your friend. We'll do what we can. Goodnight, Pin."

Pin stepped out into the humid night air and the car pulled away. He watched it depart for a moment, then made his way slowly through the back entrance of the Opera House to the dressing room that he shared with the rest of Fourth Chorus. He had thought that he was too agitated to rest, but it was not long before he fell into sleep, dreaming of golden eyes.

TWO

Mrs Pa always tried to get to the temple early, but although the setting of the cheap alarm clock crept further back each morning there were always people there before her, squatting on the steps of Emmereng Ghat in the sultry morning air. Mrs Pa had to avoid stepping on them as she hobbled up the temple steps. The clients muttered furious imprecations into the dim dawn light, rattling the *pai* cups in a frenzy and sending thin wooden spills cascading over the translucent marble. Hands were cast up around Mrs Pa's narrow shins, in elation or despair. There was already a snaking queue at the teller's counter and Mrs Pa had to wait, watching as the sun drew up over the edge of the temple roof. The last breath of unhealthy night air drifted away, and Mrs Pa's turn came. She grabbed a paper packet out of the slot, not daring to take time to choose, and shoved a coin toward the teller. Her hand shook a little as she fumbled it open. *Stupid, stupid of me,* Mrs Pa thought, and then stared dumbfounded as the slip of paper revealed the auspicious eight and lucky mountain sign.

"What are you waiting for?" a voice bawled in her ear. Mrs Pa turned to find an elderly gentleman nudging her elbow. Muttering, Mrs Pa pushed him aside and went to stand in the courtyard under the growing light. *Rude old man.* She soon forgot him, however, because the sunlight showed it clearly: *lucky eight, lucky mountain.*

The great day had arrived, just as the broker had said when she'd called last night. Mrs Pa couldn't quite bring herself to trust the broker; you heard so many stories. Still disbelieving, she inserted a coin into the counter slot. A thick spike of incense, red as embers, rattled down into the tray. *A foolish machine,* Mrs Pa thought. The incense might break. Crossing the courtyard to the brazier she stuck the stick firmly into the pan, patting down the sand to keep it upright. She touched her lighter to the tip of the incense, and a column of smoke threaded up into the polluted air. Mrs Pa watched its passage to Heaven with satisfaction. *Good. Now for the next thing.*

The courtyard was filling fast, everyone shaking the telling sticks, concentrating like mad, a possessed woman (there was always one) weaving between. Her hands were full of chrysanthemum blooms which she ate methodically, petal by petal.

Mrs Pa threaded her way between the questioners and made her way out onto Shaopeng, where she was obliged to wait forty minutes for the next tram. Finally the rails hummed, and then the tram itself rattled into view at the end of Shaopeng Street. Passengers, desperate to get to work before they got fined, wrestled their way into the nearest carriage. There were too many people; arguments broke out along the margins. Mrs Pa, unresisting, let herself be carried with the flow through the doors and found herself in the center of the car, staring up at the ceiling. She could see nothing else. How would she know when they reached Ghenret? She could not remember the number of stops. She poked a young woman in the back; uninterested dark eyes looked down at her.

"Are you going to the harbor?"

"No; Paugeng," the young woman said. She wore a technician's overalls and the scarlet badge of the Paugeng Jaruda bird blazed above her breast.

"I am," someone said. "I'll tell you when we get there."

Mrs Pa squinted up. The handsome face turned to hers was pale; the golden eyes filled with amusement. *A demon!* Mrs Pa thought, startled. It had been a long time since she'd seen one of his kind; she'd thought she had lost the gift, if gift it was. Everyone else seemed to be ignoring him: probably they really couldn't see that he was there. Mrs Pa wondered whether to summon a charm against him, then dismissed the thought. At least someone had some manners, but what a poor pass, that even Hellkind were nicer to you than your own these days.

"Thank you, young man," she said, under her breath. The demon smiled. He had sharp teeth, too, she noticed. After Murray Town, the crowd thinned out and Mrs Pa could just about see through the murky window of the carriage.

"Where are we now?" Mrs Pa asked.

"Not far," the soft voice said. "Look, there's the Senditreya Endo. What's left of it, anyway."

Mrs Pa peered through the window. The iron doors of the ruined temple appeared briefly in view; the dome of the vaults catching the morning sun. They said that the Feng Shui Practitioners' Guild was rebuilding it, and would rededicate it to someone else, but they didn't seem to have got very far. The walls were still a tumble of masonry.

"Next stop's Ghenret," the demon said.

"Thank you," Mrs Pa said again. The demon nodded and when the little knot of passengers spilled out onto the Ghenret platform, he was gone, moving quickly through the crowd.

Mrs Pa walked slowly to the market, the next stop in her preparations. It was a long walk for an elderly lady from the platform to Ghenret harbor, and she took it slowly. It was still quite early. The crowd who had got off the downtown had dispersed and the walkway was quiet. She could hear the oily tide lapping against the harbor wall. The film that coated the waves collected the light and held it, sending pale mottled shadows across the surface of the water. The warehouse go-downs filed along the edge of the harbor, dwarfed by the snaking tower. The logo of Paugeng Pharmaceuticals, identical to the red badge on the unhelpful girl's clothing, was emblazoned over one side. Up there, away from the little world, lived Jhai Tserai. But whatever they might say about Jhai, she was reputed to be generous to her employees, and she was such a pretty girl, too. They looked after you in Paugeng, up to a point, of course. Mrs Pa had wanted her daughter Mai to apply there one day, rather than becoming a cleaner like her mother, but it hadn't happened. Never mind. Her daughter would soon be settled now. Mrs Pa was conscious of a delayed relief, so enormous that she had not allowed herself to feel it that morning. She had been waiting so long that she thought it would never come, and now it had.

The go-down market had been open since four that morning. Most of the best stuff was gone, but there were still things to be found if you knew people, and Mrs Pa knew a great many. She had lived here most of her life, after all. She moved through the canopied alleys, squeezing oranges, stuffing pak choi and marsh-grown water chestnuts into her battered bag, and keeping up a constant litany of conversation with her neighbors.

"You're buying a lot today," Miss Reng probed, eyeing the bulging bag.

"A special occasion!" Mrs Pa teased her.

"What would that be?"

So Mrs Pa, making the most of her big news, told her. Miss Reng gave a shriek of excitement, making people look round.

"Mai! Your daughter, getting *married?* How wonderful!"

Mrs Pa said, "That's right. I found out yesterday. It's only to be expected, of course."

"Of course," Miss Reng agreed, a little too quickly.

The news would be all over the district by noon. Mrs Pa, well pleased, lugged her shopping home and sat in her kitchen with a boiling kettle on the stove, waiting for the neighbors to drop by. She was not disappointed. A constant stream of people knocked on the door, on one pretext or another, throughout the day. Yes, it was true. Yes, she was so pleased, although, of course, she'd been expecting it. Mrs Pa started cooking well before dusk.

Her anticipation grew. At last the phone call came.

"I'm sorry, Mother, the line's not very good. I had problems getting through." On the other end, Mai's voice was thin and disembodied. "Are you pleased?"

"Married! I can't believe it. It's wonderful. Where are you going to hold the ceremony? Had you thought?" Mrs Pa asked.

"There's a special boat… It's called *Precious Dragon*. It's coming to the city next week; you can get married on it. Ahn and I thought it would be nice."

"I'll call his parents," her mother said.

Giggling and chattering, they went into the details of the wedding. It was a terrible line, crackling as usual, but Mai explained everything twice, and then Mrs Pa told her daughter about the cooking. "I'll send it over tonight, as soon as it's ready."

"Oh, Mother! That's so good of you." Mai talked on even as the line deteriorated, but at last they hung up and Mrs Pa, as she had promised, rang the bridegroom's parents in preparation for the wedding that had, at last, arrived.

THREE

She had not left the vaults for years, and now the summons had come. Embar Dea swam out through West Iron Gate, feeling the heavy gush of water along her flanks as the gate drew to a close. The soft, muffled clang that it made as it shut behind her echoed along the channel. Embar Dea moved swiftly, seeking to overcome fear. How long had it been since she had passed this way? Thirty years? After that last journey she had been confined to the peace and silence of Sulai-Ba, before its ending. The others had told her things—tormenting the elderly being with horror stories in the darkness. They told her about the pollution; the bands of oil through which they must move like a dancer between banners, the chemicals which stung the eyes and left an acidity at the back of the throat, the dangerous wash of the canal boats and junks, so many more than in her own time. Embar Dea was afraid of these things, and afraid, too, of the people themselves: the people who lived in the world beyond the Night Harbor, their sharpness, their long hands, their little heads and little eyes.

Now, after Ayo's death, Embar Dea had been summoned to the new temple, to Tenebrae, although she did not know why. She had expected to remain here. To live out her days with the days of Sulai-Ba. But now she would have to travel through the canal system until she reached Ghenret, and then take the underground channels to the mouth of the delta, going east into the inner seas to where Tenebrae lay. It was a human name, appropriately enough for the new temple, but, strangely, a Western one. The Kingdom of Shadows. But then, not all of her kind were from the east.

Embar Dea reached the first filter, reached out with a claw, and waited for its heavy lock to swing open. The current, released, bubbled around her and she went through into Second Filter Channel. One more to go, and then she was out into the side channel that led to the canal. Already the water had a different taste, and Embar Dea, used to purity, wrinkled her muzzle at its sourness. When she reached Third Filter she almost turned and swam back; better to die a quick and bloody death at the hands of a friend in cold, clean Sulai-Ba than breathe this filthy stuff. But friends may be dead already: she did not know where Onay and Merren Ame were. Out at sea? Or dead, rolling to rot in the stinking waters of the canal or pinned to the bottom of a trawler with an illegal harpoon through the lungs? She had not heard from them for such a long time, and so she continued to swim, coming out with a snort and a gasp into the reeking water of the side channel.

When she came to the round outlet that led into the main Jhenrai, it was not so bad. The canals were supposed to be flushed every few days by opening the big sluices that led off from Ghenret. She could taste a cleaner undertone of salt through the acids and detergent, and the water seemed to be flowing fairly quickly. It was dark at the bottom of the canal; Embar Dea, afraid, had no wish to be seen making her journey. Boats tethered at the surface swung and knocked in the flow, the black bulks of their hulls rose above her in the darkness. Someone threw something over the side, an unpleasant mixture of solids and acid which drifted down through the tainted water and which Embar Dea swerved to avoid. She was following the salt, coming up toward Ghenret. Her instructors had told her when the sluice was to be opened, and she would have to pass through or be penned in the muck for another three days. Thus Embar Dea hurried, an elderly water dragon, traveling quickly and unseen through the silted canal to the harbor.

FOUR

It was evening when the visitors came for Pin H'siao. The performance had just ended, and Pin was in the process of folding up his costume when he turned to find Miss Jhin standing nervously behind him.

"Pin," she said, encouragingly. "There are some people here to see you." In a lowered voice she added, "I think they want to make a, um, a *booking*." Miss Jhin, delicate soul that she was, preferred to turn a blind eye to the more sordid activities of her chorus; he could see the distaste in her eyes.

"All right," he told her, wearily. "I'll sort it out."

"Thank you, Pin," Miss Jhin said, her face betraying gratitude. Pin tidied himself up and followed her out of the dressing room. Two people were waiting in the hallway. One was a woman in early middle age, with the trademark blackened teeth and lacquered hairdo of a professional madam. The girl who stood by her side had a pretty, empty face, reminding Pin uneasily of the lost Maiden Ming, whom he had not seen since the night of the Paugeng party. That had been two days ago now, and he had heard nothing from the policeman or the demon. And Ming had not returned. Guiltily, he could not bring himself to feel too sorry about that.

"How may I help you?" he asked.

The Madam gave a slight bow.

"We are interested in your company this evening, at a small soirée in Shaopeng. Not very far, and possibly for no more than an hour or so."

"I see." Well, that didn't sound too bad, Pin thought. But he'd been wrong before, Gods knew. "All right. Would you like me to accompany you now?"

"That would be most acceptable. We will, of course, want to come to some sort of arrangement: I have a list of the rates from your charming chorus director." Holding out the list, she indicated the higher end of the fee scale.

"Most acceptable," Pin said, echoing the Madam. If he could get more bookings like this, he thought, he might be able to start saving to get out of here. This decision had come to him on the morning after the party at Paugeng, which he had spent in a daze thinking about the demon. He needed a goal, he had decided. He followed the Madam and her assistant out into the balmy evening air of Shaopeng.

They took a circuitous route, bypassing the downtown station and heading down a maze of back alleyways to a long, low building with a red lacquered roof. A neon sign hung outside the door, and as soon as he set eyes on it, Pin stopped dead.

"You didn't tell me that this was—*that* sort of place," he protested, trying not to sound too accusing.

"Please don't worry," the Madam replied, rather sharply. "This is not the usual kind of service."

Pin stared unhappily at the sign, which bore, in bright pulsing letters, the word for Hell. He had only ever been in a demon lounge once before, but his visit had passed in a haze of narcola and panoline. The lounges catered to the more exotic end of the market; the services in which a wide range of drugs played a major role. It was said, beneath people's breath, that the inhabitants of the lounges were no narcotic-induced hallucination, but were real: minor denizens of Hell, conjured up on a short-term lease to service the clients of the lounge. It was not, by anyone's definition, safe sex.

Pin's memories of that event, which he did not care to examine too closely, were a blur of images: elegantly contorted limbs, bright, inhuman eyes, and waves of pain. It had not been an experience that he was eager to repeat.

"I'll double the fee," said the Madam, through pinched, painted lips. Pin sighed. He might as well go through with it, he thought. The money he could save would help him to escape from his life all the sooner. Taking a deep breath, he stepped through the door into the florid décor of the hallway.

The Madam's assistant led him through the labyrinth of passages into a small circular room. Here, he was invited to kneel before a low, ornately carved table, and then the assistant left. Pin waited apprehensively. At last the door opened, and a group of people filed in to kneel in a circle around Pin, arranging their robes around them. He looked warily around the room. Their faces were in shadow, but nine pairs of eyes stared back at him with a consuming eagerness. The woman closest to him, wrapped in a brocaded dressing gown, was the Madam. Her raven hair was piled upon her head with pins. She gave him a thin-lipped smile, and turned up the lamp so that it cast flickering shadows across her face.

"Now, you don't need to worry about a thing," the Madam said, kindly. Pin shivered. Her motherly concern did not reach her eyes, which were as flat and depthless as pools of oil.

"Nothing at all," one of the other women breathed in a soft, malicious voice, and giggled. Pin thought: *Ming, this is your spiritual home.* Rising, the Madam stepped forward. She held a braided crimson cord.

"Now, bow your head," she told Pin. Trying to focus on the subject of money, Pin did so. His hands were tied behind his back and the Madam placed a palm on the back of his head, forcing his head further down.

"Are you sure he's suitable?" someone said in a low voice.

"He comes from the chorus," the Madam snapped. "An artiste. A sensitive person. Of course he'll be suitable."

There was a disparaging snort of laughter.

"The other one wasn't."

"The other one was a fragile soul," the Madam replied frostily. *Ming?* Pin wondered with a sudden pang of guilt. He still felt responsible for his fellow-chorus member. Had she been brought here, for who knew what purpose? He struggled to rise.

"Keep still," the Madam hissed, adding, "Light the braziers."

The room began to fill with the acrid tang of incense, and there was something beneath the gunpowder smell which Pin thought he recognized. It was a heavy, musky odor, not unlike opium, and then he knew. It was a narcotic called sama: opium combined with nepenthe. It was useless to struggle; he would only draw more of the drug into his lungs. Raging and helpless, he let it take him, and as it did so the chanting began, rising and falling in hypnotic rhythm. The words made no sense to him, but he knew they were dreadful: they sounded forbidden and wrong. They were interspersed with a wailing incantation from the Madam in ordinary Cantonese: "Hsun Tung, great master of the gateway, minister of lightning…we summon you…we bring you in…"

The chanting rose to a crescendo. Pin opened his eyes and saw, appalled, that the world had disappeared. He was in a place that was dark and yet blinding, empty and filled with chaotic movement. He was going to Hell. Pin squeezed his eyes shut. He thought he could hear someone screaming very far away, and then everything stopped.

蛇警探

Pin found himself once more in the middle of a circle of faces. They were all looking at him, curious and predatory, and their eyes were crimson, and gold, and jade green. Pin gaped at them. He could feel the air flowing through him, as though he were made of smoke. Their faces were burnished, ebony and bronze, resembling the masks that hung around the balconies of the Opera House. One of them laughed, and it sounded like dry leaves in a winter wind.

"What are you? Where am I?" Pin breathed, but no sound emerged. One of the circle reached out toward the lamp on the table and slipped her sharp fingers into the flame. When she withdrew them, Pin saw that they burned.

She blew the flame toward him and instinctively he drew away. The fire streamed through the air and dispersed him. Then he was pulled down toward the circle, settling unsteadily into something that was hot and steaming and smelled of old blood. It was another body. Slowly, jerkily, Pin raised his hand. It was covered in a loose velvet sleeve. It had long, polished black claws.

"*Ohhh,*" everyone said, in a collective sigh. "It's *working.*" From somewhere inside the house, a clock began to strike the hour. Silently, Pin counted. It went on and on, and then at the stroke of thirteen, it stopped. Sunlight poured through the open window, but it felt like midnight. The demons looked at Pin and grinned.

They wanted him to answer questions. They asked him about people he had never heard of, places he had never visited, and Pin was utterly unable to help them.

"I don't know," he kept saying, mouthing the words with difficulty from his strange new throat.

"Tell us," they hissed. "Tell us about your city. What is happening there now?" Pin had no idea. He knew about his own small world of the Opera, and the fragments that fell into his uninterested ears at the occasional party, but apart from this he had very little knowledge of the city at large. Around him, the demon's body stretched and gasped. Pin was more interested in exploring the being that he currently possessed, but the others were looking at him with expectation. He racked his memory for details.

"It's been very hot," he said, whistling through the demon's teeth.

One of the circle got to his feet with an indignant fluttering of robes.

"What good is this? We haven't gone to all this trouble for a weather report. Send it back to wherever it came from."

"But it's only the second one we've ever reached," someone pleaded. The demon waved a dismissive hand.

"What good is it to go to all the trouble of holding a séance, to violate natural laws and face the fury of the *kuei*—if they ever find out, which lands forbid they ever will—only to summon up a being with all the wisdom of that—that tabletop! The first one could not take it and this one is an idiot. The whole thing's been a waste of time."

"Yes," Pin breathed. "All a terrible mistake! Send me back." He might plunge like a stone straight back to where he came from, but even the disquieting confines of the demon lounge were preferable to Hell itself, although he had to admit that it looked ordinary enough, apart from its inhabitants. The room was plain; the walls made of a substance that looked like waxed paper. Sunlight streamed over the windowsills, yet the demons cast no shadow. They were still watching him; their pointed faces anticipatory.

"Poor little spirit," one of them said. "Let's keep it for a bit. It might become more amusing."

Pin felt the stirrings of protest in the mind that he occupied. The demon who had spoken earlier snapped, "Do you have *any* idea of the risk we're running? This isn't a game! We have to find out what's happening on the mortal plane, to find out why the *kuei* are there; we have to seize our opportunity! If this thing knows nothing, then we must summon one who does… Send it back."

He plunged a taloned hand into the depths of the brazier, sending up a shower of bitter sparks. The eyes of his kindred glowed meteor-bright, and once again an unnatural chanting began. Pin felt himself squeezed and constricted and forced along the demon's fiery veins, racing down its twisted neural pathways. He battered behind its eyes, and it wailed and cried aloud in something that sounded remarkably like pain. The voice was female, he realized. He felt her head fall forward like a broken toy.

"It's not working!" the demon lord hissed. "Harder, harder!"

The diabolical mantras began again, and Pin was forced from one part of the demon's mind to another, but he could not break free. At last there was a terrible pause. A little, frightened voice said, "The *kuei*… I can hear them. They're coming!"

The demons panicked, throwing the table aside and rushing in all directions. Slowly the sunlit room began to dissolve. First, the paper walls peeled away and began to shred in the rising wind. Coiled filaments whirled around the table and as they spiraled past, Pin could see the patterns which marked them. It was not paper of which the walls were made, but human skin. The shreds of dermis wreathed upward and were gone. Beyond, lay a chaotic mass of cloud. It made Pin sick to look at it. The demon that held him was rocking to and fro, hands clutching at her head. With a lurch, she staggered up and sprang into the rising wind. There was the rattle of something big, above him. Horrified, Pin saw that the house had been standing on an iron column, rising out of the boiling clouds. He looked out of the demon's eyes, up into the red wind, and saw three beings, vast and armored and many-legged, coiling through the storm. The sight was so awful that his spirit fled screaming into the demon's head and stayed there, hiding in the suddenly fragile shell of her skull as his hostess fled into the depths of Hell.

FIVE

Over the last day or so, Mrs Pa had been busy, haunting the go-down markets and buying presents, flowers, and food. All the money she'd saved over the years went toward the wedding, but Mrs Pa didn't care. It was worth it, to see Mai settled at last.

On the designated evening, she visited the Kungs, as arranged. They lived in Murray Town, not far from Sulai-Ba, in a small shuttered house on the Taitai waterfront. Both parents were lab assistants, not for Paugeng, but for Somay. However, this did not affect their religious affiliations, Mrs Pa noticed. During the devotions before the celebratory meal, Mrs Kung ceremoniously opened the doors of the little kitchen shrine to reveal not only the disgraced Senditreya, holding her compass and theodolite, but also, on either side of the major deity, the severe, pretty face of Paugeng's Jhai Tserai and the pudgy features of the Somay heirs, acolytes in the home-made triptych. Worship fell where it could these days. Mrs Kung lit candles and set them in the slots at either side of the icons. The gods, old and new, disappeared in a light pall of smoke. Mrs Pa sat back and nursed her jasmine tea. She liked this family: they were sober, respectable people. She liked their pleasant, moon-faced daughter, soon to be her own daughter's sister-in-law, and the studious younger son. And, of course, she liked the bridegroom, Ahn, who unfortunately could not be here just yet; such a well-respected young man, the same age as Mai. Things had worked out very well.

"We were so pleased to receive your daughter's name from the broker," Mrs Kung confided. "My father remembers your husband well; they worked together on many occasions."

The two families fell into reminiscing about the past, the old days. The Kungs were from Beijing, a place which had become no more than a story, bright as neon in memory: the parks and the restaurants and the old city.

21

Mr Kung had left when he was a boy. Mr and Mrs Pa had come later, from Guangzhou, traded between the mining companies who were then expanding their operations to the east of Singapore Three. They shared stories, shared experiences, and then at last the two families strolled down to the dock, to wait with anticipation and excitement, and behind it all a little fear, for the wedding boat.

The sun had long set in a last rosy burst of light, and now the blue dusk was filled with the mast lights, at anchor in Ghenret and beyond, riding the evening tide. It was a mild, damp evening. That afternoon, Mrs Pa had sat in her kitchen and listened with increasing anxiety to the rain humming on the corrugated iron roof of her house. But early in the evening, the rain had stopped and the washed sky had cleared. The two families waited nervously for the arrival of the wedding boat.

"When do you think it will come?" Mrs Kung whispered.

"I don't know," Mrs Pa replied.

Along the edge of the wharf the marriage broker and her assistants had placed long tubes of incense, which flared and smoldered in the damp air. They had lit a fire in a stout iron brazier, sending a stream of sparks into the water. The broker pranced and stamped about the wharf, wheeling and clapping her hands to ward off undesirables, and occasionally striking a small, fringed drum. The amulets tied around the edges of her shawl danced with her.

"Such a lot of energy!" marveled Mrs Kung. A few faint stars rose above the city mists. There was no moon tonight. Water lapped against the wharf, loud in the sudden silence. The broker fell silent.

A junk was sailing up the sooty waters of the harbor, stealing into port. Its sails were as red as a hibiscus blossom, ragged and burning in the ship's own light. Phosphorescence trailed in its wake, a black lantern hung from its prow. From the wan illumination that it shed, the junk's name appeared briefly on its side: *Precious Dragon,* just as Mai had said. Next to Mrs Pa, the broker threw back her head and gave a long, thin cry. Mrs Pa craned her neck, trying to get a glimpse of her daughter, and then the junk was sidling against the dock. The broker threw a sudden handful of firecrackers onto the brazier. There was a series of startling explosions, and as the fire flared, Mrs Pa saw her child's pale face smiling over the edge of the deck. Mrs Pa had not actually set eyes on Mai for thirty years, since the cholera epidemic that had taken, in one long night, her husband and her three-year-old daughter, but she would have known Mai anywhere. She jumped up and down, calling excitedly, and beside Mai, the bridegroom beamed.

"Hurry!" cried the broker, and Mrs Pa and the Kung family hastily bundled all the wedding presents from their scarlet envelopes and threw them into the blaze. The little gifts went first: sweets, crackers, and cookies vanished into the fire before raining down on the deck of the junk. Then as the fire caught, the proper gifts followed. Flat paper chairs and tables, a handsome parchment bed, the paper stove and pots and pans, everything for the young couple, were consumed by the flames. They would go to the new house, to which Mai and her husband would return. Then the two families threw the money onto the fire, each note bearing the smiling face of the demonic banker and a fine representation of the Bank of Hell. The people on the junk were briefly obscured in a shower of banknotes, falling like leaves around their feet. At last it was over. The broker clapped her hands and banged the little drum. Mrs Pa saw Mai wince, and gave a sympathetic wave. The tide began to turn.

"Goodbye, Mother!" and "Phone me!"

Mrs Pa and her pale daughter cried, and then *Precious Dragon*'s silhouette crew cast off and the sails of the junk caught the incense wind and streamed out, carrying the dead beyond the western darkness, out of sight.

SIX

Chen sat toward the end of the table in the restaurant, trying to catch Zhu Irzh's eye. The demon, who sat opposite, was concentrating on the dissection of his squid. At the head of the table, Captain Sung droned on, reciting endless statistics about the decline in the crime rate, what a success the previous year had been, how the murder rate had dropped by fifteen percent...

Mind numbing. And also wrong, because the city's crime stats were massaged *ad nauseam* depending on the requirements of Singapore Three's governor, and in any case, all the data had been hopelessly skewed over the course of the last few months as a result of the disasters that had hit the city. With so many dead, a few of them *had* to be criminals. But here they were, with Zhu Irzh along as well in order to demonstrate the success of the police department's equal ops policy, for Sung to show off in front of the governor.

Without the equal ops fad, neither Chen nor Zhu Irzh would even be here. Chen had grown used to being the department's embarrassing little secret, but since he had, effectively, saved the world, Sung had reluctantly recognized that some acknowledgement of his services needed to be made.

And a demented goddess rampaging through the streets in a chariot drawn by fiery-eyed oxen tended to convince even the most hardened atheist of *some* evidence of the existence of deity.

Unable to attract Zhu Irzh's attention, Chen glanced at the governor. Ling was a saturnine, depressed-looking man—although, admittedly, he had plenty to be depressed about. Not quite as humorless as Chen had always thought, however, the governor had already made two quite amusing jokes. Chen wondered if they'd been scripted.

"...and our outreach liaison has been immensely successful," Sung was saying. "Isn't that so, Detective Chen?"

What "outreach liaison"? "Absolutely. A tremendous success." *Better agree with him now and sort it out later.*

"Chen's leading the team," Sung said, beaming like a shark. "Of course, the inspiration for it came from your own pioneering ideas in equal opportunity."

What? Chen smiled politely and willed himself not to shout. What a waste of time this was—excellent food, to be sure, but he really needed to be back at the station. He had a mountain of paperwork, several phone calls to make, and besides all the official cases, several of which were quite urgent, there was this odd matter of the young actress who'd gone missing at Paugeng's party. Chen wanted to discuss this with Zhu Irzh, but the demon had been off on a case of his own these last few days and the opportunity hadn't presented itself. Chen didn't want to phone Zhu Irzh, because what with the demon's relationship with Jhai Tserai, security had suddenly become a bit of an issue. Chen did not put it past Jhai to have Zhu Irzh's phones bugged. And anyhow, if he had to go out to dinner, he'd rather do so with his wife, although options for dining out with a female demon were admittedly a trifle limited.

Sung and the governor were both beaming at one another in mutual admiration. Chen forced himself to attend to what Sung was saying.

"…leading a small group down to Hell on a fact-finding mission, after a very kind invitation…current exchange has gone so well that we're thinking of making it a permanent post."

That made Zhu Irzh look up from his squid. Chen saw his lips move behind his napkin. *Chen? We need to talk.*

Now he tells me.

蛇警探

Back at the station, Chen focused on plowing through that paperwork. As soon as he got rid of one piece, another appeared to take its place: incorrectly filed visa applications for Heaven, a whole slew of Hell-based internet scams. Zhu Irzh had disappeared the moment they'd left the restaurant, called away on some urgent piece of business, apparently. Chen felt frustration mounting and eventually he went down to the locker room and sat in meditation for a few minutes. It helped, but not a lot.

When he came back up to the office, however, he found Zhu Irzh perched on his desk, waiting for him.

"Hi," the demon said. "Sorry I had to rush off."

"Not a problem," Chen said, although it had been. "Sung's evidently got a bee in his bonnet."

"About this outreach thing," Zhu Irzh remarked. "First I've heard of it."

"You're not the only one. I looked up a few policy statements when I got back. It's tied in with this equal ops thing. Increased connectivity between the worlds. After that episode with Heaven, the governor apparently started thinking that improving links with Hell might not be a bad idea. There's a Western saying: better the devil you know."

The demon grimaced. "I thought Governor Ling already *had* improved connections with Hell. They've been giving him kickbacks for years."

"No surprises there." *Just for once,* Chen thought, *I'd like to be taken aback by proof of someone's innocence.*

And strangely, proof was not long in coming.

蛇警探

The demon suggested going for a quiet beer, to talk things over. It sounded like a fine suggestion to Chen, after the end of a long, sticky, tedious day, but as he was on his way out the door with the demon, Sung hurtled out of his office like a human torpedo and stepped into Chen's path.

"Chen. Sorry, I can see you're leaving. Have you got a moment?"—in that tone that suggested it was not optional.

"Both of us? Or just me?" Chen asked. The prospect of a peaceful beer was receding glumly into the distance.

"Both of you."

Chen and the demon followed Sung into his cramped office and Sung closed the door behind them. To Chen's surprise, they were not alone in the office, though he had seen no one wander past for the last hour. Someone was seated in the chair on the other side of Sung's desk.

The person was small and slight and pale, smiling beneath a fall of white hair. It was hard to tell at first whether it was male or female, but then it shifted position and Chen glimpsed breasts.

She still wasn't human, though. An unmistakable, and rather sickly, waft of peach blossom floated across the room from the personage's pink and white silk robes.

"This," said Captain Sung, "is Mi Li Qi. She's from Heaven." An expression of fleeting alarm crossed his features as he spoke, as if he couldn't quite believe what he'd just said.

"Delighted," Zhu Irzh drawled. *Oh dear,* thought Chen. The demon's last trip to Heaven hadn't been an unmitigated success. He couldn't smoke, for a start, and although they clearly tried very hard to be non-discriminatory, Zhu Irzh was, after all, demonic.

"I'm very pleased to meet you, Miss Qi," Chen added.

"And you," Miss Qi said. She had a voice like a breath of wind, light and airy and slightly tinkling. Chen, seeing that Zhu Irzh was about to say something further, cut him off at the pass.

"To what do we owe the pleasure?" he said.

"This equal opportunities policy," Sung said. Chen had heard a number of ominous statements in his time (*"the assassin is on his way," "the goddess has gone mad"*) but few of them were beginning to strike such fear into his heart as *"This equal opportunities policy."*

"Chen," the captain went on. "You don't have much on at the moment, do you?"

"Yes," Chen said.

"So," Sung continued as though Chen had not spoken, "I thought this was the ideal time to strengthen connectivity, think outside the box in developing our links between the worlds…"

The management course that Sung had been obliged to attend last month had had disastrous results, Chen thought. Prior to that, Sung had been one of those fierce northern steppe people, with a low tolerance rating for bullshit. Now, he was all about ballparks and blue sky thinking. How did they do it? Did they brainwash attendees?

"Miss Qi is here as part of a team," Sung said. "The governor would like you to go to Hell as part of a fact-finding mission, work closely with the Ministry of War. The original invitation came through them, for Miss Qi, but Heaven's insisting that she be escorted and the Ministry has been really very helpful, extending the invitation at once." He nodded at Zhu Irzh. "Seneschal? How do you feel about a trip home?"

Zhu Irzh shrugged. "I can cope. As long as we don't have to visit my relatives."

"Family is *most* important," Miss Qi said, in a little disapproving breath.

"Exactly. My family *is* most important. Just not to me."

A faint frown creased the denizen of Heaven's brow. "But—"

"Miss Qi will be coming with us, then?" Chen asked, more to stave off yet another difficult discussion than out of any real attempt to clarify matters.

"She will indeed."

"What, to Hell?" Zhu Irzh said. It was the demon's turn to look disapproving. "She'll be eaten alive."

Miss Qi's frown deepened. Sung said, "No, she won't. Not if she has you to look after her. You'll be leaving at ten P.M. tomorrow; I've sorted out your papers. Chen, any loose ends will be passed on to Ma."

"Hang on," Zhu Irzh said. "What about *my* loose ends? I'm in the middle of a case, you know."

"I'll get someone to handle it. Leave the paperwork on your desk and I'll pass it on."

"But—"

"Governor's orders, Zhu Irzh. Although it's nice to see you being conscientious about things."

Chen, rather to his shame, became instantly suspicious. It might be nice, but "nice" did not adequately describe Zhu Irzh's usual *modus operandi,* which during previous cases had included sleeping with suspects, taking bribes, intimidating witnesses, and generally behaving like the vice cop from Hell. Chen did not blame the demon, he knew no better, he was what he was. But nice?

Zhu Irzh subsided, with conspicuous reluctance. Chen sighed.

"What time tomorrow? And why are we going under the aegis of the Ministry of War?"

"You'll need to be at the Night Harbor by ten in the evening. As for War, I'm not sure. I think it has to do with someone's governmental contacts. In the meantime, I'd appreciate it if you could see Miss Qi safely back to her hotel."

Chen thought of an innocent of Heaven wandering the streets of Singapore Three—one step removed from Hell itself, after all—and mentally quailed. "Of course we will," he said.

Outside, it was still hot. Miss Qi took a deep breath and staggered slightly. Chen took her arm. "Careful. It can hit you like a hammer when you're not used to it."

"If it's this hot here," Miss Qi said, faintly, "whatever will it be like in Hell?"

"Hotter," Zhu Irzh said, not without a trace of satisfaction.

Chen looked at the address given to him by the captain and saw that the hotel was very close to the Opera House. The merest prickle of engineered coincidence stirred his cerebral cortex: that was where the rent-boy came from, and the missing girl. No more had come of this and that was typical enough, in this sprawl where young people went missing every day, but somehow he still didn't like it and that in itself was worrying. He had, long ago, learned to listen to disturbing instincts.

"It's too far to walk," he said. "We'll get a taxi. Zhu Irzh, are you coming, or do you have things to do?" Forget the beer. He'd have enough to cope with during the trip, because Zhu Irzh was bound to get a rise out of needling Miss Qi, so Chen was hoping that the demon would cry off and head home on his own. Then Chen could see Miss Qi to her hotel and go back to Inari, who might—rightfully—be feeling somewhat neglected. Inari never complained, however, and would deny any feelings of neglect if charged, so it was hard to tell. Anyway, Zhu Irzh had a girlfriend of his own to placate these days.

But the demon disappointed him. "I'll come along. Why not?"

"I thought you might want to spend the evening with Jhai," Chen said.

"Jhai—let's just say that a break won't do either of us any harm," Zhu Irzh said. "She's taking a bit too much for granted."

"I see." Chen did not add: *rather you than me.* He did not like the thought of playing games with Jhai Tserai, but presumably the demon knew her better. He glanced at Miss Qi. The inhabitants of Heaven are much too refined to sweat, but Miss Qi certainly glowed: a wan, ambient light of her own that made her stand shadowless in the glare of the sun.

"Miss Qi, you're melting," Chen said. "Let's get you somewhere cooler." He stepped out into the street and flagged down a cab.

Interestingly, it transpired that the taxi driver could see neither Zhu Irzh nor Miss Qi. The demon was not infrequently invisible to humans, but Chen wasn't sure what an inability to see either Hell or Heavenkind betokened. A wilful atheism? Had the taxi driver been able to see mad Senditreya during her rampage through the city? Again, interesting, but he did not press the point and they arrived at Miss Qi's hotel in peace. At least they'd put her somewhere pleasant: a small, family-run place behind a green stand of trees, at the back of the Opera House. The girl behind the desk seemed to be expecting Miss Qi and greeted her warmly. His duty thus discharged, Chen let the demon talk him into a beer after all.

"So," Chen said, half an hour later. "This case of yours." They were sitting in a bar next door to the Opera House; a cramped little place, with hundreds of photos of opera stars adorning the walls.

To his surprise, the demon was relatively forthcoming.

"I've been meaning to talk to you about it. It's an odd one. It has to do with Sulai-Ba."

"What, the temple of Sulai-Ba? It's a ruin, isn't it?"

"It is now, yes. In all the worlds—well, I don't know for sure about Heaven. I should have asked little Miss Qi. But I made enquiries and someone told me that it has been abandoned even in Heaven."

"I've lived here for years," Chen mused, "and I've never known much about Sulai-Ba. It was supposed to be a temple to the goddess of the sea, that much I do know, and it was here long before Singapore Three grew up around it. I heard it suddenly fell into disuse, about twenty years ago."

"It fell into disuse because the goddess died," Zhu Irzh said. He curled long fingers around his bottled beer.

"Goddesses don't die," Chen said, startled. "At least—well, Senditreya isn't dead."

"No, she's a cow, in Hell. She might work her way back up to being human again one day, if they let her reincarnate. I should think she's blown her chances of ever being a deity again, though. But this goddess was called Sulai-Ba. She fell in love with a mortal—one of *those*—but he wouldn't leave his wife for her, so she killed herself. In such a way that her spirit did not go to Heaven or Hell, or anywhere that anyone knows about. She disincarnated."

"That's technically possible," Chen said. "But it's very rare. I've never heard this story. Where did you learn it?"

"I asked Mhara," Zhu Irzh said. "Thought a prince of Heaven might know, and sure enough, he did."

"Fair enough," Chen said. "But what does your case have to do with a long-ago dead goddess?"

"I don't know. You see, Sulai-Ba's been locked for years, but people have gone in and out of it all the same. And lately, it looks as though the earthquakes jarred something loose, because there's been a lot of activity around Sulai-Ba: things heard in the night by people who live near it, things seen."

"What kind of things?"

"Big things."

"Mmm," said Chen. "What do you *mean,* exactly?"

"Someone saw something huge flying around Sulai-Ba. Something with wings and a tail."

"Something dragon-shaped, perhaps?" There was one of those disturbing instincts again, smacking him right in the solar plexus.

"Well, we don't know that for *sure,*" the demon said. "It might have been something else—a trapped Storm Lord, for instance."

"That's not reassuring. I'd rather have dragons." Dragons were essentially ancient, civilized creatures, guardians of Celestial courts, keepers of old books and forgotten spells. You could reason with a dragon. They weren't like the Storm Lords, *kuei,* Hellkind's centipede law-enforcers.

"The thing is," Zhu Irzh said, "there aren't many dragons in China these days. They're ideologically unsound. Most of them left when the Communists took over. A handful in the mountains, perhaps. But otherwise, they all retreated to Sambalai, a little way off from Heaven."

"Cloud Kingdom," Chen said. "I've heard of it."

"So, I don't know whether it's a dragon or what it is. But in light of recent events, I thought I'd better check it out."

"What concerns me," Chen said, "is this missing girl from the Opera. And I don't know why. It's hardly uncommon for those sorts of people to disappear, unfortunately."

The demon narrowed golden eyes. "It isn't. But I know what you mean. I had a dream last night in which we were wandering through Hell, looking for her, but she wasn't there."

"It reminds me of Pearl Tang," Chen said. He smiled, remembering the first case that he and Zhu Irzh had worked on together. "There must be something about young female spirits that leads to trouble."

"Of course there is," the demon said gloomily. "They're women, aren't they?"

"Well, there is that," Chen admitted, thinking of Inari and feeling just a little treacherous. Goddess knew that Inari had caused trouble enough, poor love. But she hadn't meant to.

"I think we need to talk to that boy again," Zhu Irzh remarked. "I called the Opera, by the way. The girl hasn't shown up."

"We're next door," Chen said. "And there's no time like the present. In fact, there really isn't, because I've no idea how long Sung expects us to remain in

Hell on this bloody fact-finding thing."

"As long as it takes, I suppose." The demon downed the last of his beer and stood up. "Okay, let's do it."

Chen was not a lover of opera *per se* but he had always been rather fascinated by the life of the Opera House. Backstage was another world, of giant chrysanthemums, huge cardboard clouds, twirling parasols. It smelled of face powder and cigarette smoke and cheap perfume. Zhu Irzh was smiling.

"This is *fun!*"

"It's got a certain charm," Chen said. He addressed a passing stagehand. "Excuse me. I'm looking for a young man named Pin."

"Oh. The flute player. You're looking for *him*." The stagehand gave what could only be described as a smirk. "*Very* popular, he is."

"We're with the police department," Chen said.

"*Done* something, has he? Doesn't surprise me. Always thought he was up to no good. I—"

"Actually, he hasn't done anything," Chen said. "It's about a witness statement. Now, is he here or not?"

"Don't ask me. You'd need to speak to his chorus director."

"Then we'll do that," Chen said, with a faint degree of *froideur*.

"Why, no," the chorus director said, once they'd tracked her down. "I'm afraid he hasn't been in for the last couple of days. I was really becoming quite concerned." She perched on the edge of her chair, blinking behind large spectacles, her legs demurely crossed at the ankles.

Chen frowned. Miss Jhin's protestation of concern seemed genuine—a nice woman, in his professional assessment, probably born into respectability but fallen on hard times. There was something a little faded about her.

"Where does Pin live?" Chen asked her.

"Why, here, at the Opera. A lot of them do, if they've been orphaned—Pin's mother died, you see, a few years ago. She'd been one of our chorus girls, and Pin knew all the traditional songs, so it seemed natural for us to take him on. But—you see, there are so many people here, it's so busy—I should have realized sooner he was missing." She rubbed her eyes. "I'm making excuses for myself, aren't I?"

"I'm sure you did your best," Chen said. "I don't mean to alarm you, but when was Pin last seen?"

"When he went to the party."

"What party was this? Do you mean the one at Paugeng?"

To Chen's surprise, Miss Jhin blushed a deep, rusty red. "No. You see, the young people are very popular, and they get asked out a lot. Of course, we're careful, but if they *are* over age, then—"

Chen was beginning to get the picture. "I see. Who was it who held the party?"

"It was at a club. Called Cloudland, I believe. The manageress phoned me to arrange it."

Zhu Irzh leaned forward in his seat. "Cloudland? That's a demon lounge."

"Is it, now?" Chen asked, intrigued and appalled. He'd visited a demon lounge on a number of occasions in his career and none of them had turned out particularly well.

"Yes, and quite a famous one, too. I've heard mention of it in Hell—" At this point Miss Jhin gave a little squeak, although she must have been aware of the demon's origins, since she was evidently able to see him clearly enough.

"And Pin didn't come back?"

Miss Jhin blinked again. "Well—I don't know that he didn't. I'm afraid I wasn't here when the party was due to end—he was only booked for a couple of hours. But he wasn't here the next day. I thought that perhaps he'd taken the day off…" Her voice trailed away.

Taken the day off in order to recover, Chen thought. He supposed that he ought to caution Miss Jhin for what was, essentially, pimping, but he doubted whether she had any real control over the process, and anyway, he didn't have the heart. Perhaps Zhu Irzh's way of doing things was contaminating the world around him.

"If he does come back," Chen said, "or the girl—Ming?—then perhaps you'd like to call me? Here's my number."

Miss Jhin took the business card from Chen's hand as though she thought it might bite. "Thank you," she said, uncertainly. "I'll call you the moment I hear anything." Her expression became a little firmer. "Detective—I should make something plain. Pin is a good boy. He's only a—I mean, he does what he does because they're all so badly paid here at the Opera." She lowered an already breathy voice. "I'm speaking out of turn, but—it's different if you get one of the big roles, of course, but down in the chorus… Pin is a nice boy, really. I try to do what I can, but—if anything's happened to him…" Chen had the terrible feeling that she was about to burst into tears. He patted her hand.

"I know you've done your best," he said. Over Miss Jhin's shoulder, he discerned a gleam in the demon's eye, which suggested that Zhu Irzh might be about to disagree, just for the sake of it, so he added hastily, "You'll let us know, won't you?" and got to his feet.

Outside, it was still light, but only just: a deep crimson seam above the great dome of the Opera House. Chen was anxious to get back home to Inari, and Zhu Irzh, too, seemed fidgety.

"What did you think?" Chen asked.

The demon surprised him. "She's lying," he said.

"Are you sure? I didn't get that impression. I thought she was rather a nice woman, although she's working in a fairly sordid environment."

"She *is* a nice woman." Zhu Irzh made it sound like some kind of moral failing. "But she's still lying and I don't know what about, and I don't know why."

"Well, you might be right," Chen said. The demon's instincts were often spot on, and Goddess knew that he was sensitive to deceit, having perpetrated so much of it. "Do you think—" But what he had been about to say was to remain unuttered. There was a sudden whirlwind flurry in the oleander bushes alongside the Opera House. A thousand needles stung Chen's skin; instinctively, he threw an arm across his eyes. Then there came the billow of silk as Zhu Irzh flung his coat over the pair of them. A huge, hot wind ripped at Chen's hair and a roaring voice cried, "Not! Shall *not!*" Through tearing eyes Chen looked up, snatching at his rosary. Something enormous towered over them, something with insect joints and a head like a hammer. A red pinwheel eye whirled, sending out hot sparks. The image was sustained only for a moment; the creature collapsed, into a more human shape. Chen snapped his rosary at the thing but it was too late, it was charging forward and—there was the overwhelming smell of peach blossom, a lush, fruity aroma that was so strong it made Chen gag. Something blurred the air between himself and the creature, a spinning pale being, from which ribbons of pastel color were streaming outward, like silk unwinding from a cocoon.

The insect-thing toppled and fell, mummified in the pastel streamers, which swiftly collapsed inward until there were only a few faint stains of color on the sidewalk.

"Well, that was impressive," Chen heard the demon say. Zhu Irzh sounded flabbergasted.

"I am truly sorry," Miss Qi, lately of Heaven, said. She dipped her white face toward her wringing hands. "I was almost too late. I have been most remiss. If you choose to submit a complaint report, I shall admit to it at once."

"Hang on," Zhu Irzh said. "Aren't we supposed to be looking after *you?*"

SEVEN

Embar Dea reached the upper Ghenret sluice just in time. She knew by the turbulent water ahead that they were opening the gate; it was much larger than she remembered, presumably they had extended it. She could sense something big before her, perhaps the hull of a ship sailing through. Her skin felt icy cold, even above the rolls of fat that protected her from the arctic waters, and she recognized this as fear. There was a sour taste in her mouth. She tried not to think about the propellers under the hydro's hull, beating the water, tearing into her. Don't be a fool, she sang to herself, you who danced with ships as a young thing, who led them on and siren called them into silence. *Tenebrae.*

The sluice was fully open. Her tail beat the water, and turning, she shot through, grazing her side against the wall of the sluice to miss the ship's hull with inches to spare. Why was something so big coming through the gate?—and then she understood that it was the safest mooring against what she felt was to come. Someone knew, at least.

She was now in the main harbor and the soupy filth of Ghenret. She angled her way beneath the creaking boats and with some difficulty managed to locate the runoff that cut through into the delta. It was a round hole, twenty feet or so beneath the harbor's lowest level. Embar Dea remembered when water gushed to and fro, bubbling out into river and harbor, depending on the tide, the freshness of the sweet grassy water of the delta and sharp saline exchanged, back and forth, every day. Now, the runoff was silted up, thick with mud and weed. She pushed frantically at the half-concealed entrance, hoping she would not have to travel round by the harbor mouth. Gradually, a column of mud spat out into the harbor. Embar Dea could no longer see; she belled out, listening for the diminished echoes that returned and then she went head first into the runoff.

It took her a long time to force through and Embar Dea fought terror all the way. When she had been slim and young, she had bounced through the runoff like a pea down a pipe. But she had put on weight over the last thirty years, and was heavy-bodied, barrel-chested, and with slimness remaining only at her tapering tail. She was afraid of getting stuck in the runoff, unable to back up or go forward, and she would never reach Tenebrae but remain here, held fast and choking in this underwater graveyard. Determined, she forced herself on, and at last, gasping with relief, a slide of greasy mud carried her all the way down the last gentle slope of the runoff and out into the relatively fragrant waters of the delta.

Her last glimpse of Ghenret had been a pink light, the color of water and blood, filtering down from the evening sky. Out in the silent waters of the delta, it was dark. She propelled up to the surface and broke out into the warm night air. Above her, swam the stars, which to the short-sighted dragon appeared only as a smudge of light across the greater dark. The water tasted of grass and mud, the sweetness of fresh water at low tide, with only a breath of the faint chemical taint of the harbor. Embar Dea, happy to be free from the foul runoff, swam downstream and then rolled and heaved in the swift current. The stars bounced above her and at last she tired of her exercise and, traveling fast, headed for the delta mouth and the open sea.

EIGHT

Shrieking soundlessly, the demon-host fled. As she flew, Pin could hear her thoughts rushing by him like banners on the storm. He learned more about the nature of Hell and its inhabitants in a few minutes than he had ever wanted to know. The *kuei*, for example: these were the Storm Lords, the security forces of Hell. The séance had been an illegal attempt to access the world of the living—why, Pin did not know. Tentatively, he tried to glimpse further into the demon's mind, but met a series of smooth, dark walls that he was unable to penetrate.

The demon, clearly, was aware of her passenger. Her initial fright had turned to irritation; now, she was thinking only of how to evade her pursuers and evict Pin from her head. Her erratic flight took them past vast cliffs streaming with torrents of molten metal. Castles rose high along their peaks; Pin tried not to wonder what manner of people lived in them. They reminded him of the rich enclaves of Singapore Three, built on the heights above the curve of the estuary…and there was a river here, too, wide and red and smoking. A wild suspicion began to form in the grain of consciousness that was Pin. The demon flew along the bend of the river, soaring out across the span of the estuary. There, along Shaopeng, rose the dome of the Opera House, but here it was horribly distorted, and as the demon dived, Pin could see with her magnified vision that it was made out of innumerable small bones. *This is my city,* Pin thought, aghast, but everything was twisted and wrong. Then the demon turned in the stormy air and he saw Sulai-Ba.

The temple was exactly the same: a huge block of metal and black stone. Its iron doors were firmly closed. One side led onto the road that was Shaopeng in Pin's own world; behind the temple, lay a reach of the canal. As they passed over it, heading for the slums of Saro Town, Pin caught the unmistakable odor of blood. The demon landed and ran, a hobbling flight, pausing only when she reached the shelter of a nearby alleyway. Then, she stopped and looked up. Nothing was following them. The demon's chest hurt, Pin noticed. She took a deep breath, drawing the filthy air into her lungs; a clawed hand faltered to her throat. She opened her mouth and hissed with exhaustion. Pin hoped fervently that she wasn't about to have a heart attack, or whatever passed for one in demonkind; there was a possibility that her demise might free him, but he had no desire either to be free in Hell or trapped in the corpse of one of its denizens. His paranoia was not, however, justified. The demon had merely stopped to draw breath, and soon she was striding purposefully down the alleyway.

Above, the storm clouds of Hell raced overhead, revealing tatters of crimson sky. Peering through the demon's eyes, Pin could see the characters of a remedy sign appearing out of the shadows, and there was the remedy shop itself: parchment walls upon a wooden frame. The demon stumbled through the door. Inside, it was hot and quiet. The remedy man was sitting at a table, eating a plate of something that Pin could not immediately identify. On the demon's sudden entrance, he looked up. He had bright, little eyes.

"Well," he said, dabbing at his lipless mouth with a napkin. "This *is* a surprise. To what do I owe the honor of your company, madam?" He craned his neck, trying to look past the demon. "No retainers, I see. Clearly, you are in want of discretion."

"Ghost," the demon whispered. "I need your help."

"What seems to be the problem?" asked the remedy man.

"Possession."

The remedy man gave her a beady look.

"Pardon me?"

"I am possessed," the demon said, with dignity, "by a mediocre human spirit."

The remedy man stared for a moment, then began to shake with laughter.

"Well," he said at last, patting his eyes with the napkin. "What a novelty. And how ironic. Can dish it out, but can't take it, eh? Oh no—" for the demon had taken a menacing step forward. "You can't touch me. You're not one of the Great Powers even if you are an aristocrat, and I have my rights, you know. I suppose you want an exorcism?"

"Obviously."

"Well, I don't know about that…" the remedy man said. Rising, he added, "Bend your head."

Obediently, the demon did so. Pin could see the remedy man looking in at him with eyes that were like two small, red sparks.

"Hmm. Tongue."

Obligingly, the demon unscrolled the organ in question, which reached almost to the floor.

"I don't like the look of that… All right. Sit down. I need to know a few things."

The remedy man proceeded to ask the demon a great many questions, concerning her diet, her habits, and her health in general. The demon's answers were illuminating if unpleasant, particularly over the matter of diet.

"Well," the remedy man said at last. "Let's see what we can do."

He put the suffering demon through a rapid and diverse range of treatment. Needles were placed beneath her eyelids, and herbs beneath her tongue. Small cups of smoldering incense were balanced on the pressure points of her sinewy wrists. Trapped inside, listening to the supernaturally slow beat of her demonic heart, Pin grew uncomfortable but remained intact. Eventually, the remedy man said, "I don't think there's anything more I can do. Sorry. You'll have to try the Ministry of Epidemics. Good thing they're up and running again, isn't it?"

"No!" the demon wailed. "You have to help me!"

But the remedy man clapped his hands and the walls of the shop began to disappear. The books, instruments, and furniture whirled up into the storm, and the remedy man himself transformed into a boneless batlike thing and soared away. Above, among the storm clouds, was an eye, red as a coal and scanning the city below.

NINE

"Will you do it for me, Mother?" Mai's voice was strained and distant on the other end of the line.

"Of course, of course, don't worry," Mrs Pa told her. She paused. She could hear Mai listening, far away. "Mai?"

"Mother?"

"Can you tell me one thing?"

"Yes?"

"This…you didn't get married because of this, did you, Mai?"

With relief she heard Mai laugh.

"No, of course not. I love Ahn, Mother, you know that. Things are a little different here. They work in another way."

"I know that," Mrs Pa said, although she did not understand. Even in Hell, how could you get married one week, without being pregnant, and have a baby the next? Of course, it would be lovely to be a grandmother, but she needed a little more time to get used to the idea, that was all. She hadn't made any baby clothes. "Just tell me what I have to do."

Mai explained. At last Mrs Pa put the phone down, and went to the door of the shack. It was midmorning, and the light poured over the roofs of go-downs and houses alike, transforming the metal into thick silver layers. To the west, the pale brilliance of the sky betrayed the sea, light reflected from water. It was a bright summer day; the air warm and humid from the night's rain, and scented with the pungent herbs that Mrs Pa grew in her tiny square of backyard. Despite the mild morning, Mrs Pa shivered. She went back inside and collected together two of the smaller *bagua* mirrors and a charm, turning on a thread, which depicted the calm figure of Kuan Yin. She was the only one of all the gods whom Mrs Pa really trusted.

She hung the mirrors above the door, and suspended the charm between them, fixing it on its nail so that the goddess' compassionate gaze was turned outward and nothing could sneak in behind her back. More mirrors went on the back door, so that anything approaching would see its own ugly face and run screaming. She also attached a bunch of herbs above the stove and over the lavatory, just in case. Then she bent to light the spire of incense that sat in the door shrine. These precautions, against human and supernatural, having been taken, Mrs Pa brewed the blend of herbs that her dead daughter had carefully listed, drank the resultant mess, and lay down on the bed.

蛇警探

She dreamed that she was standing on the steps of the temple of Sulai-Ba, in front of the towering iron doors. The angles were somehow distressing to the human eye. How to get in? Mrs Pa wondered, dreaming. One by one, she climbed the steps, pausing to rest only when she reached the top. She looked down. The street seemed a very long way away, which was curious, because the flight of steps was not long. The people below resembled ants, in some trick of perspective.

Mrs Pa went over to the vast doors and put her hands upon them. The metal was cold to the touch, bitterly so, and rough. Tentatively, and feeling foolish, Mrs Pa knocked. Nothing happened. She stepped back and gazed around the arching doorway, and as she did so she noticed a smaller door, off to the left, sandwiched between the columns of the portal and the edge of the doorway itself. This door was ajar. How stupid of me, Mrs Pa thought. Her hands were balled into fists in her pockets. Even in the dream, the thought occurred to her: *When I was a young woman, I wouldn't have had the nerve to do this.* This was what suffering and loss did, in the end: it gave you a strength you never knew you had. Thinking of her daughter, she stepped into the temple.

Inside, Sulai-Ba was airy and quiet. There was a strong saline smell, the smell of the sea marshes along the delta, and a familiar undernote which Mrs Pa had trouble identifying. Then she realized that it reminded her of the meat market on the pier: the same salty, bloody reek. Familiarity gave her courage. She was standing between two enormous columns which ascended into the cavernous roof. Before her, were a series of connected pools: the cistern reservoirs. The dark water lapped gently against the stone. Mrs Pa walked round the cistern into the adjoining hall, and stopped short with a gasp.

In the middle of the hall, sprawled across the stone floor, lay a carcass. It was almost bare of flesh: the ribcage arched white and ghostly in the half-light, tapering off into the knobbly vertebrae, and the long skull, with its large eye sockets and sharp hunter's teeth, lay patiently on the floor, like a dog resting its head on the carpet. What *was* it? A dragon, surely. It could be nothing else.

Within the skeleton, something moved. Mrs Pa, thinking resolutely of all the times she had visited the meat market, walked toward it. She came round the end of the carcass to where the pointed bones of the tail snaked over the floor. From this angle, she was able to see into the ribcage. A solemn pair of eyes regarded her. Mrs Pa drew a sharp breath.

The child was so much like Mai at that age: the same serious eyes under the same thatch of black hair. Mrs Pa swallowed. The child's cheek bulged outward; he was sucking on something. He tucked it into his mouth and said, "Grandmother?" He got to his feet and toddled forward, ducking his head even though the bones arced high above him. Mrs Pa crouched, with difficulty, so as to be on the same level.

"Your mother told me where to find you," she said. Her voice sounded old and thin, quavery, and she spat into her handkerchief to clear her throat. "She didn't tell me your name." She tried hard not to sound accusing.

"I haven't got one yet. This one—" he gestured toward the bones "—died, but it did not leave me a name. Maybe you could give me one?" He was very articulate for his age, Mrs Pa considered... How old was he, this strange spirit child? She thought hard. She supposed she ought to give him his father's name, but it sounded too prosaic, somehow. Then, in her mind, she saw the boat that had brought Mai and Ahn to their wedding, sailing out of the salt darkness with its crimson sails hanging in wind-blown tatters.

"Precious Dragon!" she said. This produced an alarmingly big smile. "Do you like that name? All right, Grandson. Precious Dragon it is, then." She was conscious of a sudden, inexplicable relief. "Shall we go home?" The little boy nodded, and stepped forward to take her hand. He was nicely dressed, she noticed, in a puffy cotton jacket and trousers. His hand was reassuringly warm. "Come on, now."

Quickly, she took him out through the little door, closing it behind them. Outside on the steps of Sulai-Ba, the sunlight seemed to blaze, brightness consuming the air after the shadowy silence of the temple. The world seemed suddenly hot and real. Mrs Pa blinked. She looked down at the child, who smiled.

"Am I still dreaming?" she asked, unsure.

"No. You never were dreaming. The spell brought you to Sulai-Ba. You're really here."

"This is real?" Suddenly she was trembling and afraid. Reassuringly, Precious Dragon took hold of her hand.

"It's all right," he said.

Holding her grandson's hand firmly, and not knowing what else to do, Mrs Pa led him down the steps to the busy street.

There had been yet another road collapse, this time in Semmerang Anka, and none of the downtown trams to Ghenret were running. The emergency services, already overstretched in the area, were slow to react and even slower to clear the debris from the street. The collapse had brought down part of the Second National Bank, sending showers of supposedly shatterproof flexiglass into the street and severing the downtown cables. Three people were dead, a mercifully small toll this time. The collapse of the Feng Shui Practitioners' Guild had left a legacy of infrastructural problems. Mrs Pa and Precious Dragon watched the emergency services as they made their impeded way toward the Anka. The carriers bore the *bagua* symbol of the Tu Chin Trade Company; presumably the services were on private hire to the overstretched National Bank.

Wisely, Mrs Pa decided to take her new grandson to lunch and avoid the crush, but when they finally found a café whose apparent hygiene was satisfactory to Mrs Pa, they discovered that a great many other people had the same idea. Still, there was no hurry. Precious Dragon waited patiently in the queue with his grandmother. He was a very well-mannered little boy, she was pleased to see. When at last they were able to sit down, she ordered soup and noodles and bought him a fortune cookie; she had not done this for a long time. When the cookie was opened, it revealed a blank slip of paper.

"Oh, what a shame," she exclaimed in disappointment, but Precious Dragon seemed quite pleased.

"It means that anything can happen," he explained kindly. For a moment he looked completely unlike a small boy.

"I suppose anything can," his grandmother said, slowly. She found that she was enjoying herself. It was a long time since she had had a child to spoil, or had eaten out at lunchtime. She smiled at her strange descendent, sitting opposite, and he beamed back. The sweet, or whatever it had been in his mouth, was not in evidence. He was smothering his noodles with extra-hot chili garlic sauce. Mrs Pa regarded him with some alarm.

"Are you quite sure you'll like that?" she asked, doubtfully. Precious Dragon nodded, with utmost conviction.

After lunch they wandered back out along Battery Road, turning up Step Street. From the top of the steps, you could see the harbor and the long, uneven shore of Teveraya, so brilliantly illuminated at night but now almost concealed by a light mist. The sea brought all sorts of weather, for here in the heart of the city the sun was blindingly bright. They stood at the end of the steps and watched a ponderous tanker crossing the harbor.

"Are there boats where you live?" Precious Dragon asked.

"Lots, in the harbor near me, and people live on them, too. They have chickens, and cats, all sorts of animals."

"When will we get there?" her grandson said, fidgeting.

"Soon." The tram rattled past the foot of Step Street, so the service must be running again. With relief, Mrs Pa took her grandson to wait at the nearest platform. Her feet were beginning to hurt, and her joints felt stiff with rheumatism. They had to wait a long time for the downtown, and Mrs Pa, sitting on the platform bench, nearly dozed off. She came to with a start and discovered, with a terrible sinking sensation that she had not experienced for twenty years, that Precious Dragon was not by her side. Frantically looking around, she spotted him peering in through a shop window. She almost boxed his ears in relief, but as she hastened toward him he turned and looked up at her, and for a moment she felt dizzy. She could no more box his ears, she realized, than she could box those of Elder Ko of the local temple. She almost apologized, but found herself saying, "What are you looking at, Precious Dragon?"

"A tiger!" he said. His eyes shone. It was indeed a tiger, stuffed and moth-eaten. She had never seen one so close to life. It was enormous, twelve feet from head to tail, and its yellowing jaws were open wide, wrinkling the striped muzzle. A hum came from behind them.

"Quick! Here it is," Mrs Pa said. They only just caught the tram in time. Precious Dragon sat craning his head back toward the shop until it was out of sight. Mrs Pa made a decision. Despite her painful feet, she got off the downtown a stop early and took Precious Dragon into the Singapore Road General Emporium. Upstairs, they had a toy department and in it, they had tigers, with staring glass eyes.

Mrs Pa bought him one, even though she couldn't afford it. How often, after all, do you visit a demon temple and collect your only grandchild, newly arrived from the land of the dead? Precious Dragon was delighted with the tiger, and clutched it all the way home.

By the time they got back to Ghenret, it was late afternoon, and the sun was low on the water. Mrs Pa set about preparing dinner, shredding spring onions and cabbage, peppers and beef. Her grandson sat on the edge of the bed, hugging the tiger tightly and sucking something.

"What have you got in your mouth?" Mrs Pa asked. "Let me see." She held out her hand and after a momentary oblique gaze he spat it into her palm. At first she thought it was a sweet, a gobstopper or something, but it was too hard and smooth, and it glowed faintly as if lit from within.

"It looks like a pearl," Mrs Pa said.

"It is a pearl. Can I have it back?"

Normally, the last thing Mrs Pa would have done would be to return such a jewel to a child, but this was not an ordinary child and she felt disinclined to go against his wishes. She handed it back to him.

"Where did you get it from?" Mrs Pa asked, curiously.

"It came with me," he said. He returned the pearl to his mouth. "It's important," he added.

All day, Mrs Pa had desperately wanted to ask Precious Dragon about his mother. There were so many unanswered questions, but something stopped her from raising the subject. She nodded and went back to her cooking. Precious Dragon remained sitting on the bed, swinging his feet and sucking the pearl.

TEN

With Pin's spirit still lodged inside her, the demon crouched in the alleyway until the great eye had vanished, then she rose and made her way through a bewildering maze of alleys and backyards toward the city center. Carried along in the demon, Pin occupied himself with watching the scenes that passed by him. He had not ceased to be terrified, but the fear was paradoxically so great that he could almost ignore it, and concentrate on minor details.

Hell was indeed remarkably similar to Singapore Three, in terms of planning if not occupancy. They had gone up Battery Road, and crossed over into Shaopeng, but whereas in Pin's version of the city the central district was full of shops and teahouses and offices, here there was only a suggestion of life. Every building was dark and silent. Shadows watched them from the doorways as they passed and Pin sensed a growing anticipation in the air. They knew what was passing by, concealed within the demon's carapace: a small, succulent spirit, rent prematurely from its body and still warm. Now, Pin understood why they said that ghosts were hungry.

He had never failed to honor the dead. Before she had died, his mother had impressed upon him the importance of compensating the ancestors for their current inconvenienced state. He had delivered food and incense and flowers to the legion of departed relatives, supporting them in the loneliness of the afterlife and ensuring that, on those days when the dead stride the city, they would know that he had honored them and stay away. Yet Singapore Three was home to the limitless dispossessed, and when they died, who had they to comfort them? Many of the dead must be hungry indeed: forgotten by their descendants or simply the last of their lines. They waited now in the empty storefronts, and watched him with their avid gaze.

"Now," the demon said. They had come out onto the topmost landing of Step Street. The derelict buildings of Shaopeng stretched below. Where the

45

Eregeng Trade House had stood in his own city rose an immense pagoda. Its peaked roofs were wreathed in cloud. Balconies and balustrades covered its sides; carved dragons writhed. There was a subtle and indefinable wrongness about it.

"What," Pin said, inside the demon's mind, "is that?"

"That is the Ministry of Epidemics," an echoing thought replied. He had the impression that the demon was outraged at being addressed by a mere spirit.

"We're going there?" Pin asked in horror, but before he could protest, the demon had leaped from the top of the steps. Even in this disincarnate state, however, he was thankful to be leaving behind the needle teeth and hollow tongues of the hungry ghosts of Shaopeng. The city wheeled below, glimpsed through the massing clouds. It was as though someone had made a rough sketch of the landscape of Singapore Three. The main roads, which followed the meridians, were still present and he could see the dark energy lines which ran beneath them. The principal buildings of his own city were also mirrored. The pagoda towers of the Ministries of Storms, Water, Epidemics, and Fire occupied their place, named silently by the demon as they passed, and there were other buildings, too, which Pin did not recognize. The Ministry of Lust: a fat, scarlet blob below. The Ministry of War: a towering iron ziggurat, and at this the demon's heart inexplicably leaped. Fires burned blue in the spaces between the streets, and beyond, where the sea should be, stretched a troubled darkness. Pin could hear the beat of the demon's heart, like a drum in a well. The storm streamed by and the demon plunged, to come to a graceful landing on the steps of the Ministry of Epidemics.

"Where now?" Pin quavered. The demon did not answer. She strode through the double doors of the Ministry and stopped.

The queue, Pin saw, stretched down a corridor so long that the end of it was invisible. A thousand pairs of eyes turned curiously toward the new arrivals. Everyone smiled, politely, and gave a little bow. Muttering, the demon began to pace down the line. Pin looked into each face as they passed. Every manner of illness was represented here. He saw traces of smallpox and leprosy; cancer and Jiangsu fever and illnesses that he could not even name. The polite, ravaged faces turned away once the demon had passed, to resume their passive stare at the opposite wall. They were preserved in a dreadful patience. It is the manner of your death that marks you, Pin thought, not your life at all. What did anyone remember of his mother, except that she had been the chorus girl who had succumbed to a hemorrhage? How long had these spirits been waiting here? Pin wondered.

To him, the ordered line of the dead seemed sad but proper, a progression from the chaos of their last illness to this quiet hallway. Some of them wore costumes that had gone out of fashion a hundred years before, and their wearers seemed frail and thin as paper, bearing their wounds and tumors with a dignity that only the dead can attain. The demon blew lightly upon the doors and they swung open without a sound.

Inside, the Ministry of Epidemics was quiet. The demon closed the door behind her. Pin gazed around him. The fragile, courteous ghosts in the corridor seemed to present little threat. The office in which the demon stood was a cavernous room, divided by screens and cooled by fans set into the ceiling. The desks were hidden beneath mounds of paper; Pin recognized the red seals and ornate parchment coils that were thrown into the graveyard fires to placate the restless dead. Presumably, this was where they ended up.

"Oh, so much to be done," someone mused.

"I have to speak to Lu Yueh," the demon said.

From around the corner of a desk stepped a small elderly gentleman. "Good afternoon," he said.

"Good afternoon. I need to make an appointment."

"I'm afraid that won't be possible. Lord Lu is out of town at the present moment, and is not due to return until after the festival. Perhaps someone else might be able to assist you?" he asked, helpfully. Pin studied him. The administrator wore a neat, dark robe. His eyes were entirely covered by cataracts, giving his gaze a cloudy, indefinite quality. As he stepped forward, Pin looked down and observed that his feet were back to front. The toes of his elegant black slippers pointed behind him.

"I don't think so, no. I need to speak to Lord Lu. It's urgent."

"Today is a holiday, after all. The echelons of Epidemics are as entitled to their festivities as the rest of us. Indeed, I plan to go home myself within the hour."

"And no one else is available?"

"So sorry."

"Very well, then. It's always the same. If you want something done properly, you have to do it yourself," the demon snarled. Wheeling around, she headed for a door set in the wall.

"Wait!" the elderly gentleman wailed, but she was already beyond his reach. Pin could hear him shuffling forward as the door closed. They were in a lift. The demon's taloned forefinger pressed the topmost button, and then they were sailing upward, so fast that Pin found himself forced against the sides of the demon's skull. Pin had not expected to encounter laboratories, but when they stepped out of the lift and into the upper reaches of the Ministry, he could see the rows of beds and equipment through every door they passed. It reminded him of the stories about Paugeng: the endless, secret dormitories where all the intricacies of the body were unraveled and revealed, documented and stored for alchemical transformation. A thought occurred to him. He said to the striding demon, "Those people in the hallway—the ghosts—what are they waiting for? Are they going to come here, to be tested?" He thought of his mother, so savagely and suddenly torn from life. Was she here, among the ranks of the patient spirits? He had not seen her, but perhaps she had changed, worn away by death and time. It was a dreadful notion: even after the expiration of the body the suffering might not cease. The demon did not reply. She brushed aside the equipment: the silken nets of the drip feeds, the bronze crucibles and frosted tubes, as though they did not exist. The wards were empty. At last the demon reached the end of the long line of laboratories. They were in a small room, painted an unpleasant institutional green. Outside the small window, the storms of the upper air continued to rage.

As they stepped through the door of the last lab, Pin saw a young woman sitting at the desk. She was wearing a neat black uniform and slippers, and her round face, though pasty and pale, was unmarked. She looked utterly dumbfounded to see the demon.

"Can I help you?" she asked, mechanically. For the second time that day, the demon explained.

"I'm sorry. I don't think I can help. I—"

"Perhaps this might change your mind." The demon slid something into the woman's hand, a crackle of paper, and then sat in the chair before the desk.

"Oh," the woman said. She looked doubtful. "I don't know if I should— well, all right then, I'll try. But I'm only a technician; I don't know if there's anything I can do." Turning to a nearby shelf, she took down a large leather-bound book and began leafing through it, mouthing the characters silently to herself as she did so. At last she said, "Ah… Perhaps this might work. I'm not qualified to practice, you understand," she added anxiously. The demon made an impatient gesture.

"Just get on with it. I haven't got all day…"

Pin, eavesdropping on the demon's thoughts, realized that this was true. The demon was running a considerable risk in coming here so blatantly; she was counting on a swift exorcism and then flight, to her home. Presumably, Pin thought uneasily, it was only a matter of time before the Storm Lords showed up.

The woman was writing something assiduously on a long strip of paper.

"Anyone can do this, really," she said "But it needs to have the proper seals put on it…there." She stamped the paper and leaned over the demon. As she did so, Pin glimpsed a name on the little badge that she wore: her name was Kung Mai.

"Open your mouth," Mai said to the demon. The serrated jaws fell open and Mai rolled the scroll neatly beneath the demon's tongue. "Now. Close your mouth."

Encased in the demon's jaws, the scroll began to smolder and smoke. The demon shifted uneasily in the chair; Mai placed a steadying hand on her shoulder. Pin became aware that the demon's head was growing increasingly uncomfortable. Pressure was building within it like a migraine, and he was being forced against the bony interior of the demon's skull. Then he was channeled into the demon's bloodstream, flowing out into the hot, echoing cavity of the demon's mouth. Mai gave the demon a resounding blow between her shoulder blades. The demon's mouth opened and Pin's spirit shot out into a waiting flask. He glimpsed the demon rising from her chair. She had the face of an ancient skull, all bones and angularity, and her fur-collared robes were the color of fire. She was, Pin had to admit, rather impressive. She said, in an immense whistling voice, "I will not forget this," and sprang toward the window. There was a soundless blast as the window shattered and the demon was gone. Through the sides of the flask, he could see Mai's distorted face looking back at him.

"You come from the city," she said. "From the living city." Her voice sounded wistful; Pin wondered how long ago she had died.

"Yes," he said. "My name is—Pin."

"My mother is there," Mai told him. "And now my son. I can't reach my mother anymore. Do you think you can help me?"

"I don't know how—especially at the moment. And anyway, why should I?" Pin asked, whispering against the sides of the flask.

Mai glanced uneasily over her shoulder.

"Because something terrible is going to happen, and that demon who brought you here knows what it is. I don't. I only listen to rumors. Hell is in danger. And so is my son."

"Where exactly is your son?"

"He's with my mother. Her name is Pa Niang; she lives by the harbor." Her head jerked up. "I can hear something. We must hide you—" and she thrust the jar hastily into a drawer. Pin tried to speak, but it was already too late. The world had gone dark.

蛇警探

Much later, or so it seemed, the drawer was opened again. Through the glass wall of the bottle, Mai's eye looked as vast as the sun. The eye was anxious.

"Pin?" Mai said. "Are you all right?"

There were a number of sarcastic replies to this, but the question was evidently meant kindly, so Pin answered, "I think so."

"I'm at the end of my shift. I'm going to put you in my pocket. Please keep quiet."

"All right," Pin said. Light was abruptly snuffed out as Mai put the bottle inside her coat. Pin could feel the jolting sensation as she walked and there were a number of sounds around him. This seemed to go on for some time.

At last the bottle was plucked free and he was set down on a table. Pin looked around him, seeing a small room lit by lamps. Patterned shadows danced across the walls and a young man sat in a chair by the fire, reading a book.

"What's that you've got there, Mai?" he asked. He had a light, pleasant voice.

"Oh, just something I brought back from the lab," Mai said. She went over and kissed his cheek; he too looked ill, Pin thought. "I'm just going to put it in the bathroom." She picked up the bottle and carried it into an adjoining room.

"Now," she said, holding the bottle level with her face. "Tell me everything."

"I'll do my best," Pin said.

ELEVEN

Once Embar Dea reached the open sea, she swam quickly, surfacing from time to time to watch the wheel of the stars. She could hardly see them, but she could track their passage across the sky, and tell that she was still in time. The sea was calm, but she sensed the ripples beginning beneath the floor of the trench, and she could smell the sand that was stirred up from the ocean bed, dirty with chemicals and the pungent odor of fire, strange so far beneath the sea. Embar Dea rode the waves with ease. Her fear had gone; she was no longer confined within the walls of the temple, and she was young again now, riding swift upon the currents and breathing the track that led her to Tenebrae.

Night passed and the new day shone under the surface of the water, light curving and fragmented. She was coming closer to the cold waters, the ice seas of the north, and she breathed in the fresh water, snowmelt running cold along her dappled sides. A thousand words for water, the sea dragons had, describing the part of the world that was real to them, and Embar Dea sang them now: sweet water of the mountains; the acid salt up from the complaining ocean trenches; the rainwater from the forests which covered the hills of China, scented with earth and leaves, carrying fragments of the woods far out to sea.

Someone was reached by her song, responding with a note, and Embar Dea rolled joyfully in the icy waves under the sun, thinking, *Not alone, no longer alone,* coming closer to Tenebrae. She swerved in the seas and turned toward the singer, but now something came between herself and the song, a barrier that broke the water, disturbed the carrying current. The dragon dived, straight down toward the safety of the seabed, and watched the ship draw above, covering the path of the sun. She saw the square hull curve up over the swell, then in a sudden patch of gentle water the ship cast its shadow

51

over the hills of the seabed, and the guns lay like thorns along its sides. The distant song sang warning, and the voice of wisdom inside Embar Dea's head told her: *Stay here, out of sight, stay still.* Be silent, Embar Dea told herself; but she was young again. She cried out, and the sound echoed off the ship's hull, crackling through the sunlit water. The dragon sang, and the distant voice, suddenly cruel, joined hers. The ship's radar would be swinging wildly now, uncertain of its path, easy to lead it, draw it singing on. Far below, Embar Dea sang, and watched as a cloud drew across the sun and the sea swelled up around her. She somersaulted in the water and, turning, swam before the ship, singing it on, and it followed her obediently, drawn on by the deceiving instruments into the path of the gathering storm.

The arctic water was as green as a winter sunset, luminous with phosphorescence. Sea jellies, crusted with ice, drifted ghostly through the sea's depths and a single sea star coasted among them, browsing on their trailing tentacles. Embar Dea ignored the life around her. She followed the path of the stars, the underwater current which followed what, on land, would become an energy line, and then at last through the glassy water she saw a great bulkhead looming up, a rotting hull beneath the ice. Along one side, the name of the tanker was still visible, *Aluha:* the first ship lured to these icy seas by the siren dragons to sink among the icebergs.

TWELVE

It was close to nine o'clock when Chen wearily stepped onto the deck of the houseboat—a sultry evening, with an oily, yeasty smell drifting off the waters of the harbor. Inari came to meet him, ducking under the lintel of the kitchen door with a pan in her hand.

"Darling! You're home!" Some women would have made remarks about the time, questioned him as to where he'd been and what he'd been doing, but Inari was never like this. She always seemed delighted that he'd come back at all. "How was work?"

"Boring," Chen said, "and then exciting." The one breach of official protocol that he ever entertained was to talk to Inari about work. In a sense, she was part of it: Hellkind, after all, even though her heart had never belonged to Hell, or to the vast, scheming clan which had sought to marry her off to a scion of the Ministry of Epidemics. Inari was a good person; death—had she been a mortal—would surely have qualified her for entrance into Heaven.

So now Chen told her about Miss Qi, and her unexpected talent for violence. Inari's crimson eyes widened as he spoke and her small face grew even paler.

"She sounds—remarkable. But you know, there are warriors among the Heavenly Host and even Hell fears them, and the great swords that they carry. Heaven has its armies, just as Hell does."

"That's true," Chen said. He sat down on the bench that stood just outside the kitchen and accepted a bowl of green tea. Inari sat beside him, hands folded in her lap. The image of demure womanhood, and yet he knew that Inari had on occasion been obliged to fight for her life, and done so fiercely. "I suppose it's just that I haven't come across them all that much." Did he detect a slight note of resentment in his own voice? The feeling that he'd been forced to battle on, more or less alone, doing the Goddess Kuan Yin's work in the world while the warriors of Heaven sat on their Celestial backsides—

"Darling, is everything all right?" Inari was gazing at him with some concern. "There's soup if you haven't eaten," she added.

Chen reached out and squeezed her hand. "I'm fine. Just distracted." A life dedicated to Heaven's behalf and yet the most support he'd had was from two of demonkind. He sighed. "I've got to go to Hell tomorrow evening. Zhu Irzh and Miss Qi and I have been put on this equal ops visit."

"Oh. All right," Inari said. She looked momentarily downcast. "How long will you be gone?"

"A few days. Not longer, I fervently hope, and if we can cut it short, we will. None of us want to be there, not even Zhu Irzh. Will you manage all right?" Inari could and did go out to the market on her own without being recognized as a demon, but Chen couldn't help worrying about her.

"I'll be fine," Inari said. As she spoke, something low and dark trundled out from beneath the bench and snapped at a moth. "I'll have badger, after all."

"I shall look after her," said her household's ancient familiar, through a mouthful of moth. Chen rather wished that he could take the badger with him; the creature was a denizen of Hell, after all, and had proved useful in the past. But it was more important for it to look after Inari.

"Will Zhu Irzh be taking Jhai?" Inari asked. They'd spent an evening at Paugeng, at a small private reception of Jhai's. The industrialist had been charming, complimenting Inari on an admittedly beautiful dress and spending some time in conversation with her. Tserai herself had looked rather fine, dressed in a purple and silver sari with her huge eyes outlined in kohl and the faint tiger stripes of her own demonic origins just visible on her darkly golden skin. Chen could certainly see the attraction, but he would as soon have gone to bed with the original tiger. When they had emerged into the cool night air, the only thing Inari had said was, "Be careful. I don't trust her."

"I've no intention of trusting her," Chen had replied.

Now, he said, "No, Tserai's not coming with us. I'd be surprised if she ventured into Hell, quite frankly. She has—business associates there who won't be too happy with her after the debacle a few months ago. She failed to give them Heaven, effectively."

"Do you think they'll come after her?" Inari said.

"I'm counting on it. But it won't be just yet. Hell takes a long time to revenge itself sometimes. As you know. Anyway, Zhu Irzh didn't seem all that keen on having her with him. I think he feels a cooling-off period might not be a bad idea. Says she's started to take too much for granted."

Inari grimaced. "That one will always take too much for granted. She thinks she can buy people."

"The trouble is," Chen said, "she's very often right."

蛇警探

He dreamed that he had already entered Hell. Zhu Irzh and Miss Qi were nowhere to be seen and neither was anyone else, but somehow, this did not seem to matter. He was walking along a promontory of scarlet rock, the cliffs tumbling down to a crashing, iron-colored sea. On the horizon, the storm clouds were gathering and he could see the flash of the spears and eyes of the *kuei,* the Storm Lords whose arbitrary, capricious law is said to govern the affairs of Hell. But this did not matter either and Chen strolled on, admiring the view. But suddenly, a figure was standing in his path with a hand upraised: a figure that changed as he looked at it—first a small boy, then an old man, and then something that was not human at all. It opened its mouth and gave a ringing cry. Chen covered his ears, but the cry went on and on, echoing from the scarlet cliffs until the world itself began to shatter and fall apart.

Chen's eyes snapped open. The sound was still going on, although now it was the telephone. When he groped for it, dropped it, and finally answered, with the dream still so fresh around him that he could smell saltwater, Zhu Irzh's voice said, "Chen! We've got a problem."

THIRTEEN

The days had settled into a routine. Each morning, Mrs Pa and her new grandson walked down to the market. Everyone made a great fuss over Precious Dragon. Mrs Pa had been hard put to explain how, after being married for only a few days and being, in any case, dead, her daughter had somehow managed to produce a two-year-old child with the demeanor and vocabulary of an elderly gentleman, but people seemed to understand. It was pretty odd, but then so were a great many things. Her neighbors appeared to accept it, at any rate, and walking through the market, the little boy was showered with candies, biscuits, and trinkets, all of which he accepted with the gravity of a visiting potentate. After the market each day, Mrs Pa took her grandson down to the edge of the wharf, where they sat watching the boats from Teveraya. Once they had watched a tanker bound for Beijing, built to withstand the equatorial storms. It was an enormous thing, almost a mile long, and Precious Dragon's mouth fell open when he saw it, nearly dislodging the pearl.

Later in the afternoons, they would sit outside Mrs Pa's house and receive visitors. Mr and Mrs Kung came, of course, hotfoot to see the little boy who was their grandchild, too. All the neighbors came, bringing their own children. The house had been a focus of activity for days. Mrs Pa found that she was enjoying herself. The only cloud on the horizon was her inability to contact Mai. She had been trying to phone for several days now, but on each occasion the line had crackled and spat, finally settling into an electronic hum. Mrs Pa went to the temple and renewed the spells that allowed communication between the two worlds, but they still failed her. She tried to tell herself that this was no more than some occult interference, but the matter still worried her.

Mrs Pa was washing the dishes when Precious Dragon came in, holding

56

his toy tiger. He plucked at her dress.

"Grandma?"

"What is it?"

"Someone's in the outhouse."

Mrs Pa said, "How do you know?" Children, obviously, were fanciful, but it did not occur to her to treat this lightly.

"I heard them. They were scuffling about. I don't think we should go out there."

"Precious Dragon, if there's someone messing about in the backyard, I'm not just going to sit here. And I'm not going to call the police."

"I don't think we should go," he repeated. He did not have a normal child's stubbornness; this was a calm and reasoned statement.

"Then what should we do?" Without realizing it, her voice had dropped to a whisper.

"We should just watch. Put the light out. Pretend you've gone to bed."

Mrs Pa, trying not to look out of the kitchen window, crossed the room and switched the light off.

"Now," Precious Dragon said softly. They sat down on the seat by the window and waited. The sky was illuminated by the thousand lights of the city and so the yard was never completely dark, but it was difficult to see what was going on. Various possibilities were going through Mrs Pa's mind. It would be stupid to burgle her little house; there was nothing here, but someone might be sufficiently desperate or even crazy. They sent those of the demented whom they could not cure to the security fortress on the island of Moritana, but many took refuge in the disused mines of Bharulay or Orichay, or were sent for use in the hospitalization wings of the corporations. Those people, though, were the really hopeless cases, those whom the drugs were unable to reach—and not so many of them were wandering around the streets. Perhaps it was some lout having a joke, which would be on him, Mrs Pa thought. She kept a pepper spray under the sink; used correctly, it would blind. She reached for it now.

There was definitely something in the outhouse, because she could see the edges of the door rattling. Perhaps someone was stuck. But why on earth go into someone else's outhouse in the first place, if you didn't have to, of course? There were high walls between the houses, edged with razor-wire. Mrs Pa was beginning to feel rather unwell, a sick, dense pressure building up behind her eyes that she attributed to nerves, but it was most unpleasant. Unsteadily, she got off the chair and went to the back door. Outside, the light seeping from the door of the outhouse continued to grow, pulsing with the neon colors of sickness.

"Grandma?" Precious Dragon said in an urgent whisper.

"I don't know what's—" Mrs Pa murmured, indistinctly. She wrenched the back door open, and as she did so, the door of the outhouse also flew back on its hinges and something shot across into the kitchen, knocking Mrs Pa aside. The sense of pressure vanished abruptly. She shrieked. The creature was about the size of a person, but it was spinning so quickly that it was impossible to tell what it was. The air around it was streaming with light, a bloodstained red. The whirling stopped with a great rush of air. Bright eyes looked at Mrs Pa out of a pointed, black mantis face. Mrs Pa whisked the spray can up and pressed the button, releasing a stream of iridescent gas. The thing ducked its head under the spray, then, wheeling round, it made a grab for Precious Dragon. The little boy ran into the bedroom alcove and crawled rapidly under the bed, which stood on four paraffin-soaked feet to deter roaches. The creature bent, seized one small foot and pulled him out, holding him upside down over the bed. Precious Dragon yelled. Mrs Pa took one look and beat at the creature's black back with her fists. The skin looked slick, like that of a sea lion, but it felt hard, similar to horn. It opened its complex mouth and breathed, a long exhalation that singed Mrs Pa's hair and raised a wall of flame around the front door. Then it swatted Mrs Pa to one side. Fortunately, she fell on the bed, but knocked the side of her head against the cupboard as she fell. The creature shook Precious Dragon sharply.

Mrs Pa could not remember the next few minutes very clearly. There were shouts, a sudden sound like a waterfall, and then an acrid, smoky smell. The front door crashed open. She thought she recalled seeing her grandson twist in the creature's grip like a fish and spit at it. He hit it in the eye, and it wailed and staggered backward, knocking into the chest of drawers, then it span out into the garden as though reeled in on a line. The child ran after it and she heard the door of the outhouse bang shut. Someone was bending over her, speaking soothingly. Gradually, the smoke and the pepper residue began to clear and her eyes stopped watering. She looked into golden eyes, rimmed with a thin black line as though drawn by a careful pen.

"It's you," she told the demon. "From the bus."

"So it is," Zhu Irzh agreed. He squatted down on his haunches in front of her.

"Are you all right?"

"I think so." She struggled upright. "Where's my grandson?"

A man came in through the back door, holding the little boy. Mrs Pa had the impression of a pleasant, round face. Precious Dragon was choking. His face was pale and he was wheezing.

"Give him to me!" she demanded, and the man put him gently down on the bed. Other people seemed to be milling indiscriminately about her small house.

"It must be the pepper spray," someone said. Precious Dragon shook his head violently. His lips were turning blue and his eyes started.

"He's got a picture in his head," the demon said, dreamily. "Something round."

"It's on the floor!" Mrs Pa said, realizing to what he referred. She and the demon dived for the carpet.

"What am I looking for?" he asked.

"It's a big white pearl! There it is!" She could see it, gleaming in the corner under the bed. The demon slid beneath and retrieved it, handing the round object to Mrs Pa.

"It must have rolled." She stuffed the pearl, fluff and all, into her grandson's mouth. He drew a painful breath. The other man was staring, his eyebrows up near his hairline. Zhu Irzh stalked rapidly through the kitchen and out the back door. When he returned, he remarked, "There's not much damage. The carpet's wet, but the fire doesn't seem to have touched it, nor the wall. There's no one in your lavatory, either," he commented to the child, now recovered and sitting quietly on his grandmother's lap.

"Not anymore," Precious Dragon said. There was a dangerous glint in his eye.

"What happened?" Mrs Pa had time to feel bewildered now.

"One of your neighbors saw the fire and kicked the door in," the round-faced man said. "He had an extinguisher, luckily. His wife called the police precinct and they called my colleague and he spoke to me. I live on the harbor, you see, so it didn't take us long to get here." The round-faced man displayed a policeman's badge as the neighbor in question, Mr Sheng, appeared in the doorway.

"I'll ask my wife to come in," he said. His forehead was beaded with sweat.

"No, please. We'll be all right." Mrs Pa said. Her neighbor took a lot of convincing, but after many protestations of gratitude agreed to go back home. Everyone else seemed to melt away around him, apart from the middle-aged man and the demon.

"Well, I'm glad you're living here," Mrs Pa told Zhu Irzh. "Whatever people may say." In the universal human response to a crisis, she got up and made tea. When she came back in she said to her grandson, "What was that thing?"

"A demon. Like me. Well. Not quite like me. I'm from the upper levels of Hell. That wasn't. Actually, I don't know *what* it was."

"I thought it must be something to do with Hell." She didn't know much about Hell, but she knew a bit. "It's where my daughter lives, you see. She's been there since she was three."

The round-faced man frowned. "Why did a three-year-old go to Hell?"

Mrs Pa sighed. "It was a long time ago. Things are better now, they say— more regulated. But it was different then. My husband and my daughter died at the same time and I paid a funeral parlor to have the papers filled out for Heaven. That's where they were supposed to go. My husband was a good man and Mai—of course she was good, she was just a little girl. But the man who ran the funeral place took the money and didn't do what he was supposed to do—I think he had some kind of arrangement with Hell. But he's dead himself, anyway. I hope he went there. The same sort of thing happened with the Kungs' son—my daughter's husband, you know. We fixed things for my husband, but it wasn't possible for Mai—she'd already become indentured to one of the Ministries. It wasn't until years later that my husband managed to contact me, but we can't talk much, I don't know why. It seems easier to talk with Mai."

"I'm sorry," the middle-aged man said. "Things like that shouldn't happen. If you want, I can try and do something about it. It's my department now."

Mrs Pa seized his hand. "That would be wonderful." And it was. A new grandson, Mai married, and now the chance that things would finally be put right.

Zhu Irzh yawned with a snap of his fanged teeth. His companion looked at him askance, but after the events of this evening Mrs Pa was past being alarmed. They stayed quite late, talking to her. How strange it was, she thought, that this young man from Hell could still be so like her own people in some ways.

Precious Dragon, worn out, slept beside her as they talked. She checked on him occasionally, for there were things that she did not want him to hear, but he slept soundly on, his mouth open around the bulge of the pearl. When Chen and Zhu Irzh left, the dove-colored light of the rising sun was already pale in the sky behind Paugeng, and Ghenret was awakening around her. Just as well, Mrs Pa thought, because she wouldn't have gone to that outhouse in the dark for anything after all that.

FOURTEEN

After the episode with Mrs Pa's unpleasant visitor on the previous night, Chen had found himself fretting and worrying. The station house was horribly hot. Zhu Irzh was at the Opera, following up on the demonic visit of the day before.

At last, Chen discharged himself from the precinct and caught the tram back to Ghenret, finding that it was marginally cooler at the port. Ghenret was peaceful midevening, with the oily tide lapping at the walls of the docks. The light was kind to the surroundings, blurring the decay of warehouses and go-downs, throwing the monstrous architecture of the rebuilt Paugeng and the labs into sharp relief and hazing the viscous waters of Ghenret into silver. It seemed peaceful and quiet after the events of the previous night. He made his way across the harbor to the houseboat; the door was unlocked. Chen pushed it open and stepped inside.

"Inari?"

Within, the houseboat was green and cool. Water shadows rippled across the low ceiling. Neither his wife nor the badger were anywhere to be seen, but Zhu Irzh lay sprawled in sleep across the couch, one hand thrown over his chest. Chen watched, intrigued, as the demon's claws flexed in and out; he was dreaming. In sleep, relieved of the hellish charm, Zhu Irzh's face was peaceful. Chen felt a sudden unexpected wave of affection. Zhu Irzh woke up. There was a momentary flash of alarm in the golden eyes, then Zhu Irzh smiled.

"Sorry," Chen said. "Didn't mean to wake you up."

"No, that's okay." Zhu Irzh blinked. He rose from the couch and walked across to the window, where he stood stretching. "Sorry to crash out on your couch. I came straight here from the Opera and Inari wasn't here… I've slept for too long. It's time we got going, anyway."

"Yes, it is." Chen felt as though he'd been put through a mangle.

"Did you find out anything more at the Opera?"

"No. The missing kids are still missing. I couldn't find any trace of the thing we saw, either. I did some magical work—couldn't make any progress there."

"We're supposed to be meeting Miss Qi at nine."

The demon rolled golden eyes. "Ah yes. Heavenly little Miss Qi."

"I'd watch the sarcasm. She might roll you up like a moth."

"And do what? Send me to Hell?"

"You never know," Chen said. "She might decide that the time is finally right for you to enter Heaven."

Zhu Irzh's face was a study in alarm. "No thanks! I didn't enjoy it much the last time. A distinct lack of uncivilized amenities, if you ask me."

"It *is* Heaven, after all. Your mind's supposed to be on higher things." Chen picked up his small bag from the side of the couch and swung it over his shoulder, just as Inari came in with the badger at her heels. His wife wore huge sunglasses, hiding her crimson gaze and making her look rather like a pretty insect, but she took them off as soon as she entered the room and Chen could see worry on her face.

"You'll be careful, won't you?" she said to Chen.

"He will," Zhu Irzh replied before Chen could say anything. "We'll give your regards to your family if we run into anyone."

Inari sighed. "Please don't. I'm not really speaking to any of them these days."

"Very wise," said the demon. "The less I have to do with mine, the better. Although—" He stopped, and an expression of sheer horror came over his face.

"Zhu Irzh?" Chen said sharply. "Are you all right?"

"No." The demon collapsed back onto the couch.

"What's wrong?"

"I've just remembered. I *knew* there was something. It's my mother's birthday. Tomorrow. And we'll be in Hell."

"She doesn't have to know that you're in Hell, does she?"

"She'll know," Zhu Irzh sounded bleak. "She's my mother. Don't ask me how she does it."

"Can't you phone her?" Inari said. "Pretend you're still here, that the connection is bad?"

Chen looked at her with renewed respect. Every time he thought he knew Inari, she surprised him.

"It's a thought, I suppose. But *she'll know*. That's the terrible thing."

"Look," Chen said. "It's after eight thirty. We've got to get on the road; we can't keep Miss Qi waiting." Turning to Inari, he gave her a farewell embrace and then stepped out onto the deck with Zhu Irzh trailing at his heels.

Miss Qi was waiting in the atrium of her hotel, looking prim and well-rested. Chen felt disheveled in comparison, but then he always did when confronted with Heavenkind. He doubted whether they ever sweated, except for that faintly radiant glow redolent of peach blossom or roses, and they certainly never did any of the cruder things to which the human organism was so regrettably prone. But the result was that he felt like an ox next to Miss Qi.

Zhu Irzh did not seem to be experiencing similar misgivings. He said, "Miss Qi? How are you finding the city? Sleeping all right?"

"Well," Miss Qi said. "Not as well as I'm *used* to. It's rather noisy here, isn't it?"

"It's a big, human city," Chen answered. "There's a lot going on."

"I suppose so." Miss Qi looked doubtful. "And so many very unhappy people. I could feel them in the night, so restless."

"Singapore Three isn't a nice place," the demon said. "It's why I like it."

Miss Qi looked at him with an expression that, in a less refined being, might have been malice. "And now you're going home to Hell."

"Don't," Zhu Irzh said, "remind me."

"It's his mother's birthday tomorrow," explained Chen.

Miss Qi clapped pallid hands together. "But how wonderful! Will we meet her?"

"God, I hope not."

"I really don't have a very clear idea of our schedule," Chen said. "Someone's supposed to be meeting us at the other side of the Night Harbor, but I don't have a name—Sung wasn't clear. Did they give you any information?"

Miss Qi shook her head. "None at all."

Chen sighed. "Oh well. We'll just have to manage, as usual." At that, the hotel doorbell rang and Chen looked up to see Sergeant Ma's lugubrious form standing in the entrance to the atrium.

"Ma!" He introduced the sergeant to Miss Qi.

Ma looked at her with interest. "Pleased to meet you, Miss. I'll be taking you to—to the point of your departure."

"Thank you so much." Miss Qi fluttered through the door. In an undertone, Ma said, "*She's* going with you?"

"Don't underestimate Miss Qi," Chen said. "She's a Heavenly warrior."

"With respect, sir," said Ma. "Are you sure? She looks as though she'd be more at home at a tea party."

"I'm sure," Chen said. Zhu Irzh shrugged. They followed Ma out to the car.

Singapore Three, even at this time of night, was still almost gridlocked.

The city had been bad even before the earthquakes, and now it was close to impossible. Chen had thought he'd been given a tough job as liaison officer with Hell, but it was nothing compared to being a member of the traffic department. He felt almost smug as Ma took the police car the wrong way along a one-way street, up a flight of steps, and shot along the harbor road against the flow of in-bound traffic.

And then they were at the sinister black warehouse that housed the Night Harbor.

FIFTEEN

The clerk barely registered Chen's passport, which he gloomily regarded as a sign of how often he had now passed into Hell. And that was just through official channels. Zhu Irzh was waved into the antechamber with a mere gesture of the clerk's hand; he looked pardonably smug, but then in Zhu Irzh's case, immigration didn't really apply.

The processing of Miss Qi's details, however, proved to be another matter. Chen and the demon waited for half an hour in the antechamber before the Celestial reappeared. Zhu Irzh was uncharacteristically lost in thought, so Chen picked up a glossy magazine and flicked through it, finding it filled with celebrities whom he did not recognize and eulogies over movie stars of whom he had never heard. Still, he had to admit that this was a vast improvement over his previous expeditions through the Night Harbor, most of which had involved extreme discomfort and hazard. Now, they were being treated almost with respect: he supposed this was a function of traveling first class.

He was starting to become slightly concerned about Miss Qi when she came through the door, looking ruffled.

"I'm so sorry," she explained. "There was some problem with my papers—I can't think what could have gone awry. Our clerk was most careful."

"I very much doubt that there was any fault on the part of your clerk," Chen said. "I suspect they give any Celestial who ventures here a hard time. Except possibly Kuan Yin. But then, she *is* a goddess."

"And she has her own boat," Miss Qi pointed out, sitting down beside him. "Detective Chen, I can't help being worried. If it's like this in the Night Harbor, when we are still technically on Earth, then how will I be treated in Hell itself?"

Chen wanted to reassure her, but it was a question that was also preoccupying him somewhat. "How did you find your entry onto Earth?" he asked, stalling. Miss Qi's reply confirmed his fears.

"Why, it was a simple, pleasant matter. I merely stepped through into our version of a Celestial temple, and the next moment, I was in its Earthly counterpart. They were very kind to me—they brought me tea before contacting the police station."

"Well, the temple monks must have been very pleased that a Celestial being had graced them with her presence," Chen said. "But I'm afraid you're right. Hell will be a different proposition—to some extent, to Zhu Irzh and myself as well. We'll look after you to the best of our ability. And we are *honored* guests." *Well, guests, anyway.*

"That didn't seem to make too much difference to that clerk," Miss Qi said. "He practically interrogated me."

"From what I saw last night, you don't need much help."

Miss Qi looked down at her hands. "I know a few things."

"Oh, come *on,*" Zhu Irzh said. "You're a Celestial warrior, aren't you?"

"Well, yes. I am."

"So why are you pretending to be this helpless little thing?"

"It is important to be humble and modest," Miss Qi said, reprovingly.

Zhu Irzh looked as though he didn't even know what she meant. Chen said, "So, did they tell you what was happening?"

"Yes, although I had to ask the clerk several times. He said that we had to wait here until boarding was called."

Chen looked around. "There don't seem to be many other passengers," he started to say, but then he realized that this wasn't true. The antechamber in which they sat, which had previously appeared empty, was now filled with people: some apparently human, some very definitely not. Close to Chen and his companions sat two individuals, wearing full armor with war bonnets, the dress of ancient China. Beneath the helms, however, they had the faces of boar: fierce tusks and black bristles, with little black eyes like seeds. They were both staring at Miss Qi with a kind of avidity. Chen felt his heart sink; the last thing they needed was to attract attention to the Celestial, but it seemed that this was going to be inevitable. He couldn't tell whether they were aware that she was a warrior or not; nor which option was preferable.

At that moment, however, the reverberation of a gong sounded throughout the antechamber and a disembodied voice said, "Boarding for tonight's passage to Hell will commence shortly. Please have all documentation readily available."

"Here we go," Chen said. "Good." He wanted to get this trip over and done with, but then, he could have said the same about any visit to Hell. Miss Qi looked frankly alarmed and Zhu Irzh said moodily, "With my luck, my mother will be waiting on the damn dock."

Chen had forgotten about the demon's family celebrations. "I'm sure she'll be too busy."

Members of the crowd were starting to stand, and a milling throng, too disorderly to be termed a queue, was forming around a desk at the far end of the room. Chen, Zhu Irzh, and Miss Qi joined the back of the crowd and waited their turn. People were staring at them; Chen could feel it. He observed them covertly, a policeman's tricks, noting who was human and who was not. Two of the men he recognized, but he did not immediately remember where he knew them from. Then, just as they were approaching the bored, black-clawed clerk at the boarding desk, he realized. He had seen the men at the party at Paugeng the other night, the party at which the girl had gone missing.

Interesting. Chen did not believe in coincidences. He might not sense the puppetmaster hand of the gods, but that did not mean that it wasn't there. He nudged Zhu Irzh, knowing that the demon would have too much sense not to look at once. Sure enough, Zhu Irzh ignored him, but a moment later, cast a casual glance around. His gaze lingered fleetingly on the two men: human, middle-aged, conservatively dressed, and with very little to distinguish them from any other businessman in Singapore Three.

Once they had passed through the gate, Chen leaned over and whispered, "What do you think?"

"They were at Paugeng," the demon breathed back. "I don't know who they are. Jhai will know, though."

"Jhai's not here."

"I'll call her later."

Slowly, they were shuffled onto a platform, dim-lit by wall sconces.

"I've never traveled to Hell by train before," Chen said.

"I didn't know you could." Miss Qi seemed impressed. She looked around at the towering black marble walls, shot with silver; at the gleaming rails on the track beneath.

Zhu Irzh snorted. "Of course we have trains. Who do you think runs most of the world's railway services?"

Moments later, the train itself appeared, startling Chen with its speed and appearance. It was bullet-shaped, black and silver like the station, but metal and coruscated with magnificent ornamentation. Its engine was encased in the head of a centipede: of a *kuei,* and the name on its side read STORM LORD.

"Wow," Chen remarked. "It's certainly baroque."

Zhu Irzh radiated a faint national pride. "We're a high-tech society, Chen. So many new developments originate in Hell." He touched a frond of silver leaf and a door slid open. "After you."

Chen stepped inside to find a comfortable, black-velvet interior: seats that were practically armchairs, and small fixed tables. There was more than a nod to Art Nouveau. "This is certainly an improvement on the boat, that time. Or having to go through Bad Dog Village."

"I'll say." Zhu Irzh was fervent in his agreement. "I might be from Hell but the Night Harbor is bloody tedious." He selected one of the seats. "I could get used to traveling in style."

The train did not remain long in the station. There was a rushing, gliding sensation beneath Chen's feet and the train pulled out. Chen, feeling like a child, pressed his face to the window but little was visible beyond it: a gleam of sea; a bulk of shadow, that could have been the mountains through which he had traversed with Zhu Irzh and various other folk, in which Bad Dog Village lay. Then the train was shooting through rocky gorges, lit high above with flickering lights, and across vast plains and fields in which nightmare crops were growing. Zhu Irzh leaned back against the seat and closed his eyes, sleeping with that frozen quality Chen had come to associate with him. But Miss Qi appeared as interested as Chen himself, and looked out of her own side of the window, her expression wary.

"It's not like Heaven, is it?" said Chen.

Miss Qi shook her head. "Oh no. Not at all. Is it always so *dark?*"

"Not quite. Hell has its own cycles of night and day, but it never gets very light."

"Just as Heaven never becomes very dark," Miss Qi mused. "It is like the essence of Tao, a balance."

"In that case, the balancing point is Earth," Chen said. "Yet I wouldn't describe Earth as a balanced place."

"I see Earth as being the place where the dynamic of balance is worked out," Miss Qi said. "And so it is always in flux, never static, always changing. Again like the Tao. Change around a still center."

"An interesting philosophy," Chen said. "When I last had dealings with Heaven, however, there was a move to withdraw from Earth, from human-kind. Some of the Celestials disagreed: the Emperor's son Mhara, Kuan Yin. Do you know anything more of this policy?"

Miss Qi's pale face looked troubled. "I am no politician," she said. "But it is an argument that has raged—politely, of course—in Heaven for many years. I would hope that we would not withdraw. I feel we have a duty to Earth; it was formed alongside Heaven, after all. I think it would be a dereliction of our duty to abandon it."

"I hope Heaven comes to feel as you do," Chen said.

"Maybe it will. But you know, because of what we are, we cannot afford to become divided amongst ourselves. So we will believe what the Emperor decides for us."

"You mean you will choose to believe it," Chen said, seeking clarification.

"No, I mean that there is *no* choice. Once the Emperor has decreed it, we will simply believe, because we are all one."

"I didn't realize Heaven was so united," Chen said.

"That is what makes it Heaven." Miss Qi was very earnest.

If that was the case—and as a Celestial, Miss Qi would not lie—Chen was given yet another reason to be uneasy about the nature of things in the Heavenly regions. On this account, one might infer that Heaven was the ultimate dictatorship, an insect hive with all faces turned radiantly toward the Emperor. But of course, that was exactly why Heaven had survived in this form for so long. Chen wondered whether the Emperor's son, now partly resident on Earth, was subject to this policy, or whether he was permitted to have a degree of independent thought. That the Emperor's decrees were essentially benign, Chen had no doubt; the fact that debate was allowed at all was a positive sign.

But unease remained. And with it came an even more personal and disturbing thought, one that had been troubling Chen for the last few years. He was not immortal. He was a human man, in his forties and therefore middle-aged, with not all that long remaining to him even if he lived out a natural span and didn't succumb to some peril of the job (as seemed all too likely, on occasion). When he died, as a devoted servant of the Goddess Kuan Yin, Most Merciful and Compassionate, he might reasonably expect to enter Heaven himself. Okay, he'd married a demon. His right-hand man was from Hell. On a previous, unfortunate occasion, he'd used the goddess' sacred image as a battering ram. Good thing she *was* Merciful and Compassionate, really.

But did he actually *want* to go to Heaven? Even if he was reincarnated later, as usually happened? Chen was not arrogant enough to consider himself enlightened: he was a policeman, not a monk. He muddled along, but he didn't have much time to spend in contemplation and meditation, purifying his soul in preparation for removal from the wheel of karma. His meditational practice usually took place during a snatched ten minutes in the precinct locker room, not a harmonious hour in the local temple. So even if he did end up in Heaven, he was unlikely to remain there for all that long and then he'd be hauled back down to Earth, a baby again. At least it would give him a chance to get some sleep.

And then there was the central issue in all this.

Inari.

He couldn't take her to Heaven. Even if Kuan Yin swung some massive dispensation and allowed it, Chen did not think the denizens of the Celestial Realms would take kindly to a demon in their midst. Oh, he doubted that anything would be said. If anything, the Celestials would probably be too kind, and that sort of patronage would eventually grate, even on one so self-effacing as Inari. It would certainly grate on Chen. Impossible to explain that

Inari—so gentle, so kind—was really in the wrong place to start with; she would have been so much more suited as a child of a family of Heaven.

And when he was reincarnated, what would happen to Inari? This was the thing that really made Chen's heart beat slow and coldly. He would be gone, and it was improbable in the extreme that Heaven would allow her to stay. That would throw Inari back onto the highly dubious mercy of her family. They might even try to marry her off again, to the same vile personage from the Ministry of Epidemics that had led Chen to have to rescue her from Hell in the first place. Back to square one. He could think of only two choices: placing her under the protection of Kuan Yin, perhaps as a temple priestess or, at the least, a handmaiden, or placing her under the protection of Zhu Irzh.

Strangely, Chen thought that Zhu Irzh would rise to this particular challenge. He treated Inari as a younger sister these days, although Chen was fairly sure that he had at one point entertained a rather more romantic interest in her. But now there was Jhai, and Inari had become part of Zhu Irzh's adopted family.

At least there *were* choices. Also, Chen didn't want to make the mistake of treating Inari like a child; she might have equally viable ideas about her own future that simply hadn't occurred to him.

He stared out of the window and realized that the sky was lightening to an uncomfortable rosy red and that the train was coming into the outskirts of a city, presumably the sprawling metropolis that was Hell's counterpart to Singapore Three. Chen looked out onto rows of slums, weed-infested backyards in which the occasional hungry ghost could be glimpsed, narrow streets filled with litter and overlooked by towering tenement blocks. The train shot past a gap in the houses, a strip of black grass on which a rail-thin, red-eyed cow grazed. Chen thought of Senditreya, mad goddess of geomancy, who had recently been transformed into her bovine avatar and confined to Hell. He doubted she'd be happier as a cow. But frankly, who cared?

Miss Qi was looking out the window with her mouth open, revealing teeth like little pearls. "It's *horrible*," she whispered.

"It's Hell," Zhu Irzh replied, without opening his eyes.

The grim suburbs were passing by. Further on, Chen could see the great summits of the central city, the Ministries and Departments that ran the rest of Hell. He had never got to the bottom of why these buildings were here, rather than in the Hellish counterpart to Beijing—Zhu Irzh, when asked, had professed not to know—but he'd heard rumors about an enforced relocation, continual problems with the Communist administration that had obliged the Ministries to move. Singapore Three was an economically free zone, answerable to the Chinese government but largely separate from it, and Chen suspected that this in some manner gave Hell a lot more leeway.

There on the horizon was the Ministry of Epidemics, now rebuilt after an earlier disaster. That massive ziggurat was the Ministry of War, bristling now with high tech defenses and plated with enormous slabs of iron: a literally armored building around the summit of which lightning played in a constant eye-splitting panorama. That fleshy, pulpy red building was the Ministry of Lust, and around these were innumerable subdepartments, metal turrets and stone columns haphazardly placed with no regard for the harmonies of *feng shui* and monstrously displeasing to the eye.

"Are we nearly there yet?" Zhu Irzh asked.

"Take a look. You're home."

"Oh god."

"Do you want me to see if there's anyone who might be your mother waiting on the platform?"

"Yes," said the demon, opening his eyes and sitting upright. "Actually, I do want you to do that. You can look and I'll hide."

The train was slowing to a halt. It stopped, disgorging a horde of passengers, but there was no one waiting on the platform and Chen relayed this to Zhu Irzh.

"Perhaps you are simply being paranoid," Miss Qi said to the demon.

"No such thing where my family is concerned." But Zhu Irzh stepped down from the train and made his way into the station concourse with the others.

Chen kept a lookout, partly for anyone who might be Zhu Irzh's parent, but also to see who—or what—else might be lurking in the concourse of Hell station. There seemed to be a lot of shadowy forms milling around the ticket offices, an ambience of despair and disappointment, but the concourse itself was empty once the other passengers had hastened through the vast iron doors. Above, the ceiling of the concourse disappeared into what looked like a stormy sky: Perhaps there was no ceiling after all. It was hard to tell—like many of the civic buildings of Hell, the station was difficult to look at directly.

"Where must we go now?" Miss Qi faltered.

"Someone was supposed to meet us," Chen said. He followed Zhu Irzh through the doors, ushering Miss Qi ahead of him, and was hit by a blast of heat. The station was evidently air-conditioned in some manner, but this weather was typical of Hell: sultry, stuffy, humid, and stinking, with the feeling of an approaching storm continually hovering at the edges of consciousness. Miss Qi's face grew even paler and Chen noticed a film of moisture across her brow. Glowing, again.

In front of the station stretched the distant arch of a main road, with traffic hurtling along it: enormous limousines, and other vehicles, too, drawn by beasts: drays loaded with barrels, chariots, private coaches. One of these coaches was standing patiently in front of the concourse, a round black thing, with two horned beasts between the shafts. They were like gigantic, demonic deer: red-and-black-striped nightmare zebras. One of them stamped at the pavement and caused a little crack, then tossed its horned head. Miss Qi blanched even further.

On the side of the coach was an insignia: a spiked symbol that was vaguely familiar to Chen. Zhu Irzh brightened.

"Ah! That's the symbol of the Ministry of War. It must be for us."

Chen was not inclined to be as optimistic—things rarely went so smoothly in Hell—but just as Zhu Irzh spoke, the door of the carriage opened and a young female demon, wearing boiled-leather armor in spite of the thundery heat, stepped down and approached Chen and his companions.

Usually, when dealing with underlings in Hell, Chen had grown accustomed to surliness and indifference. A smarmy obsequiousness was generally the best that one could hope for, and even then it was customarily followed by an outrageous demand for money or an outright stab in the back. But the chauffeur from the Ministry of War was of a different order altogether.

"Detective Inspector Chen, Seneschal Irzh, Miss Qi? Good day. I'm glad you have arrived on time. I trust your journey was a smooth one?"

Chen was so taken aback by this that he did not immediately reply, leaving Miss Qi to say, with manifest gratitude, "Why yes. Our journey was most interesting. Have you been so kind as to come to meet us?"

"I am Underling No," the demon replied. She pushed back the flaps of her helmet, revealing a dark red face, a thin and elegant nose, small, sharp fangs. To Chen, she looked even less human than many of the denizens of Hell, and yet she was not unappealing, with huge black eyes and a bouncy step. "I have been sent to collect you, by the Ministry of War, and to take you to your hotel."

"I've never stayed in a hotel in Hell," Chen remarked, somewhat impressed, at the same time as Zhu Irzh said, "*Which* hotel, exactly?"

"The Superior Palace," No said.

Zhu Irzh arched an eyebrow. "That's—quite good."

"The Ministry is most anxious that you should enjoy your stay," No explained. Chen nearly commented that if he did, it would be a personal first, but he felt that this comment was a little impolite and might cause him to lose face. So he simply complied with Underling No's invitation and clambered up the steps into the swaying coach.

Inside, it was not unlike the train: a lot of black leather and dark red velvet. Underling No had evidently been chosen to accessorize her vehicle. Once Zhu Irzh and Miss Qi were safely inside, Underling No clucked to the deer and the coach set off at a smart pace, cantering down the sliproad to the main artery and keeping up with the rest of the traffic. The air reeked of unrefined petrol:

Hell, it seemed, had not gone over to unleaded gas. The coach bounced but Chen had to admit that it had good suspension. Miss Qi clung to one of the struts, all the same.

"The Superior Palace is one of the best hotels here," Zhu Irzh shouted above the roar of passing cars. "It's where they put all the visiting dignitaries from other Hells. A lot of diplomats stay there."

"I wasn't expecting this," Chen shouted back.

Zhu Irzh shrugged. "So far, so good."

Chen watched the scenery of the central city unfold, streets lined with sinister mansions behind huge gates and black lawns, the towers of the Ministries growing more overwhelming as they grew closer. It was odd to be treated as honored guest rather than human infiltrator and he did not trust it. But so far, it was a more pleasant stay than any he'd had in Hell so far.

The Superior Palace turned out to be situated in its own parkland, just behind the Ministries of War and Lust. Neither was attractive, but Chen could at least find a moment to be grateful that they were nowhere near the Ministry of Epidemics, which stood some distance away across the square. Having been instrumental in its destruction, he considered that the less he had to do with it, the better. But the Ministry looked just the same as it always had, as though it had never been blown apart.

"They raised its counterpart from a lower level," Zhu Irzh told him, when he remarked on this. "Caused a huge crack in the continuum fabric, apparently, and left one of the lower levels rife with unrestrained diseases, but it'll all sort itself out in a few hundred years."

Miss Qi shuddered. Chen couldn't help feeling vaguely guilty. But if the Ministry of Epidemics hadn't made its disastrous bid for power in the first place, then it would not have sown the seeds of its own destruction. A lifetime of considering karma had left Chen particular about the true causes of things.

"Here we are," Underling No called back from her seat on the top of the coach. She reined the deer to a flashy gravel-scattering stop in front of the hotel and swung down in a creak of leather armor to open the door.

Chen was obliged to concede that the Superior Palace was, indeed, superior. The coach was whisked away and parked by a junior demon, while Underling No accompanied Chen and his party into the foyer, a rich and rather overwhelming mélange of embroideries, wall hangings, oriental carpets, and mahogany.

"Delightful," Miss Qi said, faintly.

"Isn't it lovely?" Underling No's face was a fanged beam. "I'm sure you'll have a comfortable stay here."

A maid hurried forward with room keys and showed them up a sweeping flight of stairs to their rooms, all next door to one another. Chen's room turned out to enjoy, if this was the correct word, a view over the backs of the Ministries. Staring at the Ministry of War made him feel lightheaded, and looking at the Ministry of Lust, merely ill. So he drew the drapes closed and turned his attention to the room instead, a paneled chamber of no small gloom which managed to be both grand and uncomfortable. The bed seemed relatively hard, however, which suggested that at least he wouldn't have to put up with back trouble. Rather than spend too much time in the room, he went next door to find Zhu Irzh.

The demon was sitting glumly on his bed, studying a square of ornately printed cardboard in black and gold.

"What's that?" Chen asked.

"What do you think?" Zhu Irzh tossed the card toward him.

Chen picked it up from the thick pile of the carpet and read:

YOU ARE INVITED TO BIRTHDAY CELEBRATIONS
OF MADAME ZHU FENG LI
BLOODLILY MANSION, ENDLESS LANE
7:30 P.M. ON THE LAST DAY OF STIFLEMONTH.

"This is from your mother?" Chen asked. The demon nodded.

"I can't even pretend I haven't seen it." He turned the invitation over and pointed to a glittering sigil on the back. "As soon as I opened the envelope, the hex flew off, out the window. It'll inform my mother's staff that I've read it." He gave a dramatic sigh. "Just what I need. Mum snapping and bitching at Dad for buying her the wrong birthday present, my sister sulking, my little brother—god knows what he's up to these days. I don't even know if he's still living at home."

"You've never spoken much about your family," Chen said, sitting down in the armchair.

"There's a reason for that. You know, Chen, I don't think I've told you how much I've come to *appreciate* living on Earth."

"You didn't live with your family, though, did you? I seem to remember you having your own apartment."

"I did. Nice place, actually. If I ever did move back here, I'd consider trying to rent it again. Bit of an issue with the landlady over something I slew in the living room, but apart from that…" Zhu Irzh gave Chen a curious glance. "You've never said much about your folks, come to that."

"I've got very few relatives left," Chen said. "I was an only child—the one child policy, you know? My parents were getting on when they had me and they died a peaceful natural death within several months of one another."

"Where are they now? In Heaven, one assumes, not here."

"Yes, in Heaven. But in a remote part and I don't know whether they've been reborn. Their shadow-personalities may live on but I stopped hearing from them some years ago. They never knew about Inari. I haven't asked to look them up, though I loved them a great deal. Apart from that, there are a few distant cousins, and that's it. Inari is my family now."

"You are a lucky man, Chen," the demon said, and Chen replied:

"I agree. So, do you think you'll be going to this party?"

"I'll have to."

The demon looked so gloomy that Chen said, "Want me to come with you?" His motive was not simply to be supportive of a friend, but also, he admitted to himself, wanton curiosity. He wanted to see the kind of background from which someone as complex as Zhu Irzh had emerged.

"Would you?" Zhu Irzh, normally so insouciant, looked pathetically grateful. "I could use all the support I can get."

"Well, let's go, in that case. Miss Qi will be fine here in the hotel." *One hopes.* But before they were able to discuss it at any length, there was a knock on the door and Zhu Irzh opened it to reveal a smiling Underling No.

"Is everything to your satisfaction?"

Apart from the fact that I'm in Hell and have just agreed to go to a demon's birthday party. "Perfectly fine," Chen said.

"I'm so pleased. I've spoken to Miss Qi. You are to be taken on a short tour of the Ministry of War, and then you will go out to dinner."

"Sounds lovely," said Chen.

SIXTEEN

"What a horrible story," Mai said, when Pin had finished his tale. "You poor boy." She squinted into his bottle, her eyes appearing as huge as the moon. "There must be some way we can get you out of there, anyway."

"Try taking the stopper out," Pin advised. "I'm not sure if there's a spell on it or anything."

"Well, let's try," Mai said. She seized the stopper and the bottle and gave a sharp tug. The stopper flew out and Pin flew with it. His spirit surged out of the bottle and hung in the air.

"What do I look like?" he asked Mai. He felt so ephemeral, so diffuse, that he wanted proof of his own existence.

"You look like a ghost of a boy," Mai said. She frowned. "I suppose that makes a kind of sense, given that you're not actually dead, are you? You're still alive, so I suppose that makes you seem insubstantial."

Pin didn't really understand, but so much had made so little sense recently that he decided to simply accept it. At least she could see him. He sat down on a nearby couch, floating slightly above its surface.

"I don't know what to do," he said. "I think my mother is here, but I don't know where to find her." It embarrassed him to sound so lost, but Mai's kind face drew it out of him.

"How did she die?" Mai asked.

"She was ill. I thought she might be somewhere in the Ministry of Epidemics, but I don't know…"

"I might be able to find out for you," Mai said, "but to be honest, our records are in such a state—it's very hard to track people down and I'm only a minor clerk." She hesitated. "I've had associations with the Ministry for most of my life here, but it takes a very long time to work yourself up to any kind of position of power. I died of a disease, too, you see. I was three."

"Only three? Why are you here? Surely you can't have done anything bad enough to warrant being sent to Hell?"

"I'm not sure," Mai said. She sighed. "There was some kind of mix-up, my mother says. But anyway, Pin, *you* shouldn't be here. You're not dead yet; you got here by accident, from the sound of it. And you're so fragile. There are things here that *eat* ghosts."

"I don't even know what happened to my body," Pin said. Presumably it was still back in the demon lounge and he did not like to think about what might be happening to it.

"My mother is on Earth," Mai said. "I told you that. She's looking after my son. But she's elderly now—she wasn't young when she had me. She's very brave, but I don't want to ask her to go to a demon lounge. I'm sorry, Pin, but I don't want to put my family in danger."

"I understand," Pin said. "But if you could give me some advice I can't stay here with you forever, can I?"

"I'll see what I can do," Mai said with sudden resolve. "I want to help. No one should be stuck here. It's different with me—I grew up here. I don't remember Earth very well."

"How *did* you grow up?" Pin asked. He didn't mean to pry, but it seemed unimaginably difficult to him, that such a small child might be sent on her own to Hell, and survive—yet how could she do otherwise, when already dead? The horror of it struck him then, that this was a life that one could not even escape through death. If he himself died—assuming he ever made it back to his life—then certainly he would escape the Opera, but to what?

Mai sighed. "It wasn't easy. I didn't understand what had happened to me at first—one minute I was with my mother and crying because I felt ill, and then the next thing I knew I was on a boat with all these dead people, and then I was here in Hell. They just put us out on the shore and left us. I ran away and I hid for days, and then I just lived on the streets. My dad came down with me—I glimpsed him on the boat but they wouldn't let me talk to him and I couldn't find him when we got to shore. That was the worst thing. But my mother prayed and eventually one of my ancestors came and found me and took me home to his family. I lived with them until my marriage. It wasn't so bad. But they reincarnated shortly after the wedding, and their shadow-personalities have faded, so I won't see them again."

There was a short silence. "I'm sorry," Pin said.

"I'm happy now, Pin. Ahn and I love each other. And we love our son. I just wish—well, that's not your problem. Pin—are you hungry, or thirsty? I don't even know if you can feel things?"

"I'm not," Pin said. "But I am tired." As he said it, in his ghost's whisper, he realized that it was true: he was exhausted.

"Then rest," Mai said, and Pin's last memory of that night was of sinking down into the couch and sleep, as Mai spread a blanket like a cobweb across him.

SEVENTEEN

Up close, the Ministry of War was loud. The air around it snapped and whirred, humming with machinery and lightning. If Chen listened carefully, he could hear more distant sounds in between the mechanical noise: the clash of arms and the shouts of dying warriors, explosions and the whine of falling shells, as if the very building of the Ministry was some kind of recording device, set to grasp the noises of war and play them back in incessant and horrifying turmoil. Looking up to the summit of the Ministry made him feel dizzy and disoriented; Chen concentrated upon its iron flanks instead, the gun placements and missile cones that bristled from every angle. There were demonic guards at the doors, immense, hulking beings like monstrous bald bears, wearing antique metal armor.

"I always thought it was very *macho,* this Ministry," Zhu Irzh said with a sigh.

Miss Qi eyed him curiously. "Do you think that's a good thing?"

The demon shrugged.

"We are very proud of our Ministry," Underling No said, earnestly. "Let me tell you some facts."

It was clear that there was no escape. It reminded Chen of school visits in his youth, trips arranged to this steelworks or that manufacturing plant, all designed to maximize the notion of Chinese productivity and industriousness. Whatever the content of the trip had been, the young Chen had found them all slightly depressing and now they blurred in his mind into one huge all-encompassing visit. He had a feeling that this trip, too, was destined to take its place among them.

"...inaugurated over five thousand years ago by the then-Emperor of Hell, Jing-Li, and since then has had a long and illustrious history in establishing and maintaining conflict across the Oriental world..." No was saying.

Miss Qi, unsurprisingly, frowned. "Did you have any part to play in the last two world wars?"

"Of course," No assured her. "Although we must note that the seeds of those conflicts were begun in other Hells elsewhere, since the main wars began in the Western hemisphere. However, we are proud to say that we played our part in fomenting disruption across the East, too. And of course, since then, we have worked closely with the Hells of North Korea and Southeast Asia, since China has not directly been involved in conflict for some years." Underling No managed to look faintly embarrassed at this, as though the Ministry of War had been slacking.

"But you can't get a really clear picture from statistics," No went on, to Chen's secret relief. "You need to see the Ministry."

As they walked through the immense portal, decorated with gory scenes of combat and destruction from the ancient to the modern, Chen reflected that it was really quite open-minded of the Ministry to allow a human and a Celestial through its doors for a tour. Presumably there would be restricted areas, for Chen could not see the Ministry letting people wander in and out to observe its secrets. Or perhaps they were so well-established and confident that they simply didn't care… Either way, he intended to learn what he could and, if necessary, pass on the information to whichever authority seemed best able to deal with it. He was not deceived by No's pleasant manner and willingness to convey information. She was a mere lackey, after all, and her function as a liaison officer was purely to supply authorized material, the public face of the Ministry. But things were, perhaps, changing, for Chen had never known Hell's institutions to see the need for a public face before. Maybe recent events had convinced even the governing lords of the under-world that a degree of give-and-take might be required. And that, essentially, led to questions about just how much they feared the wrath of Heaven, of the Celestial powers.

An interesting question, Chen thought, strolling behind No through the colossal metal-paneled atrium, Brutalist Architecture at its most massively imposing. For it raised the issue in his own mind as to what kind of power Heaven and the Celestial Emperor wielded: one really saw it so rarely, or so it seemed. Yet Earth, though a bit of a disaster area environmentally, was improving, and there were millions of people who were not starving, disease-ridden, or murdering one another even in spite of Hell's machinations. So that suggested a more subtle balance was in play than one might otherwise consider. Either Heaven had an authority all its own, or it had none and the improvements were entirely due to human will and human ingenuity. The question remained: If Hell decided again to make a play for power across the three worlds, just how far might Heaven choose to go…?

Zhu Irzh was staring up at the panels. "Five thousand years of war," he murmured. "That's a lot of killing."

"Hell was repopulated many times through developments in this very Ministry," No assured him. "As I'm sure you know, we play an integral role in maintaining the infrastructure of Hell, and our research and development departments have proved *most* lucrative in forwarding ideas to Earth."

"I'm afraid the military-industrial complex is one of the foremost on the planet," Chen said. He could not approve, but No naturally took this as a compliment.

"That's so kind of you to say so," she said. "Now. One of the Lesser Lords has agreed to meet you. We'll go to his office."

She escorted them through a bewildering series of passageways, all lined with gleaming metal. Their footsteps resounded on stone and the interior of the Ministry was stiflingly hot, although Chen could hear a curious whirring sound throughout the place that reminded him of a large fan. Once away from the ornately decorated atrium, the Ministry was austere, with few decorations of any kind on the walls.

"Here we are," No said, in hushed tones. She knocked on a door, and after a moment, a voice barked, "Enter!" They were shown into a palatial office: If this was one of the Ministry's Lesser Lords, Chen thought, then the administrative quarters of its rulers must be opulent indeed. An armored figure was sitting behind a desk so huge and polished that it resembled a mirrored pool. Like No, his face was dark red, but he bristled with spines. Black and white porcupine quills bushed out from beneath a flared Samurai helmet and his hands were like the paws of a dog: bunched fingers terminating in short black claws. When he stood, Chen saw that he was around eight feet in height.

"Good afternoon! You may address me as Lesser Lord Nine. I am in charge of bowed weaponry and several subdivisions of the armed forces." He gestured to the opposite wall, on which rested an array of stringed weapons and arrows, from long bows to crossbows.

"Do you find much call for bows these days?" Chen asked. A usually reasonable capacity to make small talk was, he felt, deserting him somewhat during the course of this visit. With the obvious exceptions of Zhu Irzh and Inari, he was more accustomed to battling demons than making polite conversation with them. And battling was proving easier.

"Why, yes, you'd be surprised. Not just in the more—medieval—regions of Hell, but also in the inner cities of Earth. One might almost say that the weapon has been undergoing something of a renaissance recently. It's very heartening. After all, I feel that there's no real *art* in using a gun, no real *skill*."

"Glad to hear business is picking up," Chen said, with what he felt to be a palpable insincerity.

"You'll try one, of course," Lesser Lord Nine said. He charged around to the other side of the desk, clapping Chen on the back and nearly knocking him flat.

"Unfortunately an old elbow injury would prevent me from doing full justice to the weapon," Chen said hastily. He felt a bit guilty about this, even though it happened to be true. "But I'm sure Zhu Irzh will have a go."

Zhu Irzh did, in fact, appear commendably keen. "Certainly," he said. "Why not?"

"*I* should like to try, too," Miss Qi said, very firmly.

"I'm so sorry," Chen said. "I didn't mean to cast aspersions on you as a warrior. I merely thought you might not be all that interested."

"After all, Chen," Zhu Irzh remarked, "we *are* supposed to be studying equal opportunities."

Miss Qi shot him a baleful look. "The detective is telling the truth. I know."

The Lesser Lord reached up and plucked a bow from the wall, a long curving thing inlaid with gold. "First shot, then, goes to our Celestial guest!"

"All right," Miss Qi said. "Where is the shooting range?"

"Come with me," the Lesser Lord said. He led them back out into the corridor and, after a short walk, they reached another passageway, metal-lined and casting dull reflections into infinity, with an archery target set at the far end.

Miss Qi snapped up the bow, slipped an arrow into the notch, then fired, all in one smooth movement. She repeated this twice more, without apparent effort even though the bow looked heavy. On each occasion, the arrow struck the center of the target.

"Impressive," Lesser Lord Nine said.

Miss Qi bowed. "Thank you." She handed the bow to Zhu Irzh.

"I shall probably do very badly," the demon said, with what Chen felt to be a wholly feigned modesty. He raised the bow and fired, and again, sending another two arrows to join Miss Qi's in the center of the target.

"This equal opportunities thing of yours appears to be working," the Lesser Lord said. "Tell me, Miss Qi. In what other forms of weaponry do you excel?"

"I wouldn't say that I *excelled* at any of them," Miss Qi flustered. "But I am versed in the use of the long sword and the short sword, in knives, and of course, in defensive magic. However, I know very little about guns or more modern forms of weaponry."

The Lesser Lord waved a dismissive mailed fist. "Efficient, yes, but as I said a moment ago, there is no art to them. I am pleased to see that Heaven has kept to the more traditional weapons."

Miss Qi said nothing, but Chen, who was growing used to the moods that crossed the Celestial's pale face, thought he saw a shadow glide over her features.

"I hope to meet you on the battlefield someday," the Lesser Lord beamed. Chen was also becoming used to the zeitgeist of the Ministry of War and he read this not as a threat, but as a politely expressed hope.

Miss Qi, however, grew even paler. "Indeed, I trust we do not. Heaven seeks to promote harmony and good feeling between the three worlds, not bloodshed. We feel that there has been all too much of that already."

"There can never be too much!" Lesser Lord Nine declared. "Now, come and see where we make so many of our engines of destruction."

Other corridors, and many doors later, the Lesser Lord ushered them through a tall iron door, almost indistinguishable from the wall itself. Chen was expecting to find himself in yet another office, but instead, he stepped into a round, domed chamber, filled with neon-filtered light of a faintly glowing blue. Figures moved beyond a glass panel, clad in hazmat suits. One of these bustled toward the Lesser Lord and pushed up the visor of his helmet.

"Lord, I fear I must ask for documentation, for proof of permit, I am sorry, but—"

"Quite all right," Lesser Lord Nine said. "Underling No?"

"I have all the papers here." No stepped smartly forward. "I trust everything is in order?"

The demon in the hazmat suit produced a phial of gleaming blue light from an inner pocket and poured it over the papers. It foamed as it fell, like acid, and left the papers glowing in its wake.

"All is quite acceptable," the demon said. He sounded relieved. Chen could appreciate that Lesser Lord Nine was not someone whom one would wish to fall afoul of.

"Good, good," the Lesser Lord remarked. Then, to his guests: "Follow me."

Again, Chen was expecting a room, and again, he was surprised. The next door through which the Lesser Lord led them took them outside—not onto the steamy square of the central city, but out onto a vast, bleak plain. Chen stood in gray grass up to his knees; it blew in a breeze he could not otherwise feel. Above him, the sky was molten silver, racing with rags of cloud in the high upper winds of Hell, a cold and empty sky. But the plain itself was not empty. It was filled with a slow parade of moving vehicles: enormous juggernauts bristling with armaments; warships on great trolleys, sailing like black galleons across the plain; tanks that were twice the size of any Chen had seen on Earth, even during the military parades through Beijing in his youth. All of the machines were dark, some bearing the blood-red insignia of Imperial Hell, others with the symbols of the lesser Houses.

He turned to Lesser Lord Nine. "It is our turn to be impressed."

"Magnificent, isn't it?" The Lesser Lord looked gratified, though why he should be so pleased by an accolade from a human, Chen did not know. But the being was clearly proud of his establishment.

"What is it all *for?*" Miss Qi stepped a little closer to Chen.

"Why," Lesser Lord Nine said, rather blankly, "it is for war, of course."

"But I have never seen machines like this used on Earth. Where is it to be, this war?"

"We're engaged in constant conflict with the lower levels," the Lesser Lord explained. "Incursions from below mean that we need to maintain a strong military presence here. And also, such incursions provide us with a practice ground. We are able to test our military capabilities."

"I see," Miss Qi said, after a pause. Chen could tell what she was thinking, however: the military muscle before them, the great machines thundering across this barren plain, might someday be turned against Heaven. He wondered if even Heaven could withstand the onslaught, and he wondered whether this might be the real reason that the Ministry had been so open to their Celestial visitor: Would Qi be expected to return and report on what she had seen to the Heavenly authorities? Or was there another game at play? The Lesser Lord did not strike Chen as a particularly subtle being—a typical career soldier, in fact—but there was no doubt that subtlety was one of the hallmarks of his masters.

The wind rose, stirring the grass still further, and this time Chen could feel it. It lifted his hair, whipping it around his collar. Zhu Irzh hunched his black silk shoulders against the sudden wind and Miss Qi's pale mane snapped free of its braid and fluttered out like a banner.

"Ah," Lesser Lord Nine said. "You'll find this interesting." He pointed beyond Chen's shoulder. Chen looked up to see an object like a multi-bladed helicopter, but the size of a battleship, soaring over the horizon. The Lesser Lord said something but his words were lost in the roar from the sky as the flying machine came overhead. Its sides were black and pitted as though it had been struck by meteors: Just where, Chen wondered, had this thing seen active service? The lower levels? In *space?* It looked *used.* Within minutes, it was directly over their heads and then gone, roaring off across the plain and sending waves through the gray grass in its wake.

"Perhaps," the Lesser Lord said, into the sudden silence, "we should return to my office. It's a little chilly, don't you think?"

蛇警探

Just as they reached the Lesser Lord's chamber, however, returning via the decontamination unit, an old-fashioned phone shrilled. Lesser Lord Nine picked it up and listened, a frown creasing his inhuman features.

"Sorry about this," he remarked, putting the receiver down. "Seems I have to go downstairs for a few minutes. Some crisis, no doubt. There's always something. Don't you find that?"

"Almost continually," Chen said. It was possible to find some sympathy for the Lesser Lord after all.

"Wait here. I'll have some tea sent up to you. Underling No, would you see to it?"

"Of course, sir." No scurried away and the Lesser Lord strode through the door, closing it gently behind him. Chen listened for the click of a key in the lock, but there was no other sound.

They all looked at one another. Chen knew that everyone had too much sense to start a conversation about what they had just seen in an office that was almost certainly bugged.

"I should love some tea," Miss Qi said. "I hope they serve green tea. I should like to try some down here."

"I wouldn't mind some myself," Chen told her. Zhu Irzh's mind, however, was clearly far from thoughts of refreshment. He was standing by the door, with his ear to it. Next moment, to Chen's horror, he reached out, turned the handle, and disappeared into the corridor.

Miss Qi's gray eyes widened with alarm. "What—?" she started to say.

Chen motioned for her to stay put, and followed the demon out. Zhu Irzh was already at the end of the corridor, almost running. Cursing beneath his breath, Chen went after him.

When he reached the end of the corridor, he realized that the demon's hearing, so much keener than his own, had picked up the conversation that was now evident to Chen. He did not have to put his ear to the door at which Zhu Irzh had halted, however. The conversation was being conducted at full volume.

"Absolute fucking disaster!" someone was bellowing. This was said at such a roar that it was hard to tell who was speaking, but Chen did not think it was Lesser Lord Nine. Perhaps he was on the receiving end of it; though Chen, who had come almost to like the Lesser Lord, hoped not.

"What do you mean, a disaster?" An older voice, full of sibilant hissing. "The mission was an unmitigated success. We have quelled the *lung*. There will be no more incursions from that quarter, you may rest assured."

"Yes, but you haven't quelled all of them, have you? At least one remains. On Earth! It has been seen."

"If any remain, which I doubt, then they will be ancient and as such, close to disintegration," the hissing voice said, testily. "Besides, many of them have already fled from Earth."

"You cannot underestimate them! Age brings cunning." A pause. "You should know that."

"I fail entirely to see—" the second voice said, but at that point Zhu Irzh clasped Chen by the arm and hauled him back around the corner.

"Zhu Irzh, what are you doing?"

"The Lesser Lord's coming back. I heard footsteps."

They made it back into the office, where an agitated Qi was waiting, moments before the door opened and both the Lesser Lord and Underling No appeared, the latter bearing a tray on which was set a teapot and several cups.

"Now," the Lesser Lord said, all geniality and smiles. "I've arranged for a private supper to be held at your hotel. I thought you'd probably be tired. I also understand that you—" this was directed at Zhu Irzh "—have an important function to attend tomorrow night, so we will of course accommodate this. On the following evening—"

"Wait a moment," Zhu Irzh interrupted. "Might I ask how you know about that?"

"We were informed," the Lesser Lord said. "Anyway, on the following evening, there is to be a banquet here in honor of our guests." His brow furrowed. "I'm sure you'll enjoy yourselves."

"Sounds fantastic," Zhu Irzh said.

蛇警探

Chen's experience of Hell's cuisine had not, to date, been encouraging, but the supper back at the hotel was exemplary: fresh stir-fried vegetables with rice and fish in broth. Zhu Irzh was given a plate of some vile red stew with tentacles, which he consumed with every appearance of enjoyment, and Miss Qi had a bowl of something fluffily white and highly scented. Mindful of listeners, the conversation revolved mainly around food and the weather, and no one wanted a late night. Miss Qi retired shortly after the meal. Zhu Irzh and Chen wandered into the hotel bar, which was deserted, and had a Scotch each as a nightcap. The demon seemed preoccupied with his mother's party, and it was at least a safe topic. At last Chen said, "Well, this is pleasant, Zhu Irzh, but I'm afraid I'm starting to fall asleep. I think I'll go up."

"I'll do the same," the demon said. "I'd forgotten how tired this place makes me."

"Have you heard from your family yet?"

"No. But I will. The Ministry of War evidently has."

They parted company on the landing. Back in his room, Chen found that someone, probably the maid, had opened a window. He didn't know what kind of insects might frequent the night airs of Hell, so he went over to close it. The towering summit of the Ministry of War was lit by floodlights, sweeping across the building's innumerable armaments and casting a glow into the stormy skies. The Ministry of Lust, on the other hand, was a shadowy russet bulge at the other side of the square.

Just as Chen was about to close the drapes, movement caught his attention in the bushes below. Something was gliding swiftly through the hotel garden, pausing briefly beneath the branches of a flowering tree and looking up. Chen stared down into a triangular face. It struck him that there was something familiar about this person, but it was too dark to see properly. Then the figure was gone, melting back into the garden gloom. Chen pulled the drapes shut, suddenly chilled. He had the impression of something predatory, moving through the night of Hell. It made him glad to be inside.

Despite his location, he did not take long to fall asleep. Images drifted before his drowsing sight: the suburbs of Hell in endless progression, its turrets and towers; Miss Qi's alarmed face and the bristling countenances of the Lesser Lord and Underling No; long metal corridors and an arrow striking a target, sending ripples through reality like a stone thrown into a pond; raised voices—and just as Chen fell asleep, he heard someone say something about a *lung*.

And everyone in China knew what a *lung* was.

It was a dragon.

EIGHTEEN

Embar Dea, released from the prison of sluices and cities, swam through warm seas and cold seas, scenting ice and occasionally, when a dark bloom fell across the surface of the water, rising to see the chilly secret of the North Star, which is sacred to some dragons and is said, on certain days, to speak. It is said, too, that it was from the stars that the dragons had come, making their way to the sanctuary of Cloud Kingdom, but Embar Dea did not know whether this was true or not. Whatever the case, the North Star did not speak to her, but remained in glittering silence at the height of the sky. Embar Dea saw it as a friend, nonetheless, and took inspiration from it before she once more dived, and sang.

There were other voices, but they were very faint and far away. Sometimes she could not be sure whether she was hearing them at all, or whether what she was hearing was the past, swimming back through her ancient memory, just as she herself swam through the waters of Earth, when the seas were alive with whales and dragons, singing to one another. She heard whalesong now, but much less than before, and it saddened her. But some of the voices—if they existed at all—were not whales, and Embar Dea headed toward them, hardly daring to hope. She swam up straits, aware of the bulk of land on either side, once quiet and harmonious earth but now humming with technology and a sour and bitter magic. The world had changed too much, while Embar Dea dreamed in Sulai-Ba. It was better when she swam into the Sea of Japan, veering away from the land and curving past Hokkaido and then out into the open ocean. She called on her own, half-forgotten, magic as she swam, willing invisibility and causing it to wrap itself around her, keeping her warm just as it kept her unseen. Shoals of fish accompanied her, bream and mackerel, the group minds of the shoals engaging her in slow and careful conversation about currents and tides. Embar Dea drew on knowledge that might no longer be applicable and shared what she could.

It was the fish that told her about the wreck.

They did not know where it had come from, but Embar Dea knew what it was as soon as it was mentioned. The ship had glided over the sea for a great distance before it had struck something—not an iceberg itself, but the ghost of one, lingering in the northern ocean since the end of the Great Ice—and the damage it had sustained had caused it to sink.

The ship was called the *Veil of Day,* and it had set sail from Heaven many years before, but had never reached its destination—which had been Hell—and Embar Dea did not know why. It carried a treasure which had never been found and Embar Dea was amazed that this was still the case, for surely someone must have searched for it. But then she reasoned that few things could come this far and this deep: not even Hellkind.

But water dragons can dive to the bottom of the deepest trench in the ocean without injury, for water dragons are the sea itself, made of sea-stuff, and cannot be harmed by it.

So Embar Dea thanked the fish, and let them lead her to where the wreck had last been seen. She was aware of urgency, of those distant voices calling, but the thought of the wreck, if it was indeed the *Veil of Day,* nagged and twitched at her and she was too old to ignore the promptings of instinct. North and north again, she followed the fish until they reached the limits of their territory and she watched them as they shot away, falling silver down the stairways of the sea, until she was once again alone in the middle of the ocean. She rose to the surface, waited till the sea lay on that time between night and day, and then just as the moon was rising and the tides of magic were at their height, she dived, arrowing down until the faint illumination from the dying day was gone and there was only the dark.

Embar Dea's lamplight eyes shone beams ahead of her. She saw nothing for a long time, only a few strange fish, but then a moonscape land rose up to greet her and she knew that she was close to the seabed. At this depth, it was empty, no weeds or shellfish. Nor was there any sign of a ship.

The dragon swam along the seabed, seeing only a glimpse of her own writhing shadow in the light cast by her eyes. She swam for a mile or more, becoming increasingly sure that the shoal had been wrong, that there was nothing here, only acres of rumpled sand—but then she saw a glint of white in the seabed, something very small. She angled down to rest and plucked it free with one clawed toe. She found herself holding a skull. It was not human, although the configurations were a little similar. But the eye sockets were too large, the skull longer. She knew what it had belonged to: a Celestial being, one of the creatures from deep inside Heaven, who had never been born into the world.

Creatures like this had crewed the *Veil of Day.* She wondered what had happened to the skull's spirit, whether it had returned to Heaven to take on a new form, or whether it had become trapped in this lattice of water and dark. She was not skilled enough to say, versed in magic though she was. She laid the skull gently back on the seabed and swam on with renewed hope. After no more than a few minutes, the hull rose up in front of her.

She had not realized that the *Veil of Day* had been so big. The wreck was massive, a galleon, with a great curving arch of hull encrusted in turn with ghosts: little ones of barnacles and shells, of things with teeth. When she reached out a claw, it went straight through them to touch the glimmering surface of the wood. The ship was surprisingly intact, but then, the wood of Heaven took a long time to rot.

Embar Dea gathered water around her, calling on ice and tide and flow, forming a shell of protection about her body. There were still things that sought to trap dragons and she did not want to take the risk. Then she swam up, following the arch of the hull, and came to a porthole. She looked through, into a cabin gleaming with phosphorescence. One of the crew still sat at a table, a skeleton holding a pen. There was no flesh left on it at all, it glowed white, and as Embar Dea stared, its head rolled as though a sudden current had eddied through the wreck, and it said, "You are a dragon, are you not?"

"I am a *lung* of the sea. My name is Embar Dea." She spoke unhesitatingly, though it was well known that it was not wise to tell one's name indiscriminately to anyone. But this had been a Celestial.

"I would give you my name," the skeleton said, "but I cannot remember it."

"I understand," Embar Dea said. "You have been dead for a very long time. Yet you are still here, are you not? You haven't been reborn?"

"We cannot. We are enspelled around this wreck. We could not leave the ship in life, you see, not until it reached its destination and we had discharged our duty, but we did not get so far."

"And so you cannot leave at all," Embar Dea said. A great surge of pity rose in her; even she, a sea dragon, was not entirely happy so far down and in such darkness: How then must these Celestial spirits, used to light and air, feel? "I would like to help."

"You can help," the skeleton said. It leaned forward, its narrow jaws creaking. "You can take our cargo. If you promise me that you can deliver it—"

"Where is it supposed to go? To Hell?"

"To the Savior of the World," the skeleton said. "Once, that person was in Hell, but now it is likely that matters are different."

"I don't know who that might be," Embar Dea said, taken aback. "I don't even know if there is such a person these days."

"If there was not," the skeleton said, with a logic that caused that twinge of instinct once again, "I don't think you would be here."

Embar Dea had lived long enough to know when circumstances were push-ing her in a certain direction. "Very well," she said. "I accept."

Something flowed outward from the being, a pale, watery mist that took on sketchy features of the creature that the Celestial had once been. "Do you swear to me?"

"I swear," Embar Dea said, after only a brief pause. And the wreck of the *Veil of Day* flew apart.

Embar Dea, still wrapped in her magical protection, was safe from the shards and splinters of wood as they foamed through the water, but she could see little through the boiling roar of sea. Then, through the bubbles and froth, she saw a skein of brightness, a web of light that spiraled up into a twist of gold and rose and azure, and she knew it for the spirits of the crew, return-ing to Heaven at last. She felt them pick her up and carry her with them, as lightly as if she had been a small and empty shell, but the speed with which they rose sucked her remaining breath out of her. She lay gasping, floating on the surface of the sea, with a calm crescent moon above her. The spirits of the crew flashed upward and were gone. In one clawed fist, she found that she was holding an object both round and smooth. When she looked, she saw that it was a pearl.

NINETEEN

Next day, Chen, Zhu Irzh, and Miss Qi were taken on a lengthy and exhausting tour of Hell's primary industries, as related to the Ministry of War. This, too, was just as Chen remembered it from his Chinese childhood: one factory after another, endless rows of workers laboring under sweatshop conditions. Except that in Hell, all the workers were dead and there was no pretence that anyone was doing this for the greater glory of the state, or out of some zealous notion of civic duty. On the contrary, the first factory foreman to whom Chen spoke, a flickering green person in a musty suit, seemed proud of the dire conditions and appalling hours.

"They must learn, you see, if they are to progress in their next life up-planet. All of these souls are those who, on Earth, perpetrated some injustice against their fellow workers. And now, they are learning."

"Hmm," Chen said. "I'm not quite sure how this ties in with our mission statement of learning about equal opportunity policies."

Zhu Irzh snorted. "I am. Everyone's equally miserable here."

"They're here to *learn*," the foreman insisted. Listening to him, Chen realized that he had been wrong: civic duty was evident, but applied to the wider sphere of karma. In either manifestation, it wasn't encouraging.

"What do you actually produce here?" he asked. The vapid rows of workers were clearly making something, feeding pieces of metal into a series of machines, but he couldn't tell what they were really doing.

"Why, they are performing a valuable contribution to the war effort," the foreman explained earnestly.

"I see," Chen lied. Miss Qi shifted uncomfortably at this further mention of war, but Chen, although these undercurrents of ill-concealed rumor were worrisome, was more concerned with the immediate problems of the person he had spotted on the previous night, and the question of the *lung,* the dragon.

He kept telling himself that what he had seen slinking through the bushes was just one of the many hungry ghosts or itinerant spirits of Hell, but it nagged at him all the same. And the conversation they had overheard bothered him even more, especially when combined with the draconian rumors that Zhu Irzh had been investigating just before he left. Then there was the thing that had attacked them outside the Opera House and the being they had intercepted at the old lady's place. All of these things, relatively minor incidents in themselves, kept adding up, and Chen did not like it.

Plus, they had a demon's birthday party to attend later on. Chen might have agreed on going, but now—considering all that had happened so far—he liked that prospect even less.

蛇警探

Several hours later, after yet more factories—hives of military industry, all grim and all depressing—Chen and Zhu Irzh sat in the hotel bar, thankful that this part of their day, at least, was over. A present for Zhu Irzh's mother, purchased in the market earlier, sat on the table in front of them: a glass vase, hastily wrapped. Chen's contribution to the celebrations was a bottle of wine.

Miss Qi had retired to her room, saying that she would ask for supper to be sent up: she had not been invited to the birthday party, and Chen did not think he was imagining the distinct relief with which she had greeted this news.

"Lucky her," Zhu Irzh said, when Miss Qi's form had drifted up the stairs. "I wouldn't mind a nice quiet night in myself."

"I doubt you've ever had a nice quiet night in Hell in your life," Chen said.

"My childhood was fairly peaceable," the demon said. "Well, relatively. Well, maybe not all that quiet, looking back. But you don't have anything else to compare it to at the time, do you?"

"I don't know much about childhoods in Hell," Chen remarked. "Did you go to school?"

"No. The family's quite well off. I had tutors, so did my brother. I got on with most of them and they managed to teach me something, though sometimes I'm not sure quite what. My sister learned the usual domestic tasks—blood processing for the home, needlepoint, that sort of thing. Preparation for marriage, basically."

"How bourgeois."

"My sister actually has a job. Mother and I never got on all that well," the demon mused. "Not sure why. She never approved of my going into the police department. I think she wanted me to take up some more respectable job in one of the Ministries."

"Why *did* you join the police?"

"I admired my uncle—my father's brother. He was one of the heads of the city's police department. He seemed to lead an exciting life. And being a civil servant always struck me as rather dull. So the police it was."

"How did your father take it?"

"He was fine. But Dad and I have always got along. It's the only reason I'm going to this party, to be honest, to catch up with him. And the fact that my mother would kill me if I didn't." Zhu Irzh glanced up at the large clock on the wall of the bar. "She said she'd send a car. No sign of it yet."

"Maybe she's forgotten," Chen said hopefully.

"No such luck." The demon stood up. "Look, there's the coach now."

Chen looked through the window and saw a squat black coach like a night-colored pumpkin making its way down the avenue that led to the hotel. It was drawn by a horse, or, at least, by something that looked like one. As it drew closer, Chen saw that the beast had long curling teeth. Zhu Irzh went out the door and down the steps with the air of someone heading for their own execution. Chen followed him into the coach, in a silence that lasted well beyond the Ministries and which was broken only when the coach reached the beginning of the mansion suburbs of Hell.

"This is where I grew up," the demon said. Chen gazed out at the passing mansions; it reminded him of parts of Singapore Three, not too hellish at all, really, once one discounted the black and crimson grass and the oppressive overhanging trees.

"Some elegant houses," Chen said politely.

"No they're not. They're overblown Gothic monstrosities."

"If you say so," Chen replied. He had rarely seen Zhu Irzh in such a gloomy mood.

"Oh fuck," was the next thing out of the demon's mouth. "We're here."

Chen craned his neck to see. There was little to distinguish the Zhu family mansion from all the rest, apart from the strings of red lanterns that hung from eaves and branches, creating bloodied eyes of light across the black lawns. Turrets and towers, a small pagoda set slightly aside and overlooking a pond. The whole place looked top-heavy, as if at any moment it might topple over, and the pagoda was listing rather like the Tower of Pisa. The perspectives and angles were distressing to a human eye.

There were other vehicles standing outside the house, spilling guests.

"Great," Zhu Irzh said under his breath as the coach came to a halt. "My sister."

Chen stepped down onto the rough roadway and watched a young female demon march up the drive in front of them, toward the mansion. This was the sister, Chen realized, who had been referred to as having a job. Even as a human, he could probably have discerned some family resemblance: Zhu Irzh's sister had the same height, the same pointed features and sleek black hair, which fell as far as her waist in a long braid. The end of the braid twitched, seemingly of its own accord, like the tail of an angry cat as she walked.

"How do you get on with your sister?" Chen asked.

"I don't."

Chen walked with him up the drive, following the sister's back, which seemed to radiate aggression. Chen wondered what the matter was. It did not help that the only female demon he knew well was the entirely atypical Inari.

In through an elegant set of metal lattice doors, then along a paneled hallway decorated with scenes of torture. Chen winced. It was all too reminiscent of the Ministry of War. They had almost caught up with Zhu Irzh's sister now and Chen kept expecting the demon to say something, but he did not. Then the sister stopped, so abruptly that Chen nearly cannoned into her.

"Mother! I demand an explanation!"

So much for "Happy Birthday."

"Well, you're not getting one," a voice hissed, so coldly that Chen imagined icicles forming around the doorframe.

"Mother, you are mad," the sister said, with equal hauteur. Next moment, she reeled back—a series of scratches blossoming across her face. A stiletto heel almost pierced Chen's foot and he gave a cry of pain. The sister turned, snarling, one clawed hand pressed to her bleeding cheek, and saw her brother.

"You!"

"Hi," said Zhu Irzh.

"What are *you* doing here?"

"It's Mother's birthday. Remember?" Zhu Irzh held out the present, a move that turned out to be unwise. His sister struck it from his hand with such force that it spun away into the room. There was the sound of shattering glass.

"Oh *thanks*, Daisy," said Zhu Irzh. Chen barely had time to think *"Daisy?"* before a female demon in late middle age appeared, wrapped in layers and layers of silk and furs, with a face so desiccated that it looked more like a mummified skull. One hand was clutching her fur collar and she had blood on her claws. Daisy turned on her heel and stalked off down the hall.

"Hallo, Mother," Zhu Irzh said.

"Oh. You came, then."

"Happy birthday. I brought you a present, but it's in the parlor, in pieces. I'll have it mended."

"Don't bother," his mother said. She cast a disparaging yellow glance over Chen. "Who's *that*?"

"This is Detective Chen. We work together on Earth."

Chen proffered the bottle of wine. Zhu Irzh's mother looked at it as though he were trying to poison her.

"He's a human."

"Yes, Earth people generally are."

"And you brought him to my party?"

"If it's inconvenient, madam, I'll leave," Chen said. This appeared to go some distance toward mollifying Mrs Zhu.

"You might as well stay, now you're here," she said.

"Mother," Zhu Irzh's voice came from inside the parlor, into which he had stepped. "Where is Dad?"

"He's not here."

The demon reappeared. "What, he's not at your party?"

"Certainly not. I threw him out of the house six months ago."

"You did *what*? Why? Where is he now?"

"I don't know where he is! At his whore's, probably. I don't want to talk about him, Irzh. I've moved on." She gave an expression remarkably, and repellently, close to a simper. "I've met someone new."

"Are you getting divorced, or what?"

"It's in process. Naturally, there are financial issues to work out. I said, I don't want to talk about it. There's someone I want you to meet. He's not here yet; he's coming for dinner." She swept through into the parlor, leaving a stupefied Zhu Irzh in her wake.

"Oh dear," Chen said.

"I can't believe I wasn't *told*. Even with this family."

"I'm sorry, Zhu Irzh."

"I don't suppose it'll make any great difference in the long run. Except to my inheritance, but I wasn't counting much on that anyway, the way Mother fritters her way through money. Although there's the question of the house..." Zhu Irzh appeared momentarily lost in thought.

"Your mother said something about dinner."

"Yes, it's a birthday tradition with her. She throws a big dinner party and then we all have a celebration after that." As he spoke, the reverberations of a gong sounded through the house. "And that will be dinner," the demon said.

Chen and Zhu Irzh traipsed through into an enormous dining room, dimlit sconces along the wall. The room was opulently decorated with tapestries, but as Chen drew closer he saw that they had started to fray and molder, and the room itself smelled strongly of damp. It had an air of neglect and, beneath that, something much worse.

"Something happened in here," Chen murmured to Zhu Irzh, his psychic senses twitching.

"My grandfather was murdered in here by my uncle. Dispatched to the lower levels and confined there. We don't talk about it much. A nasty business."

"Quite." Chen paused and looked around, at a table groaning beneath the weight of silverware and gleaming glass goblets. "I wasn't expecting a banquet. To be honest, Zhu Irzh, I'm not sure how much of it I'll be able to eat. As a human, I mean. I don't mean the quality of the food."

"Mother has always run a very—traditional—household," the demon said, apologetically. "And her idea of a nice dinner is usually blood soup followed by a series of main courses. Boiled trotters and that sort of thing."

"Please don't worry on my account," Chen said. "I'm only mentioning it in case you think I'm being rude—I can eat when we get back to the hotel."

"I might join you," Zhu Irzh said. "I'm not fond of home cooking. At least, not at *this* home."

He motioned Chen to a seat near the head of the table. There did not seem to be any names attached to the place, so Chen sat where he was told and reasoned that Zhu Irzh could have it out with his mother if the need arose. Other people were filing in now. To Chen's dismay, the sullen, angular Daisy sat immediately opposite him and was joined by a squat escort, who favored Chen and Zhu Irzh with an oily smile.

"*So* pleased to meet you," this person said, unctuously.

"This is my brother-in-law, Sip Lu." Zhu Irzh tended introductions.

"And what do you do?" Chen asked.

"He works for one of the Ministries," Daisy said. She leaned aggressively over the table. "Lust, you know. He's *very* successful."

Chen could not imagine sharing a bedroom with anyone as needlelike as Daisy, let alone an actual bed. Perhaps Sip Lu gave at the office.

"What's your actual role at the Ministry?" Chen asked, more from a slightly desperate desire to make conversation than from any real wish to know.

"I am Thirteenth Under-Clerk to Lesser Lord Twelve. We issue licenses to demon lounges, collect fees, that sort of thing."

"Interesting," Chen said, feeling feeble.

"And yourself?"

"Lu, you know perfectly well what he does," Daisy hissed. "He's a policeman. On Earth. He works with my brother."

"Ah! Are you in vice?"

Suppressing the impulse to answer *Frequently,* Chen explained that the role of the police in Singapore Three was somewhat different to that which they played in Hell. Sip Lu nodded politely, but Chen was left with the feeling that he might not have made himself fully understood. There was something oddly stunted about Sip Lu, as though he could be drugged. He smiled and beamed, seemingly without reason. Perhaps Daisy kept him under some form of control. Looking at Daisy's long, twitching fingers, scratching nervously at the tabletop, Chen thought she was the kind of woman who would take whatever steps were necessary in order to establish her own agenda, and from the wary way that Zhu Irzh was staring at his sister, the demon thought so, too. Then Zhu Irzh glanced up and Chen saw his face freeze.

The demon's mother had entered the room, swathed in her preposterous furs, on the arm of a demon so large that he had to bend slightly to avoid brushing his crest against the ceiling. A lizardlike person, with enormously bulky limbs, a long, sinuous tail, a scaled rust-colored face with curving tusks. He, too, was wearing armor and carried with him a strong scent of gunpowder. When he turned, Chen could see that the insignia on his shoulder was that of the Ministry of War. Unsurprising.

"What the—? That's Erdzhe Shen," Zhu Irzh whispered.

"Who?" Chen had never managed to fix in his mind the various principal personages of Hell, largely because there was so much backstabbing and so many palace revolutions that personnel turnover was exceptionally high. But Zhu Irzh had spoken as if Chen should know, which suggested that this Erdzhe Shen was a major player.

"He's *only* the Minister of War," Zhu Irzh said. Chen glanced across at Sip Lu and saw that the Lust demon's face had grown watchful, overriding the expression of greasy vacancy. Zhu Irzh spoke urgently to Daisy.

"Did you know about this? Mum's new boyfriend?"

"Of course I did," Daisy hissed. "Why do you think she threw Dad out? She's been putting up with his girlfriends for years, but she didn't care—she had her own life, and you know as well as I do that they didn't share a room for years. It wasn't until Erdzhe came along that she decided to make the break. Erdzhe is more powerful than Dad ever dreamed of being." *Erdzhe.* Daisy spoke the name with a kind of complacency, a smug twitch of the lip, clearly pleased that despite her own ministerial connections, she was permitted to use the name of the Minister of War. But since her mother was now nearing the head of the table, with her vast escort in tow, Daisy fell silent. The couple took their places—Zhu Irzh's mother with a glance like a simpering skull, and everyone rose.

"A toast to the birthday girl!" the Minister of War boomed, in a voice that set glassware rattling. "To my beloved!" From the look that he bestowed upon her, it might even be true, thought Chen. How odd, though Zhu Irzh had proved susceptible to love in the past so perhaps it was a family weakness. But allegiances in Hell were notoriously unstable. Perhaps the real wonder was that Zhu Irzh's parents' marriage had apparently survived for so long.

"I don't think I can handle this," Zhu Irzh muttered.

"I don't think you've got much choice," Chen whispered back. The first course was already arriving; it was, as predicted, blood broth. He pretended to take a sip when everyone else did, but beneath the table he inscribed a careful sigil on the underside of the polished wood, holding his breath as he did so. His own magic, being goddess-given, was erratic here in Hell. After a moment, however, he saw the blood broth evaporate. It would be embarrassing if noticed, but hopefully everyone else was concentrating too much on their own dinners.

The Minister of War was attacking his food with gusto; there was certainly nothing wrong with his appetite. He finished two bowls of soup and then went on to the main course, slabs of something greenly meaty in black bean sauce, fried locusts, adders' tongues, and a number of dishes that Chen was unable to identify.

"It's deer," Zhu Irzh said in an undertone. Thus encouraged, Chen took a careful mouthful and found that the meat was revolting.

"Sorry, Zhu Irzh. Can't eat it." At least it had the benefit of killing what little appetite he still possessed. He prepared himself for executing another spell when Zhu Irzh said, "I'll have yours, then. It's not as bad as usual, actually."

Chen transferred it swiftly onto the demon's plate. Glancing back, he saw that the Minister of War's gaze, as green and reptilian as a lizard's, was fixed upon him. Chen gave a blandly polite smile and, after a moment, the Minister looked away. Chen did not know what to make of this. The Minister's gaze had been impossible to interpret: not rage, even at finding a human (and the one-time servant of a goddess, something which was surely visible to the Minister) seated at his girlfriend's dining table, nor disquiet. There had been something remote and alien and calculating about the Minister's expression and it concerned Chen.

It wasn't until halfway through the main courses that the disruption happened. Chen became aware of sounds in the hallway, distant scuffling and muffled shouts.

"Zhu Irzh? What's happening?"

"I don't know." The demon frowned, just as the door burst open and two maidservants rushed in bearing an enormous cake. It was heavily iced in red and black, appearing almost lacquered. A small figure at its summit represented, perhaps, Mrs Zhu.

"Oh god," Zhu Irzh said under his breath. "Just what we need. A birthday surprise."

Chen gritted his teeth. He hated this kind of thing, ever since being obliged to attend other children's birthday parties. He put the polite smile back in place and kept it there. The women carried the cake ceremoniously to the head of the table and placed it on a hastily cleared space. It seemed an odd time to do this; shouldn't they wait until the dessert course, or after the meal? But perhaps things were done differently here; it was Hell, after all.

There was an expectant pause. Zhu Irzh's mother leaned forward with the rapacious look of a gannet. The Minister radiated smugness. The cake burst open in an explosion of black and red icing, which spattered those guests nearest the head of the table, and a demon leaped forth. Looking back, Chen did not know quite what he had been expecting: not a naked girl, given the nature of the gathering, but certainly not a heavily armed and armored being who uttered a roar and hurled himself through the air in the direction of Zhu Irzh's mother, a glittering sword in his hand.

Zhu Irzh was on his feet in a flurry of black silk. Daisy screamed like a whistling kettle and kept on screaming. The Minister gave a bellow that temporarily deafened Chen. Zhu Irzh's mother was scuttling backward with the speed of a spider. Chen, acting before he really had a chance to think, snatched the table knife from the side of his plate and cut a bloody rune into the palm of his hand. Then, with no time to worry about whether it would work, he threw it in the direction of the sword-bearing demon, who had by this time landed squarely on the floor in front of Zhu Irzh's mother.

The rune blazed through the air in an arc of fire and struck the demon in the midriff. A ragged, smoking hole appeared in his armor and the demon looked down in fleeting dismay, before exploding in a manner similar to that of the cake, only messier.

"Well," Zhu Irzh said, picking strips of charred flesh out of his hair. "That was novel."

Zhu Irzh's mother slapped Daisy across the face. "Be quiet!" Daisy's screams subsided to a whimper, but Chen caught sight of something in her face, a swift and secret expression that, again, he could not interpret. He filed it away for later consideration.

The Minister of War turned to him. "A good shot and a quick spell! Especially from a human."

"To be honest," Chen said, "I didn't know if it would work down here."

"But so it did, and if it had not, my beloved would have been sent to the lower levels, there to eke out an existence among the creeping things."

"No change there, then," Chen thought he heard Zhu Irzh say.

"Well, I'm just glad I was here to help," Chen said, feeling like someone in a television cop drama.

"He should be rewarded," Zhu Irzh's mother remarked. Her expression was beady.

"There's really no need for that," Chen said quickly.

Zhu Irzh nudged him. "No, go for it."

"I should like Zhu Irzh to have my reward instead," Chen explained. As he spoke, he saw a flicker of light in the air, moving between himself and Zhu Irzh: the mark of a destiny spell being cast. Chen himself had done nothing, it must be some function of the proffered reward itself. *Oh dear.*

"In that case, I accept," Zhu Irzh said before his mother could react. "I should like Grandfather's heart."

"What!" That was the demon's mother.

"What?" That was Chen.

"You heard me, Mother." The spell sparkled around him as he spoke.

"Zhu Irzh? What are you doing?" Chen hissed.

"You recall I told you he was murdered here? He's been nudging me. I can feel it."

Chen expected Mrs Zhu to refuse indignantly, but he could feel the spell still working: a cool, powerful tugging at his magical senses. This was something old and strong. Zhu Irzh's mother rose as if under compulsion, and began to totter out of the room, as jerkily as a puppet. Chen expected the Minister of War to intervene, at least to make some kind of protest, but he did not. Instead, he watched, with that same remote gaze with which he had favored Chen.

"Come with me," Zhu Irzh said to Chen. Everyone else at the table appeared turned to stone. Chen, his skin prickling, followed the demon out the door.

A narrow passage, decorated with the same unpleasantness as the main hallway, then a flight of stairs, then another. This part of the Zhu family mansion seemed very ancient to Chen, it had the musty atmosphere of great age and the house seemed to grow older as they ascended the stairs. He had the sudden, dizzying sensation that he was descending rather than going upward. He did not dare ask Zhu Irzh further, within his mother's hearing, just what this business of the grandfather's heart was about. No doubt, he thought, he would find out soon enough.

Mrs Zhu stopped in front of a twisted little door; the kind of door behind which you find secrets.

"In there," she said. Her voice sounded thick and sour, as if the words were being forced out of her throat.

"Good," Zhu Irzh said. "You can open it, Mother."

Mrs Zhu gave her son a curdled look but she did as she was told. As she touched the handle, Chen heard the sizzle of a spell and then there was an unpleasant, burned odor. Mrs Zhu stepped through, followed by her son and Chen.

The room was small, and completely empty except for a large box that resembled a lacquered refrigerator. When Mrs Zhu opened it, Chen realized that's exactly what it was: it hissed apart and a cloud of cold drifted out, into the room. Inside sat a stout pot, also lacquered with a crimson so thick that it might have been made of clotted blood. In fact, Chen wondered for a moment whether it actually was a container, or the heart itself. Then Mrs Zhu reached inside and removed it and Chen could see that it had a lid.

"Here you are, then," Mrs Zhu said, bitterly. "Take it, since you want it so badly. I wish you joy of it." But her fingers were curling around the sides of the pot.

"Is this given to me of your own free will?" Zhu Irzh said. Again, the prickle of spell-work made Chen's fingertips twitch.

"Yes," Mrs Zhu whispered, very reluctantly.

"Under what circumstances?"

"You have been granted it as a reward and I am giving it to you."

"Thanks, Mother," Zhu Irzh said. "I'll take it now." He reached out and took the pot from her hands, then wrapped it carefully in a fold of his silken coat. As he did so, the atmosphere in the room lightened and lifted; Chen felt as though a thunderstorm had passed. The crackle and sparkle of the spell dissipated, leaving behind an odd sense of solidity and firmness. A little piece of destiny, Chen thought, cemented into place.

They went back down the stairs and now even the staircase seemed to have changed, appearing less gloomy. It was so subtle that Chen wondered at first whether he was imagining things, but then they reached the hallway and he saw that it was no longer decorated with scenes of torment. He thought Zhu Irzh must have noticed the same thing, because the demon's face wore a small, smug cat-smile.

"Well, Mother," Zhu Irzh said, just as they reached the dining hall. "I won't stay for dessert, after all that. Hope you don't mind."

"Given the trouble you've caused, I couldn't care less." Mrs Zhu brushed past her son into the dining hall, where everyone sat or stood much as they had been left. A strong odor of decomposition hung in the air, the last trace of the vanquished cake assassin. Daisy still stood, with the palm print and scratches from her mother's hand red upon her pale face. Only the Minister of War remained unfrozen, and he was sitting where they had left him, sipping tea.

"Beloved! You're back." As though Mrs Zhu had been for a stroll in the garden.

"Get rid of these people, Erdzhe. I don't feel much like partying anymore," Mrs Zhu said.

"Anything for the birthday girl," the Minister said, jovially. He rose and clapped armored hands. Servants began drifting back into the dining room.

"Come on, Chen." Zhu Irzh was more cheerful than he'd been all day. "If we go back to the hotel now, the bar's probably still open. I could use a drink."

Nodding to Mrs Zhu—and feeling that any protestation that it had been a wonderful gathering would fall upon stony ears—Chen went outside. After the stifling atmosphere of the Zhu family mansion, even after the demon had been given the heart, the night air of Hell seemed almost refreshing. Zhu Irzh, ignoring the carriage in which they had arrived, walked rapidly to the end of the drive and flagged down a coach that, it appeared, was a taxi.

"Thank gods that's over," the demon said piously, as they sank back onto the worn leather seats. "I couldn't have coped with much more of that. Did you see the way she was simpering at him? All right, I can't really blame her for kicking Dad out. But to take up with the Minister of War…!"

"It seems a bit—coincidental," Chen mused. The demon shot him a sharp look. "You thought so, too?"

"It's just that we seem to have had an awful lot to do with the Ministry of War over the last forty-eight hours. One can't help wondering whether these things knit together." Chen paused, glancing out across the nightscape of Hell. "So, Zhu Irzh, what's all this business about your grandfather's heart?"

"Right. That. Well, the heart has been a bone of contention—or an organ of contention, anyway—ever since my grandfather went to the lower levels. As I told you, he was sent there by one of the family, and he can't get back, because his heart was removed and spell-guarded. As you saw. To be honest, even if he could get back up here, it probably wouldn't be a very good idea to summon him, because people tend to—deteriorate—when they've been in the lower levels for even a short while. Remember Inari, when she was trapped down there? So poor old Grand-dad almost certainly isn't the man he used to be."

"So why not leave his heart where it was?"

"It didn't even occur to me when we went to dinner. And I would have left it alone, quite honestly, except for two things. One is that the spell that guarded it links the family fortunes in with the fate of the heart, so whoever holds the heart, holds the luck of the family—and the house and every other bit of inheritance, such as it is. So when I saw a chance, I took it. I don't want the Minister of War getting his claws on any of that."

"No," Chen said thoughtfully. "I don't suppose you do."

"The other thing is that there's a rumor the heart can be used for magic—but I don't know what kind of magic."

"Why was your grandfather killed—well, sent down—in the first place?"

"For challenging the rule of the Emperor of Hell. He was trying to stage a coup, but my uncle was loyal to the Emperor. That's partly why the spell guarding the heart refers to the family fortunes—all that would be put in jeopardy if Grandfather came back, so it was made to be in our interests to keep him down there. Just in case. Ah, here we are."

The taxi stopped in front of the hotel, and Zhu Irzh slid a few coins into a waiting hand. The coach was so dark and enclosed that Chen had still not set eyes on the driver. Zhu Irzh, cradling the heart, walked up the steps and into the foyer.

"I could do with a drink—I wonder if Miss Qi would like one? I never thought I'd hear myself say this, but after this evening, a Celestial would almost be pleasant company."

"You can ask her," Chen said. "It's not that late."

But when they called Miss Qi's room, there was no reply.

"Surely she can't have gone out," Chen said. He went over to the desk and queried the clerk.

"I haven't seen her." The young female demon on the desk frowned. "Perhaps she's sleeping." This seemed to be the most likely explanation, but Chen's senses were prickling with a sensation he'd come to learn to recognize. It was that of impending disaster.

"Could you come with me?" he said to the clerk. Together, they went up to Miss Qi's room and banged on the door. No reply.

"Try the door, if you would," Chen said. He was thankful that this was Hell, with fewer conceptions of other people's privacy: here, it was regarded as entirely natural to want to burst into another guest's room late at night. The clerk inserted the spare key into the lock and opened the door.

The bed was neatly made. Miss Qi's modest bag sat on the floor. The window was open, the drapes floating in the night wind of Hell, and the whole room reeked of magic, with the faintest underlying trace of peach blossom. But there was no sign at all of Miss Qi.

TWENTY

After the horrible visitor, Precious Dragon sank into such a sound sleep that he did not wake up until noon of the following day. Mrs Pa did not want to disturb her grandson, but she did shake his shoulder gently, just once, to make sure that he *could* be woken. He rolled over, breathing peacefully, a tousle of hair falling into his eyes, and she crept from the room. However, she need not have worried. Precious Dragon came into the kitchen of his own accord, just as she was making lunch.

"Grandmother? Hello."

"Hello, Grandson," Mrs Pa said. She did not want to tell him about her worries: the creature might come back, and even if she had been capable of dealing with it herself, that she might not be here. Mai—being dead—had left no provision for her son and sooner or later, given the state of the household finances, Mrs Pa would have to go back to her cleaning job. Her regular employers had been most understanding about this particular week, but she could not reasonably expect any more time off. But if she was to go back to work, who would look after Precious Dragon? And if she took him with her, she would have to warn her employers in advance—and how would they react to the presence of a small child in their homes? Badly, given the usual nature of employers.

But Precious Dragon seemed to have an uncanny understanding of her fears. He hoisted himself to the edge of the couch and sat down, swinging his legs.

"You'll have to go back to work soon, won't you?" he pronounced.

His apparent reading of her mind gave Mrs Pa such a start that she nearly dropped a plate. She was so surprised that she turned to face him and said, as if he were a grown-up, "Yes. And I don't know who I'm going to get to look after you, because I don't know whether or not I'll be able to take you with me. I think maybe your father's family is the best choice. I'm sure they'd like to see you, anyway." And she felt a pang of guilt because she had not yet contacted them with the news that their grandson had been so in danger—Precious Dragon was just as much theirs as he was hers, except that they had not been the ones asked to go to echoing Sulai-Ba to rescue him, and Mrs Pa felt a deep kind of pride at that.

"I am happy to visit my other grandparents," Precious Dragon said, very gravely. "I should like to get to know them. But there is another choice."

"What choice is that?"

Precious Dragon gave a slight frown, as if peering into a future that he could not properly see. "I do not know yet. But someone will come."

His trust in life to provide touched Mrs Pa, but even though she had seen some of her grandson's weird abilities, she was not sure that she believed him.

In this, however, she was wrong.

The knock on the door came early in the evening, a tentative, uncertain sound, so faint that at first Mrs Pa thought she was imagining things. After the previous night, she wasn't going to open the door without checking first, so she put the chain on the latch as a precaution before looking through the spyhole and then opening the door a crack.

There was a young woman on the step. She wore a pretty frock, modestly highlighting an elegant figure, and a large hat. She wore sunglasses, even though the sun was setting over the port in a smear of gold and red. She stepped back a little as Mrs Pa opened the door, and something ambled out from the shadows: a black and white shape that Mrs Pa thought at first was a dog. Then she saw that it was a badger.

"Good evening," Mrs Pa said, somewhat taken aback.

"Good evening," said the young woman. "I am so sorry to trouble you. My husband mentioned you to me—he's Detective Inspector Chen, of the city police department." She held up a picture of a round, rather surprised face. "You met him last night."

"Why, so I did," Mrs Pa said. Precious Dragon nudged her arm.

"Grandma? It's all right." He spoke with such confidence that Mrs Pa reached out and unlatched the door.

"Before I come in," the young woman said, "there's something you should know. I'm not human." She took off her sunglasses to reveal large, crimson eyes. "You see, I'm afraid I am a demon. My husband rescued me from Hell, though, and now I live here. I should quite understand if you'd rather I didn't come in."

"No, that's all right," Mrs Pa said, marveling at her own daring. "After all, my daughter herself lives in Hell. I know that in her own case it was because of someone else's corruption, but even so—not everyone from Hell is wicked."

"Hell is a wicked place," Chen's wife said with a sigh. "And so is Earth, sometimes." She took a step forward. "My name is Inari."

"I think you'd better come in," Mrs Pa said.

Inari accepted tea, and the badger had a saucer of water that it drank with a loud golloping noise.

"Please excuse badger," Inari said. "He doesn't have very human manners. He's my family's familiar."

Precious Dragon sat smiling at the badger. "He's very furry," he said.

"Yes, he is. But I'm afraid he doesn't like to be cuddled," Inari explained. "I like your tiger."

The little boy beamed. "My grandmother bought it for me."

"What a nice grandmother!" Inari took a sip of her tea. "Mrs Pa, my husband has asked me to—well, to keep an eye on you, really. He was very worried."

"That's extremely kind of him," Mrs Pa said. Pride, and the loss of face, almost made her add, *but we can manage*. She was too old for face; she could not manage. She bit the words back. "I've been wondering—you see, I have to work. I have no choice. But I didn't know if anyone might look after Precious Dragon for me… He is not the *usual* kind of child, Inari."

"No. I can see that he is not." Inari smiled. "But then, I'm not the usual kind of childminder."

"You may think it's very naïve of me, to hand over care of my grandson to a stranger—if you wouldn't mind, of course. I'm sure you're very busy."

"No," Inari said, rather wistfully. "Actually, I'm not."

"But you see, Precious Dragon seems to trust you." She turned to her grandson, who replied with a nod. "And Precious Dragon seems to know things."

"I should be honored to look after him," Inari said. Something in her voice prompted Mrs Pa to say, as delicately as she could, "Do you—do you have children of your own?"

"No." Inari paused. "You see—I'd like a child, of course. We both would. But it would be a big problem to find a hospital that would take me if anything went wrong, and I don't think they'd know what to do, anyway. I'm not supposed to be here on Earth. And if I went back to Hell to have the baby, then there would be other complications. There are problems with my family, you see. And also, well, Chen is human and I'm not. It's not so easy sometimes."

She glanced at Precious Dragon as she spoke, evidently wondering whether this was a suitable subject to raise in front of a small child, but Precious Dragon was considering her with his customary gravity. Mrs Pa said, with a sympathy that struck at her heart, "I know. It's never easy."

"Well," Inari said. "Enough of my problems. I mustn't keep you. Here's my number—let me know when you'd like me to—" Mrs Pa thought that she was about to say "babysit," but that hadn't sounded right the first time, somehow "—look after him," Inari finished.

"I will. And thank you."

Inari put her sunglasses back on, even though it was now long past twilight, and Mrs Pa showed her to the door. The badger rose, too, and moved past her, sinuous now as it slid into the shadows, and she watched them walk up the harbor path, the demon girl and the beast at her side, until the shadows swallowed them.

TWENTY-ONE

Embar Dea reached the sea palace toward dawn, when a light as faint and pure as the pearl that she still clutched in her claw was rising over the eastern horizon. Embar Dea looked out across a cold stretch of ocean, dappled with shards and fragments of ice, to where a glittering phosphorescence tracked across the sea. A rush of excitement filled her: she knew what that glitter meant, magical and beckoning—the path of dragons. And just as she saw this, they began to sing, their voices lifting up through the water and bursting into the light, as cold and eerie as the ocean itself. It was a long time since Embar Dea had given voice so boldly, but she did so now, raising her head from the water and sending air fluting through each of the bearded tentacles that surrounded her face.

When Embar Dea began to sing, the rest of the dragons stopped, as if startled, but only for a moment. Then their voices, too, began again, joining in with her song and responding in harmony to it. Embar Dea knew this meant that she had been accepted, and even though there was little possibility that she might not have been, she was still relieved. She was old, and it was long years since she had last spoken with any of her kind, apart from the now-dead in Sulai-Ba. She did not know if things had changed, for territories between dragons were subject to constant subtle shifts, and it was almost certain that the allegiances she knew were no longer in place. Dragons were benign, looking at matters over a great span of years, but dragons played games.

No games this time, it seemed. As the song from beneath the waves went on, a spire rose from the sea. It was a pinnacle of ice, a fretted turret, rising higher and higher into the wan sunlight and bringing the rest of the palace with it. Embar Dea saw huge halls and caverns, green sea ice like precious stone, marbled with silver, encrusted with barnacles and pearls, and at this, she clasped the pearl that she held even more tightly. A staircase of black ice, water gushing and rushing over its sides, surged up out of the sea in front of her and Embar Dea climbed, feeling the ice burning-freezing under her claws before her body temperature adjusted and it became like walking on sun-warmed stone.

Up the steps and into the great central hall of the sea palace. And there were dragons waiting, all nine of the remaining sea dragons of the world of Earth: wild dragons covered in limpets and weed; a dragon from the warm southern seas whose skin was chased with a thousand different colors, gold and scarlet and sea-green, gliding across it in the silent speech of its kind; dragons from the far north who looked like ice themselves, glassy and remote and chill.

Embar Dea moved between the ranks of dragons, all the way up the long hall, with its pillars and columns and lacy balconies. And as she walked, someone came to meet her.

He was black and shining, silver glistening and gleaming about his ar-mored head. Perhaps a hundred feet from nose to tail, bristling with spines, his wedge-shaped, great-eyed head swinging from side to side. Between his horns, a pearl showed him to be of Imperial lineage.

"You are the last," he said. He spoke like the music of dragons. "You are the one from the temple, from the lost place."

"I am Embar Dea," she said, for he had spoken first, as befit his status. But she was full of questions. She knew this dragon: Prince Rish, but if he was here and speaking for the assembly, then where was the Dragon Lord?

"Our King is gone," the Prince said, as if he had heard her thought, as perhaps he had. And all the dragons raised their voices in a terrible song of mourning. Embar Dea bowed her head and felt suddenly, dreadfully old.

"I have something to give to you," she said, feeling that she wanted to give up what had become a great burden. She held out the pearl from the *Veil of Day*, and explained how she had come by it.

The dragons mourned again, voices raised in icy keening. "This is the pearl of the old King," the Dragon Prince said. "This is the pearl that went missing from Cloud Kingdom, and thus stole his life away. And now we have it back, but it is too late, the old King is dead and the new King gone."

Embar Dea knew that she was not at fault, but she could not help feeling somehow to blame. "If I had been earlier—" she started to say.

"It would have made no difference. This is many years in the making. We have this now, it is returned to us and we thank you, because I believe it is a sign that we will prevail."

"Please," Embar Dea said. "What has been happening? All I know are signs of danger and loss, but I don't know why."

"No more do we," said the mottled, shifting southern dragon, in a voice that suggested that speech did not come easily to her, a voice like rusting metal. "Signs and portents, of danger and woe, but we don't know where it comes from."

"We must go to Cloud Kingdom," the Dragon Prince said, and Embar Dea's heart lifted at this, for she had not seen Cloud Kingdom since she was a child, born there like all dragons before being sent to the many worlds. "And now you have come," Prince Rish added. "We are able to leave."

TWENTY-TWO

They searched the room again and Chen performed a basic locating spell, but there was no clue, either physical or magical, to Miss Qi's disappearance.

"I don't suppose," Zhu Irzh said in the hopeless tone of the unconvinced, "that she'd have just popped out for a breath of fresh air."

"Don't be ridiculous." Worry made Chen uncharacteristically snappy. If Miss Qi had gone missing in Singapore Three, he would have been calmer, but here, with so few resources, the situation struck him as bleak. "This is Hell. There is no fresh air, and anyway, it's hardly likely she'd have popped out in it."

"How are we going to explain this to Heaven?" was Zhu Irzh's next thought.

"We're not," Chen replied. "We won't have to. Because we're going to find her."

He warded both window and door, then closed the door to the room. On Earth, his wards were stronger, since he had jurisdiction there, but not in Hell, yet they still possessed a certain degree of power and would stop any curious minor demons from entering the room, if not one of Hell's hierarchy. Zhu Irzh watched approvingly. Then Chen, followed by the flustered desk clerk, went back downstairs.

"Call the staff, please. I want to see if anyone knows anything."

He didn't hold out much hope and, indeed, what little he held was not fulfilled. The staff—a motley, shifty assortment of demons—had seen nothing, heard nothing, knew nothing. They shuffled their ill-favored feet and stared at the ceiling or the floor.

"If anyone does know anything," Chen said at last, "then you know where to find me. It doesn't matter if you have to wake me up—" not that demons would worry overmuch about disturbing other people's sleep "—as long

112

as you let me know."

"Is there a reward?" one of the staff members said, a small, ragged person with a backward-facing head. Lords knew what he'd done to deserve *that:* having your feet reversed was a common punishment, but it wasn't usual to see folk facing in the wrong direction. As it was, he had to stand with his back to Chen.

"We might be able to arrange something," Chen said cautiously.

Zhu Irzh nudged him. "Go for it," the demon whispered. "It's the only way you'll get anything out of this bunch."

Chen knew he was right, and he let the tentative offer stand. He went back upstairs with Zhu Irzh to await developments, and sure enough, they were not long in arriving, via a soft knock on the door.

Chen was not surprised to see that it was the reversed-head person.

"I saw 'er," he said, without preamble. "Your mate. They took 'er out the back."

"Who was it?" Chen asked. "Did you see?"

The demon's maltreated face became sly. "Yes, but—"

"All right," Chen said with a sigh. "How much are we going to give him, Zhu Irzh?"

"Five hundred dollars," reverse-head interrupted.

"What! You're joking. I'll give you fifty."

"Do I look like an idiot?" the demon howled. And so on. Five minutes later, Zhu Irzh was handing over fifty dollars with the promise of a further hundred.

"Right, well, there were three of them, see. I think two of them were blokes but I'm not sure about the third."

Chen was taking notes. "When was this?"

"About an hour and a half ago."

Chen did a rapid mental calculation. Given the time that the search and enquiry had taken, Miss Qi had been abducted while he and Zhu Irzh were on their way back from the birthday dinner. That meant that anyone who had been at the banquet could have taken Miss Qi and, somehow, Chen thought that this was significant.

"And what did they look like?"

"The two blokes were in black, shadow-wear. But the other one—maybe a woman, I told you, I don't know for sure—was in red, from head to foot."

Zhu Irzh, who had been listening intently, perked up at this.

"Red? A lot of people at the Min of Lust like to wear red. Lucky color, you see."

Chen decided not to investigate the implications of that last sentence. "Ministry of Lust?" Interesting. Throughout their trip, the twin threads of the Ministries of War and Lust had been interweaving. He turned to the informer.

"You're sure about this, are you?" One could hardly chastise a denizen of Hell for lying, but at the same time, one had to make sure. Chen took out his rosary and flicked it around the demon's reversed head like a boomerang. It shot back into his hand, leaving a scarlet flame in its wake, slowly fading. The informer gave a cry of pained outrage. But he had been telling the truth.

"Sorry," Chen said with a shrug. "You never know."

"Quite right, too," Zhu Irzh remarked. He rose from the seat in which he had been lounging and grasped the informer by the front of his robe. "Excuse me. I just want to try something." He spoke a word that made both Chen and the informer flinch. Fascinated, Chen watched as words tumbled out of the informer's mouth, spiky ideograms bursting like red leaves in the air. As they began to disappear, a picture formed instead, tiny and perfect as if unreeling onto a screen. Miss Qi, backed against a wall with the midnight sky of Hell far above her, fighting grimly. One of the shadow-forms went down, but the others—one black, one dressed in bloody red—stepped up behind her and threw a cloth like a fragile web over her head. It glowed briefly, and Miss Qi sank to the floor. The two demons in black, moving with a curious jerkiness, picked her up by the head and the feet and ran with her down the alleyway, followed by the lithe shape in red. Then they were gone and the image glowed once, searingly bright, then faded, leaving a little glowing coal which fell through the air into Zhu Irzh's outstretched hand.

"Impressive," Chen said. He knew Zhu Irzh had magical abilities, but he did not often see them demonstrated: the demon preferred to rely on his sword.

"Thanks." Zhu Irzh gave a modest shrug. "I had to wait until he'd spoken and you'd proved that he was speaking the truth. I can't do that on Earth, in case you're wondering. Too many restrictions on what I can and can't do. Here, it's a bit easier."

Chen nodded. It was the same for him, down in Hell.

"Can I go now?" the informer spoke with the truculence of fright.

"Yes. But not before giving us your name and your address."

The demon did so, with a very poor grace, then gathered what dignity he could and stalked off into the depths of the hotel. Chen was not confident that he'd been telling the truth this time.

"Well," Chen said with a sigh, "I suppose we're a bit further along. We've seen who took her, even if we're not sure where they come from."

"I didn't want to say so in front of our friend, but there was something familiar about that figure in red."

"Was it female, do you think?" Chen had been unable to tell although there had been a supple litheness about the red-clad figure that suggested that the informer had been right.

"I don't know. I think so."

"And do you still think that they were from the Ministry of Lust?"

"I don't know, but we can find out," the demon said. "Follow me."

Chen went with him to the room that had been Miss Qi's. He was at once praying that Zhu Irzh was right and hoping that he was wrong: he did not want to think of the pure Miss Qi in the clammy, collective hands of the Ministry of Lust, but at the same time, they needed to know where she had been taken.

"Right," Zhu Irzh said. He took the coal from his pocket and placed it on the table. Then he extracted a small *feng shui* compass from his other pocket and held it over the coal, which began to glow and expand. Once again, Chen saw the scene unfold in the air before him: Miss Qi fighting, being overcome, and carried limply away. The needles of the compass were swinging wildly, veering around the metal surface.

"Someone's putting a block on this," Zhu Irzh said, and grinned a wolfish grin. He blew on the compass, a fiery breath that sent a heatwave out into the air and caused the image to shimmer. The edges of the image shriveled, like a piece of paper held over a flame.

"This should get rid of the block," the demon said, as burning fragments spiraled down through the air and the image seemed to harden and grow clearer. The compass needle stopped its erratic wandering and grew still, pointing east. Chen went to the window, pushed aside the curtains. The Ministry of Lust stood outlined against a reddening sky, a bulbous wart against the horizon of Hell.

"Looks like you're right," Chen said. He drew the curtains closed, but not before he had, once more, glimpsed a shadowy shape disappearing back into the bushes.

"Zhu Irzh!"

"What?"

"There's someone down there," Chen said.

The demon squinted into the darkness. "I can't see anyone."

"I'm sure of it. I saw someone last night, too."

Zhu Irzh frowned. "Maybe we should go down and check."

They went back down to the lobby and the demon sidled out onto the steps, motioning for Chen to stay back. A moment later, he reappeared.

"Well?" Chen asked.

"If there was anyone there, they're not there now. Unless you wanted to search the gardens?"

Chen shook his head. "No, not with Miss Qi missing. We know where she is. I'd bet that the Ministry of Lust has sent someone to spy on you and me, though."

"They'd be pretty incompetent if they didn't," Zhu Irzh said.

TWENTY-THREE

Mrs Pa took a look around the living room and sighed. That would have to do. The polished surface of the dining table gleamed and the windows were so clear that one might have thought that there was no glass in them at all. The deep-pile cream carpet was spotless and all the silverware mirrored the light and sent pale reflections dancing across the walls.

Mrs Pa felt a modest pride in her diligence as a cleaner. It would not do to lose humility, but on the other hand, she was good at her job. A pity that this was not her own home, prepared for the use of her own family, but then you had to be thankful for what you had. And she was very thankful indeed for Precious Dragon, last seen sitting placidly on the deck of the houseboat belonging to Detective Chen and Inari, sucking his pearl and guarded by the badger. Mrs Pa felt that Precious Dragon was as safe as he could be at present and this had allowed her to get on and do a good job on the Pang's living room after what appeared to have been a fairly riotous party.

Some of the things Mrs Pa had found in the living room had been…surprising. She had put them all in a plastic bag, thankful that she was wearing rubber gloves.

So much for the living room, anyway. Now, she planned to turn her attention to the three bedrooms and the bathroom. This took a further two hours and was even more distasteful, especially considering whatever it was that she found under the bed. It looked as though it had been organic, like a lump of ancient meat, about the size of a human head, but green and fluffy. She then scoured the bathroom, which was filthy, and cleaned all the traces of white powder from the black marble surfaces. Nasty stuff. Detective Chen might be interested in some of the things that she had found, but then again, there was the question of her employer's privacy: Mrs Pa was a strong believer in minding her own business.

At last the house was clean from ceiling to floor and Mrs Pa felt a great sense of satisfaction at what she had achieved. Making order out of chaos, that was a wonderful thing to be able to do, even if it was something as small as washing up. She peeled off the rubber gloves, put all the cleaning materials tidily away beneath the sink, and wrote down her hours for Mrs Pang on a piece of paper. Mrs Pang might have some very odd parties but she paid her bills on time and Mrs Pa would receive the money next week when she called again. She'd already collected last week's wages. It was good to be working again, to feel that she was helping not only herself, but her grandson and Mai.

She walked out into the steamy afternoon and waited for the downtown tram. It was now about half past five, with her shift timed to end shortly before Mrs Pang returned home from work. The house was high in the foothills, with a faint breeze from the sea adding thousands of dollars to even the most average property, and from the vantage point of the tram stop she could see out across the whole city, to the harbor where her own little shack stood and where Precious Dragon sat upon the deck of a boat, and beyond to the shadowy blue humps of the islands. From here, with the sound of the downtown traffic muted and the lush vegetation swaying in the sea breeze, Singapore Three might almost be a pleasant place to live.

Almost.

The tram arrived, only a few minutes late, and Mrs Pa squeezed her way on. All the way down to the city she thought about what she might buy Precious Dragon as a treat, and when she eventually got off the bus, she found a bakery near the entrance to the harbor and bought everyone a steamed bean bun. She could afford it now, and Inari deserved something for her kindness. She even bought one for the badger, though she wasn't sure whether this was really appropriate. But she did not want to leave him out. Then she made her way in the evening sunshine to the walkway and out across the decks of the boats. The Chens' houseboat was moored close to shore at the moment, the result—so Inari had informed her—of a recent typhoon warning, and one reached it by stepping precariously across the decks of other moored craft. Mrs Pa wondered whether the Chens' neighbors knew about Inari's demonic origins: they must see her at fairly close range. But perhaps the sunglasses and the hat were enough. It seemed quiet enough, anyway: there was no one about. Mrs Pa climbed the steps onto the main deck of the houseboat and called out, "It's only me! I'm back."

There was no reply. Perhaps they were around the other side. Mrs Pa walked around the deck, but there was no one sitting on the bench. She began to feel uneasy. She knocked cautiously on the door that led to the inside of the houseboat, but again, there was no answer. Mrs Pa opened the door and went down the narrow stairs, finding herself in a long room decorated with batik images of waterbirds and boats. It was a lovely, calm place, the floorboards scoured and sanded until they were almost white, and everything in tranquil shades of blue and green. It was a world away from the vulgar opulence of the Pang's living room and yet its emptiness was not having a calming effect on Mrs Pa: the reverse, in fact.

"Precious Dragon?"

A bedroom, curtained off from the main room, revealed nothing except a stack of paperback books on both sides of the bed. A small bathroom was equally tidy, but bare. Mrs Pa found that her hands were starting to shake as she replaced the bedroom curtain; she felt an overwhelming sense of dread, a black cloud swimming through the quiet, hot air and enveloping her in its shadows.

She'd felt so strongly that she could trust Inari. Now, she wondered how she could have been so stupid. She didn't even have real proof that the demon woman was Chen's wife: she could easily have stolen a photograph of the detective. Precious Dragon had seemed to trust her, too, but despite everything, he was still a small child and maybe he had made a mistake. The blackness was churning her sight. She sat down heavily on the couch, still clutching the bag of buns.

"They are not here," said a voice like earth. Mrs Pa leaped, nearly dropping the bag. She looked down to see the badger staring up at her. The black and white head was sleek and damp, as if the badger had been swimming. The badger's eyes were as black and opaque as those of a skull.

"Where are they?" Mrs Pa faltered. With a crossness born of fright, she repeated, "Where's my grandson?"

"They are not here," the badger repeated. "They are close by. We had to leave this place."

"Why? Inari told me that she wasn't planning to take Precious Dragon anywhere."

"An assassin came," the badger said.

"What?" Mrs Pa's heart sank in dismay. "Oh no. Like the thing the other night?"

"Perhaps. This thing was not human, but not a demon either: we do not know what it was. It was fierce and fast. I bit it in the leg." The badger's eyes glittered in what might have been satisfaction. "It fell into the harbor, and then it proved it could not swim. It sank like a stone. We waited, but it did not come back. But where there was one, there will be others, and so Inari has taken your grandson into her keeping and is hiding nearby. We need to go back to the shore."

"What do we do then?" Mrs Pa asked. She would do anything to keep Precious Dragon safe, but her age weighed down on her, pressing. If only she were younger...

"That is for my mistress to say. We are to head for the trees that line the shore. She will see us coming. Carry me, please."

It was not a suggestion. Mrs Pa was about to protest that she couldn't bend down and pick up a creature as heavy as the badger, but then there was a dark sparkle in the air, and she blinked. The badger was no longer standing at her feet. Instead, a large and somewhat battered iron kettle stood there instead.

"Well," Mrs Pa said aloud. "That was a surprise."

She picked up the kettle gingerly by its handle and carried it up the stairs to the deck. She was apprehensive, but all was quiet. With the buns in one hand and the badger-teakettle in the other, Mrs Pa clambered back over the decks to the shore, and whatever might be waiting there.

TWENTY-FOUR

Chen tried to snatch an hour of sleep, but the dreams kept chasing themselves through his head, an endless, wearying round of Zhu Irzh, his mother, Daisy, Miss Qi, and various Ministers, all running in and out of a vast mansion like some kind of operatic farce. He felt more exhausted when he actually awoke, than if he'd not slept at all. He went into the little *en suite* bathroom and splashed rusty water over his face. It did not help. Then he went next door and knocked.

Zhu Irzh took several minutes to answer and when he did, he looked as fatigued as Chen felt.

"Couldn't sleep a wink," he said in answer to Chen's enquiry. "Kept thinking about things, and I can't help feeling that something's *getting* at me."

"Wouldn't surprise me," Chen said. "What kind of something?"

"That's just it, I don't know. I kept thinking there was someone in the room, that I was being watched. I even got up and checked behind the curtains and under the bed like a kid, but there was no one there. It's just paranoia. Probably seeing my family has done it."

"We've got to focus on finding Miss Qi," Chen said, although he was thinking of the thing in the garden on the previous nights. He was certain they were being watched and he knew that Zhu Irzh would agree. Then a thought struck him and he wondered that he hadn't considered it before; he was not used to being in Hell on legitimate non-crime-related business, that was the problem. "We'd better let the Ministry of War know what's happened. They've probably got something planned for us today."

"I'd forgotten about the Ministry of War," Zhu Irzh said, and sighed. "Believe it or not."

The Ministry of War, however, had not forgotten them. When Chen and Zhu Irzh went downstairs, they found a bright and cheerful Underling No

120

waiting in the hall, perky in her stiff leather armor.

"Detective! Seneschal! Is Miss Qi not with you?"

"No, she's not," Chen said grimly, and explained what had occurred.

Underling No appeared genuinely dismayed. If Zhu Irzh was wrong and it was not the Ministry of Lust who was behind Miss Qi's abduction, then Chen seriously doubted that Underling No had anything to do with it. Either that or she was an excellent actress: she was a demon, after all. He thought of that lithe figure in red: Could it be? But Underling No seemed too stocky, too solid, although it was difficult to tell under all that ornate armor.

"But this is appalling!" Underling No exclaimed. "And worse, it is an insult to us. The Lesser Lord must be told immediately. The Minister must also know." She raised her wrist to her mouth. A metal frog, open-mouthed, was inlaid in the cuff of her armor. Underling No spoke briefly into it, using some manner of code. A moment later, a voice came out of the mouth of the frog.

"Report to the Ministry immediately. Bring our guests with you."

Chen had the sensation of being caught up in events and swept along, and to his mild surprise, this was not displeasing. Before, on his visits to Hell, he had grown used to acting alone, apart from Zhu Irzh and whoever else had been along for the ride. But their power had always been limited: solo battles against supernatural might. Now, with the Ministry of War seemingly eager to become involved, Chen felt that he actually had a measure of support.

Best not to let yourself become too trusting, though, Chen thought. *This was still Hell.*

At the Ministry of War, battle stations appeared to be well underway. The immense iron doors swung open as Underling No's carriage clattered up to it, the hooves of the deer striking sparks from the stone. The carriage shot straight up the steps and through the doors into the atrium, where the Lesser Lord was waiting, barking orders amidst a milling crowd of warriors. He looked even more bristling than before; layers seemed to have been added to his already decorative armor.

"Detective, Seneschal. I understand we have a problem."

"Miss Qi is missing, Lesser Lord," Chen told him. "She was taken from our hotel last night as we were returning from Zhu Irzh's family gathering. There are indications that the Ministry of Lust is behind the kidnapping."

"I'll show you," Zhu Irzh said. "We've got a recording."

"Not here," the Lesser Lord said quickly. "In my office."

He ushered them upstairs, and Zhu Irzh took the coal from his pocket and activated it. The Lesser Lord and Underling No watched in silence as Miss Qi was, once again, stolen away.

"That red person," Underling No said. "I'm sure I've seen her before."

"It's a woman, then?" Chen asked. "We weren't sure."

"Definitely female," Underling No confirmed.

"The shadow-masks," the Lesser Lord said. "Those are used by the Ministry of Lust. Each Ministry has its particular style of armor and weaponry, you see: it is an ancient dictate imposed by the Emperor, to make sure that everyone can be identified."

"Our informer didn't seem sure," Chen said.

"Your informer is merely a staff member at the hotel, not a civil servant. Ask anyone involved in administration and they would have been able to tell you, others, probably not. But I can say with some certainty that these people come from Lust. And that creates a problem."

Chen sighed. He'd thought as much.

"You see," the Lesser Lord said, with a degree of embarrassment that suggested he was aware of a loss of face, "there's always a delicate relationship between the Ministries. I'm sure you understand. Power in Hell is always an unstable thing, with various governmental departments enjoying a closer or more distant relationship with the Imperial Court. At present, the Ministry of War is enjoying some degree of support, but the Emperor is always more wary of our department than of others, and to be honest, most of the previous Majesties have been close to the Ministry of Lust and this administration is no exception. I'm sure you can understand why."

Chen thought that he understood very well. The Emperor didn't trust the Ministry of War, because War was the obvious Ministry to stage a coup. The Imperial Court approved of Lust, for reasons that were, indeed, perfectly obvious. If the Ministry of War started a campaign against Lust, particularly one that revolved around the presence of a Celestial and thus was likely to bring the Imperial Court into even worse diplomatic odor with Heaven, then the Emperor was going to be displeased with War. And that would probably result in loss of funding for War's currently massive campaign, perhaps a change of Minister (which might directly impact upon poor old Zhu Irzh, quite apart from anything else, given his recent familial connections), and who knows: obliteration of War from the central square of Hell and relegation to some even more squalid lower realm. It might be farfetched, but a rather similar fate had recently befallen the now-rebuilt Ministry of Epidemics, after all.

"So the situation will have to be handled with an element of *diplomacy,* as regards our esteemed absent guest," the Lesser Lord was saying, and Chen heard: *We're not sticking our heads above the parapet for some Heavenly bint.*

"The Ministry will of course support in theory any actions you may wish to undertake."

You go and get her back and we'll deny any knowledge of it if you screw up.

"And we look forward to welcoming Miss Qi back within our portals."

Just get on with it, all right? And I don't want to hear about it in the meantime.

"I commend your subtle approach," said Chen. *Very well, then, you lily-liv-*

ered Hellspawn, we don't have any choice but to let you off the hook. "I'm sure the Ministry will act honorably in supplying us with any relevant information, however." *How do we get into the Ministry of Lust?*

"I have spoken with the Minister and, naturally, he understands the situation." The Lesser Lord gave a relieved nod toward his desk, on which sat a scroll. The Lesser Lord then turned and stared hard for a moment out of the window, during which Zhu Irzh leaned forward and neatly appropriated the scroll. "I don't think we have anything further to discuss."

"I appreciate your delicacy in this matter," Chen replied.

"Underling No will show you out. You might like to visit one of the blood cafés: you'll find them on the other side of the square. Jin's does a rather pleasant lunch."

Chen and Zhu Irzh, with fulsome protestations of gratitude designed to restore the Lesser Lord's diminished *face*, followed Underling No back down to the atrium.

"I'll take you to Jin's," Underling No said. "My cousin runs it. It's a nice place."

Rather curious, Chen agreed. They needed to formulate a plan of action, preferably somewhere in which they could not be easily overheard, although given current magical practice it was difficult to say how realistic that was. But he did not understand why Underling No was being so helpful, nor did he trust her.

They crossed the square. Chen glanced back at the Ministry of War. It had been nice to feel that he'd had some support, even though it had lasted only as long as a conversation and he hadn't really believed in it anyway. He glanced at Zhu Irzh, striding along with his black silk cloak whipping around his heels, and once more thought how strange it was that the two people closest to him were demons. Inari, he could understand: there was love there, and gratitude. But Zhu Irzh had owed Chen nothing, been owed nothing, and he'd still put himself on the line on a number of occasions. The demon dismissed it with a characteristic insouciance, but even so, Chen thought it was significant. To their left, the Ministry of Lust rose in bloated opulence. Chen hoped that the Lesser Lord had slipped them some information that was actually useful, like a map. The thought of breaking into the Ministry was daunting, but he'd done worse. It was just a bigger version of a demon lounge, wasn't it? And they'd been in plenty of those. In his gut, however, Chen knew that this was not quite true. The Ministry of Lust was a primary source of much of the world's corruption. Horrible, to think of poor Miss Qi incarcerated within its fleshy walls.

"It's this one," Underling No was saying. Chen looked out across a range of blood cafés, all with their telltale barrel signs and characteristic dark crimson awnings. They all looked the same to Chen, but Underling No led them to a café at the end of the row and ushered them to a seat. To Chen's relief, this was outside. There was not just the issue of potential eavesdroppers to consider, but also the question of the smell. Blood cafés and emporia smelled of, well, *blood,* and Chen found it fairly nauseating after prolonged exposure.

"What can I get you?" asked Underling No, transformed into an anxious, if unlikely, hostess.

"Just some tea," Chen said quickly. "Ordinary black tea. Or green, if you have it." *Anything but red.*

To his surprise, Underling No bustled away without demur and returned a few minutes later carrying a teapot, along with a bottle of blood beer that she set in front of Zhu Irzh.

"We'd better have a look at this so-called information," Chen said.

Zhu Irzh, after a glance around, took the scroll out of his pocket and rolled it out onto the tabletop. To Chen's relief, it was indeed a map.

"Yeah, this is it," said Zhu Irzh. "It's definitely the Min of Lust. Look, here's the central dome."

Chen studied the map. It showed a number of levels and stories, including one at the bottom that appeared to depict the cellar.

"Makes sense to go in below ground," Chen said, grimacing. He'd had rather too much experience of Hell's sewer system. Then, he was startled as a mailed hand shot out and grasped his wrist.

"Take me with you," said Underling No.

TWENTY-FIVE

Embar Dea stood on a shelf of ice, looking upward. They were to leave in an hour, when the sun sank down across the western ocean, one of the halfway points of the day when the veils between the worlds were thin. Embar Dea worried about the journey. Her strength had already been sapped by the voyage here, by the cold of the seas and the struggle through the ocean currents, as well as by the burden of the pearl. She did not know whether she could make it as far as Cloud Kingdom, but she had no other choice. She could not stay on Earth, the Dragon Prince had explained to her. The dragons must act as one, now, in the face of the oldest of enemies; it had been decreed.

Embar Dea understood this and there was a kind of peace within that understanding. If she died on the way, plummeting out of the heavens and back into the ocean like a cold comet, then it would be worth it. She was the oldest; she would have to die someday. The souls of dragons do not pass into Heaven or Hell, for they are already travelers between the worlds. Once she died, Embar Dea knew, she would be extinguished, forever gone, but a little soul-fragment would remain, passing into the group soul of dragonkind, and that was enough. But the worry was still there: even dragons have a lingering fear of mortality.

So she waited on the ice, watching alone, until the other dragons emerged, one by one in the greening light, and joined her.

The Dragon Prince Rish was the first to fly. He leaped from the ice shelf, spreading black-silver wings and soaring out across the waves. The falling sunlight caught the water, glittered red, and then the dragon from the south followed him, shooting like a blazing coal into the sunset. One by one, the others left, until only Embar Dea remained on the shelf as the others flew overhead, circling around and around, singing encouragement to her. The sea thundered against the ice shelf, the waves rising to a froth in the growing wind, and the sky was filled with the rattle of scales.

"Embar Dea!" the Dragon Prince called. "Embar Dea!" and then he cried out her name again in the ancient tongue, the tongue that dragons used before the coming of humankind and the coming of the ice, when demons and Celestials alike roamed the plains of the great continent of the changing world, and the dragons held sway over ocean.

When she heard that name, Embar Dea was compelled to respond and the Dragon Prince knew it: he had seen the need to help her. He called out the name again and again, and the other dragons picked it up and sang it back to her, so that the air reverberated with the power of her name and Embar Dea spread her creaking wings and let the power drive under them and lift her upward.

The ice shelf fell away, dwindling beneath her to a tiny patch in the middle of the waves; from this height, the domes of the sea palace looked like a handful of mouse skulls, fragile and frail. Embar Dea spread her wings further and rushed out across the sea, diving until the spray spattered her scales, and then she rose, following the Dragon Prince who was rising now into the darkening sky, as distant as a blown leaf.

She was flying for the first time in years, free in the airs of Earth. It took a great deal of will power to go after the Prince, not to soar off across the waves, leave the twilight world behind. But the Prince sang her ancient name, weaving it into a tapestry of the names of the other dragons, words that could not have been spoken in a human voice, and she rose and followed and flew.

Up and up, until the sea palace was no longer visible and the sea was a great dark curve against the wall of night. Embar Dea saw the last rim of the sun, a rind above the curve, and then it sank and was gone. The stars blazed, mirrored now by the scatter of the lights of Earth, the cities of the world. As they rose, Embar Dea drew closer to the other dragons, flying in tight spirals now, winding themselves up from the Earth and out of its magical field. Embar Dea looked up and saw that the veil that parted the worlds was drawing aside, a glowing shimmer of light across the sky, hiding the stars.

Up and up and the veil was all around them, hiding the world from view and Embar Dea felt the wrench and tug as the magic of the human realms vanished and they were through into the upper levels. Heaven lay ahead, a line of bright shore, but before that were towers of cumulus, huge sweeps of cirrus cloud against a burning blue sky, anvil thunderheads around which the lightning of flame dragons played in bursts and lashes of light.

Cloud Kingdom. Memories thousands of years old came rushing back: riding the winds of Heaven, dancing on the shores of the sky. Her mother, the Mother of Dragons, a vast, sinuous shape against the cloudscape, rarely glimpsed and always a sign of great change. There was a new Mother of Dragons now, drawn from the heart of Cloud Kingdom long after Embar

Dea and her siblings had come to Earth. Embar Dea did not know her; it seemed strange, to have a Mother that was younger than herself. But she did not care about that. She was thankful to have reached the end of her journey, to have made it alive. With the others, she glided through the sparkling air between the clouds. Other dragons were coming to meet them, coiling and curling through the air, and Prince Rish flew to meet them like a black arrow. Embar Dea followed, going home.

TWENTY-SIX

Mrs Pa stepped onto the shore, still holding the buns and the iron teakettle. No one had paid her any attention as she crossed over the decks of the boats—there were some advantages in being a harmless old lady—but her skin prickled all the same at the thought of what might be watching. She hoped it would take her for the cleaner. As she took a careful step down onto the sandy shingle, the teakettle jumped in her hand. Startled, Mrs Pa dropped it and, as it fell, the teakettle flowed into a badger once more. The badger, foursquare on the shore, gave itself a violent shake.

"Where are they?" Mrs Pa whispered, feeling horribly vulnerable.

"Not far, I think," the badger said. It sounded rusty, as iron would if it could speak; perhaps the creature retained aspects of its other form. It trotted swiftly into the scrub and trees beyond the tideline and Mrs Pa followed, stepping over driftwood and floats, dead fish and the oily scum that marked all of the city's shores.

She was glad to get under the shelter of the trees, where it was shadowy and cooler. The sun had now almost set and a faint refreshing breath sighed from the sea, which glowed with its own light as though a captive sun lay beneath the waves.

"Ah," said the badger, and Mrs Pa saw two huge red eyes floating in the darkness between the trees. "Mistress."

"Grandmother!" Precious Dragon ran forward and Mrs Pa reached down to give him a hug, her heart hammering in relief.

"Precious Dragon. You're all right."

"Mrs Pa, I'm so sorry." Inari looked strained, her face gaunt and even paler than usual. "Something came up out of the water. I did my best to fight it off—it wasn't a demon, not of any kind that I know."

Mrs Pa gripped her hand. "You looked after Precious Dragon and kept him safe. That's all that matters."

"The creature was unpleasant," Precious Dragon said. He sounded grave and measured, like a middle-aged man commenting on a regrettable business lunch.

"Do *you* know what it was?" Mrs Pa asked her grandson.

"I have never seen anything like it before. It was strange, as though the form it took was not its natural form, but a shell which it wore."

Inari stared at him. "You didn't tell me that."

"I have been trying to work things out."

"We can't go back to the boat," Inari said. "It might come back or something else might come, and you see, Mrs Pa, I am not a warrior. And my husband is not here. I'm sorry to be so feeble."

"You're not feeble at all," Mrs Pa said. "But I am. I saw what came to my house. I couldn't do anything to stop it."

"If it came to your house," the badger said with slow logic, "then it knows where you live and we cannot go back there, either."

"Then where can we go?" Mrs Pa asked.

"The temple of Kuan Yin," said Inari. "My husband used to be under her protection."

Mrs Pa stared at her. "*Used* to be?"

"Yes. Unfortunately, he disobeyed her instructions when he rescued me from Hell and she renounced him. She *has* helped him since, however."

"Well, so I should think," said Mrs Pa. "After all, she's supposed to be merciful and compassionate. It doesn't sound very compassionate to renounce your servant because he helps someone else."

"Gods are weird," said Inari. There was a short silence.

"Anyway," Mrs Pa said. "You still think that her temple is the place to go?"

"It's the only place I can think of," Inari said. "Unless—oh, wait! I have an idea." She sank down onto a nearby tree trunk. "Last year, Chen and Zhu Irzh helped some people. One of them was the son of the Celestial Emperor."

"My word," said Mrs Pa faintly. "That's quite something."

"He had a friend, a human woman. She died, in a battle. But because of the friendship, she's still living here in Singapore Three. There was a ruined temple to the Emperor's son—he didn't like being worshipped so it fell into decline. But his friend decided to restore it and now she's its priestess. We went to see them once, at the Water Festival last year. It's a nice place now. I think we should go there rather than bother Kuan Yin again. You see, I don't have any other friends here. Chen and I can't socialize, because of what I am."

"Well, it sounds like a plan," Mrs Pa said. She felt rather stunned. First, all this business with Mai and Precious Dragon, and then here she was, about to start hobnobbing with the son of the Celestial Emperor. But someone of that status would surely be able to protect them from unknown demonic assassins. Wouldn't they? "Where is it, this temple?"

"That's the only problem," Inari said. "It's on the other side of the city. And it's dark now, I don't want to start wandering about, especially after what's just happened. You must know how it is with Hellkind. Some humans can see us, like yourself, others can't, but I don't want to take a risk."

"Well, we'll wait until morning, then," Mrs Pa said. She sat down beside Inari. "Would you like a bun?"

"Mrs Pa, you must have been sent from the gods yourself," Inari said with a wan smile. "I'm hungry."

Precious Dragon curled up beside Mrs Pa after they had eaten, and the badger sat next to Inari, eyes glittering in watchfulness. A day's cleaning work, and then the excitement of this evening, had made Mrs Pa exhausted, but she could not sleep. Inari's head drooped and Precious Dragon's breathing deepened, but Mrs Pa and the badger sat wakeful late into the night, until the stars hung low over the harbor and the mournful hoots of passing boats sounded out across the water.

Much later, however, Mrs Pa woke. At first she was completely disoriented, then memory came back in a rush. The badger was growling low under its breath.

"Badger," Mrs Pa whispered. "What is it?"

"Something is on the boat," the badger replied.

Mrs Pa could just see Inari's houseboat through the bushes and with dismay she saw that the badger was right. Something—no, *several* things—were swarming up from the water and onto the deck of the houseboat. Mrs Pa nudged Inari, who woke with a start.

"What are they?"

Inari shook her head. "I don't know."

They moved like human beings, but even from this distance, in the uncertain lights from the harbor, Mrs Pa could tell that they were not. They made her senses prickle. Precious Dragon had been right: it was like looking at shells, at simulacra of human beings. They wore slick black outfits like sealskin, and if it hadn't been for that terrible sense of wrongness, Mrs Pa would have assumed they were human divers. But instead, she had the impression that she was seeing their actual flesh.

And they were exactly like the thing that had invaded her home a little while ago.

"Inari," she murmured. "Is there any way that they can track us, do you think? By smell?"

"I don't know. I hope not."

One of the things was on the roof of the houseboat. It stood and looked around, then it crawled face down along the wall to the lower deck. It moved with unnatural speed, reminding Mrs Pa of a spider or crab. A moment later, all the things returned to the waters of the harbor with barely a splash.

"I think we should move," Inari said. Mrs Pa thought so, too.

"We could climb a tree," she suggested. It sounded so futile, but looking around, they didn't have many other options. There was a ruined pier further down the shore, but the scrub had petered out at that point and the shore was exposed. Behind the trees was a high wall, a concreted cliff that would be impossible to climb.

So Mrs Pa hoisted Precious Dragon up into the branches, and then Inari helped her up, with some difficulty.

"I'm too old to be sitting in a tree at my age," Mrs Pa said ruefully. She clutched the trunk. It seemed a very long way to the ground. Inari shinned lithely up beside her, followed by the badger.

Then they waited. At first, Mrs Pa thought that it was over. The things had merely wanted to check the houseboat and had returned to the water. But then the badger, crouching beside her on a branch, stiffened, and she saw a narrow wake out in the harbor, heading fast for shore.

"Precious Dragon," she murmured. "Don't even breathe." But her grandson was already as still as stone.

The wake reached the shore and one of the black beings glided out of the water. Closer to, it looked nothing like a human being. Its limbs were too thin, but the muscles and veins were hideously prominent. Round black eyes like lenses were set into its shiny skull. A small circular mouth opened to reveal needle teeth and a long probing tongue that snaked over the shore, testing and questing. Its hind legs were jointed the wrong way, bending backward, and its feet were long, razor-edged paddles. It came quickly up the shore and left no trace in the sand.

Mrs Pa and her companions stayed still and quiet. The thing investigated the place where they had slept. Then it looked up. Mrs Pa found herself staring directly down into the black lenses and it was like looking through a gateway, into a vast dark land where everything was storm and cold. She gasped and the thing was already swarming up the tree. Inari kicked out and her foot connected with its head. The head snapped backward, as if its neck was made of rubber, and righted itself. The thing gave a little curling grin. It seized Inari by the ankle and threw her out of the tree. She landed heavily, but the next moment was up again and grasping for the creature, trying to avoid the sharp, flailing paddle of its left foot. The badger bit into its arm and hung on. The thing, still grinning, tried to dislodge it but the badger clung solidly.

Something pushed past Mrs Pa and she almost lost her grip on the trunk. Precious Dragon stood precariously in the fork of the tree. He was mumbling the pearl, working it inside his cheek, and as Mrs Pa watched, aghast, he spat. A long stream of glistening white saliva shot out and plastered itself over the thing's face. It screamed, a discordant shrieking which delighted Mrs Pa's heart. She would have struck at it herself but she was afraid of falling out of the tree. The saliva was burning, eating away the creature's face like acid and revealing a thin sheen of bony skull that soon dissolved. Inside, at first there wasn't anything, and then there was everything: a whole world. Mrs Pa was looking through a gap in the air, the size and shape of a human figure, and beyond it was that immense, storm-riven land. She was looking down through the clouds, a distance of thousands of feet and all at once she felt she was falling. She screamed and clutched at Precious Dragon and then they did fall, but out of the tree. Mrs Pa felt a sickening crack at the back of her head and then there was nothing.

TWENTY-SEVEN

"It started with my mother," Underling No said. They were still sitting at the café table. "She worked for the Ministry of War all her life, it's in our family. She was a warrior." No banged the table with her mailed fist for emphasis. "Then one year there was a dispute between War and Lust—the two Ministers fell out over something. There were raids between the Ministries, and a raiding party from Lust overpowered my mother and her unit. They took her into the Ministry and we never saw her again, but we knew what had happened to her because they sent us photographs. Big ones. Full color. She was raped and put to work. Can you imagine how humiliating that is for a warrior? For *anyone*?"

"I'm so sorry," Chen said. He had to restrain himself from reaching out and putting a hand on No's arm; he did not think she would appreciate it. He felt, at gut level, that she was telling the truth. Zhu Irzh made a tutting noise.

"Dreadful business. Happens a lot between Ministries."

"I know that," Underling No said. "But Lust has additional weapons. At least with Epidemics, for instance, all you get is some foul disease. You're not *broken*."

"Very true," Zhu Irzh said. "I've never liked Lust. Well, you know what I mean. The Vice Department had a lot of dealings with them, obviously; we had to carry out their remits. It was always a pain in the ass. They were always getting on their high horse about something or other, always whining."

"Also, your brother-in-law works for them," Chen reminded him.

"Yes, well, that doesn't exactly endear me to them. Daisy worked for them for a bit, too, before she landed her bureaucrat and started giving herself airs and graces. She was a secretary. In fact, come to think of it, as a family we've probably had more dealings with the Ministry of Lust than with any other department over the decades."

Chen bit back what he had been about to say, but he knew that both he and Zhu Irzh were thinking the same thing: Given those connections with Lust, what was Zhu Irzh's mother doing with the Minister of War?

"I can understand why you're not a fan of Lust, in that case," Chen said to No.

"This is why I want to come with you. Miss Qi—I don't know her, of course. She is a Celestial, our enemy. But sometimes enemies can be closer than one's friends and I saw what kind of a person Qi is—she is like my mother. A warrior, too—I saw her with the bow. And I do not like to think of her in the hands of Lust. I couldn't save my mother, I was too young. But perhaps I can help you save Miss Qi, and maybe, if I can get into the Ministry, I might also be able to find out what happened to my mother. She might even still be alive."

"Have you tried before?" Chen asked.

"Twice. Each time, I failed. I did not have this map—I was surprised that the Lesser Lord gave it to you."

Chen sighed. "I'm afraid demons don't matter, Underling No. Miss Qi is a Celestial and they're too scared of a diplomatic incident with Heaven not to give us some help, at least."

"Then you'll take me with you?" Underling No asked.

"Yes," Chen said. "We will." He did not know whether it was wise to put any faith in Underling No's story, but you had to trust your instincts some time, and Chen's had already told him that the demon was telling the truth. Besides, they could use her help.

"Good!" No leaped to her feet. It struck Chen that in many ways, No was the mirror image of Qi: both warriors of integrity, one mild and one ferocious, one serving Heaven and the other Hell. It gave him the discomfiting feeling that the worlds might all have their counterparts: Was there a Celestial version of Zhu Irzh? Of Inari?

"I shall bring more blood," No announced. "We will drink to our success!"

"She's very keen," Zhu Irzh remarked as No disappeared in the direction of the café's interior. He leaned languidly back in his chair and looked in the direction of the Ministry of Lust. Chen followed his glance. The Ministry seemed to have swelled.

"You can see why."

"There's a fair chance her mum's still in there, unless she's been dispatched to the lower realms. If you ask me, she's coming along for the ride simply to find out what happened to her mother. I doubt she gives a toss about Qi."

"Very probably you're right," Chen said, though he wasn't entirely sure about that. "Do you have objections to her coming along, though? She could be useful."

"No objections. I agree with you. I think we'll need to keep an eye on her, though. She's likely to go running off at a crucial moment."

Underling No came back with drinks, and they resumed a study of the map. The most promising entrance lay at the back of the building, in the grounds. Chen remembered the extensive shrubberies that he had seen in the gardens of the hotel: both the grounds of the hotel and those of the Ministry adjoined one another.

"We're going to need some kind of disguise," he said. "We can't just pretend that we're going back to the hotel. Someone will be watching."

"I have a method of temporary invisibility," No said. "It's standard use among the troops. It won't work once we're inside the Ministry itself, though. They have protections against that sort of thing."

Chen shrugged. "Sounds good enough to me. As long as we can actually get inside the Ministry, we'll take it from there. If we go back to the hotel and use your method, then we can slip out again. I'm reluctant to leave this any longer."

"So am I," Underling No said. She grimaced. "You didn't see the photos of my mother."

Zhu Irzh downed the last of his drink and got up. "Let's get on with it, then."

They made their way back to the hotel in silence. It was now close to what, in Hell, passed for noon, and the sky was a brassy, brilliant red, baking with heat. The hotel foyer was empty apart from a bored and unfamiliar demon on the desk. She did not look up from her magazine, but slapped the room keys down on the desk in front of Chen and continued studying what appeared to be celebrity photographs. Chen, Zhu Irzh, and Underling No went up the stairs to Chen's room.

"We need to stand and touch hands," No said. "There are other ways of doing it, but this is the quickest."

"Ah," said Zhu Irzh. "I know what this is."

Underling No spoke a word that made the walls of the room tremble. A black spark of magic traveled down Chen's spine, making the scars on the palms of his hands ache momentarily, and then buried itself in the floor. Chen saw no difference until No broke her grip and he turned to look in the mirror. He was a shadow on the air, nothing more.

"Invisible," Chen said, and the word was a whisper. He heard it inside his head, echoing.

"At least until we reach the Ministry," Zhu Irzh replied. Chen glanced in his direction. The demon, too, had become a sharp shadow, easier to see out of the corner of the eye than directly.

"We can see one another," No informed him, "but not be seen by anyone else. At least, that's the idea."

They went back down the stairs, through the foyer where the bored clerk did not glance up, and out into the steaming afternoon. They had all agreed that it would be safest to walk through the gardens, avoiding the main avenues, just in case. So they moved through the black-spined trees that skirted the grounds of the Ministry of War, shrubs with leaves like sabers that hissed in the wind, bulbous-trunked palms the shape of hand grenades. The air smelled faintly of gunpowder, of smoke, the bracing odor of the battlefield's edge.

As they drew closer to the Ministry of Lust, however, the foliage changed from black to red, becoming fleshier and more pliable, moist, with clefts and folds that secreted a glutinous mucus. The scent of the air changed also, now heavy and filled with musk. Chen found both kinds of vegetation disturbing, and the smell revolted him, but he refrained from voicing his opinion. As the gardens of the Ministry became more formal and increasingly decadent (crimson and mauve-veined fungi, vines loaded with mammary fruit), they stepped into a narrow, artificial gorge cut between contoured rocks. The gorge was fringed with red-fronded ferns; there was little doubt what it was intended to represent. There was a snort of disapproval within Chen's hearing: he attributed it to Underling No, who seemed far too stern for any sexual activity.

When they were halfway through the gorge Chen became convinced that someone was following them. He nudged Zhu Irzh, still visible to him but not, he hoped, to anyone in pursuit.

"Zhu Irzh! There's someone there."

The demon paused and looked round. "I can't see anyone."

"There. Do you see where those fronds are moving?"

"You keep seeing things. It's just the wind."

"Then why is everything else so still?"

"You might be right," Zhu Irzh breathed, after a moment's contemplation. "Do you want to check it out?"

"I think we'd better."

But when they made their way back up the gorge, there was no one there.

"All right," Chen said. "We carry on. But keep your eyes open."

He did so himself, turning swiftly every so often to see if the person was still behind them. He thought of the shadow he had seen in the parkland in front of the hotel, slipping into the night. Hell had spies everywhere; it was only a matter of determining where they came from.

The gorge ended. Chen and the others stepped out onto a red squashy expanse at the back of the Ministry, which rose now before them.

"The entrance isn't far away," Underling No said in Chen's ear. "Just around these rocks."

It was another artfully constructed cleft, this time filled with the phallic, mauve fungi. They moved slowly, drifting in the damp air like clams, their blind heads seeking.

"Don't let them touch you," Zhu Irzh warned.

"What will they do?" asked Chen.

"To be honest, I don't know, but I doubt it would be good."

As they reached a quarter of the way along the cleft, Chen thought he heard something, a faint muffled cry. He swung round but no one was there. He was sure they were still being followed. Then they came to a large cluster of the fungi, a phallic phalanx that stood rigid and quivering.

"You go first," said Underling No. "I'll distract them." She was standing at the entrance to what looked like a small cave, a hollow in the rock. This, too, was lined with vegetation. a kind of dank, black fern. Chen and Zhu Irzh, careful not to touch the sides, inched their way into the hollow. Ahead shone a dim phosphorescence. Chen glanced back. The phallic fungi were twisting and turning, seeking No and paying little attention to Chen and Zhu Irzh. After all, reflected Chen, she *was* female. The fungi did not appear able to see, but then No was invisible. Could they smell her? Chen was not sure. But if such things were to be found outside the Ministry of Lust, then what was it like inside? Grimly, Chen reminded himself that Miss Qi had already found out.

Zhu Irzh was striding ahead, his black cloak outlined by a silvery glow. Chen turned to make sure that Underling No was still behind them and was relieved to discover that she had left the fungi and was close on their tail. They were in a tunnel, which seemed to have been deliberately carved from the red rock: its walls and the low roof were smooth, disquietingly fleshy, like the cliffs outside. The floor seemed hard enough, but Chen was not inclined to touch the walls, especially when they were some distance in and the tunnel gave a sudden convulsive contraction.

Zhu Irzh stopped abruptly. "What was *that?*"

"Keep going," Underling No advised. "From the map, we're almost at the end."

They walked on. After a few minutes the tunnel began to narrow, convoluting into labial folds. Chen began to feel claustrophobic: He didn't think he'd suffered any birth traumas, but who knew? He certainly had no desire to go through the process again. Another series of folds, coated with beads and globules of moisture, so narrow that Zhu Irzh had to turn and sidle sideways. Then, suddenly, the tunnel widened, arching far above their heads in a blur of pink and rose, and Chen's vision filled with light. They were inside the Ministry of Lust.

TWENTY-EIGHT

Mrs Pa's head felt as though it was a melon, about to burst. She groaned.

"Lie still," said a worried female voice. Mrs Pa made the mistake of opening her eyes and in between the explosions of light saw that Inari was looking down at her. "Precious Dragon?" Mrs Pa heard Inari say. "Can you do anything?"

"Wait." Precious Dragon sounded very authoritative and calm. Mrs Pa felt something smooth and round travel across her brow and it drew the pain with it like a veil being pulled gently aside. She blinked and sat up. Precious Dragon was putting the pearl back in his mouth. Inari sat by her side and the badger was some distance away across the little glade. Mrs Pa looked up into the branches of the tree and saw that they were empty apart from the graying light of dawn.

"Thank you," she breathed to her grandson. To Inari, she said, "What happened to that—that *thing?*"

"I don't know." Inari sounded bewildered. "It just seemed to open up the air and fall through it. Into Hell, I think. It looked like Hell. It *felt* like Hell."

"And we might have gone with it," Mrs Pa said, shivering at the recollection. "Inari, I was so *stupid*. I panicked."

"Oh, Mrs Pa," Inari said, visibly shocked. "Don't blame yourself. You were confronting a demon that was trying to kill you. You didn't see me on the houseboat. *I'm* a demon myself and I very nearly ran and hid under the bed. If it hadn't been for Precious Dragon, I would have done so. I'm no warrior."

"I nearly got Precious Dragon hurt," Mrs Pa said. Even the most supernatural of children might injure themselves falling out of a tree. But her grandson shook his head.

"I was perfectly safe, Grandmother. I was more worried about you."

"If we all look after each other," Inari said firmly, "then we will be all right."

"It's nearly light," Mrs Pa said. "How long was I unconscious?"

"Only a few minutes," Inari said. "It was nearly dawn when the demon came."

Across the glade, the badger turned. "And twilight when they came the last time."

Inari frowned. "The bleed-times between day and night. They seem to appear then."

"And they may come again at noon," the badger said. "Or midnight. The high and the balance points of the day."

"We should try to get to the temple before noon, then," Inari said. "Just in case."

She made Mrs Pa rest for a few minutes more until they were sure that she was well enough to travel. Then they set off along the woods of the shore, with the badger scouting ahead and Inari bringing up the rear.

"I am so sorry," Mrs Pa said over her shoulder. "If it wasn't for Precious Dragon and myself and our problems, you'd be waking up on your own boat and thinking about nothing worse than breakfast."

Inari laughed. "Mrs Pa, given where I come from, and given my husband's job, there's always *something*. If it wasn't you and Precious Dragon then believe me, it would be something else. And to be honest, although we're in danger and I don't like that, helping other people makes me feel useful."

"You *are* helping us," Mrs Pa said. She reached out and squeezed Inari's hand. Inari took her arm and supported her. It was now quite light, with the rim of the sun just starting to rise over the tops of the skyscrapers across the harbor. As they left the trees and set foot on the shore road, Mrs Pa looked back at the houseboat. It rocked gently in the middle of the harbor, with nothing out of the ordinary about it. But the sight of this peaceful scene made Mrs Pa shudder all the same and she was glad when they reached the end of the harbor road and made their way into the maze of alleys that was the southern end of Ghenret.

"Do we have to walk all the way?" Mrs Pa asked. "Couldn't we catch a tram?"

Inari sighed. "You can, but I can't. After the problems last year, the city's governors put a demon-block on public transport—if I set foot on it, I'll set off an alarm. Then I'd be arrested and the police department would find out my connection with Chen. But Mrs Pa, if you want to, you go on ahead without the badger and myself. I don't want to make you walk all that way."

"I'd rather we stuck together," Mrs Pa said. "I'd feel safer. Anyway, I don't know where this temple is. Is it difficult to find?"

"It's not very easy, I'm afraid. I suppose we could put you in a taxi."

"I don't have enough money for a taxi all the way across town. It's miles and miles. Do you have any?"

"No," Inari said, frustrated. "I left the boat in such a rush, I didn't pick up my bag."

"Then we'll keep together. I don't mind walking."

Inari pointed upward, to a block that towered over the shanties and roofs. A red bird blazed across the structure and some of the scaffolding was still up.

"Paugeng," Inari said. "My husband's police partner is going out with Jhai Tserai."

"He must be a very brave young man," Mrs Pa mused. "Although I suppose he *is* a demon."

"He's either brave or foolish," Inari said. "But one might say the same about Jhai. I wish I felt able to trust her. But I just can't. This might sound strange, coming from me, but she's had too many dealings with Hell." She lowered her voice when she spoke about Jhai, Mrs Pa noticed, and understood why. The companies had ears everywhere.

"I heard so many rumors, when there was all that trouble with the *feng shui* place," Mrs Pa said. "But this city is full of rumors and it's hard to know what to believe sometimes. Wasn't Jhai supposed to have been behind that goddess who went mad?"

"It was a bit more complicated than that," Inari said. "But she did kidnap the Celestial Emperor's son and conduct experiments on him."

"But that's terrible! And she got away with it?"

Inari grimaced. "I think they struck a deal. That's the trouble. Sometimes Heaven can be as cold as Hell. It's all a question of diplomatic negotiation."

"And this poor experiment is the person—the being—whom we are going to see?"

"That's right. Maybe he'll tell you about it himself."

"I should have thought," said Mrs Pa, "that it was something he'd be keen to forget."

They were trying to keep out of sight as much as possible, walking as quickly as they could beneath the shadows of shop awnings and away from the main streets. Most of the folk whom they passed paid no attention to Mrs Pa: just a little old lady out for a walk with her grandson. But sometimes Mrs Pa saw a head go up and the person would stare sharply at Inari, then down at the shambling black shape of the badger. Once, the badger hissed, displaying sharp, yellowing teeth, and the man who had come too close backed hastily away.

"We're too visible," Inari murmured. "If anyone asks, they'll know that we passed this way. But there's no other way to get to the temple."

"At least it's morning," Mrs Pa said. "If this was nighttime we'd be in even more danger and not just from demons."

Inari nodded. "People think that where I come from is Hellish. But this city, sometimes, seems far worse to me. Demons don't have much choice to be as they are but even then some of us prefer to do the right thing and not the wrong. But humans all have a choice, and so many of them choose wrongness."

"It's just the way it is," Mrs Pa said. "All you can do is go your own way and not worry about other people."

But that, she thought, was easy for her to say: Inari had fewer options.

By late morning, they had left the reconstructed Paugeng building far behind. The dome of the Opera House rose now above the tiles. Inari stared at it uneasily. They were entering the Pellucid Island district, one of the more bohemian quarters of the city and a place where Mrs Pa only ever went to undertake cleaning work.

"My husband was attacked near here the other night," Inari said. "You hear stories about the Opera House, too. I'll be glad when we're on the other side of the city."

Mrs Pa agreed. She bought three boxes of noodles from a street-side café, no more than a cluster of children around an iron wok, and consulted Inari about the badger's requirements. She did not want it to feel left out, but she need not have worried. The badger ran off behind the café, returned with a squealing rat, which it devoured headfirst.

"He prefers meat," Inari explained.

"I like insects," the badger said, through a mouthful of rat.

"At least he can fend for himself," Mrs Pa said.

By midafternoon they were more than two-thirds of their way across the city, through Pellucid Island and Shaopeng, skirting Bharulay and Peng Ti.

"Are you all right, Mrs Pa?" Inari said. "You can still take the train if you want."

But it was Precious Dragon who answered. "We are safer together," the little boy said. "Even if you are not a warrior, Inari, we are still safer."

"I don't quite see how," Inari said. "I'm getting a little worried. It's not all that long until twilight and you've got blisters on your feet, Mrs Pa."

"Nothing happened at noon," Mrs Pa said hopefully.

"No. But maybe badger is wrong. Maybe it's not the high points of the day, but only the in-between times that we need to watch out." She pointed to the sun, now sinking down between the distant tower blocks of Ghenret. "Another hour and a half, and it'll be gone."

"Let's keep going," Mrs Pa said. "As quickly as we can."

But whatever Precious Dragon might really be, he was still in the form of a small boy and small boys cannot walk for miles across the hard streets of a city, not without a break. So Inari, belying her fragile appearance, had been carrying him for the last hour or so. And Mrs Pa, as Inari had correctly observed, did indeed have blisters. Her feet burned with every step; even in the comfortable old slippers that she used for cleaning, she was not used to walking so far. *Nearly there,* she told herself, as though she was the small child and not Precious Dragon. *Nearly there.*

And it was true. As the sun sank further, with every hurting step, they were drawing closer to the temple and Mrs Pa kept herself going by imagining what it would be like. Inari had told her that the temple had been ruined but was in the process of being restored, and she envisaged it as being a little like the temple in which she had first learned about Mai's marriage. Big statues of the gods, fierce with their swords, a stone floor, a courtyard beneath a curling, tiled roof. A large, once-splendid place. It must be, if it was dedicated to the son of the Celestial Emperor. There was a temple to the Celestial Emperor himself, after all, and that was enormous. She had been there only once for its inauguration, many years ago now, and she had only been permitted to enter the outer precincts, along with all the other ordinary people, as the elite of the city filed through in their magnificent robes into the inner courts. This place must be very similar.

So when they came onto the crest of a hill, to see the downtown area stretching behind them to the harbors, and the hillside suburbs before them, Mrs Pa was surprised to hear Inari say, "There it is," and point to a ramshackle little building on a slight rise some distance away. The building was covered in vines, glowing golden in the sunset, and even from this distance it looked as though part of the roof had fallen in.

"Is that really it?" Mrs Pa asked, disappointed, and Inari said, "Why, yes. The most powerful places are not always the largest."

"Is that so?" Mrs Pa said. The idea had not really occurred to her before and she was not sure that she agreed. She looked back. Paugeng's red bird floated above the other towers of the downtown area, highest of the high. She knew that this was power. It did not seem equivalent to the tumbledown place before them.

"We need to hurry," Inari remarked, with an anxious look back at the sun. Its lower rim was touching the sea now, casting a gilded path across the waves that seemed to flow right across the city and catch the little temple.

"I'm going as fast as I can," Mrs Pa said. The blisters had burst now, and she could feel the wetness in her shoes. Every step was like walking on needles. Inari's free hand was grasping Mrs Pa's arm, but the other was holding onto Precious Dragon. A normal boy would have been asleep by now, head lolling on the grown-up's shoulder, but Precious Dragon was staring out across the city with narrowed eyes. Beyond the temple, beyond the point where the built-over foothills started to rise and climb, the light was already dying over the mountains, and they were purple and in darkness.

Nearly there, nearly there. They were hastening now down a narrow street where the stalls mainly sold cooking wares: pots and woks and steamers. Mrs Pa looked at the things hanging on hooks, the burnished kitchenware, to try to take her mind off her feet. Now that they had come down from the rise, the temple was only just visible on its slight hill, the shattered, vine-covered roof a glimpse through the awnings and tiles.

Nearly there—but then Inari cried out and the badger growled and Mrs Pa turned to see the creature coming fast over the rooftops, leaping across the tiles like a great black ape, its curling mouth set in a red needle-grin and its eyes two glittering black lenses. Twilight was falling and the demons had found them.

TWENTY-NINE

Blinded by unexpected radiance, Chen stood blinking in the vast hall of the Ministry of Lust like a foolish owl. Zhu Irzh grabbed him by the arm and dragged him behind a nearby column. As his vision cleared, Chen saw that it was a twirling pink spiral of meat, pulsing in the same unwholesome rhythm as the tunnel through which they had just come. That was when he realized what he had hitherto been only dimly conscious of: the Ministry was alive.

"This row of columns leads to this passage, see?" Underling No was explaining. Chen peered over her shoulder at the map which Zhu Irzh held open, and saw that the huge circular space in which they now stood was clearly depicted.

"Where are we?" he asked.

"This is the main Ministerial chamber of Lust," Zhu Irzh said. "They're on recess now, lucky for us."

"I don't see any seats," Chen said.

Underling No shot him a curious glance, which Chen thought he could interpret as embarrassment. "It's not that sort of Ministerial chamber."

Any explanations that might have been forthcoming were abruptly cut off by the sound of footsteps. Chen and his companions kept very still. Peering cautiously around the side of the pillar, Chen saw two female guards walking past: both tall, willowy demons clad in the minimum of clothing and carrying spears. One of them stared suspiciously at the pillar from emerald compound eyes, but neither of them stopped.

"I think we need to get out of this chamber," Zhu Irzh murmured.

"Does the Ministry itself know we're here?"

"Actually, I doubt it, although it probably knows that we're walking about on it. I don't think it can tell who we are, though, or that we don't belong to it."

"Is it sentient?"

"Not really, as far as I understand it from Daisy. It's apparently highly sensual, but not capable of much actual thought. I mean, if you think about the function of the Ministry, and the bits to which it corresponds—"

"Are you telling me that we're standing in some kind of semi-aware testicle?"

"Basically, yes, in a manner of speaking. Or a kind of womb."

"I don't know why," said Chen, "but I don't find that nearly as repulsive."

Zhu Irzh shrugged. "You can see the Ministry personnel as being sperm or eggs, or both."

"I hesitate to ask," Chen said, "but where do we go now?"

"Upstairs. From this map, and from what Daisy's let slip, the upper stories of the Ministry are where the cells are. It's sort of spongy upstairs, like a hive."

"Where does the Minister actually have his office?"

"Ah," Zhu Irzh said. "Here, I see we have a misunderstanding. The Minister of Lust is a woman."

"It hasn't always been the case," Underling No said earnestly, suddenly regaining her equal opportunities hat. "The previous Minister of War was female, one of our greatest warriors. And the Minister of Lust was a man."

"It tends to go in opposites," Zhu Irzh said. "Traditionally, they're said to complement one another. Doesn't really bear thinking about."

He began to walk along the rows of columns, which grew closer together and more intertwined as they went on, until Chen had to duck beneath sticky pink tendrils. Eventually the web became too close and cloying and they were forced to step out into the main hall again, first checking to see that no one was in sight. Chen felt very small and vulnerable in the enormous cavity of the central hall, and he hastened after Zhu Irzh and Underling No with all possible speed until they reached the point indicated on the map, where they could dive into another narrow passage. Here, there were more of the mauve fungi, but the Ministry at this point appeared blighted and rotten, for the fungi were covered with weeping yellow sores.

"Lust and Epidemics had a disagreement some years ago," Underling No whispered. "Epidemics released a sexually transmitted disease on the Ministry of Lust. Hundreds of people are still in the lower levels; it was a terrible thing. The Ministry itself almost collapsed but they found a cure."

"A not entirely successful one, though," Zhu Irzh added. He nodded toward the blighted fungi. "That's the result."

"I've always wondered whether my mother was one of those affected," Underling No said. Her face grew fierce. "If I can find her—"

"We'll help as much as we can," Chen said firmly. "But we need to find Qi first."

They made their way past the livid fungi and toward the end of the passage.

The map was correct. A flight of what passed for stairs led upward: short, yielding steps formed from a kind of membrane, lit by the same phosphorescent light that Chen had seen in the first tunnel. They climbed, feet sinking into the membrane. It felt very unstable, as though at any moment the stairs might give way and precipitate them downward. Chen saw Zhu Irzh disappear through an opening in the ceiling above, and moments later, he was able to follow.

Here, the passages through the Ministry of Lust were extremely narrow, obliging even Chen to bend his head. The Ministry was also hot, and now sweat was streaming down the back of Chen's neck, causing his shirt to cling clammily to his spine. Zhu Irzh remained as cool as ever and it was hard to tell whether Underling No's thick crimson skin was overheating or not. Chen kept glancing back, expecting to see one of the insect-eyed women close behind, but the passage remained mercifully empty.

"We're not far from the cells, according to the map," Zhu Irzh said over his shoulder. "Should be there in a minute."

"We'll need to watch out for guards, in that case," Chen reminded him.

But when they came to the cell area, they found that it was not as they had thought. As Chen and Zhu Irzh peered around a gristly outcrop, they saw that the first cells—small cavities in the wall of the Ministry—were decaying. The flesh of which they were formed had turned to a grayish green, with a strong smell of rotting fish. Zhu Irzh wrinkled his elegant nose and Chen clapped a handkerchief to his mouth to prevent himself from retching. There was no one in sight.

"This looks like it's been abandoned, Zhu Irzh," Chen muttered from underneath the handkerchief.

"I think you're right." The demon, followed by Underling No, stepped out from behind the outcrop and began to investigate the cells. "No, there's nothing here." He poked at a thick stain on the floor with the toe of his boot. "I wonder what this was? Or who?"

Chen gave him a curious glance. "Do you think these cells might have digested their occupants?"

"I've seen weirder," the demon replied.

They walked on, leaving the decaying cells behind, and turned a corner. The smell of rot filled the air. Zhu Irzh, in the lead at this point, dodged back behind a column of gristle.

"What is it?" Chen hissed.

"More cells," the demon answered, "but these ones are occupied."

Before he could stop her, Underling No shouldered past Chen and craned around the column.

"I can't see anyone," she said.

"Look. There." The demon pointed. Chen glimpsed a foot, clad in a red velvet slipper. It was motionless.

"I have to see!" Underling No declared, and stepped into the room.

"Wait!" Chen commanded, but it was too late. As soon as No set foot on the floor of the room that contained the cells, a sticky weblike substance fell from the ceiling and enveloped her. Chen felt something long and sharp touch his throat. Turning, he found himself looking along a spear's length into the grass-green insect eyes of one of the guards.

THIRTY

Mrs Pa gave a faint scream. Inari turned to see what had happened, and echoed it.

"Come *on!*"

The black demon skittered over the roof and down to the ground. It bounded along the road toward them, moving on all fours like an ape. With Inari's hand clamped to her arm, Mrs Pa broke into a hobbling run just as a monochrome streak rushed past them and confronted the bounding demon.

"Badger, be careful!" Inari cried but the badger growled only, "*Run.*"

The temple was not far ahead now, but knowing what was behind them made the distance seem like a thousand miles. The badger's growls were terrible but Mrs Pa knew that she and Inari and Precious Dragon were not going to make it. And if she died now, with none of the proper paperwork, slain by a demon, she would go to the place that it came from. At least she would see Mai again, Mrs Pa thought as Inari dragged her along, but then came another dreadful thought: perhaps that was the essence of Hell, for you to know that you were in the same place as your loved ones, and to be unable to find them.

Something flew through the air, a ball of dark, and hit the wall of the temple with a thud. It fell into the surrounding bushes and again Inari cried out: "*Badger!*" Mrs Pa, even used to heavy shopping bags, could not have lifted the badger up in his animal-aspect and yet the pursuing creature had thrown him like a football. She felt a hot breath on the back of her neck and terror made her tear herself free of Inari's grasp, but her foot turned on a stone and her ankle gave way under her. She fell heavily, sprawling on the dusty tarmac. The thing shot over her head: it must have sprung at the instant that she fell and missed her, but now it was between them and the temple.

148

She struggled up. The thing was crouching on its heels in the road. It spun round to face them and she saw again its wet, red grin. But then the temple door opened, with such force that it banged against the white plaster wall, and a voice cried out, "*Stop!*"

It was so loud that for a moment Mrs Pa had a vision of the entire city shuddering to a halt, trams and cars stopping, people arrested in mid-motion, and even the waves ceasing to crash on the shore. Yet the next moment, she wondered whether she had even heard it out loud at all.

Someone was standing in the entrance to the temple. Not a very tall person, or a very imposing one. Someone slight, with a fall of dark hair and eyes that, even from this distance, Mrs Pa could see were blue. He was dressed in an old-fashioned suit, indigo with a Mao collar. He raised a hand.

The demon was still grinning, but it remained in a crouch and Mrs Pa had the impression that there was some huge force pinning it down so that it could not rise. It turned, with painful ponderous slowness, and the figure at the doorway of the temple held out its hand, palm upward.

The creature sprang, bounding toward the temple and as it did so, Mrs Pa saw a young woman come running around the side of the building. She shouted when she saw the thing and immediately it leaped at her. She cried out as it lacerated her throat and in horror Mrs Pa saw her fall. The demon stood up.

"Go back," the figure at the door said. "Go back!" and he turned his palm face downward. At that moment, the demon shrieked, and once more it split, losing all features and becoming a black rent in the air. Storms raged, sending a gust of lightning-scented wind through, into the world of the city. There was a thunderous crack and the demon was gone. The air closed, but it looked jagged and trembling as if with heat, slashed by the demon's passage. The temple stood untouched, in a last glow of evening sunlight, and then the sun slipped beneath the horizon and the shadow of night crept over the temple from the mountains.

At the side of the building, the young woman rose, touched a hand to her slashed, bloodless throat, and sealed the flesh with a movement of her finger.

"You'd better come inside," the figure at the door said.

蛇警探

Out of everything that had happened, Mrs Pa found this the hardest thing to believe: she was sitting in a temple in the city in which she had lived for so many years, being served tea by the son of the Celestial Emperor.

He had not introduced himself as such.

"My name is Mhara," he said. A calm, quiet person, Mrs Pa thought. She'd have liked him if she'd met him on a bus. She liked Robin, too—somehow, she'd have thought that a priestess of the son of Heaven would be different, but this girl looked ordinary, exactly like someone you *might* meet on a bus, come to that, and she was dressed not in flowing robes and a headdress but in cut-off jeans and a blouse. There was now no sign that her throat had recently been ripped out by a denizen of Hell, and she had dressed the cut on the badger's head with the kind of competence that one might have expected of a veterinary assistant, in spite of the badger's growls.

Mhara moved with a deliberateness that was hypnotic to watch. He set the tea down in front of Mrs Pa in a way that was almost ceremonial.

"Thank you," Mrs Pa said faintly.

When he next spoke, Mhara addressed Inari, but he favored Precious Dragon with a very sharp glance, as though he recognized the little boy. Precious Dragon stared back placidly.

"Now," Mhara said. "You'd better tell me what's been going on."

When Inari came to the end of her account, she was knitting her hands together, and again Mrs Pa realized how great a strain Inari had been under, and what a responsibility she had taken on to bring them here: burdening herself with an old woman and a small child, when she could have been sitting on the deck of her houseboat.

"…and I don't know what these things are. They must be some sort of demon, but I've never seen them before," Inari concluded.

Robin shook her head, but Mhara said, "I know what it was. As soon as I saw it, I knew, but I haven't seen such a thing for a very long time."

Robin asked, as curiously as Mrs Pa felt, "What are they, then?"

"They are *kuei*."

Inari's mouth opened in shock. Robin said, "What? Surely not."

"What is a *kuei*?" Mrs Pa asked.

"They are the Storm Lords. They are the beings who carry out the laws of Hell, such as they are. Perhaps it would be more accurate to say that they carry out the whims of Hell's Emperor."

"But a *kuei* is huge," Inari said. "I've seen them. They're like great dragons, centipede-things—*bigger* than dragons. That thing was no bigger than a man."

"They're not allowed to set foot on Earth in their natural form," Mhara explained. "They would be too disruptive. So at Heaven's mandate, they are forced to keep to Hell, and on the very few occasions that they enter the world of Earth, they must take a smaller form. But they still have powers."

"If the *kuei* are after me—" Inari faltered, but Mhara interrupted her.

"Not after you, I think. They're after *him*."

And everyone turned and stared at Precious Dragon.

"I know you," Mhara said. "But who are you? What are you?"

"That's just it," the little boy answered. "I don't know."

"He's my grandson," Mrs Pa said. "He's the son of my daughter, Mai."

"He may have incarnated somehow as your grandson," Mhara said, "but I don't think this is the spirit of a small child."

Mrs Pa kept quiet. She didn't think so, either.

"How did he come here? How did he enter this world?"

"He came through Sulai-Ba," Mrs Pa said. "Through the ruined temple."

"Then I think we should go back to Sulai-Ba."

"We were hoping to seek sanctuary here," Inari said. "If the *kuei* are after us—"

"If the *kuei* are after you, then this won't be a safe place for you."

"But you're the Celestial Emperor's son," Mrs Pa said. She had to bite back the words *young man*. How quickly familiarity came! But Mhara's quiet demeanor did not seem like that of a god. Mind you, from the little she'd actually seen of gods, that might be no bad thing. Mad Senditreya's rampage through the city hadn't impressed anyone.

"I have limited powers. I defeated one of the *kuei*; I don't think I could defeat many of them if they came all at once. You see, my father and I have had a disagreement. We still cherish one another—we are from Heaven, after all. But my father thinks that Heaven should be distancing itself from the human world; he thinks that humans have chosen Hell and taken their own path. And he thinks that if I insist on living on Earth, then I should have a palace where everyone should come and worship me."

"And he doesn't approve of me, either," Robin said. "As you might have gathered earlier on, I'm actually dead."

"Inari told me," Mrs Pa said. "I must say, you look quite healthy for a dead person. But of course I saw—well, your throat. I don't mean to be rude, but if you're dead, what are you doing here?"

Robin grimaced. "Special dispensation. I should have gone to Hell, really—I didn't lead a particularly great life. I used to work at Paugeng, for Jhai Tserai. But for various reasons, I wasn't sent to Hell but I can't enter Heaven either. Or at least, I can, but his family doesn't like me. I'm a human spirit, not a Heavenly princess."

"Ah," Mrs Pa said. "You're not just his priestess, then."

"No, she is not," Mhara said. "But she is much loved."

"Just not by your folks," Robin added. Impatiently, she brushed dark hair back from her brow. "The thing is, Mhara can't really help your grandson, Mrs Pa, unless he knows what your grandson *is*."

"And that's why I suggested we go to Sulai-Ba," Mhara said.

"It's dark now," Robin said. She pushed back the blind and looked outside. "They might come back."

"They'll be at their strongest at dawn and dusk," Mhara said. "That's when the veils between the worlds are at their thinnest and the *kuei* can draw upon Hell for their power. But that doesn't mean to say that they're not dangerous at other times, especially if they act in a pack. It depends how many of them there are."

"I wish I could help," Precious Dragon said, "but I can't."

"Can you remember anything?" Robin asked him.

"I remember being born. And my mother and father, of course, and our house. I think I chose to take this form but I can't remember why."

"People sometimes choose to incarnate as something different in order to hide," Mhara said, with another sharp glance. "To escape from someone who is pursuing them. If the *kuei* are after you, then it's likely you were someone important, and chose to incarnate as a baby so that they wouldn't find you. You'd be hidden by the newness of your form, you see."

"Then who was I?" Precious Dragon was frowning. "I wish I could remember, but—I recall rain. And a thunderstorm. I was outside and on my own, so it must have been before my birth. But that's it."

"You must be exhausted," Robin said to Mrs Pa. "Mhara, they can't go to Sulai-Ba tonight. We'll just have to do the best we can if something comes at dawn—the temple is warded, after all."

"I am so sorry," Mrs Pa told her. She hadn't wanted to make a fuss. "But I don't think I could walk any further tonight."

And so they stayed, enveloped in the thick darkness that surrounded the temple, with the lights of the city seeming very far away.

THIRTY-ONE

The insect guard looked most surprised. Chen couldn't blame her. He'd have looked a little startled, too, if, one minute, he'd been holding a spear to a captive's throat and, the next, had been seized round the head and dragged off into the shadows.

"What the hell?" Zhu Irzh asked, wild-eyed. Chen was already running forward, sweeping Zhu Irzh and Underling No with him.

"Never mind what it was! Do you really want to meet it?" Given the characteristics of the Ministry of Lust thus far, he was having visions of some crevice-dwelling arachnid, a great louse lurking in the moist, rotting walls. Zhu Irzh appeared to agree; after a moment's reflection, he sprinted after Chen, with Underling No creaking along behind.

Another passageway, this time one that opened into a domed atrium. There were cells on the far side of it but Chen did not have time to study them properly: as they entered the room, one of the insect-eyed guards dropped from the ceiling in a flurry of red silk robes. Her eyes were the color of rubies. She carried a long scimitar that whistled around her head with a sound like the north wind.

Underling No gave a tiger-growl. She kicked out and upward at the guard, sending her flying. Another guard dropped from the ceiling and when Chen looked up he saw that there were three more, clinging to the meaty surface of the roof and bouncing gently like mosquitoes. Chen ducked as Zhu Irzh's sword hissed over his head. The sword caught the guard neatly across the abdomen, black guts spilled out and the guard shrieked and shriveled as if sprayed with insecticide. As she blackened and withered, her soul snatched down to the lower levels of Hell, a third guard dropped silently down to take her place. Chen threw a hasty spell: it snapped the guard backward and spun her, twisting her in whirlwind formation until she bored down through the floor in a bloody splash and disappeared. The entire Ministry shuddered and quivered, throwing Chen to one side.

"Must've hurt," Zhu Irzh said, wincing.

Regaining his balance, Chen jumped across the hole and sent another spell glancing upward. It knocked one of the guards from the ceiling, but failed to accomplish any lasting damage. Zhu Irzh stabbed at the guard but she brought her own scimitar round; Zhu Irzh leaped out of the way and the guard wielded the scimitar back and caught Underling No across the chest. No gave a gasping cough and staggered backward.

"No! Are you all right?" Chen shouted, but Underling No was coming forward again, snarling, with a ragged tear across the front of her leather armor. She reminded Chen suddenly of a small, fierce dog. Seizing the guard, No crushed her. The guard gave a startled squeak and was dropped limply through the hole in the floor.

The fourth guard laughed. She undulated toward Zhu Irzh and No, lazily spinning her scimitar. Then, without warning, she struck. Zhu Irzh blocked the blow but the guard was fast; with her second strike, she drove him backward against the wall. Chen sent a spell but it sputtered and fizzled into a small drizzle of ash. No was engaged with the final guard, fighting desperately. They had, Chen thought, saved the best for last. He aimed another spell but he could feel the magic running out of him now, draining away as the Ministry itself began to marshal its decaying resources and issue protection. There was a slapping sound as Zhu Irzh's sword flew from his hand and hit the floor. Flesh oozed over it as the Ministry tried to digest an alien object.

"Hey! Get back here!" Zhu Irzh yelled. The sword pulled and tugged but could not break free. Underling No's swing took the head off the guard she was fighting: it bounced across the floor, lamenting and coughing obscene spells. Sparks flowed out of its mouth and spiraled up into the air, forming a glowing character: the word for death. Chen kicked the head like a football across the annex and it dropped through the hole in the floor, which was now starting to close.

Movement caught Chen's gaze and he saw something sharp and bright sing through the air toward Zhu Irzh and bury itself in the remaining guard's left eye. The guard dropped like a stone, starting to wither and rot before she hit the floor. Someone stepped forward, out of shadow.

Zhu Irzh was staring, open-mouthed.

"What the fuck," he managed to say, "are *you* doing here?"

THIRTY-TWO

Morning burned red in Hell. Pin woke groggily, wondering where he was, and then he remembered. *Oh.* He crawled off the couch and found that Mai was pottering about in the kitchen.

"I've made rice porridge," she said. "Do you want some? Do you think you can eat?"

"I'm not really hungry," Pin told her, but as he spoke he realized that this wasn't true: despite his ghostly form, or perhaps because of it, he was ravenous. "No, wait," he added. "I *will* have some."

Mai placed a bowl in his hand. The porridge itself looked gray and shadowy, but it was surprisingly good.

"I spoke to my husband last night," Mai said. "He told me that there's a remedy man who understands ghosts, but he's not very close to here."

"I think we'll have to risk it," Pin said, although the idea of venturing out into Hell again was horrifying. He fought the impulse to ask Mai if he could just stay here. Forever. "We have to find some sort of solution. Although the other demon tried a remedy man, and he couldn't do anything." A thought struck him. "Where is your husband now? Has he gone to work?" Pin spoke in between mouthfuls of porridge.

"Yes. He's a technician, but not at Epidemics. He works for Malaises."

Pin frowned. "How is that different?"

"Malaises isn't quite so bad. It's a step down, to be honest. He used to work in Epidemics but he refused to do something—they were working on a contagion and he couldn't bring himself to do the experiments they asked him to do." Mai grimaced. "They were horrible, actually. He had to dissect things from the lower levels—everyone says that those sorts of beings can't feel pain, but I know they can, from what my husband said. So he was sacked, and luckily he managed to pick up a job in Malaises, because someone else

155

got fired from there the same week. It's like that in Hell. We say: *dead men's shoes.* That's a little joke, you see."

Pin managed a smile. "I'm sorry about your husband," he said. "But I admire that. I think it was a brave thing to do."

Mai's own smile lit up her sickly face. "I think so, too. That's why I love him," she said. "Have you finished your porridge? Then perhaps we ought to go."

In the brassy light of morning, Mai's part of Hell was run-down and partially ruined, though no worse than some parts of Singapore Three, Pin supposed. An oily canal ran through the backstreets, clogged with rubbish and things that looked dead, but might not have been. Many of the buildings looked like old warehouses, long since derelict and abandoned, their windows lined with broken glass. Some of the roofs were glassy and dripping, as if they had once been melted.

"What happened there?" Pin asked. Mai gave a shrug.

"I don't know. There's been a lot of conflict in Hell—mainly between the Ministries. I think War was trying out a new weapon. They used to do that sometimes before the Emperor made them practice somewhere else. And sometimes they missed."

She fell silent and they walked on, along an alley that led down to the side of the canal.

"I don't like going down here," Mai said. "But we don't have a choice—the other streets were blocked off when one of the buildings collapsed."

"What's wrong with it?" Pin started to ask and then he leaped back. Something was rising from the oily water of the canal: a thing with woman's breasts and an empty gouge where her face should have been. She was covered with glistening black oil but as she rose, the oil oozed away to reveal only the sketchy outline of her form. She held out beseeching, groping hands. Mai motioned Pin back.

"Don't let her touch you! She's a hungry ghost, she wants to eat you."

"With what?" Pin quavered.

There were more of them now, a host of dozens, swarming up from the polluted waters of the canal. Mai and Pin ran, fleeing along the canal side until they reached an alleyway that could lead them up into the city and safety. The water ghosts fell behind.

"They're the spirits of the drowned," Mai explained. She was panting for breath, but Pin had run faster and harder than he'd ever done in his life and he felt no different. "The ones who did not lead good lives."

"What a horrible existence," Pin said.

But as they walked on, in between the wrecked warehouses Pin caught glimpses of a different Hell: little houses, neatly kept, occasionally with a small black lawn and shadowy flowers. And Mai's own home had been better than anything Pin had ever known. Perhaps he *should* just stay here, after all.

He was trying to work out how to say this, and how to ask Mai what she thought, when they turned a corner and Pin saw the red sign of a remedy maker ahead of them.

"There it is," Mai said, pointing. "I think that's the place—yes, it is. Shi's."

Now that they were finally approaching their destination, in spite of the unwelcome attentions of the hungry ghosts, Pin found himself dragging his feet. This was a dreadful place, but he was becoming increasingly unsure that he wanted to go back to his life. Mai, however, did not seem prepared to give him a choice. She ushered him through the door of the remedy shop.

But although the door was open, the shop appeared empty.

"Where is the remedy man?" Mai asked, frowning. She pushed past Pin, leaving him to examine the many fascinating shelves of herbs, roots, insects. In spite of its location, it was very similar to the remedy shops that he had visited with his mother during her desperate, and unsuccessful, quest for a cure. The remedies had been there, but Pin's mother had not been able to afford them, any more than she had been able to afford a hospital bed or, before her illness, the insurance to pay for it. It was, she told Pin, just the way things were.

While Mai went back behind the counter to look for the remedy man, Pin picked up a jar and peered inside it. Something was moving, deep within. He put the jar down hastily—just as well, he thought later, because he would probably have dropped it in response to Mai's shriek.

"Pin!"

Pin ran around the counter in the direction of the shriek and found an open door. It led to what was evidently a storeroom: a dusty place, lined with huge jars. Some of them were cracked and the contents were oozing out over the floor, creating a pungent mélange of odors that Pin was a little surprised at being able to smell. Mai stood in the middle of the floor, looking down at a body.

"Pin—he's *dead*."

"Oh dear," Pin started to say. Unfortunately, this was not the first dead body that he'd seen and it probably wouldn't be the last. He was about to add that these things happened, before he remembered that this wasn't Singapore Three—it was Hell, where you were supposed to be dead already.

"What?" he said. "He can't be." And then, "How can you *tell?*"

"Breathing and pulse are obviously not an option," Mai replied, rather tartly. "Just look at him."

Pin did as he was told and saw that the remedy man was tiny and old, almost mummified. His body was curled around itself. His skin was stretched tightly over the bones of his face and his open, staring eyes were like small black seeds. His mouth was open, the discolored tongue protruding.

"He certainly looks dead," Pin concurred. "But how can he be? This is Hell."

"Exactly," Mai said. Her bloodless face looked even paler. "The only powers here who have the ability to kill those who are already dead—not just send them to the lower levels, which is usually what happens—but to *kill*, are the *kuei*. This means that the *kuei* have been here, Pin." Her voice was a whisper.

"*Have* been here?" Pin asked sharply, because a sudden icy shiver was crawling through him, not just his spine, but his entire shadowy body. He'd once heard that you know if you're about to be struck by lightning, because your body senses the bolt before it comes and tries desperately to escape. This felt as he imagined it to be. "Or still are?"

He saw Mai as if through a sheet of heat. Her mouth opened and he thought he saw her say his name. Then her pale eyes opened wide and she looked up, as though her head was being dragged forcibly back. Pin followed her gaze and wished he hadn't. The dingy roof of the remedy shop was unscrolling like a tin can, revealing a racing storm across the crimson sky. A huge, hot wind poured in through the gap, knocking the bottles from the shelves and sending them rolling and tumbling across the floor. All the dust in the storeroom whirled up into a choking cloud, which took on a vague form of its own, complete with two red eyes. The dust looked upward, wailed, and fled. Mai was shrieking but Pin could barely hear her above the wind. Then his perspective changed, and he saw that what he had considered to be the red eye of the storm was the eye of something huge and living.

The *kuei* opened an immense pincered mouth and emitted a shriveling blast of heat. Mai and Pin ducked behind the fallen jars but Pin felt his essence beginning to unravel, a dreadful tugging sensation. On the other side of it lay nothingness and he knew that his soul was starting to be undone, unpicked from the weave of life and death and dissipated upon the burning air. Mai's hair streamed out from her head and all at once he could see her component atoms, spinning about their nuclei, like the diagram he'd once seen on TV. She was being unmade, too, and he felt grief that he had been responsible for snatching away what little life she had.

The *kuei* opened its mouth once more and Pin, with a last remaining scrap of consciousness, knew that this was the end. Then something cried out, with a vast and desperate love, "*No! You shall not!*"

Beneath Pin, the floor of the remedy shop opened up. He saw limitless chasms below him and then he and Mai were falling, blazing like a pair of comets into the lower levels of Hell. Even with what lay below, Pin had a sudden sense of exhilaration: they were free, they had escaped. But that was before, twisting, he looked up and saw that he'd been mistaken.

The *kuei* was coming, too.

THIRTY-THREE

"Sorry about that," Jhai Tserai said. She was lounging against the opposite wall, absently cleaning the dagger that she'd plucked from the guard's shriveling body. Hell was taking its toll on Jhai, Chen observed with interest. It had brought out her true inner form, her tiger nature, the form that Jhai was so keen to conceal from the human authorities of Singapore Three. There were laws against those of demon stock from holding interests on Earth—not that the regulations couldn't be surpassed by a generous bribe, Chen was sure. But for whatever reason, Jhai had chosen to do things the hard way. She probably enjoyed the risk.

So now the industrialist still regained her elegant sari, her expensive earrings and delicate bangles, but these were accessorized by tiger claws and tiger teeth. Jhai's eyes were a deep dark gold, hidden fire, and stripes shadowed her skin. A tail flickered about her ankles.

"What are you *doing* here?" Zhu Irzh asked. Jhai's sudden, lethal, appearance seemed to have rattled the demon more than anything else on this trip.

"I got bored," Jhai said. "Company's doing its thing, rebuilding is progressing as planned, life was normal. So I thought I'd come and see what *you're* doing."

"Are you checking up on me?" Zhu Irzh said.

"Why? What have you been doing?" Jhai raised a painted eyebrow. "Actually, you don't have to answer that. I pretty much know."

"It doesn't really matter why she's here, does it?" Chen said, hoping to forestall a domestic tiff. "She saved your life."

"Thank you, Detective," Jhai said. "And it's lovely to see you, by the way. We never seem to have enough time to chat." Jhai was always heavy with the charm, but the trouble was that she seemed to mean it.

"Unfortunately, that includes now," Chen said. "We still haven't found Qi and the Ministry knows we're here."

"*You* haven't found your Heavenly friend," Jhai said. "But I have. I took a quick detour while you were hanging about commenting on the décor back there. She's one level down, in a holding cell. It was pretty obvious who she was. That peach blossom smell's a dead giveaway."

"Is she all right?" Chen said, and at the same time Zhu Irzh asked, "Why didn't you free her?"

"Too many guards," Jhai said. "And I don't know whether she's all right or not. She was sitting up and she didn't look pleased."

"We need to get down there," Chen said.

"All right," Jhai agreed with a shrug. "No time like the present, eh?" And with a flick of her tiger tail, she jumped through the hole in the floor. Zhu Irzh, with a curse, started after her.

Following, Chen descended into a passage very similar to the ones through which they had just come, but more dimly lit. Fragments of insect guards littered the floor. As Underling No dropped through the hole, the light from above was abruptly cut off as the hole closed. Jhai led the way down the passage, moving swiftly. Chen and the others followed.

"I can't believe she's bloody here," Zhu Irzh muttered. "She followed me! Can you credit that?"

"She must care more than you think," Chen said. He didn't want to get caught up in a disagreement between Zhu Irzh and Jhai. He had a feeling Jhai might win.

"That's the trouble," Zhu Irzh said.

"I heard that," Jhai remarked, without turning round. She put out a warning hand. "Careful."

It wasn't clear whether she was referring to the present circumstances or to her dispute with Zhu Irzh. They had come to another door, and the sibilance of voices beyond it. Chen checked for magic—an inward turning, a moment of focus—and to his consternation, found none there. The Ministry had blocked him.

"I'm useless, magically," he said quietly to Zhu Irzh. Underling No turned, frowning.

"But you can still fight, yes?"

"Yes, to some extent. I'm trained in Hsing-I. They teach it to the infantry on Earth." No defensive maneuvers, no blocks. Just a fast forward striking, lethal in the right—or the wrong—hands.

"Good," No said with evident relief. Chen wondered what she'd do if she ever met someone who was not capable of fighting. Perhaps she would literally be unable to see them.

"You're going to need it," Jhai said. "I think the Ministry's marshaling its troops. There are at least six guards in there."

"And more on the way," Zhu Irzh said. Just as he spoke, Chen could hear feet running along the corridor behind them. No choice, then.

"In," he said.

Jhai kicked the door open and dived. Inside, something shrieked. Blood, black and sticky, spattered Chen's face as he went in after her. Zhu Irzh brought the scimitar down and around in a sweeping rush and cut two of the guards in half. The whole room stank of sudden rot.

"Detective!" a familiar voice cried. "Seneschal!"

Jhai had been right about one thing, then. They'd found Qi.

"Let me out!" the Celestial demanded. Chen struck a guard hard above the eye, let her crumple. He rushed to the cell and started tearing at the lock, eventually ripping it free from the wall, which began a slow seep of blood.

"Miss Qi, are you all right?"

The Celestial turned to Chen with eyes the color of bruises. A dreadful weight hung over her like a psychic pall.

"No," Miss Qi replied.

But she did not have time to explain further. A guard was on them, stabbing out with a needle dagger. Miss Qi knocked the dagger from her hand, seized the guard by the throat and the jaw, and with careful deliberation, tore off her head.

"Wow," said Jhai, momentarily distracted. "She's not as delicate as she looks, is she?"

Miss Qi gave Jhai Tserai a look of deep disdain. Her usual humility seemed to have disappeared, scoured by recent events. "I am a Celestial warrior. Deal with it."

The guards fell back, and Chen felt a fleeting sense of satisfaction, before realizing why. There wasn't any need for the guards to risk further destruction. More of the insect-eyed women were pouring into the chamber, carrying bows. Chen and his companions were confronted by a ring of glittering arrowheads. The ring split, briefly, to allow a woman to walk through.

She wore rubies. Her hair was as red as blood, as were her slanted eyes and full lips. Her garnet tongue flicked out, thick as a toad's, and the air became dreamy and filled with desire. Chen hadn't been so much at the mercy of his hormones since he was a teenager; he took a deep breath and concentrated on a Zen meditation. Behind him, he heard Jhai give a small snort; Miss Qi was blushing furiously.

"Visitors!" said the Minister of Lust.

蛇警探

Chen had, on a couple of occasions, been invited to parties where someone had tried to kill him. But he'd never found himself facing a swathe of weapons only to be invited to a party. He mentioned this to his companions.

"Believe me, it won't be much of a party," Underling No said bitterly from across the cell. "More like an orgy."

Jhai, lying flat on a bench and to all intents and purposes asleep, murmured, "It might even be entertaining."

"You don't understand," No said. "The only ones doing any entertaining will be us."

Chen could not avoid glancing at Miss Qi, who sat statue-still with her face turned to the wall. He had not yet dared ask what had happened to her.

"Use it as an opportunity," Zhu Irzh said. "We'll be together, presumably, and we'll be free to move about."

"How do you know that?" No demanded. "How do you know they won't tie us up in some kind of bondage session?"

"I don't," Zhu Irzh said, discomfited, "but we have to think positively."

"To be brutally frank," said Chen, "it's hard to think at all around the Minister."

"I'd forgotten that you hadn't met Su Yi," Zhu Irzh said. "She's difficult to deal with. For obvious reasons."

"Well, I don't find her remotely attractive," Jhai said. "All that red is *so* last century. And that sexual magnetism is a well-known trick of the trade—you take pheromonal enhancers to boost your appeal."

"One assumes that you would know?" Underling No said, but politely.

"I would, actually. I come from a long line of Keralan courtesan demons. We know how to big it up, if you'll pardon the expression. Normally, I take suppressants to dim it down: it's not very helpful in the lab. And I don't think it's terribly businesslike, to be honest."

"If that's the case," Chen said, "then is there any more indirect way in which you might be able to fight the Minister? After all, you're not taking the suppressants now, are you?"

"No," Jhai said. She opened her golden eyes and stared at Chen. "That's an interesting suggestion."

"Moving between the worlds changes people," Chen said. "My magic is different down here. Zhu Irzh's abilities alter when he comes to Earth. And it's impossible not to notice that your own inner nature is more strongly aspected, the longer you're here. You're more tiger than you were when I first saw you a while ago."

"It's definitely bringing it out of me," Jhai agreed. "But I'm not losing sentient awareness. I'm still me. And it has a limit, obviously. A few more stripes and I'll be there fully."

Miss Qi turned an arctic face in her direction. Reflecting on it, Chen did not think that Qi's *froideur* was completely due to recent events: Jhai had, after all, been crucially involved in a plot to help Hell overcome Heaven not so long ago. One could hardly blame Miss Qi for not holding Jhai in very high regard.

"A curious aspect for a courtesan," Miss Qi said, "that of a tigress."

Jhai shrugged. "What can I tell you? Keralans must like stroppy, fierce women."

"But is there anything you could do?" Chen persisted.

"I don't know," Jhai said slowly. "I can certainly try. The Minister is a lot more powerful than I am. She's a lot older, for a start."

"What if someone were to distract the Minister?" Chen said. "If you could influence the guards, Jhai…"

Zhu Irzh looked up in alarm. "What do you mean, 'if someone were to distract the Minister'? Like who?"

Chen grinned. "I gather that you are reasonably appealing to the ladies."

"Hang on," Zhu Irzh said. "I'm not coming on to Su Yi."

"You might not have to. She might come on to you." This was not entirely out of the blue; Chen did not think that he had been mistaken in noticing a slightly speculative glint within the inhuman gaze of the Minister of Lust.

"Well, one thing's for certain," Underling No said gloomily. "We have to do *something*. Because either they'll kill us after the orgy, or we'll wish they had."

THIRTY-FOUR

Mrs Pa woke to find that it was morning: not dawn, but full into the day with the sun burning through the blinds of the room in the temple annex and the smell of jasmine drifting through the air like a scented sea.

"Here," Inari's voice said. "I've brought you some tea."

Mrs Pa struggled into wakefulness; she felt as though she'd been asleep for years.

"Precious Dragon—?"

"Precious Dragon woke not long ago and now he's sitting outside with Mhara and Robin. He's quite safe."

"Nothing came in the night?" Mrs Pa questioned.

"Nothing came," Inari reassured her. But in that, Mrs Pa soon discovered, Inari had, unbeknowingly, lied.

They might not have noticed the footprint if Precious Dragon hadn't spotted a bird in the bushes and gone over to look at it. His exclamation of surprise brought Robin running, and caused Mhara to turn his head and walk slowly over. Inari and Mrs Pa, hearing some commotion, rushed outside.

"What is it?" Inari breathed. The footprint was at least eight feet long, a spined, spiked ridge: if it had not been imprinted so clearly in the soft earth around the temple, Mrs Pa might have taken it for erosion.

"It is a *kuei*," Mhara said, crouching down by the footprint and holding out a hand. His face was very grave.

"But how can that be?" Mrs Pa asked, bewildered. "I thought you said they'd taken human size, like the ones we saw."

Mhara's blue gaze came up to meet her own. "I thought they had."

"But if this great big thing was outside, why didn't we hear it? Why didn't it attack us?"

Mhara raised a hand and gestured toward the outer limits of the bushes.

Mrs Pa blinked. A blue glow was visible, the color of a summer sea or an azure sky, perhaps a hundred yards around the perimeter of the temple, just inside the clawed end of the footprint.

"I put this place under heavy wards last night, the strongest that I know," Mhara said. "I've also sent a message to my cousin Kuan Yin and asked for her protection. She is held back in much that she tries to do these days, but I believe she has done *something*, for we were not touched as we slept. I don't think the *kuei* that made this footprint was any larger than the *kuei* that you saw, but it is a message: they are powerful and they are on their way. We need to get to Sulai-Ba, therefore."

"I will do my best," Mrs Pa said. The idea of another long walk made her heart sink. "But I'm afraid that I'll slow you down."

Mhara smiled. "You'll be traveling in a lot more comfort than you did yesterday, Mrs Pa. I've sent for a car."

蛇警探

"Goodness me," Mrs Pa said faintly, when the car arrived.

Mhara had the grace to look embarrassed. "It's not the sort of thing I'd normally choose to travel in," he said, as they stood in front of the gleaming white and silver limousine. It was at least twenty feet in length. "I'm afraid it's the kind of official vehicle that Heaven thinks I should have, as the son of the Emperor."

"What sort of car do *you* think you should have?" Mrs Pa asked

"Something small that runs on ecological fuel. Or a bicycle. My Heavenly clan is living in the past, you see. They're much too grand."

"Perhaps you should ask for a bicycle."

"I did. They sent me this."

"Oh dear," Mrs Pa said, but secretly she was rather impressed by the big car. At least they could get everyone in it, although Robin stayed behind to look after the temple in Mhara's absence. Mrs Pa worried about that, but then again, Robin couldn't actually be killed and that was encouraging. Neither could Inari, who was also staying behind, at Mhara's insistence. She had wanted to come, but the Emperor's son said that it would be better if they went alone to Sulai-Ba, because the *kuei* were more likely to follow them there. But even though Inari could not be slain, she could still be sent back to Hell, and Mrs Pa worried about that, too.

Precious Dragon sat with Mrs Pa in the second row of seats in the limousine. The back rows stretched behind them, fading into dimness. The limo seemed much longer from the inside than it did even from without, and the rows of seats made Mrs Pa uneasy, as though she might look back and see something suddenly sitting there.

Then Mhara joined her in a flurry of indigo garments.

"Who is driving?" Mrs Pa wondered aloud. But as she spoke, a shadowy form appeared in the driver's seat and a beautiful face looked calmly back at them. Mrs Pa couldn't tell whether it was a man or a woman, nor how old it was. It had pale golden eyes and white hair, but its face was unlined. Of course, it must be from Heaven, and things were different there. Mrs Pa felt a sharp pang, a sensation familiar to her in the years after Mai's death. This is where Mai should have been, not Hell. The thought of everything that had been denied to her daughter made her heartsick. *You cannot let yourself be bitter,* she thought. *Look what has come of that old mistake,* and she turned her gaze to her grandson instead. The pearl made a small bulge in his cheek.

"Are you all right, Grandma?" Precious Dragon asked, with that penetrating gaze, and she lied as she answered, "Why yes, I'm fine."

Doors closing, said the limo. The driver put a gloved hand on the wheel and they glided out into the suburbs toward the city center. This was much better than walking. Mrs Pa was even able to enjoy the view of the passing shops; normally, she did not have the time to look, but as the limo sped toward Sulai-Ba down long, tree-lined boulevards she marveled at the chic designer clothes in artful boutiques, the well-dressed people sitting at pavement cafés over long, cool drinks. That was the sort of life that her employers enjoyed. It must be nice, she thought. But none of them had a grandson as marvelous as Precious Dragon, and none of them was riding in a limousine with the son of the Emperor of Heaven. The life of an elderly cleaner was not without incident, after all.

They passed the Opera, which looked far more splendid than Mrs Pa remembered, and then the beautiful designer homes in the district just beyond Sulai-Ba, finally drawing to a halt in a neat little street in front of a small park. Hibiscus blossoms blazed red in a hedge and jasmine spilled down onto the sidewalk.

"We'll have to walk from here," Mhara said. "There isn't room for the car around Sulai-Ba itself. Can you manage, Mrs Pa?"

"I'll be fine," Mrs Pa said. Mhara helped her out of the car, just as the Celestial chauffeur melted away.

The street was really quite run-down, and several of the houses were boarded up and derelict. Litter was strewn about the sidewalk. The lawns of the little park were yellow and dusty in the heat; the jasmine shriveled and wilting. Only the hibiscus still blazed redly in the hedge.

"That," Mhara said quietly, following her gaze, "is another reason why I'm not keen on using the car. It—changes things."

He led them through the little park. Mrs Pa sighed. It had been such a wonderful city, and yet it had all been illusion. She'd once heard that the Buddha had made a similar journey when he was still a human prince; his father had made sure that he saw only the most beautiful things along the way, sweeping the beggars aside. Then the Buddha had realized how things really were and renounced all his wealth. It seemed Mhara had similar views and she respected him all the more for that. She could see now why he'd been so keen on a bicycle.

"We're not far from Sulai-Ba," Mhara said, clearly wanting to reassure Mrs Pa. But her blisters had healed overnight, and the walk was not nearly as painful as it had been on the previous day, even though she was still stiff. Besides, she could see the ruined temple now above the heat-bleached trees, the shattered roof rising in a dark arc over the city. She reached out and took Precious Dragon by the hand, not knowing what else they might find inside the vaults of Sulai-Ba.

THIRTY-FIVE

Pin thought that he was never going to stop falling. He twisted and turned in the air until it was almost relaxing, traveling down through the dimly glimpsed layers of Hell like someone in an elevator, passing different floors. He saw lands that were nothing but windswept iron plains, lands that were all fire, with volcanoes spurting sparks the size of stars. A million hands reached out, beseeching, but it was too late: Pin had passed.

Below him, Mai also fell, downward like a leaf with her skirt billowing out around her. Occasionally, she waved. Pin thought that she was trying to keep his spirits up.

And above them, the *kuei* also fell. It was far enough behind that Pin could see the entire serpentine-centipede shape of its length, the thousand legs like metal pilings, and the huge curving jaws at its head. Its visible eye rolled frantically in crimson panic, and it roared so loudly that Pin was soon deafened and could hear nothing at all. After a while, he noticed that the *kuei* looked smaller, diminished, but he thought that this must just mean that it had slowed down and was further away.

Down and down. And finally Pin realized that there was a limit to Hell after all and it was coming up fast. Unlike some of the levels they had passed, this was a bright land, a sandy expanse. Pin caught sight of ragged yellow mountains and then a canyon. He hit the sand at maximum velocity, was splattered out across a mile or so. This was painless, but bewildering, with only a tiny scrap of consciousness remaining, and then there was an even more confused period during which he reassembled. Mai was struggling up between the rocks a short distance away. There was no sign of the *kuei* at all.

"Pin," Mai shouted. Her voice sounded reedy and distorted. "Are you all right?"

Pin fought back hysterical laughter. "What do you mean, 'all right'? I've just fallen into the depths of Hell and exploded."

"Well," Mai said shakily, as she approached him. She did not walk, but moved with an odd gliding motion, her feet not quite touching the ground. "You look much the same as you did upstairs, if that's any comfort."

"So do you," said Pin. He looked around. This place seemed more like Earth than the city above; the sky a brassy gold, the yellow mountains and thick, sticky earth. Like somewhere in the depths of China, perhaps. Pin had the sense of great age. "What happened to the *kuei*?" he asked.

Mai shook her head. "I don't know. Didn't you think it was getting smaller as we fell? It looked like it to me."

"Me, too," said Pin, "But I thought it might just be slowing down."

Mai looked dubious. "I don't know. Perhaps you're right. Maybe it got stuck on one of the levels above us. I hope so."

"I hope so, too," Pin said, shuddering. The memory of that centipedal shape twisting and writhing through the skies of Hell was one that he'd far rather forget. But even worse was the dawning understanding of what had happened to them. "Mai, what are we going to *do*? Look at this place. There's nothing here. Do you know where we are?"

Mai's face was contorted with dismay. "I think I do know, Pin. This is the bottom of Hell. It's where everything else came from—this is the distant past, not just another level, and it's where the rest of Hell came from—where it grew out of. As for nothing being here, I'm afraid that the legends disagree with that. It's where the first demons came from, too." She ran a hand through her disheveled hair. "There's one thing, though—in every level, including this one, there's a place where you can move between the levels themselves. We can go back up."

"Even given what's waiting for us?"

Mai sighed. "I don't know what else to do, Pin. The *kuei* are after us and they'll find us eventually. We can either stay here or try to run. I'd rather run."

"Then I'll come with you," Pin said.

There was no plant life in this part of Hell, just pools of oozing yellow mud that occasionally emitted a sulphurous geyser, and the endless, stony earth. Pin had never seen a bleaker place. They trudged on toward the mountains, which seemed to grow no closer no matter how much they walked. There were some benefits, however: Pin did not feel hungry, and neither did his feet hurt—like Mai's, they did not seem to want to touch the ground.

Gradually, the brassy sky darkened and an ominous night fell over the canyon.

"I think we should stop," Mai said uneasily.

"Are you tired?" Pin asked. He did not feel that he would sleep; it was as though the descent had sent him into even more of a state of limbo than he had been previously.

"No, I'm not," Mai replied, "but I have the feeling that there might be things that come out during the night that we haven't seen during the day."

"Even if they do," Pin said in despair, "We can't fight them off. We've got no weapons." The hungry water ghosts had been bad enough and that was in the upper level of Hell. He told himself that Mai might be wrong, that they'd seen nothing so far and that really did mean that nothing was there, but he could not believe in his own reassurances.

"We'll just have to hope that they won't bother with us," Mai said, but as she spoke a blood curdling yell came from the rocks above them.

"What was that?" Pin whispered.

"Oh Pin," said Mai, "Let's just hide."

They found a crack between two large boulders and crouched inside it. It did not afford much protection but any was better than none. The yell came again and something large bounded down the canyon wall and past the boulders. The sky was dark now, but a dim yellow glow came from the rocks of the canyon and when Mai wonderingly held out her hand, Pin saw that it, too, was glowing. He looked down and found that he was lit up like a beacon.

"It's like radiation," Mai exclaimed.

So was the thing that had gone past them. It was larger than a human, though it moved upright and wore a flapping cloak, and it had a narrow, pointed head. It was sleek and quick, moving with lizard speed against the rocks.

"Do you think it's seen us?" Pin hissed.

"I hope not."

But Mai was wrong. Next moment, the thing turned. It leaped up the canyon, covering six feet or more with each spring, until it was crouching at the entrance to the crack, directly in front of Pin. Its eyes were like boiling yellow fire. Mai and Pin both screamed. The demon's jaws snapped open and it spat. A sticky web shot out, enveloping both Pin and Mai in its folds. The thing seized a handful of its web and, without any discernible effort, threw the web with Pin and Mai in it over its shoulder and strode off.

THIRTY-SIX

The guards let him keep his original clothes, which was a substantial relief to Chen when he discovered what Zhu Irzh had been given to wear. The demon, who had been led out of the cell half an hour previously along with Jhai, returned in what Chen assumed to be standard male harem attire. He was bare-chested, with a satin cape attached around his neck and a pair of billowing silk trousers. He also wore an expression of extreme distaste.

"This is so cheesy."

Chen thought of making a snide remark and decided against it, purely on the grounds of kindness. "Yes, it is," he said.

"I don't see why I have to wear this, and you don't."

"I suspect that Underling No, Miss Qi, and myself are required to appear in our actual roles," Chen said. "My humiliation will probably have more of an impact if I'm in my working gear."

"You're right," Miss Qi said. "That's what they expected of me, when it was my turn."

Silently, Chen berated himself for behaving like a coward. He'd pretended to himself that he was being sensitive, but in fact, he just could not bear to learn of what had befallen Miss Qi. But now, with Jhai still absent, he felt that he had no choice but to ask.

"Miss Qi, I am so sorry to ask, and I understand that you must have had a harrowing time and loss of face. But what exactly happened to you?"

"I was not raped, if that is your concern," Miss Qi said, and at this Chen released a breath he did not know he had been holding. "I was taken into a—they called it a party but you were right, it was an orgy. I thought it would be horrible, decadent, and disgusting. But at first everything seemed very civilized. The Minister and her demons sat around drinking tea and talking. About the weather and such. All of them were female and that made me feel a little more comfortable. They invited me to sit down and I did so. Then one of the demons handed me a cup of tea. I thought it might be poisoned, but they were all looking at me and I thought that if I refused to drink it, they might force it on me and that would be worse: at least if I drank it myself I still had some degree of control, if that makes sense." Her voice was stilted and hoarse, hinting at either an iron willpower, or impending breakdown.

"Perfectly," said Underling No. "It's what I myself would have done."

"Nothing happened at first," Miss Qi said. "They all went on talking and I just listened, but gradually I became aware that I was experiencing—" She stopped. "I'm sorry. This is very difficult."

"We understand," Chen said.

"I'm not sure if you do, Detective. I have known desire before, but relationships are not encouraged among warriors and therefore I suppressed it; it was easy enough to do. We are taught to maintain our purity and it is little hardship to do so, in Heaven. But all too clearly, this is not Heaven. I looked at Su Yi and I wanted her as I have never wanted anyone. My desire grew stronger and stronger until it was like a bursting wave in me and I threw myself at the Minister's feet and begged her to—" the control was faltering "—to make love to me. She refused. I'm sure you can appreciate how humiliating this has all been."

"Miss Qi," Chen said, "I'm so sorry."

"Su Yi really is the proverbial bitch from Hell," Zhu Irzh remarked.

"I'll help you kill her, if you want," was No's contribution.

"They all laughed at me," Miss Qi went on. "After that, the Minister ignored me, but I could not seem to stop myself, I pawed at her clothing like a dog and eventually she said to one of the guards that since I clearly couldn't control myself during a genteel tea party, I should be taken away. They brought me back here and shut me in."

"If it's any consolation, Qi, this is what the Minister does," Zhu Irzh said. "You heard that conversation about pheromones. It's how she controls people."

"I am a warrior of Heaven," Miss Qi said. "I have been through experiences requiring great fortitude and endurance, and I have always come through. But this demon has reduced me to a quivering wreck with the aid of a few biochemicals. I should make it clear—it is not the fact that she is female that revolts me. Love between women, or between men, can be a pure thing. It was that she controlled me so easily. If she's done so once, she can do so again."

"She could do it to any of us," Chen said, "except perhaps Jhai and that's why I'm counting on her."

As if on cue, Jhai appeared. She was naked apart from a golden thong. Her tigress aspects had come even more to the fore and despite her nakedness, she was so striped that she looked almost dressed. Miss Qi looked away, but

Jhai appeared unconcerned by her unclad state.

"Suits you, darling," Zhu Irzh said. Jhai shot him a grim gilded glance.

"You, too, Aladdin."

"Please," Chen said wearily. He looked through the bars of the cell to where the guards were congregating on the other side of the room. "We need a battle plan."

"We *need* one," Jhai agreed, "but I'm not sure whether we can *formulate* one until we actually get in there."

"It should be simple," Zhu Irzh said. "One of us can distract the Minister with our manifold charms and the rest of us will overpower the guards."

"I have a feeling," Jhai said, "that it just isn't going to work that way."

蛇警探

Jhai was right. A few minutes later, they were led from the cell and down a short passageway into what turned out to be the main hall. Chen could not work out the inner configuration of the Ministry: it was as though the building was turning around on itself in some painful contortion.

And it was immediately clear that this was to be no tea party.

The hall was filled with demons, most of them naked and some of them already engaged in acts that made even Chen, who had seen many things during his career with the police force, look away. Miss Qi gave an audible gasp.

"It's like something out of Hieronymus Bosch," Chen said.

"Who?" Zhu Irzh frowned.

In the middle of the hall, the Minister reclined upon a divan. She, too, was naked apart from her fall of red hair.

"At least the carpet matches the curtains," Zhu Irzh remarked.

"Zhu Irzh, please," said Chen. "Heaven forbid that I should ever be a prude, but I've experienced quite enough crudity for the moment."

Jhai gave Zhu Irzh a nudge. "You even think about trying something with one of these trollops and you'll be as dead as a demon can be."

"Darling," Zhu Irzh replied, "at the moment, quite frankly, it's hard to think about anything else."

Chen saw Jhai repress a grin. She strolled forward, to where Su Yi reclined.

"Hello," she said, hands behind her back. "We met a little while ago. I'm Jhai Tserai."

"I know who you are," the Minister said. "What are you doing in my Ministry?"

"I came to check up on my boyfriend," Jhai said.

"I see." The words fell from the Minister's ruby lips like little stones, yet Chen had the impression that she was not unamused by Jhai's answer. "I did not know," the Minister said next, "that you had demon blood."

"Not many people do," Jhai replied.

"That might be useful. If you live."

"Su Yi, I have every intention of living and if you're thinking about black-mail, forget it. I have connections in the Hindu Hells and believe me, not even you want to mess with them."

"Ah, but you see," the Minister purred, "I'm not without connections there myself. One does *have* a social life, you know."

"Besides," Jhai went on as if the Minister had not spoken. "I'm thinking of coming out of the closet when I get back home. After all, it's so important to have *authenticity,* don't you think? I've never approved of living a lie."

The trouble was, Chen thought, that Jhai almost certainly believed what she was saying.

"You're really quite attractive," Su Yi said. She was now eyeing Jhai with a different kind of speculation. Over the Minister's shoulder, a conga-line of copulation was forming. Given the lithe sinuousness of the women, not to mention the fact that he had a head start in sleeping with demons anyway, Chen was slightly surprised that he was not more aroused. Perhaps it was the jaded weariness on the demons' faces as they engaged in their yogic eroticism that was putting him off, or maybe it was the memory of Inari, who though naturally a modest person, could be startlingly inventive once the bedroom door was closed. Whatever the reason for it, he was grateful. It helped him to think.

"Thanks," Jhai said. "It's the stripes."

The Minister rose and undulated over to where Jhai stood. Demons or no demons, not even Chen was immune to Su Yi. He found himself literally unable to take his eyes away from her. The Minister wound her arms around Jhai's neck. Jhai grinned with tiger teeth. An expression of mingled chagrin and consternation crossed Su Yi's lovely face and then it was Jhai who was gasping and stumbling forward. She regained her balance almost immediately but it was the Minister's turn to smile.

Then Jhai reached out and drew a delicately clawed finger between Su Yi's breasts. A thin trickle of black blood followed and the Minister sighed. Her crimson eyes half-closed and she swayed forward.

"Su Yi," Chen heard Jhai murmur. "Why don't we get rid of all these people?"

"But darling," Su Yi said. "I *always* have an audience."

"Time you tried something new, then," Jhai said, and kissed the Minister on the mouth. Chen had to drag his gaze away; it was that embarrassing. Zhu Irzh's eyes were like saucers, Chen could see him mentally racking up different possibilities. Miss Qi's face was almost as red as the Minister's hair but there was a kind of fierceness in her expression, the look of a woman presented with a real chance of revenge.

Chen stared at the opposite wall, beyond the columns, in an effort not to look at the Minister and Jhai. But then he saw something that effectively distracted him from any thought of lust.

Someone was standing in the shadows, a crimson-clad form, lithe and strong. It was familiar, too, and when the figure shifted a little and its angular features fell briefly beneath the light, Chen understood why. The figure was Zhu Irzh's sister, Daisy. Chen nudged the demon.

"Zhu Irzh! Look!"

The demon took some distracting, but finally he glanced up, just as Daisy moved back into the shadows. But Zhu Irzh had seen.

"That's my sister!"

"Yes, and did you see what she was wearing?"

Zhu Irzh gave a grim nod. "Looks like Daisy's our girl for the kidnapping."

Chen frowned. He wasn't sure whether Daisy would have had time to bolt back after her mother's birthday banquet in order to stage a principal part in the kidnapping of Miss Qi.

Daisy melted back behind the pillars. She must have seen her brother, but there had been no change in expression that Chen had been able to discern, which suggested to him that Daisy was already fully aware of the course of events: more evidence of complicity, in Chen's eyes. He glanced reluctantly back at the scenario before him. As Jhai took the Minister in her arms and swung Su Yi around, Miss Qi raised a hand. Chen thought at first that she was merely gesturing, in horror, perhaps, but then he saw long, glistening claws, the color of pearls, slide out from beneath Miss Qi's fingertips. Before the guard at her side could stop her, or Chen offer a word of caution, Miss Qi stepped swiftly forward, sliced out with her pearl-clawed hand, and tore out the Minister's spine.

"Bloody hell!" Zhu Irzh said, appropriately enough. Black ichor fountained over the floor, over Jhai, over the guards, who stood as if paralyzed. Su Yi flopped to the floor and lay twisting and gasping like a dying fish. Miss Qi let the spine fall to the floor with a gristly rustle.

"No, don't let it go!" Jhai yelled. Chen, fighting severe revulsion, dived at the spine at the same time as one of the guards. They collided and Chen punched her as hard as he could in the face. She fell back, clutching her jaw, and Chen seized the spine.

"Come on!" he shouted, and made a run for the entrance to the passage. But the floor of the Ministry heaved like the deck of a ship and threw him to the ground. He did not let go of the spine, but it was close. The guards, the copulating demons, stood where they had last been, frozen. Only the Minister moved, in increasingly rapid convulsions. The Ministry mirrored her movements, bucking and twisting. Above Chen, a large lump of meat became detached from the ceiling and plummeted downward, narrowly missing him. Zhu Irzh grabbed him by the arm and hauled him upright. Together, they dashed for the exit, followed by Miss Qi and the others. Zhu Irzh, with unusual chivalry, shoved Jhai ahead of him.

"I can manage, thank you!" she shouted back, and her flying tiger feet made short work of the passage and Chen did his best to keep up with her.

"Miss Qi! Are you all right?"

"Yes! *Much* better now!" the Celestial called back. Not a very Heavenly thing to do, ripping out someone's spine, but then she had been born to battle demons and Heaven knew, she'd had a lot to put up with recently.

When Chen looked back, Zhu Irzh was nowhere to be seen. Where had the demon gone? Jhai, registering that Chen had stopped, doubled back.

"What's the matter?"

"Zhu Irzh."

"Shit!" Jhai paused, indecisively. "Look, you go ahead. I'll go and look for him."

"I don't think that's—" Chen started to say, but at that moment, Zhu Irzh reappeared around the corner at a run, carrying something flapping and dark.

"You went back for your *coat?*" Jhai said. "You really are the vainest man I've ever met."

"There's something in it," Zhu Irzh said, and Chen was reminded that the demon still carried his grandfather's heart.

"Is it in there?" Chen asked him in an undertone as they raced along.

"Yeah, they didn't bother to search the pockets. Sloppy lot, the Min of Lust."

The passage, however, was closing in on them, the fleshy walls seeping blood and making the floor increasingly slippery. As Chen turned a corner, he heard a wet thump behind him and glanced back to see Miss Qi struggling over a bulwark of fallen flesh. He reached out a hand and pulled her through. The claws were no longer in evidence.

They ran back through the phallic gorge, the fungi now drooping in impotent purple clusters. Back through the first passage, which was now narrowed and stinking. As they neared the exit, Zhu Irzh dived into an alcove with an exclamation, and returned with someone, gripped firmly by the hair.

"Let go of me!" Daisy hissed, clawing and spitting.

"Who the hell's that?" Jhai said.

"Jhai, darling? Meet my sister." Zhu Irzh punched Daisy straight in the face and slung her over his shoulder.

And then, finally, they were out into what, for Hell, passed for fresher air. It was close to night. The parklands behind the Ministry were peaceful beneath a turbulent red sky. Chen, panting, stopped and looked back.

The Ministry's bulbous efflorescence was slowly collapsing in upon itself like a slowly deflating balloon. It stank as it collapsed, hissing rancid air into the already pungent twilight. It reminded Chen of some enormous, noxious fungus, the kind you come across unexpectedly in a damp portion of forest, that releases its spores with a stink and a sigh when you poke it with your toe. Chen felt a distinct sense of triumph as he watched the Ministry of Lust detumesce into a boiling mass of flesh. He wondered whether matters on Earth would be any different as a result. The Ministry's collapse represented no loss. But the sight of Minister Su Yi, writhing about on the floor with a bloody channel running where her spine had once been would, Chen knew, stay with him for too long a time. He looked down at the thing in his hand, the long curve of bone, the knobbled, bloody vertebrae.

"Well, congratulations," Zhu Irzh said, still in his ridiculous harem outfit. Dropping Daisy unceremoniously onto the ground, he twitched off the cape and threw it at Chen, a covering for the Minister's spine. Then he searched pockets that weren't there, finally remembering to rummage in his rescued coat. That didn't seem to satisfy him, either. "This is the second time you've been personally involved in the demolition of an entire ministry. I'm going to have to buy more cigarettes. And I want my sword back. I'll look for it later, in whatever's left. Assuming we've not been arrested by then."

But what Chen said in return was, "Where's Underling No?"

THIRTY-SEVEN

"So," Zhu Irzh said, some while later. "We've not only managed to destroy another Ministry and fatally wound a governmental minister; we've also lost an employee of the Ministry of War. They *will* be pleased." They were grouped in the demon's hotel room. Zhu Irzh had effected a change of clothes from his own luggage; Jhai had improvised a bedspread as a sari. Her tigress accessories seemed to have diminished somewhat. Su Yi's spine, wrapped in the ridiculous cape, lay on the floor at their feet. Occasionally, it twitched, a convulsive movement like the tail of a cat, mirrored by the still unconscious form of Daisy.

"Underling No came with us of her own accord," Chen said. "Not that I expect War not to make as much political capital out of it as they can."

"I am very sorry," Miss Qi said. Her ethereal features were crumpled with distress, which in Chen's eyes was an improvement on the frozen glaze of a few hours before. Qi, he thought, and not for the first time, was a lot tougher than she looked. "I had some regard for Underling No."

"I bet she stayed behind to look for her mum," Zhu Irzh said. "It's why she came with us, after all."

"Do you think," Jhai said slowly, "that Su Yi will really be missed?"

"I don't even know where she'll go," Chen said. "What happens when that sort of thing—well, happens to a person? You'd go to the lower levels, wouldn't you?"

"Usually," Zhu Irzh said. "But Su Yi's a minister. And she was assaulted by a Celestial. For very good reasons," he added hastily, "but it's really going to complicate matters. I'm surprised we haven't been picked up already. The Ministry of War won't offer any further support, for the reasons they gave us."

"I am prepared to stand trial," Miss Qi said. She raised her chin defiantly.

"If necessary, I'll take full responsibility. I shall make sure that everyone understands that I was acting on my own initiative, while the rest of you were being held prisoner."

"This is Hell, dear," Zhu Irzh said. "No one's going to care whether we were really involved or not, they'll just prosecute us anyway."

"Perhaps I could bribe someone," Jhai said.

"Not even you are rich enough to put forward the kind of money Hell would want for this," Chen said. "But it's a generous offer."

"What happened to 'you have to act with authenticity'?" Zhu Irzh asked.

"I *am* acting with authenticity."

At this point, Daisy began to stir. Miss Qi eyed her with distaste. "I cannot be certain," the Celestial said, "but I believe that is one of the people who kidnapped me."

"Daisy's always had an eye to the main chance," Zhu Irzh said. He gave his sister a little push with his foot. As he did so, she blurred. A second Daisy appeared a few feet away.

"Well," Jhai said. "Looks like your sister's got some magic of her own."

Zhu Irzh snorted. "It'll be borrowed, you can be sure of that." He leaned over the unconscious girl and shook her. The second Daisy shimmered and was gone. "Daisy! Wake up!"

Daisy stirred again, moaned, hauled herself upright against the bed. "What—?" She looked up at her brother. "You *fucker*, Irzh."

"You're a fine one to talk," Zhu Irzh retorted. "I'm not the one who's been in the pay of the Minister of Lust, am I? What were you, Daze, some kind of hired help?"

Daisy spat out a small, glowing coal that sizzled a burn in the carpet. "Screw you. While you've been swanning off on Earth, Irzh, *I've* been the one trying to keep the family together in the face of Mother's treachery."

"Daisy, what are you talking about?"

"The Ministry of War, Irzh, is what I'm talking about. Remember Granddad's coup? I suppose you were very clever, getting hold of the old bastard's heart like that. But Mum's been trying to stage a coup of her own."

"I think you'd better explain," Chen said, quietly, but his tone seemed to reach Daisy in a way that her brother's antagonism had not. Something like fright glittered across her face.

"A while ago, not very long, something happened down here in Hell. I don't know what it was, but it caused no end of a stir. Suddenly the *kuei* were everywhere, asking all manner of questions—of everyone, even respectable families. People became very frightened. The Emperor hasn't done much for years, and suddenly, all this activity and interest."

"Like stirring a hornet's nest," Chen said.

"And then a whole section of the *kuei* disappeared. Went to Earth, to that city of yours. Looking for something, or someone. Mum got the wind up. She was really shady about what she was doing, but eventually I found out—stupid bitch had been playing politics and attracted the attention of the *kuei*. When they went to Earth, she and a bunch of other people held a séance—can you believe?—tried to summon up a human spirit to find out what was going on. They managed to finish off the first one, some little girl from the Opera—her spirit ended up in Lust, that's how I know all this. Then they tried to get hold of someone else and Mum ended up being possessed—what a mess."

"Those men at the party," Jhai said. "I *thought* they were gate-crashing."

"So mother is involved in a plot," Zhu Irzh said. "Why does that not surprise me?"

Jhai snorted. "Sounds like *my* mother."

"Are you saying," Chen said slowly, "that your mother has been involved in some kind of anti-Imperial coup?"

Daisy nodded.

"Like I said," her brother remarked, "doesn't surprise me. Mother's always been ambitious. And if she was stupid enough to attract the attention of the *kuei,* then the Minister of War's the only one powerful enough to protect her. And possibly not even then."

"About my kidnapping," Miss Qi said. Frostily, she drew herself up.

"All right, I'll admit it," Daisy said, very sullen. "I've been trying to get hold of Grandfather's heart for a while, in case Mum tried to do something stupid with it. Then you got hold of it, and I panicked. I cast a replica of myself at the banquet and arranged the snatch."

"But you seemed surprised to see me," Zhu Irzh said. "You must have known we were here, along with Miss Qi."

Daisy spat out another coal. "Of course I knew. I started keeping tabs on you when we first found out you were coming to Hell."

"Which raises the question," Chen said, "as to why we were invited." Chaperones to Miss Qi, to make sure she was granted passage? A legitimate excuse, for War to bring a Celestial down to Hell? What had been planned for Miss Qi?

"I think this robs us of any real support from War," Miss Qi said. "Detective Inspector Chen, we have to leave. I have been through enough."

Chen agreed. "If we can," he said. But when they opened the curtains, they found out the answer to that.

蛇警探

"My gods," Jhai said, staring out over the hotel parkland. "There's a lot of it, isn't there?"

"Reminds me of Beijing, on military day," Chen said as they watched the tanks roll past. The parkland, which previously had been almost pleasant, was now a wasteland of churned mud and clouds of dust, thrown up by the tank treads. Like the other engines of destruction that they had seen on the plain, the machines were much larger than their human equivalents. Chen had no idea whether the hotel management had been consulted on the sudden transformation of their gardens into a military test site; one assumed that they hadn't. The tanks rolled over what was left of the Ministry of Lust and left bloody smears of flesh behind, trampled into the soil. Hell was a better place for the destruction of the Ministry, in Chen's opinion, but he also wondered what the repercussions were going to be.

Overhead, aircraft of proportionately massive size thundered along, leaving billowing fumes in their wake. There were hundreds of machines, both aircraft and infantry, a rolling panoply of military might that moved through the heart of the city.

"What prompted all this?" Chen asked. "Surely not the destruction of Lust?"

"It would be helpful if we still had Underling No," Zhu Irzh said. "Assuming she'd tell us. But they've been building up to this for a long time. Remember what we saw inside the Ministry of War? Those planes? Something's been on the go for a while."

"Told you so," Daisy said.

Someone hammered on the door, making Miss Qi leap.

"What is it?" shouted Zhu Irzh. "We're in a meeting."

"For gods' sake," Jhai muttered. "That's not going to put them off, is it?"

But a voice said, "Oh, sorry! We'll come back later, then."

Zhu Irzh turned to Jhai and was about to say something, but next moment, the entire door burst inward in a shower of splintered wood, and the Lesser Lord of the Ministry of War appeared in the gap, holding a weapon like a howitzer.

"You lot," the Lesser Lord said with remarkable cheerfulness, "are coming with me."

THIRTY-EIGHT

Pin and Mai's demonic captor loped across the yellow plain for what seemed like hours. Pin, bonded uncomfortably to the sticky web, eventually drifted into a kind of doze that was closer to unconsciousness. Beside him, Mai's head also drooped and caught against the net.

When Pin came round again, he saw that the sky above them was beginning to lighten, but this time it was boiling with cloud, a yellow-gray billow, moving fast. Then the demon turned and Pin saw that it wasn't cloud at all, but smoke, roaring out of the chimney of a sprawling factory.

"What is *that?*" Mai whispered.

The factory covered the floor of a wide valley. Pin saw great derricks reaching out of the soil, gouts of flame shooting out of refinery chimneys, and huge open containers in which fires blazed. The churn and pound of industrial processes filled the air. It was like an amalgamation of every heavy industry that Pin could imagine: mining, steelworks, oil refineries....

Soon, they came upon the freight rail: a group of sweating, panting demons, their skin burned and cracked to black, pulling a cart behind them. The cart was loaded with yellow ore.

"Pin," Mai whispered. "Remember how we glowed? I think this might be some kind of uranium mine."

"In Hell?" Pin asked, but then he thought: *Where else?*

The demon strode alongside the track. More and more carts were coming out of the mine, all of them heavily loaded.

"Where are they going?" Pin asked.

"I don't know. I've never heard of such a place even being here. I thought this level was empty."

"Silence!" the demon said in a voice as thick as the yellow earth. "Your chatter is annoying me."

Pin and Mai shut up. They were moving between the chimneys now and it was difficult to see what lay ahead, with the smoke pouring out into the already soupy air. Then the air cleared a little and Pin saw that they had entered a compound: an ordinary looking place, like any of the hastily erected warehouses and office sheds that appeared so readily in Singapore Three. The demon walked straight into one of the office sheds without knocking and threw the net down on the floor.

"Couple more for you."

"Thanks, Oshi," a voice said. "Where'd you find them?"

Footsteps approached. Squinting up, Pin saw a squat demon in a leather apron, with tough yellow skin and a flat head, as though someone had sat on it. Pendulous breasts, however, proclaimed the demon's gender.

"Out in the desert," Oshi said.

"Whatever were they doing there? These are ghosts." The new demon bent close over Pin and sniffed. "No, wait. This one is not even dead. Odd."

"Is that so?" Oshi sounded only mildly surprised. "All sorts of shit finds its way down here. You know that."

"Curious." The demon stood. "Undo the net, Oshi, if you would."

Oshi stretched out a hand and the net unwound itself and flowed back up the demon's arm beneath the skin, forming alarming twists and bulges. Then it disappeared. Oshi shook himself like a dog.

"I am Foreperson Tung," the squat female demon said to Pin and Mai. "You're to be placed on cart detail and kitchen; we're short a couple of workers."

"What happened?" Oshi said.

"They ran off into the desert last night. They won't get far." Tung gave a snuffling laugh. "There's nowhere to go from here, after all. They'll be demoted to toilet detail when they get back, though. Get up, you two."

Mai and Pin did as they were instructed. It was surprising, Pin thought bitterly, how stiff you could become even when you didn't have a proper body. He stifled a grunt of pain.

"Never mind!" Tung said, clapping him on the shoulder. "You'll soon get fit. It's not a bad life for a lad down here. You'll soon work your way up through the ranks. You might even make Foreperson someday! And you," she turned to Mai. "Can you cook?"

"Yes."

"Good. We have provisions sent down by elevator from the upper levels, so you'll actually have something to cook with, you'll be pleased to hear."

"Tell me," Mai said. "What is this place?"

"This?" the Foreperson looked surprised. "Why, this is the feed-mine for the Lowest Level Nuclear Plant. We power the whole of Hell."

"Hell runs on nuclear power?" Pin asked blankly.

"What else? Where do you think your electricity comes from?"

"I thought it might be magic," Pin said.

Tung roared with laughter. "Magic! That's a good one. I'll have a laugh today about that—wait till I tell the lads! No, Hell used to run on woodburners in the old days, then coal, then steam. But now we're fully modernized and up-to-date under the Ministry of Industry. Who do you think introduced atomic power to Earth?"

And thinking about it, Pin supposed that was logical.

蛇警探

The next few days passed in a routine that was almost peaceable. Pin had never undertaken hard physical labor before now, unless one counted prostitution, although the routines of the Opera could be rigorous. He wondered occasionally whether he would have held up so well if he'd still been in his actual human flesh, now who knew where. He suspected that he would not. Here, in this incorporeal form, he rarely suffered from tiredness or hunger, except in moments of a curious ravenousness that had to be assuaged in the kitchen. He could not bruise or bleed, although strangely, he still seemed to sweat. The worst thing about lugging the ore-laden carts from the feed mine through the gap in the mountains to the plant itself was the tedium, but given that his life had been somewhat too exciting so far, Pin didn't mind this. He kept to himself and the demons with whom he worked were undemanding company, enjoying a joke and a bit of a laugh. Given a choice between the kind of teasing favored by Maiden Ming—now also who knew where—and the demons, Pin found that he had a marked preference for the latter: they chuckled when he fell over or dropped something, rather than making spiteful remarks that stung like needles, and quite often they'd give him a friendly slap on the back afterward. He didn't miss the artistic temperament, either; at the mine, people woke up and got on with their work rather than indulging in endless personal dramas which ran for weeks and ended in a blazing row. In ways, Pin thought, he wouldn't have minded staying here all that much, had it not been for his guilt about Mai and his worries about the *kuei*.

They still had not seen the *kuei* that had fallen with them through Hell, and Pin was beginning to hope that Mai was right, that it had become trapped on one of the higher levels and had given up. But the thought of it still nagged him at night, and sometimes he dreamed of centipedes.

He caught sight of Mai occasionally in the kitchens, but she was always busy. It was clear that he was not exactly a prisoner, however, so one evening, Pin went to the kitchen doors and sought her out. She was scrubbing dishes vigorously.

"Hello, Mai," Pin said.

"Pin!" She gave him a thin smile. "How are you getting on?"

"All right," Pin said with a shrug. "I don't mind it, to be honest. How's the kitchen?"

"Much the same as any kitchen. Prepare food, cook food, serve food, clean up after food. It's not as interesting as Epidemics but I've always enjoyed cooking and they certainly appreciate it. And you don't get the politics. To be honest, the worst thing about it is that I miss Ahn and talking to my mum. I'd really like to know how my son's getting on—I worry about him dreadfully."

"I'm sure your mother is looking after him," Pin said.

"She will if she can," Mai said doubtfully, "but she's old and if the *kuei* are after me—I can't stop thinking about it, Pin."

"You've heard nothing about the *kuei* that came after us?" Pin asked.

"No, and I have made enquiries. I spoke to Tung, who's not a bad old sort. I didn't say why I wanted to know, just that there had been rumors in the kitchen. She said she hadn't heard of anything but there's all kinds of shit out in the desert and maybe it had been one of the oldest demons, from the far past. They're very big, apparently, but very slow and they're afraid of the plant so they don't come near it."

"So we've heard nothing of the *kuei*," Pin said. "Well, that's good."

But it was not long before they did.

THIRTY-NINE

"I hope you don't take this personally," the Lesser Lord said, as he and a group of warriors ushered Chen and the others through the corridors of the hotel. "As you've probably noticed, we've got a few things on our plate at the moment. But I've been instructed to take you into custody over the little matter of the destruction of the Ministry of Lust. Not that I'm concerned about that myself, you understand. Good job! Thorough infiltration, no messing about, straight to the heart of the matter, and what I understand was a very effective surgical strike. The Minister's undergoing medical care right now, having a new spinal column grown for her, but she won't be Minister again after this debacle. And that's not a bad thing, in my view. We've got her spine, thanks to you, and that means that if we need to work some antithetical magic with it, we can. So jolly well done all round."

"I'm not with them!" Daisy said. "I'm an employee of Lust!"

"Not anymore," the Lesser Lord pointed out.

"You seem," Chen said to him, "to be remarkably well-informed about all this."

"Underling No, you see. Very efficient young woman. Of course, I've had to place her on a reprimand for unauthorized activity but under the circumstances it's not much more than a slap on the wrist. When she and her mother escaped from the collapsing Ministry, they came straight back to War and submitted a full report. No's mother's a wreck, of course. Won't hold office again."

"At least No found her," Miss Qi said. "I'm glad."

"She was very complimentary about your input," the Lesser Lord said. "I don't suppose you'd like to consider a move sideways? Or in this case, downward? Of course, given your attempted assassination of a government official, we'd have to keep quiet about it for a bit, but I'm sure we'd manage to get round the problem somehow."

"I don't think I could," Miss Qi said. "But it's very kind of you to offer." She managed to sound almost regretful, to Chen's admiring ears.

"Lesser Lord," Chen said. "What exactly is in store for us?"

"I'll have to take you with me, except the young lady from Lust—she's due for custody," the Lesser Lord replied, over Daisy's protest. "Can't risk you escaping." He gave Chen a jovial clout on the back. "Might come back to find War in ruins, eh? No, we're instructed to get the battle over and done with and then bring you back up to stand trial. Might be no more than a formality. Possibly."

"What battle?" Jhai said.

By this time, they had passed through the foyer of the hotel and out into what remained of the gardens. The air was choking with tank fumes and dirt, but when he looked up, Chen saw something that froze his blood.

There weren't just planes in the sky. Above the level of the aircraft, distant and yet still huge, writhed the forms of the *kuei*. Chen had seen them before, but only singly, never in such numbers. There must have been dozens of them. As Chen watched, one of the smaller craft cruised a little too high and a wingtip touched the trailing leg of one of the Storm Lords. The plane flipped over, spun, and dived, out of control, toward the ground. There was the distant crump of an explosion and a column of fiery smoke rose from the cityscape.

"Damn," the Lesser Lord said, wincing. "That's twice this morning."

"About this battle," Jhai said, in tones of ice.

"Ah, yes. You asked. Well, look above you. The *kuei* are out in strength. What does that tell you about who they will be fighting?"

"Something big?" Chen said. He felt as though he was back in the classroom.

"Correct! Today is the day that Hell goes to war with Heaven. The *kuei* will be defending us against dragons."

蛇警探

"Zhu Irzh," said Chen, a little later. "Do you know where this battle is going to be? How they plan to enter Heaven?" Despite the joviality of the Lesser Lord, he had bound their hands and had them loaded into an army truck, which was now bouncing and jolting across the plain at the very edge of the city.

"No, I don't," Zhu Irzh said. He leaned over and nudged the bored guard, a demon in an ill-fitting tin hat with a cigarette in its loose-lipped mouth, with his shoulder. "How about you? Where are we going?"

"The lower levels, s'far as I know."

"Hang on," Chen said. "That doesn't make sense. How do you expect to gain access to Heaven from there?"

The guard stared at him. "We're not going to Heaven."

"But the Lesser Lord said the battle would be with Heaven's forces."

"Yeah, it is, but we're not going there, are we? They're coming to us, see. They're the ones doing the invading."

"What?" Miss Qi said. "That's not possible."

"Sorry, love, but the alert came a few weeks ago that this was on the cards, hence the buildup. Heaven's planning to strike at the very heart of Hell. Way I heard it, they're sick of dealing with humanity, don't want to dirty their precious Celestial hands anymore with nasty demons either, so they're going to destroy Hell and let the humans stew. No offense, miss. I can see you're one of them but I know you're just a grunt, like me."

Miss Qi appeared too stunned to speak. Chen had a hard time believing this as well, but it tied in rather too neatly with what he had recently learned about Heaven's changing policies.

"But if Hell goes," Zhu Irzh said, "and I *have* got family here, even if I despise them, and a home, even if I hate it, but quite apart from all that—what happens to humans who die?"

"They won't," Jhai said. "They'll either not die at all—which isn't great news, given how fast the population of Earth is increasing, or they'll have to convert to some other religion which, one presumes, won't be affected by this—or they'll die and just shuffle about like zombies. Whatever happens, it'll cause havoc. You'll get people converting the other way, because they've got terminal bloody cancer and they don't want to end up in the Christian Hell, or the Hindu one, or whatever."

"I just can't believe Heaven could do this," Miss Qi said. Her modest friendliness had now entirely disappeared and along with it her traumatized aloofness of the previous day. She looked as close to tears as Chen had seen her.

"Unfortunately," Chen said, "I do. The son of the Celestial Emperor is a personal friend, not that I like to name-drop, and he's not all that happy with the way things have been going. Neither is Kuan Yin."

"It's the Emperor's say-so, though, isn't it?" Jhai said. "Heaven's a dictatorship. A benevolent one, but still a dictatorship. What the Emperor says, goes."

"But that's dreadful," Miss Qi said.

"If you're starting to consider the Lesser Lord's job offer, I'd go for it," Jhai said. She looked appraisingly at Miss Qi. "If you don't like the idea of living in Hell, I could offer you work as a bodyguard. Frankly, the idea's beginning to grow on me."

"I—I don't know," Miss Qi said. "I've never thought of living anywhere other than Heaven, or doing any other kind of work."

"Decent pension? Not that it'll worry you, you're an immortal. I could find you a really nice apartment, great pay..."

"Do you think," Chen said, "that you might want to wait until we actually survive before you start debating terms of employment?"

"It's a thought," Jhai said. "But you know, Detective, I always work on the principle that survival is a given in my case. Otherwise I'd never do anything."

"I wouldn't take it as a given right now," Zhu Irzh said, craning his neck out of the blowing tarpaulin that made up the side of the truck. "Not when you see what's happening."

Chen squirmed over until he could look past the demon's head.

"Dear merciful Heaven," he said, even as it struck him that this might be an unfortunate choice of words right now.

The world was opening up. In front of the convoy, which lay along a colossal sloping plain several miles distant, was a black hollow, a void in the heart of Hell. The convoy was pouring into it like a column of ants through a gap in the soil, flowing onward without pause.

"The lower levels, mate," the guard said, taking a last drag on his cigarette and tossing the burning stub out of the truck. "Told you that's where we're going."

There was silence after that. Jhai appeared reflective, chewing her lower lip between teeth that were still slightly tigroid, until a drop of blood oozed out. She flicked it away with her tongue and went on chewing; Chen was sure that she was plotting something. He hoped it wasn't anything too rash, but with Jhai, one never knew. Zhu Irzh stared at his boots and Miss Qi seemed to return to being traumatized, although Chen couldn't blame her. He sat tight in his seat in the truck and waited for Hell to drop away.

FORTY

Mrs Pa was relieved when they reached Sulai-Ba, although this time they were coming through the back entrance rather than the front steps. It brought back a strong feeling of déjà vu, although last time she had been to the temple, to collect Precious Dragon, there had been that odd detached sense of dreaming. And now it was as though everything was hyper-real: the dome of Sulai-Ba etched against the sky in sharp relief, iron-gray against morning gold. She felt that she had lost track of the time, somehow, that it should be evening, or a different season. She had been cast adrift on the world and she was glad that Mhara was there. Apart from Precious Dragon himself, Mhara seemed more real than anything else.

"What do we do now?" she said to Mhara, who was waiting for her to catch up.

"We go inside." He put out a hand and steadied her. "Are you all right?"

"I'll be fine," Mrs Pa told him, "as long as Precious Dragon is."

"Grandmother?" the little boy said. His eyes were round. "I'm starting to remember things."

"What sort of things, Precious Dragon?" Mrs Pa said.

"Clouds. And storms. Having to make a choice. But I don't know what it was."

"Do you still want to go back in here?" Mrs Pa asked. Now that they were actually standing before Sulai-Ba, with the iron wall of the temple rearing up over their heads to the broken dome, she suddenly thought: *What if he goes away?* He had come to this world through Sulai-Ba, after all, Mai's child from Hell. What if this whole strange and uncomfortable journey was no more than the mechanism to send him back where he belonged? She was about to voice her doubts to Mhara when Precious Dragon swung around and looked at something beyond her, something behind—and Mrs Pa looked, too, and saw a sight that made her mind up with lightening speed, for the blackened avatars of the *kuei* were standing there, in broad morning sunlight, eleven of them in a row and grinning red.

Mhara said, "Go. Go now, I'll hold them as long as I can."

Mrs Pa hesitated, but only for a moment. Then she clutched Precious Dragon by the hand and dragged him as quickly as she could up the back steps to the temple entrance. The door was ajar. With a last look back at the *kuei,* she forced her way in, shoving Precious Dragon ahead of her. Then she slammed the door shut with all her strength. The last glimpse she had of the outside world was of Mhara on the steps, a blue-clad figure drawing the powers of daylight into himself, as the *kuei* closed in.

蛇醫探

Inside the temple, it was calm and quiet, just as before. Mrs Pa and Precious Dragon did not stop, but ran through the vaults, past rows of skulls on top of enormous jars, past strange skeins of what might have been moss. In one of the vast inner chambers they came across something that resembled a shed skin, still faintly gleaming ivory and blue: scales skimming across the stone floor in a slippery mass. Precious Dragon stared at it and Mrs Pa had to pull him away.

After a little time, they found themselves on the bank of a canal. There was no way across and it looked dark and deep.

"What are we going to do, Precious Dragon?" Mrs Pa whispered. She cast a fearful look over her shoulder, expecting to see the shadows of the *kuei* slink around the corner, but nothing was there. The temple was silent, echoing with the lapping of water.

"I—remember something. Down here."

Precious Dragon led Mrs Pa through a small, cramped entrance. "I've been here before," the boy whispered.

Mrs Pa was about to say that this was surely where she had collected Precious Dragon that first time, from the skeleton of whatever beast had lain here, for the columns of the vault looked the same. But then she saw that the floor was empty; there was no skeleton here.

"This is the place," Precious Dragon said with conviction.

"Which place is that?" Mrs Pa asked. Precious Dragon pointed.

"Look."

There was the statue of a dragon on a pedestal in the far corner of the room. An Imperial dragon, with whiskers and open mouth and bulging eyes, rearing up on two stout hind legs and holding up a clawed paw. The paw was empty.

"That's it," Precious Dragon whispered.

As he spoke, something rustled at the door through which they had come. Mrs Pa turned and her heart dropped. A *kuei* was crouching in the entrance, with one hand placed on the ground. Its lensed head swung to and fro, but the lenses were fixed on Precious Dragon.

"Grandson?" Mrs Pa said.

"We'll find out, won't we." Precious Dragon said, in response to a question that she had not asked, and he ran forward. The *kuei* opened its red mouth and gave a weird whistling cry. Another bounded through the entrance to crouch beside it. Mrs Pa put her hand to her mouth, too frightened to even scream. Precious Dragon clambered up the pedestal but he could not reach the statue's empty paw.

"Grandma!"

Mrs Pa had not known that she could move so swiftly. She picked Precious Dragon up in her arms and hoisted him high enough to reach the claws of the dragon. The *kuei* moved, as if her own motion had broken whatever spell they were under, but as they bounded forward, Precious Dragon spat the pearl into his hand and placed it between the dragon's claws.

Time stopped. Mrs Pa looked directly down into the storm-riven eyes of the *kuei*. Out of the corner of her eye she saw the dragon and her grandson blur, whirring as swiftly as a hummingbird's wings as they merged. She cried out. Precious Dragon vanished, as completely as if he had never been. But the stone dragon was coming alive, stretching, roaring, growing, and seething, down from the pedestal toward the *kuei*.

The *kuei* shrieked. Roiling clouds of darkness boiled out of the lenses of their eyes and enveloped Mrs Pa. Blindly, she groped out and touched something cool and scaled and huge, that still somehow reminded her of a small child. She clutched at it and found herself falling forward, over the top of a round, hard surface. There was a snarling roar and a sudden iron smell. Thousands of legs stretched out over Mrs Pa's head as the *kuei* shot above her, and she ducked down onto the dragon's back, hanging on for dear life. The clouds cleared. Mrs Pa was carried up high beneath the ceiling of Sulai-Ba, the stone floor a dizzying span far below. The *kuei* were gone, the vault filled with coiling centipedal forms, bigger than anything she had ever seen, and that was when the floor of the temple gave way.

FORTY-ONE

The dragons were the last of Heaven's warriors to leave their home, and of the dragons, Embar Dea was the last to go. She did not think she would see Cloud Kingdom again. The Mother of Dragons had once told her that you can feel your death approaching, and Embar Dea did not think it would be long now. But it was an honorable way to go: to battle the *kuei,* ancient enemies of dragonkind. The *kuei* were planning to invade Heaven, so Prince Rish had been informed by the Emperor; they must strike first.

The older a dragon becomes, the closer it draws to the truth. Rish was too young, but as soon as Embar Dea heard this, she knew it to be a lie. It surprised her, that the Celestial Emperor should lie to his oldest allies, but then such things had happened before. So she went to Rish and told him.

The Prince was silent for a long time after Embar Dea had spoken. They were alone in the great mist-filled hall of the Cloud Palace, the seat of the Dragon Kings. An opalescent light swirled through it, like liquid pearl, concealing the old dragon and the young.

"Do you believe me?" Embar Dea said in a moment of terrible doubt, for it had also been known for old dragons to go mad.

"I believe you," Rish said, slowly. "Of course. But what are we to do about it? This kingdom was granted to us thousands of years ago by Heaven, it is the only place in all the worlds where we can build a home. Hell won't have us, because of the *kuei* and the old enmities. Earth will not—they would hunt us down and exhibit us in zoos, you know that. And we are too big for the pastures and orchards of Heaven. If the Emperor takes Cloud Kingdom away from us, then where are we to go?"

"We should not be under the mandate of another," Embar Dea hissed in frustration.

"Indeed we should not. And yet, we are. Embar Dea, you are the oldest of us all and I have great respect for you—" and here Prince Rish, to Embar Dea's embarrassment, bowed his great head "—but you were born in a time when politics was not so important, when China respected Heaven and when dragons were honored within it. Now the world of humans has forgotten us and Heaven is closing in upon itself and only Hell is still the same, or so it sometimes seems to me."

"So you are saying that we must do as the Emperor asks," Embar Dea said. She sighed, and the mist rose and sparkled at the touch of her breath. "Then I will go with you."

蛇警探

And now she was flying at the end of the great skein of dragons pouring out from Cloud Kingdom. She did not look back; there was little point. Instead, she stared straight ahead, at the golden, the green, the scarlet, all manner of dragons, with the silver-black shape of Prince Rish at their head. Embar Dea knew there had been lamenting, that the King of All Dragons was no longer there to lead them, but times were different now. She flew on.

Cloud Kingdom fell away into the soft, clear light of Heaven. Embar Dea looked down and saw fields and rolling hills below, small temples on summits, rocky crags with pouring waterfalls. A wild, yet managed, land, mirroring China itself. They flew over a wall, snaking across the hillsides, and soon they came to a great plume of water cascading down a mountainside that marked the start of the river that on Earth was known as the Yangtze. As they flew on, it widened, until the landscape beneath them was recognizably populated with small cottages, large mansions, orchards filled with blossom and fruit and the faint light of floating stars. Embar Dea looked ahead and saw the edge of the Sea of Night, a dark line in the distance, and before it lay the Eternal City, with its fortress walls and its palaces.

Around the city gathered the troops of Heaven, mounted on unicorns and lion-dogs and deer. Beyond them, were immense engines: catapults and creaking wheeled citadels. Hell had tanks and guns, Heaven had arrows and bows, yet Embar Dea knew that, somehow, they were equally matched. Heaven had a strong, clear magic; she wondered whether this was still the case, or whether it now carried undercurrents and shadows, the betraying trails of secrets and lies.

The lion-dogs raised their chrysanthemum heads and roared as the dragons flew overhead, the sound reverberating out from the city walls and causing, somewhere, a ringing sound like a gong. Moments later, as they came in sight of the Imperial Palace, Embar Dea realized that it was indeed a gong: a circle of bronze the size of a house, situated at the summit of the citadel itself. It was the signal for the descent into Hell.

FORTY-TWO

The truck containing Chen and the others trundled forward toward the lip of the chasm, picking up speed as it did so. Even Jhai's normally shuttered face wore an expression of alarm, which Chen was sure mirrored his own countenance. Miss Qi looked simply resolute.

"Here we go," said the guard, and there was a sudden lurching sensation, rather like a plane taking off, except that the nose of the truck dipped slightly instead of rising. Chen, unable to hold onto the sides of the truck because his hands were still bound, and reluctant to place faith in the rather frayed old seatbelt that circled his waist, could not hold back the thought that they might all fall out. Given that he, at least, was human and still alive, the thought was not an appealing one. He tried to wedge himself as tightly as possible against Zhu Irzh, and the demon seemed to understand what he was doing.

He need not, however, have worried. The descent was jerky, but it did not feel as though they were plummeting. Looking out the sides of the truck, Chen saw that they were part of a huge convoy of falling vehicles. A tank drifted past, made of red iron and covered with graffiti and images of devilish faces. A picture of a scantily clad female demon adorned its engine casing. Beyond, where Chen could dimly glimpse a fiery shore, a jet hurtled downward, nose-diving into Hell's heart. The air was filled with the sound of humming engines.

"Are we nearly there yet?" Zhu Irzh asked. Chen suppressed the momentary urge to strangle him. Perhaps it was a good thing that his hands were still bound.

"Dunno," said the guard. "ETA was supposed to be seven P.M. upper level time but nothing ever happens on time round here."

"It's four now," Zhu Irzh said, squinting at the watch on his bound wrist. "Three more hours of this. Great."

195

"At least there's a view," Jhai said, but negated her own words by closing her eyes and leaning back against the seat. Chen admired her fortitude.

"I had not thought," Miss Qi mused bitterly, "to see so much of Hell."

Something jumped against Chen's arm and made him start.

"What was that?"

"Sorry," Zhu Irzh said. "Think something just bit me." He shot Chen a warning glance and Chen realized what it was that had moved: the heart in its container, still stashed in the inside breast pocket of Zhu Irzh's coat.

"Don't worry about it," Chen said. "Made me jump, that's all."

"Lot of insects on some of them levels," the guard said, not without sympathy. The nose of the truck tilted and Chen looked downward through the flapping tarpaulin. The convoy stretched out below, growing more ragged now as they descended. There was no sign of any ground.

FORTY-THREE

Pin was asleep when the alarm sounded. It was so loud that it felt as though he'd been picked up and slammed against a wall. He sat up with all the normal physiological reactions of shock: heart hammering, head pounding, sweat icy down his spine, before he remembered that he didn't actually possess a body. It didn't seem to make much difference at this particular point. The dormitory was a seething turmoil of startled demons. The crew was not the most organized group of people at the best of times and this sudden incursion threw them into complete chaos.

"Shut it!" Forceperson Tung yelled, barreling in through the door, pendulous breasts swinging unappealingly from side to side. "Get yourselves together!"

"What's going on?" someone shouted.

"The plant is under attack," Tung said.

"What?"

"I didn't hear anything!"

"Why weren't we told?"

"You weren't told because we've only just had the communication. Heaven's army is on its way."

Pin's imaginary heart leaped at this. If Heaven's warriors were coming, then perhaps he stood a chance of being rescued. But why would they bother? And did he really want to be rescued?

Demons clamored and lamented at Tung's words and Pin felt suddenly very sorry for them. They were a decent bunch, as demons went, and they had their own little lives here, just as he had. His sympathy was followed by a flood of anger: What right did Heaven have, to come in and disrupt everything? But that was the way of it everywhere: there you were, getting on with things, minding your own business, and suddenly some arsehole

197

decides to start a war.

"Look, calm down!" Tung shouted. "You're not on your own. Hell's forces are coming. They'll reach us before Heaven does. They'll protect us—they can't afford to let this plant be shut down. If it does, then Hell itself shuts down and we might as well all pack up and shuffle off the Wheel. Just bleeding *think,* for a change."

A slight sigh of relief spread through the room.

"What are we going to do then?" someone asked.

"That's better," Tung said. "That's more like it! We've had clear instructions, for a change. You're to stay put, and go where you're told in order to defend the plant if necessary and keep an eye on things. So we want everyone on a cart and out of this compound."

"What if they *do* blow up the plant?" came a voice.

"Okay, it won't be pleasant. It'll get a bit hot. But think about it—you won't die. You can't even be sent to the lower levels, because you're *in* the lower levels. So you'll probably have a nasty couple of hours and then that will be it, and we'll have to see what Heaven does with us at the end of it. We're at war now."

With the rest of the crew, Pin piled onto a cart and, within minutes, they were hurtling out of the rail gates of the compound toward the mountains. He wished he'd had time to say goodbye to Mai; he hoped she'd be all right. But there simply hadn't been a moment.

It was still dark. Behind the hurtling cart, the railway tracks glowed bright against the desert earth and the compound and the mine were outlined in a sickly, glimmering radiance. It was lit up like a bloody beacon, Pin thought in dismay. Unless some form of magic could be utilized, Heaven could hardly miss it.

The cart shot through the mountain gap, rattling between the now-familiar rocky outcrops, and down toward the plant. More carts were coming fast behind, propelled by frantic demons, and more lay ahead, thundering down the slope and into the compound of the nuclear plant itself. Minutes later, Pin's cart joined them. Immediately, he was ushered off the cart and up to one of the big observation towers that stood on the four corners of the plant, there to stand guard with the rest of the crew. Below, the plant was a hive of activity, demons scurrying to and fro like insects. He looked anxiously up, but saw nothing, only the dim vastness of the sky. Might as well sit down, Pin thought, and did so.

Toward dawn, Pin was once more roused from a doze, this time by a shout.

"Something's coming!" A demon clambered to her feet and pointed.

This time, the sky was not empty. Its bronze expanse was filled with tiny specks that grew rapidly larger.

"What are they?" Pin asked.

"Planes!"

Moments later, the air above the plant was filled with hurtling jets, shrieking overhead and across the mountains. They dispersed quickly, then regrouped above the mountain wall to fly in tight formation, circling the basin of the valley in which the plant stood. They were followed by the infantry, tanks and trucks which shot past the plant and then, just before they hit the ground, slowed down, landing with a series of thuds and puffs of dust all across the plain. Within the hour, the plain was filled with grinding, trundling columns of vehicles, moving slowly into position until they formed rings around the plant itself. Pin had never imagined such an army: it looked as though the whole of Hell had been militarized.

Then, he saw that the rings of trucks were parting slightly, leaving a low track that led directly to the plant. An enormous tank advanced down the track, with a kind of awning on top in which two people sat. Both were demons. One was a huge being, armored, bristling with weapons like a lobster. It had the face of a lizard.

The other was female and, despite the heat, wearing a fur coat. Her face was pinched and bitter, sour as an old plum, but she still managed to radiate a faint air of pride.

"Workers!" the bristling demon shouted, through a loudhailer. "I am the Minister of War! As you know, Hell is under an unprovoked and unjustified attack by the forces of the Celestial Emperor. This plant is, as you also know, crucial to the smooth running of the kingdoms of the Emperor of Hell and we shall not let it fall. Keep to your posts and let the army do its work. Don't be afraid! If you look above you, you will see that the strongest forces of Hell are there, about to battle for your safety."

And when Pin again looked up, he saw that the skies were gristly with the multiple legs of the *kuei*. Somehow, he did not find the sight reassuring. But perhaps it did not matter, for beyond the *kuei*, he could now see a glowing mass falling slowly down the sky. The forces of Heaven were coming.

FORTY-FOUR

"What the fuck is my mum doing on a battlefield?" Zhu Irzh said.

Jhai gave him a wary glance. *"That's* your *mother?"*

"Yeah, she ditched my dad, threw him out of the house, and started seeing the Minister of War. I forgot to tell you. In all the excitement and that."

"And I thought my family was dysfunctional," Jhai sighed. They were still sitting in the truck, still bound. The tank containing the Minister of War and his consort had just rumbled by, heading for the industrial plant that, so Zhu Irzh had recently informed Chen, formed the main power source for the whole of Hell.

Chen leaned to one side and spoke urgently to Zhu Irzh. The guard had shuffled down from the truck by now and was having a quiet cigarette over by the side of a tank.

"I'm not at all keen on being captive while there's a battle going on. We won't even be able to make a run for it."

"I agree," Zhu Irzh said, and the women also nodded. "I couldn't do it while that guard was watching, but if you move round…"

Chen did so. He felt the demon's sharp claws sawing against his wrist and then a sudden sensation of freedom.

"Good. Thanks."

Meanwhile, Miss Qi had freed Jhai. Chen felt at a distinct disadvantage, with ordinary human fingernails. He did a cautious inner check, assessing the status of his own magic. Down here, furthest away from the home of the goddess Kuan Yin, the original source of his powers, the magic had dwindled to no more than a thin trickle, like the faintest source of moisture in the depths of the desert. A human among demons, Chen knew that he was worse than useless.

But he still possessed cunning. Better than nothing, wherever you found yourself.

Zhu Irzh gave him a nudge. "Look up there."

Chen did so and, had he known it, had the same experience as Pin on the watchtower: the *kuei,* and the glow and gleam of Heaven beyond.

"Do you think there's any chance of Kuan Yin putting in an appearance?" Zhu Irzh asked.

"I don't know whether any of the gods will be coming themselves or whether they're relying on the army," Chen said, but Miss Qi added:

"No, she won't. I heard before I left Heaven that she had gone into retreat and was not expected to emerge for several weeks."

"Lying low because she doesn't go along with the Emperor's plans," Zhu Irzh said. "Can't blame her."

"Neither can I, but she's the one person who might have been able to help me out," Chen said.

"Never mind," the demon replied. "You'll just have to rely on us."

FORTY-FIVE

Still flying at the end of the formation of dragons, Embar Dea dived low, keeping in the center of the void that led down through the levels of Hell. Rish had instructed them to keep close to the middle, rather than the edges, where missiles might be aimed at them from the Hellish shores.

Embar Dea's doubts had been burned away on the dive, as Heaven fell far behind and a crack opened up in the Sea of Night to let the Celestial armies through. Embar Dea had one last glimpse of Earth, serene and blue from this great height, half-concealed behind the veil that separated the worlds and that no radar or other human equipment would ever show. The moon, at which Embar Dea had often gazed, was even less clear, hidden behind a bright smear of light, its own magical field. Then they were through the veil again and flying down toward Hell. They were not, Embar Dea knew, doing the right thing, and yet it was the thing that had to be done.

Now, she could see the land that lay at Hell's floor, wrinkled and yellow like a beach from which the tide has only just drawn back. They were so high that Embar Dea knew that the sandy ridge was a mountain range, the hole, tiny enough to have been made by a child's toe, was in fact a colossal crater, and that the little sandworm coils above the surface of that sand were the *kuei*, flying between the dragons and the troops of Hell's Emperor.

At the sight of the *kuei*, Embar Dea's whiskers bristled and her mouth opened in an old, involuntary cry of war. The *kuei*: bred to fight dragons—bred, some said, *from* dragons, in one of Hell's unnatural experiments eons ago when monsters roamed the human world itself. Embar Dea's cry was picked up and echoed by Rish and the others and it circled the walls of Hell, reverberating in a dreadful consuming howl.

"Dive!" commanded Rish. "Dive!" and they went down and down, arrowing toward the waiting coils of the *kuei*.

FORTY-SIX

"Grandson!" cried Mrs Pa. "Where are we?" She was hanging on for dear life to one of the streaming whiskers at the back of Precious Dragon's remarkably transformed head. It seemed somewhat inappropriate to address this huge beast as *Grandson,* but what else could she call him? One minute, he had been that strange, placid small boy, and the next, he was something else entirely.

But a rumbling voice came back all the same. "I don't know."

It was a very uncertain place. Dark, but shot with roils and curls of color, which billowed like clouds in a chemical experiment. Yet unlike smoke, they passed straight through solid objects like a kind of light, without taste or sensation or smell. And it was echoing with odd sounds that were like the booming of distant machinery. There was no sign of the transformed *kuei,* and that was a substantial relief to Mrs Pa.

"I am flying," Precious Dragon's rumbling voice said. "Hold on!"

The dragon's four legs shot out, claws extended. He was the color of metal, Mrs Pa saw: gold and copper and bronze, with a gleaming ruff of scales that was almost a dark green. He turned his head and revealed a vast fiery eye.

"Where are you going?" Mrs Pa asked. She did as he had instructed, and clung on. Seizing one of the thinnest whiskers, she wrapped it around her waist and tied it tightly.

"Down. The air is pulling me down."

But Mrs Pa could feel no breeze against her face and when she held out a tentative, shaky hand, the air was hot and still. Far in the distance, there was a line of light, almost like the coast seen from far out to sea.

"I did not know..." Precious Dragon said.

"Did not know what, Grandson?"

"That this is what I am."

"I should think not!" said Mrs Pa. "A dragon, indeed! What an idea. It's a pity you didn't realize sooner—you could have made mincemeat of those *kuei*."

Precious Dragon gave a huge booming laugh. "I did not know how to change into this form."

"I can't work out why you were a child in the first place. And my own grandson!"

"I have a memory now," Precious Dragon said. "Things are beginning to come back. I had to hide, from Heaven—I could not stay in Cloud Kingdom. I don't know why. But I decided that the best place to hide would be in Hell, because no one would follow me there—I forgot about the *kuei*. I suppose one of them smelled me out and then my mother sent me to you."

"But whatever can you have done," Mrs Pa said, "to make Heaven come after you?"

"I made someone angry," her grandson replied. "Dragons often do."

FORTY-SEVEN

Standing on the observation tower of the Lowest Level Nuclear Plant, Pin had a ringside seat for the first clash between the dragons and the *kuei*. Both converged on one another, and then two were battling it out in the sky above him while the rest were hovering back, as if by some ancient and recognized law of combat.

When Pin had watched all those battles in the Opera—it seemed years ago now—he had never thought that he might witness something similar in real life. The Opera had been melodramatic enough, but this was truly dreadful: he watched, appalled, as the *kuei* twisted round and gouged a long weal in the dragon's flank. The dragon shrieked, filling the air with a sound that grated on Pin's spectral ears like a blade scraping down glass. Drops of hissing hot blood spattered down around the observation tower and one of the demons screamed with pain as the blood fell across his shoulder.

"They didn't warn us about this!" someone said.

"Get an umbrella," said another voice. Pin did not think the blood could hurt him, but you never knew. He scrunched against a stanchion of the observation tower and tried to keep out of the way. The dragon leaped across the sky and buried its teeth in the *kuei*'s spine. The *kuei* began whipping to and fro, causing dust storms in the desert and a blasting wind that made the observation tower start to sway. Demons moaned and clung on.

It struck Pin that, sooner or later, one or both of these creatures would drop out of the sky.

And this was only the first fight. There were many dragons, many *kuei*.

Sure enough, this was exactly what happened. The dragon and the *kuei* had wound themselves into a raging knot. One of the *kuei*'s sharp pincers tore into the dragon's wing and the dragon could no longer sustain its height. It fell, and Pin saw the *kuei* struggling to free itself, but it was too deeply entwined with its foe. Both the dragon and the *kuei* plummeted with the noise of a downed fighter jet. Below, troops scattered as they realized what was happening, fleeing from the estimated point of impact. Some of them did not make it in time. The fighting creatures struck the floor of the valley with a tremendous reverberating echo and the entire nuclear complex shook.

"What in hell happens," one of the demons shouted, wild-eyed, "if one of those fuckers falls on here?"

Pin decided, straightaway, not to think about that. He looked out across the valley to where an immense crater had appeared, behind walls of billowing yellow dust. The bodies of the dragon and the *kuei* could still be seen, writhing. A jet streaked across the sky, undertaking reconnaissance.

"Well." Someone had evidently decided to reply to the demon's question. "It's not going to be pretty."

FORTY-EIGHT

Chen, Zhu Irzh, together with Jhai and Miss Qi, had sidled one by one out of the truck and bolted to the makeshift shelter of one of the tanks.

"Wish we still had No's invisibility spell," Zhu Irzh said. "I just tried to replicate it. Can't. Can't do much down here, it seems."

"Do we even have a plan?" Jhai asked.

"Yes," Chen said. "Stay out of the way of the action."

"That's not going to be easy."

Chen pointed to the rocks, the ragged boulder field that led into the mountains. "Not a lot of people up there."

Jhai squinted narrowly. "No, you're right. In the absence of anything better, let's go for it."

Each of them broke cover from the tank and sprinted across the short strip of desert that separated rocks from army. Chen, as he did so, felt that at any moment the alarm would sound and bullets or spells would be shrilling at his heels. The reality was a welcome anticlimax. He reached the rocks in safety and was hauled down by Zhu Irzh. The women were already there.

"This feels safer," Miss Qi said.

"Qi, that's a nuclear plant," Zhu Irzh told her. "You won't be used to that, coming from Heaven. If that thing goes up, we'll be fried. We're well within the blast zone."

Miss Qi looked understandably uneasy. "What will happen to us then? We will not die."

"We'll probably just glow for the rest of our lives," Jhai said. Then she pointed. "Fuck! Look at that!"

They watched as *kuei* and dragon hurtled toward the valley.

"See what I mean?" Zhu Irzh said. A second dragon was flying in to take the place of the first, a *kuei* in hot pursuit.

"Do they battle it out first?" Chen asked.

"No." It was Miss Qi who replied. "This is ritual combat. They will continue until no dragons or *kuei* are left. See? Everything else is taking place around them."

She pointed to a line of dust advancing across the desert. Chen shaded his eyes against the glare and saw white and gold shapes in the front line, great prancing creatures with glittering manes.

"Kylin," he said. "Heaven's using lion-dogs."

"Must have just landed," Zhu Irzh said. Hell's tanks were turning, forming a wall, but one of the lion-dogs, complete with an armored rider, raced ahead of the rest and leaped up and over a tank, leaving dented footprints in the metal. Inside the hastily improvised blockade, it set about tearing demons to pieces, dismembering pieces of scattered limbs that crawled blindly about of their own accord. There was the shriek of machinery as someone brought a rocket launcher around and fired. The missile hit the lion-dog broadside and blew it to pieces in turn. Bits of hairy flesh shimmered and disappeared.

"It will return to Heaven," Miss Qi said, sounding suddenly quite calm, as though she were discussing a game of chess. "It will not see the rest of the battle."

The main line of the lion-dogs had come within yards of the tank wall now, and the creatures were either leaping across or being torn apart. Something like a long iron spear shot screeching down from the sky and buried itself in a puff of dust not far from Chen and the others. It stood, quivering and emitting a mosquito-whine.

"What in gods' name is that?" Chen said.

"Leg of a *kuei*," Zhu Irzh answered. "Dragon's winning this time."

More iron legs showered down from the sky like giant needles, impaling luckless demons and spearing a tank through its engine casing. The machine howled. Steam poured out of the vent made by the *kuei*'s leg and the tank glowed red hot. Demons fled as it exploded.

"It strikes me," Zhu Irzh remarked, "that Hell's not doing all that well at the moment."

"I don't know," Chen replied. "There's a dragon down."

蛇警探

Two hours or so later, Chen and Zhu Irzh were still trying to formulate a plan of escape. The demon's latest notion had been to seize one of the small planes that had now landed across the desert and fly it back up to the higher levels. This idea suffered an early termination when it transpired that no one knew how to pilot an aircraft.

"Besides," Jhai said, "you'd have to get past the rest of the air forces, and that lot." She gestured upward. Five of the *kuei* and three dragons had now perished, although it was rather difficult to tell how many of each remained through the clouds of smoke. Now the *kuei* had retreated to one side of the sky, where they formed an enormous writhing knot, and the dragons to the other. Qi thought that they had agreed on some kind of breathing space while the rest of the forces went into battle, but Zhu Irzh disagreed.

"*Kuei* don't give up," he explained. "They're relentless. There must be some other reason."

Jhai half-rose, shielding her eyes. "What's that plane doing?"

One of Hell's bombers was shrieking across the desert, low over the shadowless sands, heading in the direction of the mountains. The sound of the battlefield—lion-dogs and the big spike-horned, moon-colored unicorns that had made mincemeat of several rows of infantry—had diminished to an ominous hum.

Chen and the others watched the bomber until it became no more than a speck on the horizon. Then it began to grow larger again.

"It's coming back," Chen said.

Zhu Irzh surged to his feet. "It's heading *here!*"

Moments later the bomber roared overhead, sending a hailstorm spatter of bullets down into the rocks. Chen and his companions threw themselves flat. The wail of the bomber was retreating again but Chen, glancing up, saw that it was turning. Beneath them, the ground shuddered, casting a shower of little stones down the hillside.

"For fuck's sake!" Zhu Irzh said, bitterly, brushing dust from his coat. "So much for staying out of the action. An entire battlefield to choose from and they pick on a bunch of noncom escapees."

"Zhu Irzh," Chen said. He'd just seen what was rising out of the shaking ground, beyond the demon's shoulder. "I don't think it's us they're aiming at."

FORTY-NINE

After a while, Pin grew less frightened than bored. He had a nasty moment when one of the *kuei*'s severed legs shot down into the nuclear plant, but it fell short of the reactor and speared a small hut instead. The bulk of the tanks were keeping Heaven's forces well away from the plant itself, although from his vantage point on the observation tower he had an excellent view of lion-dogs and unicorns and various other beasts in Celestial zoology. It still reminded him of various performances and if he ever got back to Earth, what an opera he would be able to write!

Above, with dragons and *kuei* fighting, the air forces were in a quandary: no additional aircraft could take-off from the ground, and those in flight couldn't get through to the lowest level. So, for the time being, Pin felt reasonably safe, even in such a precarious position. Some of the demons still clung nervously to stanchions, peering out across the desert, but a number of them were crouching in the shade. A card game was in progress.

Then, Pin noticed that dragons and *kuei* were drawing back. He did not know why this should be. The observation tower shook a little. One of the demons engrossed in the card game looked uneasily up.

"What was that? Earthquake?"

"We don't get earthquakes here," somebody else replied. "There's nothing underneath us."

Pin was thinking that this was surely likely to produce more quakes, not less, when one of the other demons shouted and pointed toward the rocks. "Look!"

At the summit of a band of rocks, a ridge was appearing under the soil. That they could see it from this not-inconsiderable distance suggested that something huge was breaking through, like some enormous worm. Then a black many-pincered head broke the surface, scattering a burst of yellow soil in all directions, and a segmented body shot up after it, towering some thirty feet or so above the rocks.

"It's a *kuei!*" a demon said. "Where did that come from?"

Four little figures—presumably demons—had broken cover from the rocks and were now racing across the desert toward the nuclear plant.

"Maybe it's one of the ones that fell from the sky," a demon replied.

Pin said nothing. He knew where the *kuei,* now rearing in a column of waving legs high above the desert, several times the height of the observation tower, had come from. It was the *kuei* that had pursued him and Mai down through Hell and had, so it now seemed, buried itself in the sands of the desert. And now it was back.

FIFTY

Chen could not only hear the *kuei* rustling and chittering behind him; he could also smell it, a rank, foul odor like cat's piss magnified by several thousand degrees. A fetid wind blew past him, causing him to stagger on the already uncertain footing of the desert: the *kuei,* exhaling. Chen did not think that centipedes breathed, but then, this was not a centipede as such and neither was it the time for naturalistic speculation. He mustered a burst of speed that took him level with the sprinting Zhu Irzh.

"Chen!" the demon panted. "Fuck off!"

"What?"

"Go *away*. It's me it's after! Get clear and I'll try and draw it off."

"How in the world do you know that?"

"Because I can feel it in my head. It's like it's moved into my mind. *Go away.*" Zhu Irzh veered off to the right, charging toward the wall of the nuclear plant. Chen risked a glance over his shoulder and saw that, horribly, the demon was right: the *kuei* was coming in a scuttling rush across the sand, aiming its blood-eyed, pincered head directly at Zhu Irzh. Slightly ahead of Chen, Jhai had noticed the same thing.

"Zhu Irzh! Watch your back!" She stumbled as she spoke and Chen caught her arm. "Shit, why is it going for *him?*"

"I don't know." They were almost at the fence of the compound. Above, Chen was dimly aware of demons congregating along a walkway and clustering on the observation turret at the corner. Then, amazingly, someone called his name.

"Detective Chen!"

Chen looked up and saw a thin, small shade. A boy, perhaps sixteen years old, gesturing wildly.

"Detective! It's me! It's Pin H'siao!"

The boy from the Opera. Chen felt a surge of dismay. So the boy was dead—except, wait, no, he wasn't. The faint spirit carried an unmistakable sense about him, not a smell, not a color, but something in between that tugged at the remnants of Chen's magical abilities and spoke to him of life.

"Pin!"

The boy was shouting something to his fellow demons.

"Open the gate! Open the *gate!*"

A rusty metal gate swung open. Zhu Irzh, however, was running in the opposite direction along the compound fence. The *kuei* ducked its head and snapped at him, taking out a chunk of fence. It reared back, fragments of metal trailing from its pincers. Chen shoved Jhai and Qi ahead of him into the compound; he seriously doubted whether they were any safer there, but it gave the illusion of sanctuary, at least. Out of the corner of his eye he saw a tall, dark shape swarm up and over the fence: it was Zhu Irzh, as the *kuei* leaned back for a second snap.

Chen turned. Someone was shouting through a loudhailer, but in a language that Chen did not understand. Then he saw the tank, with the howdah containing the Minister of War, thrust through to the compound in a flurry of sand, and then Chen realized that it was the Minister who was doing the shouting.

Zhu Irzh was nowhere to be seen. The *kuei* appeared to think better of its attack. It remained, half-raised, swaying menacingly to and fro.

"Stay there," Chen said to Jhai and Qi. Jhai started to ask where he was going, but Chen did not give her time to finish. "Wait there!" he shouted to the shade of Pin H'siao, and ran off behind the sheds in the direction of Zhu Irzh.

The demon seemed to have disappeared completely. Chen scouted around the sheds and saw a series of boot prints in the dust. He was not entirely sure that they belonged to Zhu Irzh, but lacking any other clue, he followed them. They led him under a flapping tarpaulin into a building that looked like a storeroom: metal containers were stacked against the far wall. Chen stopped and listened. He could hear voices coming from behind the containers—no, a single voice, unknown and whispering, and then Zhu Irzh saying loudly, "Where are you?"

"Zhu Irzh?" Chen called.

"Over here!"

Chen went cautiously around the side of the containers—it was not unknown for demonic predators to mimic someone's voice—and discovered Zhu Irzh standing in the middle of an empty space, apparently having a conversation with himself.

"The fucking thing came straight after me! What was I supposed to do?"—and then—"Well, I didn't *know* that."

Then he turned and saw Chen.

"Chen, meet my granddad."

"What? I thought your grandfather was dead—or whatever. Isn't that his heart you've got there?"

"You know I told you he was dispatched to the lowest level after attempting a coup against the Emperor and had his heart removed." Zhu Irzh explained. "And now we're here and so is he. He's come in search of his heart. But I can't *see* the old bastard."

"Oddly enough," Chen told him, "now, I can."

FIFTY-ONE

Pin squeezed into a small hole by the stanchion on the observation platform, trying to keep out of sight of the *kuei*, which paced on its many legs just beyond the perimeter fence of the compound. He had a feeling that this was useless, that it would know he was there even if it could not see him—but he just didn't want to draw attention to himself.

Then there came a shout from the other side of the fence, across the ranks of troops. "Look!"

If Pin had still possessed a heart, it would have stopped, for over the mountains was coming another *kuei*. It was far larger than the one just beyond the fence, or even the *kuei* that Pin had watched doing battle with the dragons in the skies. Its length must have been close to half a mile and it carried something on its back.

A demon by Pin's side nudged him and whispered, "That's the oldest, that is! With the Emperor."

"The Emperor?" Pin said.

"The Emperor of Hell!"

The *kuei* was moving with the speed of an express train and now Pin could see that an awning was mounted upon its back, like the howdah in which the Minister of War was seated. Inside it, sat something hunched and wizened and old—Pin did not understand how he knew this, because the *kuei* was still some distance away—but it was as though the being sent an aura of age ahead of it, making the air stale. If this part of Hell had contained any plants, Pin thought, they would have withered. He glanced at the demons around him and they seemed to have aged, too. A hissing rustle passed through the troops below: *He is coming, the Emperor is coming.*

And not only the Emperor. A great shadow passed over the valley. He looked up and saw that the sky had been blotted out by something huge and bronze-green and glistening. A dragon, but a dragon as large as the *kuei* that bore the Emperor. The troops grew still and hushed. The dragon flew on.

FIFTY-TWO

The shade of Zhu Irzh's grandfather was standing in the corner of the room.
Dust motes spiraled through him and the wall was clearly visible on the other
side, but to Chen, at least, he was still reasonably visible: an elderly demon,
very similar to Zhu Irzh in countenance, but with a pencil moustache and
an even shiftier expression.

"How do you know it's Grand-dad?" Zhu Irzh asked, apparently still unable
to see his departed relative.

"The gaping hole in his ribcage is a bit of a giveaway," Chen said.

"Ah."

"Who are you?" the spirit said in a subvocal rasp.

"My name is Chen. I am a friend of your grandson."

"My grandson has my heart," the spirit said.

"He took the heart from your daughter," Chen told the spirit.

The spirit turned and, invisibly, spat. "My daughter! She never did know
anything about magic. Do you know what it's like to exist down here, day
after year after day, knowing that your essence is still in the worlds above,
frozen and misused?"

"You're going to have to explain to me this business about your heart," Chen
said, casting an uneasy glance back toward the compound. There seemed to
be some kind of conflict going on; he could hear shouts. "It's not a piece of
human magic."

"Do you know why my heart was taken from me?" the spirit asked.

"I thought it was to keep you down here," Zhu Irzh said.

"Not only that. I defied the Emperor of Hell," the spirit said. "I sought to
lead a rebellion against him."

"Yes, I know that bit. For any particular reason?"

The spirit spat again. This time, the spittle sizzled into the dust and left a small smoking hole in the floor. "All he cared about was the Ministry of Lust: its pleasures, its intrigues. Hell rarely saw him. He spent most of his time inside the Ministry."

"It's the same Emperor," the demon said. "He's not changed much. The Ministries run things. Except, by the way, Lust's gone, for the moment. Long story."

"I have the means to destroy the Emperor," the old spirit said. "My daughter knows this: she seeks to overthrow the Emperor in turn. But she does not know what the means is. So she has kept my heart, trying to summon me from these levels, always failing."

"What, you mean Mum's been trying to bring you back? Not keep you here?"

"Did you prompt Zhu Irzh to ask for the heart at that dinner?" Chen asked. Zhu Irzh started to say something, but then stopped.

"I did. I knew he could succeed where my daughter has not. Tell him to put the heart down," the spirit stated.

"I don't think so," Zhu Irzh retorted. "Sorry, Grandpa, but I don't think you can be trusted."

The spirit hissed in frustration. "If I am reunited with my heart," the spirit said, "then I will have the power to defeat the Emperor. I was granted that power during the rebellion, but the spell was on the condition that the power would last as long as my heart continued to beat in my body. During the rebellion itself, I was captured by the Emperor's forces and my heart was torn out. I was cast down here, but my heart was stolen by a person loyal to me and returned to my family."

"Defeating the Emperor isn't really the issue," Zhu Irzh said. "Given that we're under attack by Heaven."

"If I had succeeded during the first rebellion," the spirit said, "Heaven would not now be in a *position* to attack us. The Emperor of Hell is weak, and he must be removed."

"I think that might be about to happen anyway," Zhu Irzh said.

FIFTY-THREE

"Grandmother," the dragon said. "I will have to put you down."

Mrs Pa looked at the landscape beneath her, unfolding at speed. She should be blown about all over the place, yet the high airs of Hell were windless and still, as if Precious Dragon flew through a vacuum.

"I don't have a parachute," she said.

She thought she felt the dragon smile. "You won't need one."

He veered upward, coiling through the yellow clouds. Far ahead, Mrs Pa saw a platform.

"What's that?" she asked.

"You'll be safe there," Precious Dragon said. As he flew alongside, Mrs Pa saw that the platform was large, and that people were standing on it, holding parasols. They wore red and gold; they were women with quiet, grave faces. Several of them ran forward to take her hands and pull her onto the platform.

"I will see you soon, Grandmother," the dragon said. The gleaming back curved as the dragon dived.

"Be careful!" Mrs Pa shouted over the edge of the platform, and his voice came back, faint now:

"I will!"

FIFTY-FOUR

Pin watched in horror as the *kuei* on which the Emperor rode rose up from the ground, its legs writhing. It rose up and up until its hindquarters left the ground and it was airborne. It shot past the great bronze-green dragon with a snap of its pincers. The dragon coiled away, but just a little too late: a pincer tore open a strip along its flank and sent boiling green blood spattering over the assembled troops below. A cheer went up, even from those who'd been scalded. But the dragon was turning. It roared down out of the sky, coming so close over the observation tower that everyone standing on it ducked, and struck the *kuei* a glancing blow. The *kuei* spun, momentarily out of control, and the end of its spiny tail flicked the observation tower. It was as though the tower had been struck with a giant hammer. It did not collapse, but reverberated, catapulting everyone who stood on it either down into the compound or out among the troops.

Pin, light spirit that he was, floated down like a leaf and landed on the hood of a tank.

"Off there!" shouted a voice from within. Pin scrambled down. Above, both *kuei* and dragon had surged off toward the mountains, readying themselves for another battle. Pin backed away from the tank.

"You're familiar!" a voice said. Pin turned and saw a pair of golden eyes in a severe and beautiful face.

"Jhai Tserai! I mean—I'm sorry, madam, I—"

"Jhai will do," she said. "Under the circumstances." She frowned. "You came to one of my parties."

"You've got a good memory," Pin said.

Jhai smiled. "Oh, I remember people. It's often useful. I'm looking for someone. A demon, the man you met at my party. Have you seen him?"

"Yes, he's here. I saw him in the compound. He was running toward the reactor."

Jhai exchanged glances with her companion who looked, Pin thought, too ethereal and pale to be a denizen of Hell. "What's he up to?" Jhai said aloud. But Pin did not know.

The ethereal person—surely she could not be a Celestial?—was looking up.

"That's the King of dragons!" she said. "Wherever did he come from?"

"From Heaven, I assume," Jhai said.

"No, he could not have done so. That's the whole point. He was exiled from Heaven."

Jhai frowned again. "Exiled?"

"Yes. I never found out why. I just heard rumors that there had been a terrible argument between Cloud Kingdom and the Celestial Palace, and that the Dragon King had been sent away, or had chosen to leave."

"He might have been sent into exile," Jhai said, shading her eyes with her hand as she stared into the skies, "but it looks as though he's come back."

FIFTY-FIVE

Embar Dea watched as the King of the dragons, the lost and exiled lord, snaked through the dusts of Hell's skies. He was directly beneath her now, with the great *kuei* that carried the Emperor streaking toward him. *Our king will prevail*, Embar Dea thought. *He has to*. Then the *kuei* gave a hissing whistle that scraped across her hearing and more *kuei* poured down out of the sky. A cry of protest rose up from a dozen dragon throats—this was ancient law, now violated, but who says Hell has to play fair? Embar Dea thought bitterly.

The *kuei* fell in a writhing knot upon the bronze-green shape of the Dragon King. Embar Dea watched as he twisted and bucked through the air, trying to shake off the pincered forms, but as he did so, his jaws gaped in pain and the pearl that gave him his power shot out from his mouth.

In horror, Embar Dea watched the pearl as it fell; hurtling down through the grimy airs of Hell like a round, white grenade. An Imperial dragon would not last long without it and the *kuei* knew this, too, for they dived, racing after the descending pearl. Embar Dea's gasp sent a shiver through the clouds but she could not take on the *kuei*, so many of them all at once.

And the Dragon King was in trouble: still flying, but writhing as he began to suffocate, unable to breathe without the magical properties of the pearl. The *kuei* had sensed this, Embar Dea knew. One of them continued to streak after the pearl, but the other Storm Lords headed back, to attack and to rend. The *kuei* who had gone after the pearl reached it; there was a grinding sound, a screeching shriek, and then a vast soundless explosion as the *kuei*'s pincers met across the pearl. The pearl splintered into dust. It disembodied the *kuei* that had destroyed it, blasting it apart into a mass of legs and vertebrae, but it was too late: the pearl itself was gone.

Embar Dea saw, suddenly, not yellow dustclouds, but a thin light through a cold sea, the pale shapes of ghosts drifting across the seabed, the black bulk of a hull rising ahead of her, encrusted with ancient shells. She saw the pearl she had rescued from the *Veil of Day*, the sunken ship of Heaven, resting in shimmering perfection in her own old claw.

"Rish!" Embar Dea shouted. "Rish!" She arrowed across the sky toward the Dragon Prince. "Give me the pearl!"

He knew what she was going to do and did not hesitate. His trust in her stirred her heart and then the pearl was once more back in her claws. Embar Dea dived after the Dragon King, into the writhing mass of the *kuei*.

Their iron pincers streaked her sides but she was barely aware of it, barely aware, too, that the hot rain that spattered the desert sands of Hell was her own blood. She looked down into a golden glazing eye.

"Here!" she cried. "Take it, it's yours by right."

And the King of All Dragons reached out and took the old king's lost pearl from her claws. It was the last thing that Embar Dea saw in the three worlds. The *kuei* closed in and she felt no pain, only triumph, and a growing sense of wonder at the last glimpse of the Wheel of Life, before she drifted from it into the soft and glowing dark.

FIFTY-SIX

The *kuei* was coming straight down now out of the sky, arrowing with its legs folded against its sides until it looked like a great black spear. The Emperor—staying on by some kind of magic, Pin thought—was a tiny hump against its back. It headed for the revived Dragon King like a missile, flattening out before it hit the ground and streaking over the plain. But the dragon saw it coming. The dragon turned, spinning in air, evading the *kuei* that surrounded it, and pounced like a cat. Pin somehow had the impression that the Emperor's *kuei* had not been expecting such a direct attack. It rolled over and over as the dragon struck it, bringing both beasts almost directly overheard. Demons scattered as the *kuei*'s iron legs began to shower downward. Something small and nodule-like flew out from the battling mass and hurtled into the compound. A gasp went up: *"The Emperor!"*

"Well," said Jhai, shielding her eyes. "That's a bit unfortunate."

The *kuei* was definitely getting the worst of it. Many of its legs had been splintered away in the dragon's attack and now stood quivering in the ground, or embedded in machinery. The dragon's claws tore at the sides of the *kuei* and the ground was slick and slippery with ichor and blood. Pin stood with Jhai and the strange woman, unable to look away. Jhai hauled at his sleeve.

"Better get out of the way."

Pin, mesmerized, agreed. He ran between the tanks, following Jhai, but kept glancing up at the battle. The dragon's head, above, was twice the size of the huge tanks: rushing across the sky like a machine, eyes wide and fire-filled, mouth gaping. Both its front legs were outstretched, talons reaching for the *kuei*'s side, and in its mouth gleamed something round and white, like an enormous mint, thought Pin.

The *kuei* tried to turn but the loss of its legs appeared to be impeding its movement. It emitted a high whistling scream, reminiscent of a boiling kettle, and then the dragon broadsided it. The impact carried them both back above the nuclear plant but the dragon seemed to be struggling to drag the *kuei* away. Perhaps it was afraid that they might both fall into the compound. The dragon seized the back of the *kuei*'s neck in its jaws and thrashed it to and fro. Its body whipped across the compound, removing two more of the corner observation towers. But Pin, though unfamiliar with the *kuei* as he was, could tell that it was failing. Black ichor bubbled at the corners of its mouth and its red eyes were glazing over.

The dragon spread fringed wings and leaped, taking the *kuei* beyond the reactor and over the reach of the army. Then it plunged the *kuei* into the ground, driving it down under the dust. The dragon rose, snarling, then bit down. The *kuei*'s body arched up, like a snake trying to bite its own tail, and then it fell back and lay still. The dragon stood, behind a cloud of dust.

Jhai dragged Pin and the Celestial-looking woman around the side of a tarpaulin tent. Demons were shrieking in dismay. The Minister of War's tank barreled around the compound, as he shouted instructions, gesturing toward the sky. Now that the way had been cleared of both dragon and *kuei*, Pin could see a skein of bright objects descending from the heavens, at first as distant pinpricks, sparks against the storm-cloud skies, and then coalescing into chariots, silver-white vehicles drawn by unicorns: shaggy, goatlike creatures with a thick spike rising out of their forelocks. They were not much like the slender, graceful unicorns that graced the backdrops of the Opera. These looked fierce and the figures they bore carried spears. There was a burst of light from the ground as a rocket launcher fired; one of the spears spat flame. The site of the rocket launcher disappeared in a gout of dust and fire.

Then the Dragon King was spiraling upward—to join the chariots, Pin thought at first, but then he saw that the lead chariot had veered to avoid the swipe of the dragon's claws.

"What the hell—?" Jhai asked.

"He's attacking our air battalion," said the Celestial woman. "But—he killed the *kuei*, too. I don't understand! Perhaps the Dragon King has gone mad."

Pin did not understand it either but he was relieved that the dragon was now some distance away and not rocketing overhead. The flying chariots came in for another swoop and were, again, rebuffed by the dragon. One of the chariots, knocked aside, spun out of control down into the mountains: there was a distant puff of smoke. A muted cry came from the skies, a roar of many voices raised in anguish and outrage, the protest of Heaven.

"This is terrible!" The Celestial woman was wild-eyed. "Why is he doing this?"

"Who cares?" Jhai said. "It's keeping Heaven from attacking. And I've got a demon to find."

FIFTY-SEVEN

Chen, coughing, picked himself up from the floor of the warehouse.

"What in the name of the unholy was *that?*" Zhu Irzh spluttered, some distance away. They had been in the middle of conversation with the demon's grandfather when the roof of the warehouse had caved in, sending them both sprawling. The beams and girders of the roof now curled inward like the legs of a large spider, blasted apart.

"Must have been a missile," Chen said. He helped the demon to his feet. There was no sign of the Irzh ancestor: the spirit had either disseminated or fled.

"But where did it go?" Zhu Irzh groped in his pocket for the heart and was evidently reassured that it was still there. "Is Grandfather still here?"

"No, he's not. I don't know where he's gone. I can't see him."

"Do you think the old bastard was telling the truth about his heart?" Zhu Irzh asked.

"I've no idea. I don't know much about that kind of magic. It sounds plausible."

"It's certainly true that he was involved in a rebellion," Zhu Irzh said, dusting off his coat.

"Might even have been in the right," Chen said. Usually, he kept out of political conflicts, motivated as he was by a feeling that both sides were as bad as each other. This might very well be the case here, but given what he'd seen of the Ministry of Lust, and also what he knew of the Emperor's relationship with that governmental department, he had more than a slight sympathy for Grandpa Irzh's original goals.

Beside him, Zhu Irzh said, "What was that?"

Chen frowned. The sound had come from beyond a partition on the other side of the warehouse, or what was left of it: a curious hissing, as if someone was letting the air out of a balloon.

"Let's have a look," Chen said.

But when they reached the partition and looked cautiously around it, there was no one there.

"Someone's been here, though," Zhu Irzh said. He pointed to a line of small footprints in the dust. "Hard to tell when they were made."

"Only one way to find out," Chen said, and they followed the footprints.

They were soon out of the warehouse itself and into a series of catacombs, a warren of passages that must, Chen estimated, surround the reactor. The nuclear plant might run according to the principles of physics but there was nonetheless a powerful magic at some level. The place reeked of it, ancient and earthy and primitive.

"Can you feel that?" Chen asked the demon, as they hurried past one particularly potent spot.

"Hard to miss," Zhu Irzh replied. "Lower level magic, if you ask me. Really old stuff."

"What's it doing here?"

"At a guess, protecting the plant. I'm not sure how much security they actually need—not much gets down to these levels, or at least, didn't before Heaven showed up. It didn't seem very great in terms of demonpower, so they must be relying on something else to keep the plant safe."

A layman, Chen thought, might have associated the magic of Hell inextricably with evil, yet although this place was frightening, it did not have the hallmarks of some of the darker magic he had encountered in the course of his career. It was just very, very old: a primordial force that had nothing of the human about it. And Chen could not help wondering if this was in part the source of the current situation: that Heaven, so elevated, lofty, and sophisticated, had not grown too far away from the physical world, so far that it could no longer sympathize with those who sweated and bled and struggled. Hell might, indeed, be hellish, but at times it seemed closer to the human realm than did the Celestial powers. Did that grant Hell, too, the possibility of redemption and improvement? Looking at Zhu Irzh, striding ahead of him along the passage, and thinking of his own wife, Chen thought that it might.

He could hear the hissing again, a sibilant muttering, and this time he thought he recognized the voice. Zhu Irzh's grandfather was, it seemed, back. He caught the demon by the arm.

"Zhu Irzh. I think it's your ancestor."

The footsteps led beyond a narrow door, marked with a symbol that was either magical or the demonic equivalent of a biohazard sign. Zhu Irzh pointed.

"We're nearly at the reactor."

"I think your grandfather is *in* there," Chen said. The hissing was louder now and he was able to place it: the syllables and cadences of a spell. It was rising. Chen could feel the power building up and for a horrifying moment he thought the reactor was going to blow. Zhu Irzh evidently sensed the same thing because he grabbed Chen by the arm and pulled him to the floor. The door of the reactor room blew outward on a blast of magic, which shot overheard and down the corridor like an invisible fireball.

"Shit!" Zhu Irzh cried. "What was that?"

Chen did not know. There was a power in the room ahead, nearly as ancient as the ground on which they walked, but this time it was entirely sentient, not the ancient earth energy but something active and malign. And it was working. He felt it beginning to counter the spell that Zhu Irzh's grandfather had just launched through the door.

"Who is that?" Zhu Irzh asked, eyes narrowing. "I've felt that before."

"Can you remember where?" Chen asked. He was conscious of stalling for time. He was as reluctant to go into the reactor chamber as if the room had been on fire.

"Yeah," Zhu Irzh said. "The Imperial Court."

He looked at Chen in sudden wild surmise. Then they raced through the door.

Chen had never set eyes on the Emperor of Hell, but he knew what he looked like, so when he saw the person who was standing on the railed walkway above the reactor, facing Irzh Senior, he knew immediately who it was.

It was said that the Emperor of Hell breathed magic like air. He had placed himself outside time, a pocket of protection that kept him from even Hell's curious temporal forces. He was neither old nor young, but cycled endlessly between, now having the smooth face and bright eyes of a boy, now the seamed countenance of an old man, but the two were blurred and shifting so that it was impossible to say which he favored at any one moment.

If this had been a legend, Chen thought, then perhaps the Emperor might have been described as the embodiment of evil, darkness incarnate—he was, after all, the Emperor of Hell—but things aren't that simple. There was simply the aura of great age, and a kind of experience that no living thing should really have, and that in a way was worse than evil, because it still transcended the natural law of any world, and as such, it was obscene.

Zhu Irzh's grandfather was chanting now, his face a picture of hate and concentration. He raised a hand and Chen saw a line appear down the center of it, a ragged strip in ghostly flesh. The gape in his chest was painfully apparent; Chen could see the ribs peeled back like the struts of a ship. He managed to throw a spell, drawn out from the hole in his hand, but it was a little, sputtering thing.

Chen thought he saw the shifting face of the Emperor change again, into a smile. It reminded him somehow of the Minister of Lust, something small and cruel, that sipped at pain because that was the only sensation left. And what Chen next thought was: *You've lived too long.*

He was never quite sure, later, what prompted him to act as he did, whether it was the magic foaming and boiling in the air, or the memory of the Ministry of Lust and how it had decayed, or the decadence that had played its part in leading the self-righteous armies of Heaven down to Hell, or just an impatience with Emperors, an upswelling of rage that his own life and Zhu Irzh's and Inari's and everyone else's should be so disrupted by these *bloody* people—whatever the reason, Chen stepped forward, opened Zhu Irzh's coat and, before the startled demon could stop him, snatched the heart from its pocket and threw it like a ball across the reactor to Zhu Irzh's grandfather. It burned Chen's hand when he touched it, the pain of magic transgressed.

Irzh Senior hesitated for only a moment. Then he gave a great, incredulous shout and caught the heart in his cupped hands. He slammed it into the hole in his chest and the hole healed, ribs folding in like flower petals closing, the old flesh closing over it, ragged robe hiding ragged scar. The Emperor stopped changing; an old man's withered face peered across the reactor and Zhu Irzh's grandfather leaped. He hit the Emperor full on, grasping and clawing at him, and they both fell over the rail.

Zhu Irzh turned to Chen, standing transfixed and nursing his burned hand. "Run like fuck, I'd say."

Chen agreed. They bolted out of the reactor room, down the corridor, back into the warehouse, leaping over the fallen girders and beams, their flying feet sending dust spiraling up into the air. Out into the compound and Zhu Irzh was shouting now.

"Run for it, you lot! The reactor's going to blow!"

Chen felt the build-up behind him, magical pressure with physical consequences. There was a hiss like a steam train and the air grew suddenly moist. Zhu Irzh was out of the compound, fighting his way through a group of panicking demons, and Chen followed. The hissing was growing louder. Someone—Chen thought, the Minister of War—was bellowing incomprehensible orders through a megaphone but the troops were breaking rank, tanks and trucks revving up and veering off every which way. Chen saw Zhu Irzh leap for a tank and hang onto a stanchion; Chen barely had time to think, *Every demon for himself,* when the tank swung around and Zhu Irzh reached out a hand and pulled him up. Chen clung on, balancing on the top of the tank tread and feeling the rumble of the machine below his feet. Then the tank was thundering across the desert toward the rocks.

Chen and Zhu Irzh gripped the stanchion above their heads and tried not to fall off. But the tank was old, the treads threaded and laced with rust, and the vehicle lurched alarmingly from side to side. The tank was climbing now, heading up into the foothills. Chen took a look behind him and saw that the entire compound of the reactor was swathed in what looked like mist, a sparkling gray pall that must, he thought, be escaping steam. Around the compound spread a widening ring of vehicles, heading fast into the desert and beyond; above the mountains, flew a dragon larger than any Chen had ever seen, glimpsed bronze-green through the cloudscape. There was no sign of the forces of Heaven. He couldn't blame them for keeping out of the way. After all, Hell seemed quite capable of destroying itself.

The tank lurched again, reeling to one side like a town drunk. They were heading up between the huge boulders now, on a path that was itself strewn with rocks, and the tank's passage was becoming increasingly uneven. Chen's grip on the stanchion tightened just as the tank rolled over a boulder. It stopped, teetering.

"Jump!" Chen cried. It was his turn to give the startled Zhu Irzh a shove off the tank tread. They hit the ground, rolling over and away as the tank tottered and began to topple. Dismayed shouts came from within. Chen and Zhu Irzh flung themselves down behind a rock just as the tank fell. And then the reactor blew.

Chen covered his eyes but he could still see the reactor as it went up: a display on the magical part of his mind, distant but still vivid. A searing flash of white light burst forth as the compound vaporized, then a ring of gleaming blackness rose from a gaping crater. This was not, Chen felt, the usual result of a nuclear explosion: this was something else, something magic-based. He found that he was crouching flat against the floor, shielding his head.

Zhu Irzh raised himself cautiously from the ground and peered over the top of the rock.

"It's gone," he said.

"I know," Chen replied. He joined Zhu Irzh and saw the crater with his actual sight. A ring of exploded tanks and trucks, a mass of twisted metal like some huge anarchic sculpture, littered the plain.

"And that dragon's coming back." Zhu Irzh pointed in the opposite direction.

Moments later there was the rattle of wings and something immense glided overhead.

"What's that?" Zhu Irzh asked, frowning. Chen looked in the direction of his pointing finger. A square of bright light was descending from the sky, like a glowing elevator.

"I don't know—" Chen started to say. But then there was a kind of click inside his mind, like a switch being turned on. From the arrested expression on Zhu Irzh's face, the demon had experienced a similar phenomenon. Upon Chen's inner eye, there appeared the figure of a man: elderly, dressed in red, with a thin white beard.

"It's the Celestial Emperor," Chen said. He had seen Mhara's father once before, during a previous trip to Heaven. You do not easily forget the countenances of gods.

The Celestial Emperor—visible both in Chen's inner sight and outer—waved a hand. A ripple passed across the blasted plain, and it changed: Where the crater had stood, containing the remains of the nuclear plant, a series of grassy hollows appeared. Lily ponds lay at the bottom of each. A ring of rosebushes now replaced the twisted remnants of tanks. An artfully constructed landscape.

"Well, it's very *pretty*," Zhu Irzh said after a pause. "But it doesn't really make things better, does it?"

This so aptly expressed what Chen himself was feeling that he simply nodded.

"One wonders if it's still radioactive," Zhu Irzh remarked. "I suppose not."

"We could find out," Chen said. He was conscious of the urge to go down and see for himself what the Celestial Emperor was really up to. Appalling, to discover that he had as little respect for Heaven as for Hell.

"I want to find out what's happened to Jhai," Zhu Irzh said.

"And Miss Qi. And Pin." Chen did not know what had befallen the people closer to the blast site, but even given the peculiar theological ramifications of their locale, he still hoped that no one they knew had been down there. He set off down the hill at a rapid pace, accompanied by Zhu Irzh.

The question as to what had happened to Jhai and Miss Qi was answered as they reached the bottom of the slope. Chen heard someone call his name and looked up to see the two women picking their way between the boulders.

"There you are," Jhai said. She pointed to where the crater had stood. "Did you do that?"

"No. It was my grand-dad."

Jhai gave the demon an odd look. "I see. For some reason, I get the impression that you are not being sarcastic."

"I'm not. His spirit showed up. Had a fight with the Emperor. Fell into the reactor and it blew."

"Shh!" Miss Qi said. "The Celestial Emperor is speaking."

"…preparing for the annexation of Hell," the Celestial Emperor was saying. He had a remote, reedy voice, Chen remembered, like the worst kind of priest, all piety and no substance. Above, the great dragon still glided, circling the rim of the mountains. "Now that the power source of Hell is destroyed, it only remains for us to banish the remaining demons."

"What?" said Zhu Irzh. "Banish them where? There are billions of us!"

"…another realm will be designated for demons—the place of the existing Earth. Those humans who die will therefore remain upon the Earth itself.

Meanwhile, Heaven will expand and—"

"I think," Chen said to Miss Qi, "that your Emperor might, in fact, have gone completely mad."

Miss Qi said nothing. She stared numbly at the glowing figure before them on the plain. Jhai gave her a nudge. "Job offer's still open."

But they were not, it seemed, the only ones to disagree. From the sky, a great booming voice spoke out. Chen, watching the glowing figure, thought that it took the Emperor by surprise: he seemed to start.

"You shall not!" it said.

"It's that dragon," Jhai exclaimed, shading her hand with her eyes.

"I should remind you, O my lord dragon," the Celestial Emperor said icily, "that my word is the law of the worlds."

"And I should remind you," the dragon replied, "that your word is law up until the point of the death of a living being. According to ancient law, if anyone should take such issue with your word that they would die to gainsay it, your power will wither."

"This has never happened," the Emperor said, with contempt.

"Obviously not," the dragon roared. "But is this right? To wage war on another empire upon a pretext, and when it tears itself apart, to saunter in and take the spoils? To cut off Heaven from the millions of human souls who choose to live rightly and still will have no reward? Do you think that is just?"

"Humans who live rightly have still not succeeded in making right of their world," the Emperor retorted. "Let Heaven secede from the Three Realms, let us live in our own way in peace."

"This is not why Heaven was created!" the dragon said. "As an exclusive paradise for those who disdain to take further trouble."

"Perhaps not," the Emperor replied. "But it is what Heaven will become."

Zhu Irzh leaned toward Chen. "Bit like a golf club," he whispered. Chen nodded.

"But you do agree," the dragon said, "that the old law still stands? That if a living being should give its life in protest at your word, then that word and all the ones that follow it will become no more than dust on the wind?"

"I agree," the Emperor said, very sourly, after a very long pause.

"No choice," Zhu Irzh said in Chen's ear. "That law was a binding spell."

"Then I will choose death," the dragon said, triumphantly. "My death, to void your word!"

"Ah!" the Emperor said. "But you cannot. You are no longer living! I have been informed of recent events. You died, and were reincarnated in Hell, a little boy. You might have changed shape, but you are still a denizen of Hell and as such, no longer a living being."

"A technicality!" the dragon said, but Chen could tell it was rattled.

"But still true. And there is none other here—look around you. All you will see are immortals, or demons. So unless there is a living one to speak—"

"Oh shit," Zhu Irzh said, and he looked at Chen.

Chen thought of Inari. He thought of the city, of Earth, teeming with millions of hapless souls, some of them fairly dreadful, it's true, but most just trying to do their best and get by. He thought of Earth roaming with thousands of hungry ghosts, swarming with dispossessed demons, of the Night Harbor closed down and proper access to the other realms suddenly denied. Earth would be a hell, far more so than anything Hell had produced so far for itself.

One living being.

Chen stepped forward.

"You can't," Zhu Irzh said.

Chen opened his mouth to speak. And as he did so, he heard, with bemusement, the dragon say, *"Oh Grandmother."* He looked up, and saw something small and huddled hurtling through the air, from a gleaming platform high above the clouds. The body of an old lady, falling.

FIFTY-EIGHT

He did not see her hit the ground. Chen and Zhu Irzh watched as the dragon dived, a flurry and glitter of wings and then a surge of dust as it landed.

Zhu Irzh said, "What was that all about?"

"I don't know," Chen murmured, but as he spoke he saw again with inner sight: the shining presence of the Celestial Emperor, turning with a snarl of fury, and then the great spread of the dragon's wings shivering, folding, diminishing—until a little figure was standing in the dust and Chen recognized him.

"It's Mrs Pa's grandson," he said. "It's Precious Dragon."

"Aptly bloody named," Zhu Irzh said, after a moment, and Chen could only agree. The Celestial Emperor raised a hand and Chen felt the surge of a spell, an incantation he had only ever encountered once before: the conjuring of a thunderbolt. The Emperor's hand flickered but the air was empty.

"He can't do it," Miss Qi said, stunned.

"Just as well," Chen remarked. "That was aimed at the child. Or whatever he is."

"He is the Dragon King," Miss Qi said. "The Emperor of Heaven just tried to kill the Dragon King."

"*Former* Emperor of Heaven," Jhai said. She pointed. A battalion of the unicorn cavalry was floating down from the sky. They surrounded the Emperor briefly, and then they were floating up again, as serenely as if they had been gliding through the skies of Heaven itself. The Emperor was gone. Further across the plain, however, so were the small boy and the small, crumpled body beside which he stood.

Miss Qi turned to Jhai. "I think I'll take you up on the job offer, if that's still all right with you."

"Fine. You're on the payroll as of now." Jhai hesitated. "All we have to do is get back to Earth."

That, thought Chen, was likely to be their biggest problem. But in this, he was wrong.

"Zhu Irzh!" A harsh voice, easily recognizable. Chen and the demon looked up to see a tank coming toward them. On it, somewhat battered and dusty, sat a canopy and beneath that, stood the Minister of War and Zhu Irzh's mother. "What are you doing here?" Mrs Zhu demanded.

"There was an issue. With the Ministry of Lust."

"Never mind that," Mrs Zhu said. "This family is allied to the Ministry of War now."

"Now that the Emperor's gone," Chen said, "I suppose the Imperial connection with Lust is no longer an issue either."

"Lust will be rebuilt," Mrs Zhu said. "But it will be under our control."

"Hang on," Zhu Irzh said. "What do you mean by 'our'?"

"We," Mrs Zhu said grandly, "are the Emperor now. Since Erdzhe and I are to be married."

Chen had often wondered if there was anything in any of the worlds that was capable of rendering Zhu Irzh speechless and now he had found it. It wasn't the only thing, either. Jhai stepped forward.

"Mrs Zhu, what a pleasure. Allow me to introduce myself. Jhai Tserai. I'm Zhu Irzh's fiancée."

"What?" said Zhu Irzh.

An expression of what might, in a less icy countenance, be described as delight crossed Mrs Zhu's features, a faint thawing. "Why, I've *heard* of you. A *very* old family." Not Chinese, the expression seemed to say, but never mind. It was clear to Chen that Mrs Zhu was dynasty building.

"Wait a minute," said Zhu Irzh.

"But this is wonderful news," Mrs Zhu said to her son, with unaccustomed sweetness. "I'm so pleased you've decided to settle down."

"And congratulations on your own fiancé's appointment," Jhai said, warmly. Mrs Zhu wasn't the only one. Jhai had seen a chance to mend relations with Hell and she was grasping it with both professionally manicured claws.

Mrs Zhu looked frostily gratified. "Why, thank you. Irzh. Now. About your grandfather's heart."

"Right. We gave it back to him. He took on the Emperor of Hell, they went into the reactor together. That was why it blew."

"So," the Minister of War said. His lizard voice hissed out across the plain, sibilance sending sand skittering over the ridges and ripples. "A new Emperor in Hell and a new one in Heaven."

"We don't know who that will be yet," Mrs Zhu said.

"I think I do," Chen said. His mind went back to a little, half-ruined temple on the outskirts of Singapore Three, a calm young man, and the ghost of a girl. Mhara was next in line and Heaven was known to be highly traditional. "He's got rather different views about the relationship between Heaven and Earth." Thank God. Literally.

"Hell is in disarray," the Minister said. "We need to return."

"You're going up?" Chen asked. "If so, we'll hitch a ride."

It seemed that the order had already been given, because Hell's troops were beginning to rise, the tattered remnants of trucks and other vehicles lurching up from the floor of the plain and drifting upward into the clouds. Chen was looking around for Pin H'siao, but the spirit was nowhere to be seen.

"Come on," Zhu Irzh said in his ear. "Looks like we're leaving. Including my *fiancée*." Chen could not tell whether the demon was displeased or not. Jhai and her new bodyguard were already taking their place in one of the trucks, which were forming a disorderly queue behind the Minister's tank. Zhu Irzh swung up and Chen followed him. The truck started to rise.

FIFTY-NINE

The reactor was gone. Pin could not believe it. He and the other demons came back down from the rocks and wandered around the little pools, the gentle hollows, the lilies. The reactor had been hideous but at least it had produced something, it had been *useful,* and this pretty landscape was not. He was at a complete loss. Everyone seemed to feel the same way; no one was saying very much. He came over the crest of one of the hills and looked down, and his heart gave a jump.

Mai was kneeling in the middle of the hollow, by the side of one of the lily pools, and in front of her was a little boy. As Pin started to hasten down the side of the hill, the child reached out a grave hand and touched Mai's bent head. She shimmered and began to fade.

"Wait!" Pin cried. Mai had done so much for him, given up so much for him, that he could not bear to think of her leaving before he had a chance to say thank you. But as he reached the floor of the hollow, Mai was gone.

"*Mai!*"

The child looked up and Pin saw that his eyes were completely blank and dark, like looking into empty space. For a moment, he looked like something else entirely, but Pin could not have said what it was.

Then the child blinked and the world changed.

They were somewhere else. The place had the familiar smell of the dressing room: powder and the musty odor of the ceremonial costumes, mingled with sweat and cheap perfume. Pin thought that he was sitting on the edge of one of the divans on which the actors rested, but it was too dark to see properly. He felt heavy and hot. He raised a hand and it seemed incredibly weighty. He smelled of meat and there was a weird thumping in his chest, a whistle as he breathed in. It took him a minute to realize that he was back in his own body.

There was a brief flare as someone lit a lamp. He blinked until his eyes adjusted. The little boy came to sit beside him, swinging his legs against the bed. Pin looked around him wonderingly at the seedy comfort of the dressing room.

"I'm back," he said. "This is the Opera, isn't it?"

"Yes, it is," the child answered. "I have brought you home. You should never have been in Hell. Is this where you want to be?"

Pin shrugged. "I don't know anymore. In Hell—it wasn't so bad. There were more opportunities, that's for sure. At least I had some *dignity*." He looked down at the small figure next to him. Now, the child's eyes caught the lamplight and held it, burning a smoky yellow somewhere far within. They reminded him of the demon's.

"Can I make a suggestion?" the child said.

"Sure."

"Go to the temple of the son of the Emperor of Heaven. It's now the Emperor's own temple. Say that I sent you and give them this." He placed something in Pin's hand. Pin looked down: he held a shining bronze-green scale, like the wingcase of a beetle. "Things are changing. You'll find they have opportunities. I think that Hell might be rebuilding, too. They'll want people who know how things worked. And Pin, your mother is there. She's still looking after you, you know, as best she can. She saved you from the *kuei*. She wants you to take this chance."

"I think," Pin said, swallowing hard, "I will do that."

He saw the Opera with new eyes: not as a trap, but as a beginning. Somewhere to start, and somewhere to leave. "What time is it?" Pin asked.

The child gestured toward the heavy curtains. "Go and see."

Pin pushed the curtains aside. There was a faint pale light over the city.

"Morning's coming," the child said. Pin nodded. It seemed a good time to make a move. He looked up at the skyscrapers and saw that the sun was touching their sides. When he looked back into the room, the child was gone.

Pin opened the door and made his way to the front entrance of the Opera. There was only one person in the foyer, a cleaner, who paid no attention to Pin. He went through the main doors of the Opera and out onto Shaopeng. The café owners were just beginning to put their tables out, setting menus down. Pin made his way among the first trickle of morning commuters, heading up Shaopeng, away from the Opera. He did not look back.

SIXTY

At Inari's suggestion, Zhu Irzh held his Earthly engagement party on the houseboat. The Chens had been invited as well to the party in Hell, but did not know if they would attend. Chen was trying to be diplomatic, but he needn't have bothered.

"Don't come if you don't want to," Zhu Irzh said. "I wouldn't, if I didn't have to. It's being held on the lawn of the Imperial Palace. Mother's hired a marquee."

"Zhu Irzh," Chen said. "Do you actually want to go through with all this?" They were standing on the deck of the houseboat, a little distance from the main gathering which, by necessity, was small: some acquaintances of Jhai's, plus Sergeant Ma, Inari, and Robin Yuan, who was treating it as her last social engagement before heading up to Heaven in the wake of Mhara. Still recovering from what had apparently been a nasty encounter with the *kuei*, Mhara was now Emperor of Heaven.

"Might as well," Zhu Irzh said, gloomily. "She's certainly the most interesting girlfriend I've ever had. And I suppose one has to settle down at some point. Besides, I've committed myself now. I actually broke down and asked her to marry me. Bit late, admittedly. But it's done now." He did not look altogether miserable, Chen thought, despite the air of gloom. "Anyway, we're staying here on Earth. Jhai's got a business to run. And I've no wish to go back to Hell, not with my mum running things alongside that lizard."

"There'll be a place for you," Chen said. "The captain's over the moon. Thinks there's a chance of some real possibilities, what with the son of the Empress of Hell working for the police department."

"Equal opportunities?" Zhu Irzh asked, smiling.

"Perhaps." What an odd trip to Hell that had been, Chen thought. He did not feel that they had got anywhere near to the bottom of things. Why *had* the Ministry of War invited Miss Qi to Hell, to go to so much trouble to bring down a Celestial, then without demur, let her go again? Whatever the rights and wrongs of recent events between Hell and Heaven, it was not like Hell to be accommodating and conciliatory. War had wanted Miss Qi's presence for a reason, and Chen did not like not knowing what it had been.

Zhu Irzh had evidently been following a different line of thought. "Not to mention Robin over there as the Empress of Heaven," he remarked.

Robin had been standing several yards away, but she appeared to hear this. She wandered over. "Don't know how much of an Empress I'll be," she said. "Mhara's mother is still the Dowager Empress."

"How much of a say will she have in things, though?" Chen asked.

Robin grimaced. "Not much, if I have anything to do with it. She's in favor of this detachment from Earth thing. Guess what? I'm not."

"I think," Chen said, "that we'll all be having a lot more to do with one another in the future."

He looked thoughtfully down the deck of the houseboat. Three demons, one Celestial (Miss Qi, shadowing Jhai, in her new Paugeng uniform and looking not displeased with the way things had worked out), one ghost—shortly to become a major Celestial power—and a handful of humans. Three worlds it might be, Chen thought, but who's counting?

EPILOGUE

A little bedroom in a house by the harbor, with the shutter tightly drawn against the onset of night. Precious Dragon was swinging his legs over the side of the bed.

"Thank you," he said at last.

"Oh, that's all right, dear." Mrs Pa was looking distractedly around her. "I just want to make sure that the place is tidy before we go, although it's not easy to pick things up without flesh.... I ought to thank *you*. I feel as though I've done something constructive, after all these years. And of course, I'm so looking forward to seeing your grandfather again."

"You're sure, now?" he asked her, and she put her hand beneath his chin, tipping his head up.

"Yes, quite sure," she said. She took a last look around. "That should do. Shall we get on with it?"

蛇警探

A little while later, the old lady gratefully accepted the bowl of steaming black tea.

"This is a nice house you have here, Mai."

"It's not so bad," the girl said, deprecatingly. "It's a lot bigger than the old house in Hell. And now that we have all your wedding presents...you must have gone to so much trouble." Swiftly, she bent to kiss her mother on the forehead. "Making me feel guilty."

"Things always work out," her mother mused. She had recovered her composure now, and sat sipping her tea. "It wasn't so bad, after all. Dying."

Mai laughed.

"My son usually seems to know what he's doing."

There was a single rapping knock at the door, like a thunderclap. The girl hastened to the door, while her mother gazed around the well-appointed

241

room. The winter rains had stopped now. Outside, through the half-shuttered window, the golden light streamed in across the clouds and carried with it the scent of thousand-flower, almost burying the tang of gunpowder tea in its sweetness. Mai opened the door to the sunlight and someone entered.

"My goodness," Mrs Pa said, after a startled moment. "You've changed again." She set down her cup from a suddenly shaking hand and leaned forward, admiring. "It's a little difficult to get used to," she added, after a minute. Her grandson smiled. From the window, the gilded light fell in banners across the floor, illuminating his scales, round as rice bowls and glistening with rain.